MW00790127

DISCARD

BEFORE AND AFTER YOU

The Leffersbee Series Book #2

HOPE ELLIS

www.smartypantsromance.com

COPYRIGHT

This book is a work of fiction. Names, characters, places, rants, facts, contrivances, and incidents are either the product of the author's questionable imagination or are used factitiously. Any resemblance to actual persons, living or dead or undead, events, locales is entirely coincidental if not somewhat disturbing/concerning.

Copyright © 2021 by Smartypants Romance; All rights reserved.

No part of this book may be reproduced, scanned, photographed, instagrammed, tweeted, twittered, twatted, tumbled, or distributed in any printed or electronic form without explicit written permission from the author.

Made in the United States of America

Print Edition
ISBN: 978-1-949202-64-9

DEDICATION

For Karon and Manny. Their enduring love still lives.

CHAPTER ONE

Leigh

When I was in fifth grade, our teacher told us to choose a social crisis and prepare an oral presentation for the class. Most of my classmates presented familiar ills: hunger, homelessness, illiteracy. I decided on a different tack.

I chose a topic for which I'd already collected significant supporting data, thanks to my own direct observation. At ten years old, my adoration for my father had begun to curdle. Promises like "this time is different" and "I've turned over a new leaf" were no longer bright and burnished with the opportunity for a fresh start. I'd come to learn there was no escaping our family's recursive loop, in which my father begged my mother for yet another chance and then temporarily subsided into good behavior. It was only a matter of time before the next woman came along. Maybe it was the lady who came to his garage to get her oil changed, maybe my mom's Mary Kay rep. And then, inevitably, there was always the crushing discovery that he was lying his ass off, bringing the worst kind of chaos and upheaval to our family.

Given the uncomfortably cold state of affairs between my parents and my mother's ban on any discussion of the infidelity that landed us in my aunt's house, yet *again*, I didn't hesitate in picking my topic. If being unable to trust your own parent wasn't a crisis, what was?

"People don't keep their word," I informed the class, watching my classmates' eyes glaze over as my teacher's penciled eyebrows rose higher and higher. "And something needs to be done about it."

In retrospect, I probably could have gotten away with the unconventional presentation inspired by my dysfunctional family. My teacher was known for her lax approach to classroom management, and for lunch hours spent frantically chain-smoking in her tiny, smog-choked car. But I've never done things in half-measure, so I drove my point home using one of the favored gristly expletives bandied about my father's garage.

"Keep your fucking promises," I said, capping off the speech. "Because when you don't, life gets fucked up for everyone around you."

Whoo boy.

Had I caught it for that one. My teacher took pains to ensure I enjoyed very little of the remaining school year. After suffering through a public apology to the class and writing an essay reflecting on my use of profanity in school, I was barred from recess. For the rest of the year, my lunch hour was spent inside under the glare of my teacher while I pretended not to hear the delighted shrieks of my classmates on the playground. My mother, who held the record for perfect attendance at mass, was horrified not only by my coarse language, but also by my unintentional airing of our family's dirty laundry. My punishment had been swift and severe: six months without friends, television, the phone, or playing outside. It was a depressing, joyless summer. Yet even in the midst of my misery, I'd been grateful for my older sister, Lucia, who got my sentence commuted down from six months to three.

"Never be afraid to tell the truth," she'd counseled me. "Nobody's perfect, and it's not wrong to hold someone accountable for what they've done. Next time, just try to find a way that doesn't leave quite so much carnage behind."

My sister's advice still rang in my head whenever I felt a wildfire of rage threatening in my chest. And even after so many years, it still pissed me off when someone lied, didn't keep their promise. Especially when it impacted a child.

Can't help it this time, Sis, I thought. *This time there will be carnage.*

The same grim determination that had driven me to deliver that presentation in fifth grade powered each of my fury-filled steps across the pediatric in-patient wing of Knoxville Community Hospital.

When I finally get my hands on that kangaroo, I'm going to squeeze the stuffing out of his upholstered neck.

I pinned the corners of my mouth up in a benign smile for passersby, doing my best to convey a pleasant expression. After all, Child Life Specialists are harbingers of hope, purveyors of peace. Best not to telegraph my plans for Muppet murder.

Slowing to a more leisurely pace, I snuck furtive glances into each patient room I passed as I internally prayed for a miracle. On the wall above me, a massive analog clock screamed the time in garish primary colors, its furry red and yellow arms marking off each minute, each second that brought colossal disappointment that much closer to an expectant little girl.

All because Karney the Kangaroo hadn't seen fit to show up. As promised.

Once I was sure the oversized, puke-green kangaroo wasn't hanging out in a patient room, I detoured to the nurse's station.

Time for a back-up plan.

I gathered the heavy weight of my unruly, corkscrewed dark hair and wound it into a bun using the elastic on my wrist to secure it in place. The wall-to-floor window at the end of the hallway reflected my swift approach, and I took a moment to stop and regroup as I looked out over the serenity garden below.

I'm calm now, I thought, lying to myself, struggling to slow the rapid tattoo of my heart. My reflection didn't so much resemble an even-tempered health care professional as it did the angry, defiant kid who stalked the sidewalk in my old New Jersey neighborhood ready to meet the challenge of the neighborhood bully. That same battle-ready flush stained my neck and cheeks red, and my blue eyes were narrowed to slits beneath my dark heavy brows.

That kangaroo was going to pay today, I vowed to myself as I continued to the nurses' station. I'd just made the first turn around the corner when a familiar voice called my name.

"Ah, look who's here! General D'Alessandro."

I swallowed back a growl of impatience and stopped. Layla and

Aaron, kick-ass hospital chaplains who were also my coworkers and friends, crossed the hallway to greet me. It took every fiber of my mental fortitude not to pretend I hadn't heard them and dart away to finish my mission. But I didn't have it in me to ditch a rabbi and a reverend. With the almost nonstop barrage of bad news about the hospital's impending doom now besieging us on a daily basis, it was important for us to be present for each other. We were more than a team. We were a family.

"What regime are you about to topple?" Layla asked, her usual sunny smile in place. "I've seen that look on your face before. I'm worried about the other guy."

"Don't be," I told her. "He has it coming. Trust me."

"We were hoping we would run into you," Aaron said. He ran a restless hand over his salt and pepper beard, always a sure sign he was circling a topic with an abundance of caution. "Layla should have been off hours ago. She stayed for a five-car pileup. Since she's here, she wanted to get your opinion about something."

"Guys, I really do need to go put out a fire—"

"It'll be quick," Layla insisted, waving her hand.

I bared my teeth in an imitation of a smile. "What's up?"

"It's my hair." One of her hands stole up to pat awkwardly at her graying tight curls.

Seriously?

"I've got a hair appointment later today, and I wanted your honest opinion about whether I should re-do my perm."

I couldn't help wincing. Behind her, Aaron mimed washing his hands of the topic.

"That's a spouse kind of question, Lay. Why don't you ask Carla?"

"I tried. She chickened out. I don't think anyone is telling me the truth. I know you will."

I sent a desperate look back at the clock. "Is this one of those situations where I'll end up having to do days of friendship repair work, or are you expecting me to be polite? You know I can't read the difference. Please put me out of my misery and just tell me."

She lifted her chin. "Give it to me."

"I'll do the aftercare," Aaron promised.

I laid a hand on her arm. "No more perm. Not unless you plan to get a round office door and apply for citizenship in the Shire."

She stared at me for a breathless moment before her face creased into a smile. I took off, striding away from Aaron's strangled laughter.

"It's just ... when you first got it done the curls were so *tight*," I heard him say as I finally made it to the nurses' station.

The enclosed pod was a hive of activity. Patient care advocates fetched Styrofoam cups of ice water, nurses trailed back and forth to the dry erase board, casting brief glances to the roster of patients on the monitors overhead.

"Leigh. What's up?"

The charge nurse, Ruth, headed in my direction. I felt the faintest stirring of reassurance ... and worry.

Things were looking up if it was her shift. Ruth was an outstanding nurse, loved by all her subordinates, and a powerful ally of mine. She, like me, was perfectly willing to shank anyone that messed with one of our kids here on the floor.

My already outraged state escalated a bit when I remembered that soon she'd be waging war without me. Given the recent acquisition of KCH and the well-founded layoff rumors, I'd been proactively searching for other positions. Child life programs, good ones, weren't that abundant. I'd been fortunate to score an interview in New Jersey later in the week. But what would happen to my kids here? And did I really want to go back? To New Jersey? My fingers itched for the cigarettes I'd given up five years ago. I'd have given anything to feel the numbing, soothing surge of nicotine in my bloodstream at that moment.

I waited until she drew closer before I dropped the bomb.

"The kangaroo is not here."

My meaning took a moment to register, but then her blue eyes narrowed dangerously.

"What's today?" She let out a little breath, making no effort to consult the wall calendar behind us or the monitors above our heads. I didn't blame her. There is a great deal of solace in denial, but we couldn't hide there for long. We had to deal with that was shaping up to be an ugly reality.

"It's the fourteenth." That's all I had to say. We both knew all the other pertinent details. I knew the case file by heart because I knew the patient and her family by heart. Madison Bowers, age five. Hospitalized for three months to manage treatment for severe burns, scheduled for yet another skin graft. Today.

Which also happened to be her birthday.

If ever there was evidence that life was patently unfair, this was it. Over two weeks ago, I'd led the nurses, doctors, and Madison's family members in a strategic social media campaign to lure Karney the Kangaroo to the hospital for a visit with Madison. She loved that hideous, high-voiced character on PBS Kids, proving once again how children could be amazingly intuitive while also having appallingly bad taste. But ... she *loved* that ugly marsupial. And I wanted her to have something good to look forward to. She was only a kid after all, facing an ordeal that had already required herculean strength. When we'd gotten confirmation that Karney (or the reedy-voiced man inside Karney's costume) was indeed confirmed for a birthday visit, we'd rejoiced.

But here we were at the appointed time. With no Karney.

"Maybe he's just late." Ruth's eyes hadn't moved from mine.

"Then he's two hours late."

"Damn it—"

"And a few cases got bumped in the OR and they want to send her down early."

"I'm being nosy, but what're y'all talking about? Who's late?" Ebony, one of my favorite nurses, sidled up to us. In the taut silence, she looked between the two of us, frowning. "What's going on? Y'all are scaring me."

I studied my clogs. "Karney the Kangaroo. He's MIA."

She gaped at me, then said in a voice loud enough to halt all activity in the pod, "*Say what?* Did you just say that dingy kangaroo had the nerve to not show up? On that little girl's birthday? Before she has *surgery?*"

Her expression hardened in the face of our answering silence. "Oh, hell no. This is some bullshit. I'm gonna need him to—"

"Hell no is right." Simon, a ridiculously handsome, muscle-bound nurse flanked us on the other side. "I'm still washing all the glitter out of my truck and hair after working on that 'How Many Sleeps' calendar with Maddie. Where is he?"

"I don't know. I don't know where he is." I lowered my voice, hoping they'd follow suit. Madison's room was at the other end of the hall, but still. "I called Development, but they're stonewalling. I'm going down there. Ruth, can you—"

"Already on it," she said as she reached for the phone receiver. "As many times as we've dealt with their delays, OR can work with us for just a little longer. You go see what's what."

"Thanks, Ruth. Hopefully I'll be right back. With a kangaroo."

"I'm not surprised," Ebony said through pursed lips. "I told you all before, people love to glorify overgrown rats. And everyone knows, you never trust a rat. Even if it's dressed in a polka-dotted dress like Minnie or a tuxedo like Mickey."

"It's a kangaroo," Simon returned, and I heard the trace of laughter in his voice as I started down the hall.

"It's an overgrown rat that jumps," Ebony countered, and I couldn't help my reluctant smile as I hustled to the elevator.

Overgrown rat or not, I needed to get him to Madison's room. Ruth would only be able to delay the OR for so long, and I doubted Madison would remember or enjoy Karney's visit in the afterglow of recovery under a cocktail of anesthesia and pain meds.

Besides ... I'd promised. I had to keep my word, even if Karney the Asshole didn't keep his.

Five minutes later, I stood outside Development empty-handed and desperate. There had to be *something* that could be done.

No one had heard from Karney or the PBS representatives, but it seemed Karney had at least intended to show up. The kangaroo suit had been couriered to the Development office the previous day.

Everyone in the office took turns trying on the suit—myself, the receptionist, and even an average-height Development Officer, but it hadn't worked. The suit required someone well above average height to fill it out and stop the head from sagging and flopping forward.

There has to be another way.

I headed for the south bank of elevators further in the bowels of the hospital. I was so lost in my musing, my attention glued to the highly shined floor, that I didn't see the man at the end of the hallway. Not at first. But when I finally looked up, I realized the man's identity almost immediately as my gaze moved over his tall, solid form. I recognized that familiar tilt to his head, the one that meant he was in deep thought. His head was bowed, expression obscured as he studied the neon orange paper he held in one hand. His other hand was shoved into the pocket of his pants, and a sports jacket was neatly folded across his strong forearm.

I stopped in my tracks, my breath catching in my throat.

Walker Leffersbee.

Damn it.

Indecision glued my feet to the floor, halting my progress as I stared at his frozen profile. I briefly considered turning the opposite way and retracing the same route I'd used coming down.

It wasn't that I didn't want to see him.

That wasn't the case.

Well, not exactly.

But there were several reasons why his sudden appearance was damned inconvenient.

First, Walker was the older brother of my best friend in the world, Zora Leffersbee. But I didn't consider Walker to be my brother, not by any stretch of the imagination. Through all the years we'd known each other, our relationship had continually evolved. He was as supportive of me as he was of Zora. But we both knew he didn't think of me as a sister.

Which led to the second problem.

Walker Leffersbee was sexy. Sexy as hell. The kind of sexy that always took my brain captive with the grimy bass line of a 90s R&B song and thickened my blood for the heat of inevitable battle. We were always locked in some kind of mental combat, our traded barbs and jabs never quite masking the powerful current of attraction between us. He would have been easy to ignore if my attraction to him were based solely on his physicality. I'd bounced on more than one pretty man in my day and managed to keep my brain cells unscrambled. But he was hot as hell with all those intriguing *layers*. Damn it. I didn't have brain space to deal with Walker right now.

"Leigh?"

I stiffened, surfacing from my thoughts. Walker straightened and ambled closer. He moved with the lumbering grace exclusive to big men, a very slight bowleggedness lending his walk a kind of deliberate, sexy swagger. Advancing, he squinted slightly as if trying to make me out in the muted lighting of the hospital's basement floor. He stopped only three feet away from me.

I disciplined my eyes, sternly instructed them away from the just-right fit of Walker's huge shoulders in his white broadcloth shirt. I did not allow my eyes to notice how the tip of his conservative navy tie arrowed the path to his tapered waist and the slightest imprint of powerful thighs just visible in his dark slacks. I refused to dwell on how beautifully his perfectly sculpted dark goatee contrasted with the deep mahogany of his skin.

My fingers clenched against the empty wish for a cigarette.

He wasn't nearly as circumspect, making no effort to disguise the frank assessment in the gaze that slowly crawled upwards from my clogs in slow degrees. I didn't miss the banked heat in his eyes when his stare finally met mine.

"Golden Boy," I said, feeling a perverse pleasure at having launched the opening salvo and earning the answering curl at the corner of his lip. He hated that name, I knew. Hated it whenever I reminded of him of who he was. Son of the richest man in the county, heir apparent to a growing banking empire in Tennessee. Why this bothered him, I'd never know. It was hardly a secret, not with him and his father on billboards advertising his family's bank around Knoxville and Nashville. But that didn't make it any less fun to pick at him.

"Umbridge."

I feigned surprise. "What, have you exhausted all the Disney villains? We're into the Harry Potter lexicon now?"

His answering smile was sharp and wicked. "You know, there are just so *many* names for the devil. I don't think I'll ever come up empty-handed when it comes to you."

"Good to know. What are you doing here?" I flicked a pointed glance at the doorway to Radiology he'd evidently just come through, and I noticed the orange paper had somehow disappeared into his pocket by the time he greeted me.

And ... cue the third complication.

Walker Leffersbee and I shared a secret, and seeing him here had just made it much more, well, complicated.

I hadn't seen him since he abruptly passed out right in front of me at Zora's wedding almost two months before. He'd gone down like a felled tree with no notice at all, almost smacking his head on the cement floor. As I leaned over him praying he wasn't dead, Zora walked in and assumed she'd caught us in the throes of passion. I instinctively covered for him by letting her believe that, and once he regained consciousness, I allowed him to convince me to keep the truth of the episode between the two of us. Neither of us wanted to burden the family with stressful information on such a happy occasion.

Zora had been away on her honeymoon for more than two months, during which I'd seen not hide nor hair of Walker. That was quite a feat in Green Valley, the small town outside of Knoxville where we all lived, and even more impressive considering he'd previously been a regular visitor at the duplex Zora and I shared. It worried me. He'd promised to seek medical help to identify whatever the hell was wrong with him. Looking at him now though, he seemed perfectly fine. But I also couldn't help but notice the way his eyes shifted evasively at my question. The hand in his pocket tightened around what had to be that orange paper.

He was hiding something, something important, and I was the only one who knew anything was potentially amiss. Great.

This was why I hated secrets. In my experience, they never ended well.

You won't be here that much longer anyway.

"What did you say you were doing here?" I prompted again, realizing with no small amount of uneasiness that we'd both been silently contemplating the other while I was absorbed in my thoughts.

"Bitterly regretting that I left my crucifix and garlic at home," he said, a familiar teasing note entering his voice.

I smirked. "You think I'm going to let you get away with this weak-ass evasion?"

His smile dropped.

"Hi, Leigh."

We both turned to see a scrubs-clad woman waving to me as she approached. I recognized her as one of the nurses from the burn unit. I gave her a smile and threw my hand up in greeting, noting her gaze was now sliding over Walker. Walker glanced at her, turned back to me, then did a double take, his head craning sharply to take in the apparently entertaining twitch of her ass as she passed. She glanced back over her shoulder and met his assessing stare with her own bold regard before continuing onward to the elevators.

Walker was slow in returning his attention to me, a sly smile sitting on those deliciously full lips when he finally faced me again.

And here was perhaps the biggest problem. Yes, I had an itch for Walker, and had ever since he showed up in our dorm room all those years ago to check on Zora. It was an itch I'd probably have a lot of fun scratching before I wisely moved on. But Walker was the equivalent of community dick: never short on female companionship and seemingly averse to even the most casual of attachments.

A memory, the worst kind of haunting, assailed me as I stood looking at him. Me at ten years old, sitting in the passenger seat of my father's lovingly restored Ford Mustang, waiting for him to come out of his auto repair garage. He'd somehow forgotten the night deposit, he'd said, and needed to jet in and pick it up. *Shouldn't take more than a second, Lee-Lee.*

It had, in fact, taken more than a second. More like thirty minutes. He'd emerged from the shadowy interior of the shop adjusting his belt, the new, pretty, young receptionist close at his heels. Her shirt was misbuttoned.

Only a few days prior, my mother, sister, and I had returned home after several months spent cramped with my aunt and cousins. He was sorry, he'd told my mother. It wouldn't happen again.

I'd delivered that presentation to my class a week later.

I'd worked my whole life to avoid men like my father. Nonetheless, eight years ago, I'd managed to marry a different flavor of the same treachery. Six years ago I'd moved from New Jersey to live with my best friend in a tiny Tennessee town, all to avoid the unrelenting presence of the unfaithful man I'd married and thankfully divorced. And here I was, standing in front of yet another version of the same man.

Knowing all of that, why did Walker appeal to me on any level?

Maybe you're no good at keeping your word to yourself. That would the worst betrayal of all now, wouldn't it?

Maybe it was time to stop running from the mistakes in my past. With any luck, I'd be back in Jersey soon, resettled with a new job. I needed to start a new reality.

"Leigh?"

Startled, I glanced up at Walker and found him frowning down at me, his expression grave. "Are you alright?"

"I'm fine," I said, with more bite than I intended.

His frown deepened. "You haven't been this cranky since they ran out of ribs on all-you-can-eat day at the Rib Shack."

"Sorry. It's just ... we had something fall through with a patient. It's really disappointing and I've got to figure out how to fix it."

I delivered a friendly punch to his arm, but he easily absorbed the blow, those dark eyes steady on mine.

"This is worse than the Rib Shack running out of ribs, if you can believe that," I admitted.

His gaze sharpened. "What's wrong? How can I help?"

"You can't. We were supposed to have the Karney the Kangaroo show up—"

"Who?"

I shook my head. "It doesn't matter. No one over the age of seven would know. But he was supposed to show up for a patient. I promised, and he's not here."

Walker appeared to think this over. "Well, can you arrange for something else instead? Another—"

"No." I shook my head. "Her heart is set on this. And all we've got is an empty suit."

"You've got the suit?"

"Yeah, none of us can fit it—" And then it hit me. "*We've got the suit.*" I turned my wrist to check the time, then looked back at him, running an eye over his height.

"You know I'm certified as a volunteer—"

"That's right!" Maybe God was about to answer my prayer.

"Walker ... do you think—"

"You need me in the suit, right?" His smile was wry.

"Do you mind? If it worked out, it would mean so much to this little girl—"

Shrill beeping from his pocket interrupted me. He pulled out his phone, glanced at the display, winced, and quieted it before returning it to his pocket.

Oh, that's right. Walker likely had vice president-y things to do. Come to think of it, I was surprised to see him away from the bank during business hours.

"It's fine if you can't," I said, wanting to give him an out but almost choking on the words.

His gaze flitted to his watch, then back to me. "Naw, I can do it. I need to be out of here soon though, so we need to get a move on." Another fitful glance at his watch as his hand seemed to close longingly over the phone in his pocket. "So. Are we doing this?"

I jerked a thumb behind me to indicate the Development office down the hall, but now found I couldn't quite work the explanatory words up my throat. *Are we doing this,* he'd asked, and the words suddenly carried unexpected significance. Walker Leffersbee was about to do me an enormous favor, and I'd already done him one. Was it really wise to get in the habit of trading favors with him now?

What's wrong with you? I had a precious little girl upstairs who needed her kangaroo. Why was I hesitating?

"Yeah," I said over my shoulder, "We're doing this."

~

"SOMEHOW, I don't think this is Karney."

"What was your first clue, Sherlock?"

Ebony, Ruth, and Simon stood in a semi-circle around a costumed Walker, gaping at him. I couldn't decide if I wanted to laugh or cry.

Right now, laughter was winning out.

"More like Highwater Hal." Ebony gestured to where the stubby legs of the kangaroo costume abruptly ended before a large patch of Walker's smooth brown skin began. Even more disconcerting were the thin, gray business socks and highly shined dress shoes he wore with the ensemble.

He looked like a giant toddler in an absurdly undersized kangaroo onesie.

It was hysterical. I couldn't see Walker's expression behind the dark mesh of the oversized grinning kangaroo head, but I knew he would enjoy punishing me later if I laughed.

"Highwater Hal," Simon repeated, finally letting his laughter spill over. He and Ebony high-fived each other and cracked up.

"Why does he have kangaroo hands but not kangaroo feet?" Ruth asked, blinking at him in apparent amusement. I shook my head, trying not to cackle. The fully-exposed length of Walker's well-developed forearms ended in giant green kangaroo paws.

"The kangaroo slippers are supposed to cover his shoes, but they were too small," I explained.

Ebony glanced back to me with a sly smile. "Well, now we definitely know we're dealing with a different man." Her brows quirked at me. "A much bigger man. With *big feet*." She turned back to him and offered her hand. "I'm Ebony. I'm one of the nurses here on the Peds floor. I work closely with Leigh."

Walker awkwardly maneuvered the oversized mitt until it smacked against her extended hand. "I'm Walker." His voice was now somehow deeper than usual. I rolled my eyes.

Ebony gave a dramatic shiver. "My, what a deep voice you have."

Simon elbowed me. "How did this suddenly take a creepy turn?"

"Never mind that," Ruth said turning to me. "You did it. God knows how you pulled it off, but you did. Although, there's the issue of his voice. There's no way he can change it, and he doesn't sound like Karney. And the fact that the suit is too small—"

"It'll work," I said. There was no other choice, and we were so close. "We'll cover the exposed parts of his arms with ace bandages. It'll be just like the doll I use to teach the kids about the medical procedures they're having. And ... he just won't talk."

"We've got to figure it out fast, then. OR will be on their way up any minute now," Ruth hissed.

Fifteen minutes later we watched, hearts in our throats, as Walker lurched toward Madison's room. Ebony had run down to another floor to fetch an adult gown large enough to fit over the arms of the costume. It rode up over the protruding kangaroo paunch with comical effect.

"I hope this works," Ebony whispered in my ear, echoing the same worry currently pinging through my gut.

"It's gonna work," I whispered back with a confidence I didn't feel.

A loud cheer went up in the room as soon as Walker crossed the threshold. I followed behind him just in time to see Madison spring to her knees as she let out a loud squeal.

"Karney! You came!"

Madison's parents jumped to their feet, looking relieved. Mrs. Bowers's eyes widened as she took in Karney's rag-tag appearance, and her gaze shot to mine. I nodded to her and mouthed, *Go with it.*

She nodded back.

As planned, I pulled up next to Walker with my box of teaching materials in hand. "Karney, Madison is so excited you're here. How do you like the welcome sign she made?"

Walker gave an oversized nod, wildly gesticulating his approval. I took a step back before one of his paws gave me a concussion.

Madison, possibly one of the cutest kids in the world, shrieked as she told him all about how she'd made the banner with the help of floor nurses. Seeing the giddy light in her brown eyes, the excited quiver to her ginger ponytails, and the wide smile persisting despite the contracture of the scar tissue covering her left cheek, I let out a relieved sigh.

This would work. We'd kept our promise.

"Karney, since you have a sore throat today and you can't really talk, would you like to learn about the surgery Madison is having today?"

Karney nodded emphatically, and Madison's face lit up.

"Madison, do you mind showing Karney what's going to happen with your surgery today?" Madison nodded, and used my Patty the Patient doll to explain it. Walker stood next to her, nodding his oversized kangaroo head often. I was suffused with pride as Madison took Walker through all the things I'd taught her about the upcoming procedure. Throughout her lecture she patted Walker on the arm, gazing adoringly at Karney's goofy grin.

"Listen to her, she's got it down," Simon said in my ear, and I nodded. "That's got to make you proud, seeing how much your education has helped since she got here. She understands what's going to happen, so she's a lot less anxious. Hell, she's calmer than her parents right now."

He was right. "Sometimes telling kids a version of the truth they can handle is a lot more effective than their imaginations running riot with all the worst-case scenarios."

"Good job getting Karney here too," he said, giving my back a quick pat. "This is a way better send-off for the surgery, and that's thanks to you."

"You're buttering me up. You must want something."

"I guess I've been missing you. Sure I can't talk you into a celebratory nightcap, a friendly sleepover? For old times' sake?" Simon aimed a boyish grin down at me, and I lightly elbowed his ribs.

"I prefer to leave the past in the past. As much fun as it was, our run is up."

"Too bad."

I winced at the genuine disappointment in his eyes. I'd really had some good times with Simon. Not only because he had the body of a Greek god and remarkable stamina when it counted the most, but because he was a genuinely good guy. But he wasn't the guy for me.

I was leaving anyway, whether because of the hospital's implosion or for another job. I sighed and turned my attention back to the scene in the room.

Walker gave Madison a hug. My heart clutched.

By the time the orderly showed up to take her down to surgery, Madison was ready.

"Bubble parade!" I tossed tiny vials of bubble solution to the assembled nurses and orderly, and we all let out a cheer.

"We'll be here waiting for you, Maddie," her father said, managing to flatten out the faint tremble in his voice.

"Yes," Madison said matter-of-factly. "You're going to get me something to drink. 'Cause I might have a sore throat when I wake up. But it won't last forever. Just for a little while."

"That's right." Her mother leaned over to plant a kiss on her forehead, her husband quickly following suit. Walker gave Madison one last hug then stepped out of the way as the orderly sorted out wires and wheeled her bed away from the wall. I caught her parents engulfing Walker in a huge hug just before I left to join the cheerful, singing procession down the hallway. Madison joined us in blowing bubbles as she sang. She held my hand the entire way down to the OR, frequently giggling at the jokes and funny noises we made along the way.

The relief I felt when she was safely delivered to the OR was immense. I'd kept my promise, and I had Walker to thank for that.

On the way back up in the elevator, I wondered how I'd find sufficient words to express my gratitude.

But, as it turned out, I didn't need them. He was already gone.

CHAPTER TWO

Walker

I guided my car into the reserved spot in front of the bank, parked, and let out a relieved sigh. It felt good to just sit for a while. I needed a moment to recover from my encounter with Leigh and the unexpected visit to the Peds ward, and I had to gather my mental reserves before walking into whatever crisis was likely waiting for me inside the bank.

Used to be I looked forward to a workday at any of our Leffersbee Savings & Loan branches. We'd managed to cultivate the same small-town feel of our Green Valley branch in larger cities like Knoxville and Nashville, and each branch felt like coming home to family. My soul relished the rhythm of a well-worn routine, and running the bank usually provided exactly that. Same schedule, same procedures, same friendly neighbors stopping in to check on their account or just chew the fat. However, the recent arrival of my sister Tavia, twin to my much more reasonable sister, Zora, had had the jarring effect of a live wire dropping into an otherwise placid pond. Chaos had quickly ensued in the wake of her efforts to "modernize" the bank, to refashion us as formidable opponents against our banking competitors. Trouble was always on a slow simmer at the Knoxville branch nowadays, always threatening to boil over. For some reason, I seemed to be the only thing standing in the way of that.

I gave in to the tired, surrendered to what had become in recent weeks a constant low-frequency hum of fatigue, and allowed my eyes to close. Just for a second. Unbidden, the memory of Leigh bloomed to life against the darkness of my closed lids. All my careful efforts to avoid her the past few months proved futile when she suddenly appeared in my path, wearing that same mocking smile, and filling those puppy scrubs out in a way that surpassed even my most lurid imaginings of her. Leigh, my little sister's best friend, was still the only woman who provoked that unsettling blend of frustration and attraction. *I must be crazy*, I thought blearily, resting a hand against my eyes to block out the aggressive sunlight. I had no business even thinking in Leigh's direction. Our relationship was already muddy.

All the playful, silly flirting that marked our early acquaintance in Leigh and Zora's undergraduate years had evolved over time, eventually deepening to solid friendship. I genuinely liked Leigh, appreciated her sarcastic commentary and quick wit, all while managing to keep my eyes to myself. Most of the time. But when Leigh moved to Green Valley from New Jersey after her divorce, it was clear things had changed.

Leigh had changed.

Her teasing had acquired a razor-sharp, scornful edge. She never hesitated to deliver her opinion of my dating life with a pin-pricked honesty and disdain that often left me baffled.

Enough. I had more than enough to worry about without remembering how the tip of Leigh's tongue had slid out, snake-like, to slowly dampen the curve of her upper lip.

Like returning the call I missed when she suddenly appeared in the hospital hallway.

I used the car's voice command to dial Miles Green, my long-time friend and now business partner in our house-flipping side hustle. He answered on the first ring.

"'Sup, Walk."

"I need a line on the executive housing you mentioned the other day. I know I missed your call about the online auction this morning."

"House needed too much work anyway," he said, with his usual equanimity. "You mean the place I send my family when they come for the holidays?"

"Yeah. So much for southern hospitality, huh?"

"Those jokers come for weeks at a time. 'Guests, like fish, begin to smell after three days.' That's what Benjamin Franklin said. Separate accommodations mean a happier holiday for all involved. What, you need the place for yourself? Your brother-in-law's rental can't be too much of a hardship, at least until we find our next work in progress."

I shook my head, as if he could see me. "Zora and Nick are back in town."

"So?"

"They're fresh off their *honeymoon* and back."

"*Oh.*" His drawn-out response indicated he got it. "So your ass is definitely smelling fishy, then."

I did not want to remember the atrocity I'd witnessed on the kitchen table the previous night when I walked in on their surprise return.

"Accurate."

"Might be we need to rethink our arrangement. I like you living in our in-progress units just as much as you do. Best security money can buy, and our bottom line always benefits from all your stress projects. We've flipped, what, ten, twelve more houses since you sold yours?"

"About."

"This has gotta be the first time we've found ourselves without a project."

"Yeah, it's bad timing, but as gracious as Zora and Nick were to let me use their rental while they were away, I need to find something else soon."

"I don't know, Walk. Maybe it's time." A sly, teasing note entered his voice. "Time to settle down. Put yourself out to pasture. Eat your last oats or sow them, whatever the saying is. Leave the game to the experienced men like me." He guffawed openly. "Give up your player's card."

"Don't you have something better to do right now?"

"Turn in the transitory life for a five-bedroom Tudor. Fill it up with a wife, 2.5 kids, and a dog."

"Torpedo your own life and leave mine alone." I didn't really have this kind of banter in me right now.

"You sound tired. You alright?"

A beep sounded, indicating another call was coming in. I cracked open one eye to peer at the phone display.

"Gotta let you go. It's my sister."

"Which twin? It's not Tavia, is it?" he whispered.

"Zora."

"That's alright then," he said, audibly brightening. "If I don't talk to you before Friday, see you then."

"Bet."

I ended the call and immediately switched over the line.

"What's up, baby girl?"

Zora's voice flooded the car. "Hey, big brother." She sounded sheepish, and I couldn't help but laugh.

"It's okay, Zozo. Although, after last night, it's clear you aren't all that little of a sister anymore."

"I'm so embarrassed," she whispered, and we both cracked up. "Although," she said after catching a breath, "I would say we're even."

I opened my eyes. "In what world? When have you ever walked in on me having sex?"

"Well. Okay, maybe I didn't walk in on full-blown sex. But I did discover you and Adele Longbottom in your car in the driveway that time."

That name was a blast from the past. And Adele's bottom had lived up to her last name, in the very best of ways.

"We weren't having sex."

"She didn't have on a bra, Walker. And your hands were on her—"

"I'm traumatized for life. I saw your husband's ass."

She made a dismissive noise. "You think that makes you special? You're not the only one. You and Jackson James can compare notes." Her voice lowered. "It *is* an excellent ass, though, isn't it?"

"Please, you're making me sick." But inwardly, I was glad to hear the new lightness, the joy in her voice. I'd known her husband since he'd been a very young boy and considered him my brother, but I still felt significant relief hearing she was so happy.

She hadn't been happy for a long time before Nick returned.

"You'll survive. Leigh and I have heard and witnessed your exploits for years."

I sat up a little at the mention of Leigh, my mind suddenly just a little clearer.

"Speaking of Leigh," she continued, and I batted away the thoughts of Leigh standing in front of me, her eyes sparking with the usual challenge. "I wanted to invite you to dinner tonight. My place. Well, my old place. Eight o'clock. Can you come?"

"Yeah, I can swing it. What's on your mind?"

"What makes you think I have an agenda? Can't it just be what it seems on the surface? An innocent—"

"Nope. You're all giddy, so you've got something up your sleeve."

"Dang, you know me too well. Okay. I have an idea, a plan I'd like to propose. All I ask is that you hear me out."

I smiled. I loved all three of my sisters, of course, but there'd always been something special between me and Zora. It wasn't that we were all that alike, or at least I didn't think so, but my mother had always described us as kindred spirits. That was probably the best description of our closeness, the quiet knowing we had with each other, but I'd never admit that to my mother. Telling our mother she was right had the unpleasant side effect of making her even more smug than she usually was.

"I'll hear you out," I said, and smiled at the clapping I heard in the background.

"One last thing."

"You promise?"

"Shut up, this is the last thing. Leigh's going to be there."

"Of course she is. Isn't she always?"

She sounded exasperated. "No, I'm asking if things are going to be weird between you two."

Now I was all the way awake again. "Why would they be?"

She was suddenly tentative in her approach, seeming to pick her words with care. "Well, I know the two of you had that *run-in* at the reception, and I don't know how far things went ..."

I smiled at her obvious attempt at fishing. Obviously Leigh hadn't disabused her of the notion that something had happened between us. That wasn't necessarily bad—it was the best cover.

It was also very interesting, considering.

I let her open question sink into the silence.

"So it sounds like you two are fine then." Her voice was colored with disappointment. I smothered a laugh.

"All good here, baby girl. Don't you worry about a thing."

"Yeah, yeah. See you tonight."

"See you. And tell Nick I said to keep his ass in his pants this time."

I hung up the call and leaned back in the seat. I'd just close my eyes for a second more, just a minute, and then I'd go in ...

Loud rapping filled my ear, and I jerked up.

Now what?

I turned to my left and faced the glaring woman on the other side of the glass. She raised her fist again as if to knock, and I lifted a staying hand.

With my heart still hammering from startlement, I lowered the window to face the wrath of Mrs. Thelma Watkins. She and I had been playing this game of cat and mouse for as long as I could remember. She'd started managing the bank alongside my father before I was even born, and knew its history, its roots. There were many upsides to her working closely with me in my role of VP. She knew the bank and the community we served as well as my father did. She was an excellent source of counsel whenever I encountered a hiccup. One significant drawback I was acutely aware of in this moment, however, was the fact that she often came across as a mother collaring her wayward child when her ire was raised.

Ever since my sister Tavia had found her way back to the bank with questionable motives, her ire was raised often.

"Morning, Mrs. Watkins," I said, working up a pleasant expression.

"More like afternoon," she fumed, fixing me with the trademark glare that sent lesser employees and customers scrambling. "And here you are in your car, sleeping it away."

I opened my mouth to protest. It had only been a little after eleven when I pulled into the spot, and both calls had taken less than five minutes. But a quick glance at the in-dash digital readout of the time showed she was right. It was almost one o'clock.

I'd been asleep? Here in my car, for almost an hour? How had I lost time like that?

My mind strayed to that bright orange paper in my pocket. Just one more test result to wait for and I'd have a clean bill of health. I wanted everything to be fine, but I also wanted an explanation for the leaden heaviness weighting my limbs right now.

Maybe there was something to my doctor's theory that it was stress-related. Could be. Right?

I lassoed my attention back around to the matter at hand.

"I'm coming, Mrs. Watkins." I unlocked my seatbelt and returned the seat to its upright position as proof. "I closed my eyes for minute, talking to the Lord, and must have drifted off in the middle of the conversation."

This was not, by the way, strictly untrue. I did recall thinking, *Help me, God,* before I apparently nodded off.

"Amen," Mrs. Walker said, raising one heavily ringed hand in a waggle, and I heard the predictable stomp delivered to the cement outside. "Keep your mind stayed on Him. But uh," her eyes narrowed at me, "carry your ass in this here bank with me. Now."

I smothered a laugh.

"Alright," I said, and she backed away enough to allow me to open the car door and step out into the parking lot. I took my time straightening up, pausing to let my head re-acclimate to the adjustment in pressure before I straightened fully.

She squinted at me in the strong afternoon sunlight. "You been drinking?"

"No, ma'am. You know I'm not much of a drinking man."

"I know. But you look a little peaked."

"I'm fine," I said, moving past her towards the bank's entrance. "Now, what's going on?"

"I'm sure you saw I called you on that cellular phone of yours."

"I saw it," I acknowledged, trying not to smile at our reflection in the bank's double doors. Her little legs were moving triple time to keep up with my long stride. I slowed to make it easier for her. "But I was in the middle of something and I couldn't answer."

An atrocious green kangaroo costume, if you can believe it.

"It's about your sister," she huffed, going through the door I now held open for her. I followed in her wake, swallowing back a groan.

Of course.

We made our way in, and I ran an eye over the lobby. Nothing was amiss. All three tellers sat behind the raised counter, one helping a customer. Deposit and checking slips were stacked in neatly regimented columns, and the caddies of pens were full. The night cleaner had shined the marbled floor to a blinding finish, and the original cherry woodwork of the counters gleamed dully with polish. Above us, the original clockface my grandfather had installed all those years ago presided over us like a giant moon, a constant amid ever-changing times. A familiar sense of comfort and reassurance settled on my shoulders as I walked across the lobby. I remembered visiting my father and grandfather here as a kid, and Mrs. Watkins plying me with Dum Dums suckers. Root beer had always been my favorite flavor. I'd tuck it into my cheek wanting to save it, to draw out the flavor as long as possible while I sat on my grandfather's lap. He'd explain whatever happened to be on his massive desk in that big back office.

All these years later, the wheel of time had finally turned enough revolutions so that I could clearly see that one day, this would be my mine. Third in a line of Leffersbee men managing this bank. It was birthright, my father always said. My birthright, before I was even a thought. My duty. No matter how fervently I might have wished otherwise at times.

We made it past the old-school glass-paned door into the administrative space. I cut a quick look at the office on the immediate right, noting the bar of light below the door. My sister had commandeered it upon her return, effectively upending the employee break room and forcing displaced employees outside. We'd tried to intervene, Mrs. Watkins and I, only to have my sister turn cold, accusing eyes on us. *My last name is Leffersbee too, Walker. What, are you saying I don't have a place here?*

I smothered a sigh. Time for another round.

"I have *told* that girl," Mrs. Watkins said, continuing on with her tirade, clearly still worked up. She stopped and turned to face me, the better to deliver her sermon. One hand went up to tug compulsively on her wig, upsetting its balance. "But she doesn't listen. She will, though, mark my words. She doesn't think fat meat is greasy and water is wet, but she'll learn."

I winced at her words as I held her in place, awkwardly patting her wig back to its original position. Dear God. If she was borrowing from her endless repertoire of country sayings all while tugging on her wig, we really were in trouble.

I stuck the key in the lock to my office and shouldered the door open. Mrs. Watkins followed closely behind me and planted herself in one of the chairs opposite my desk.

I sat on the desk, positioning myself directly in front of her. "What's happened, Auntie?" Here, I could be informal.

She sat back and related the tale. By the time she was done, I was angry too.

"I'll take care of it."

"I know you will." For the first time since she'd corralled me in the parking lot, her voice and expression softened. "And I'm sorry you're the one in the position to do it. Should be your father, but ..."

"When was the last time you saw him? Here?"

She gave me a speaking glance. "That's an excellent question."

I let out yet another sigh, and my gaze caught on the framed picture on the opposite wall. Me, aged ten, and my grandfather, out on the lake in my grandfather's favorite old rowboat. My grandmother had taken the picture from the end of the pier, I remembered, then pretended to fuss about cleaning the haul my grandfather and I had brought in, our chests puffed with pride.

I missed those days. I wished I could go back and sit on my grandfather's lap again as a child and turn the present mess over to someone else.

Mrs. Watkins tracked my gaze on the picture and sat forward. "You're just like him, you know. Same strength of will, same integrity. The love your granddaddy had for this bank, you've got it too, even if you don't always think it's there."

She stood and straightened her blouse. "Ain't always easy to lead, Walker. That's why not everybody can do it. But, you? You're up for it."

She stared at me meaningfully for another beat, then opened the door.

My sister stood on the other side.

"Come in," I said, trying to work up a pleasant expression, but I was sure it held little cheer. "What's going on, Sis?"

Tavia didn't reply as she studied me from the doorway, motionless.

I looked back, stifling the urge to throw up my hands in exasperation. Where the hell was my sister, the one who'd moved away to New York? Who smiled, even if it was at the tail-end of stinging sarcasm, and laughed. Joked even. Who had we gotten in her place, this stranger with the angry eyes and barely suppressed rage?

"Don't bother with the niceties," she said, entering to take the seat Mrs. Watkins had just vacated. "I know you've been tasked with delivering my spanking. Thought I'd come to you, save you the effort of walking down the hall."

Her smile was bitter and her eyes were hard. My stomach turned. I just wanted to be her brother. To finally coax out of her what had happened in New York and who had put those shadows in her eyes. But she didn't want my concern. She was Tavia, and so she pushed, and she would continue to push. Sometimes it seemed she wanted to provoke a reaction from me, to prove a point. But to me, or herself?

Didn't matter. Today, I would be patient. Deliver the truth in love, right? That's what my mother would tell me right now.

"Mrs. Watkins said you've been pushing the tellers to recommend financial products to our customers, even when they don't necessarily need them or ask for them."

"God," she snapped. "You make it seem like I'm pushing heroin on them."

I pushed back from the desk and rested my elbows on my thighs, locking eyes with her. "It's not much different to me. These are not just our customers, they're our community members. Our neighbors. They trust us. For us to take advantage of that trust, to manipulate them into making choices that only benefit us—"

"*Please*, Walker," she spat, and I was strongly reminded of our father and his bullish ways as she jutted that same dimpled chin forward, eyes squinting. "I'm not doing anything different than other banks are doing nowadays—"

"We're not any other bank—"

"So you keep reminding me. Clinging to the nostalgia, never wanting to change anything. You'd keep all the cobwebs from when Grandpa ran this place if you could, wouldn't you? I'm trying to bring us into the present, into the future. I don't want people to look at Leffersbee Savings & Loan and see the past. I want them to see us as progressive, as cutting edge."

"And how do you define that, exactly? That we're just as good at being dishonest, at draining clients' accounts with every miscellaneous fee you can think of? By tacking on services that don't mean a hill of beans to them?"

"You're stuck in the past."

"And I don't accept what you're proposing as our future." My gaze snagged on the photo again, and seeing the planes of my grandfather's smiling face strengthened my resolve. "It can't happen again."

Her eyes widened, and she sat upright. "What ... you're *telling* me?"

"You're my sister and I love you, but I won't let you tear down what our father and grandfather worked so hard to build. I've made room, I've made concessions, I've done everything I can think of to make it clear that I want you here, that you have a place here. I've listened. I heard you when you said I was stuck in tradition. I've been open to your ideas. But not this."

She slid forward on her seat, fists clenched. "Stop acting like I've offended your delicate sensibilities, Walker, or attempted some kind of crime against our members. It's called upselling, and if RadioShack could teach their high school employees to ask if a customer needed batteries before checking out—"

"Because they're still in business, right?"

Her expression darkened. "You say there's a place for me, and then you sit there like a dictator and order me around." Her voice had risen on a steady current of rage, and I counseled myself to relax, to sit still. I was still bitterly disappointed in myself for that time I'd yelled back. My grandfather had drilled into me that real men, honorable men, didn't behave that way. No matter the circumstances.

"When you came back, you said you were developing your own corporate consulting service. I supported that then and now. We never agreed you'd interfere with the day to day running of the bank."

"Just because Mrs. Watkins goes crying to you—"

"Careful," I said, very quietly. "She's more than an employee to us, and has been our entire lives. She loves us, God knows why, and she only wants the best for us and this bank. I don't know where your manners went when you left New York. Hell, I don't know where *you* went. But you'll respect her, Tavia, and all that she means to us."

She stood, fists still clenched, lips working bitterly. "You're sitting on so much potential, Walker. You could have so much—"

"I don't want to be a richer man. I want to be a good man."

Our gazes met in heavy silence. She turned, finally, and headed back to the door.

I'd almost relaxed my shoulders from around my ears when she turned back for a parting shot. "I wish you would remember I want what's best for this business too. It's a sad day for me, knowing my own brother doesn't trust me." And with that, she took off down the hall, the echo of her high heels telegraphing her anger.

I sat still, unable to move my eyes from the doorway she'd just vacated.

It was a sad day. She was my sister. But I did not trust her.

CHAPTER THREE

Leigh

ora!”

“Lee-Lee!”

Zora’s arms closed around me the instant I stepped into her side of the duplex. I’d missed my best friend, I realized, holding her at length. Far more than I’d expected to after just two months.

“You look so good!” Better than she’d looked in years, since our undergrad years at Northwestern, even. Her eyes held a new sparkle, and she’d gotten fuller in a way that showed just how content she was. Even her wild mane of curls looked happy and well-conditioned. She wasn’t the same Zora who had always been exhausted, running on fumes, and hollow-eyed. She looked relaxed. Rested. Happy.

She’s changed.

“So do you.” She grabbed my arms, shaking me, and I grinned.

“I know, I do look good. So, what’s the verdict? You’ve spent two months with your bear of a husband. You ready to ditch him for another twelve years?”

“No chance of that happening,” a deep voice said from behind Zora. I met the green-eyed gaze of her new husband. Nick was absurdly tall and vaguely reminded me of a big, sleekly dark-haired, jeweled-eyed cat, with the same stealthy qualities. He was the childhood love she’d been separated from so many years ago. Zora and I had both been under the impression he'd cheated on her in undergrad. Years later, however, we'd learned the full extent of Nick's story and the devastating circumstances that had kept them apart. Now, knowing he'd been faithful and seeing the extent of his devotion, I trusted him with Zora.

Given my past, that was saying a lot.

"I'm not losing this woman ever again," Nick said. His gaze was intent yet kind as he watched us both. "She missed you," he said quietly to me, and the way he looked at Zora then, with such tenderness, warmed my heart.

Zora was such a beautiful person, one of my favorite people. She deserved all the love I saw in his eyes. Here, at least, there was some justice in the world.

"I told you it would be like a scene from *The Color Purple,*" a familiar gravelly voice said, startling me, and I was surprised to see Walker leaning against the far wall of the kitchen. He was out of his suit now, in jeans and a yellow retro NASA T-shirt. I stopped short when I observed how the T-shirt hugged his biceps just right and skimmed over his tight abs. My heart stuttered just a bit as he sauntered toward me, and the jukebox in my head was kind enough to supply a guitar-lick heavy Carlos Santana joint to accompany his slow swagger.

"Walker."

"Maleficent. You done picking the flesh and bones of vanquished enemies from your teeth?"

I laughed despite myself. "I thought we'd exhausted the Disney canon."

Walker smirked. "With three younger sisters, Disney is indelibly burned in my brain. It was traumatizing. I didn't get near enough time watching *He-Man* as a kid."

"Oh, don't even try it. All those times you kidnapped our Cabbage Patch dolls if we didn't let you watch stupid *He-Man*." Zora headed over to harass her brother, trying to pinch him despite his skillful evasions.

"You hungry?" Nick gestured to the large paper bags that covered the counter. "We brought dinner."

"I'm always hungry." I shrugged out of my lightweight jacket and snagged it on the hook next to the door. "Feel free to feed me."

"Consider it done." He opened a cabinet and retrieved a stack of plates. I took them from him, and we worked in tandem setting the small table for four with cutlery and glasses. When Walker's shrill cry mingled with Zora's bloodthirsty shout of triumph, a rare, unguarded smile grew across Nick's face.

"It's good to be back," he said quietly, handing me a stack of Styrofoam containers. "I missed them, all of the Leffersbees and their assorted crazy."

I nodded, settling the containers and reaching for more.

It was strange, being here in Zora's house again when it was full and bustling with activity. In the space of only a few months, so much had changed. Now her side of the house sat empty. If things went according to plan, I'd be gone soon too. I glanced around the kitchen, wanting to preserve the moment, to commit it to memory.

"I know how much you miss her."

I pulled up short, surprised to see Nick studying me as he set napkins on the table. "I want you to know, you're always welcome. Wherever we are. There's always room for you." His gaze was steadfast, his voice surprisingly reassuring.

I might actually like *this bastard*, I thought, hearing the sincerity in his voice.

"Nick, we're just friends. Despite our adult sleepovers and occasionally braiding each other's hair, our relationship is strictly platonic," I teased.

Walker's disgusted snort sounded near my ear. "Please," he said, his voice strained as he pulled out a chair and gestured for me to sit. "Please don't get them started with any sex talk tonight." He threw Nick a dry look. "It doesn't take much to get them started, apparently." He pulled out the chair next to me and sat with a long exhalation.

Zora settled across from me, next to Nick. I couldn't help but notice they'd both fallen silent at Walker's comment. Nick's face was now faintly awash with color. Zora bit her lip as she studied the empty plate at her setting.

"Ohhhhh. There's a story here. What happened?" I looked between all of them, waiting for someone to crack.

"Who wants Mongolian beef?" Zora's voice was overloud as she popped the top to a container. "Or roasted eggplant?"

"Nuh uh. I want the story," I said, leaning forward to open more containers. Braised lamb, stuffed grape leaves, roasted squash. Yum.

"This looks really good." Walker peered over my shoulder, nodding in approval at the food. With him so close, I easily picked up his scent. Something layered and complex, musky and delicious. I averted my traitorous nose.

"Where'd you pick this up?" Walker asked.

"Nope. We're not changing the subject." I looked between the three of them. "What is going on?"

Walker let out a groan.

"Please, no," Zora said, looking pained.

"I need to know what has all of you cringing so hard," I pressed.

"I walked in on them," Walker said from beside me. "In, let's say, a 'compromising position'," he added with obvious difficulty. I turned to him, mouth hanging open in shock, and met those dark brown eyes. He blinked at me, once, twice, before his gaze moved down to my mouth and got stuck there. Something down low in my nether regions clenched.

"You. Are. Lying."

"I wish I were," he said with what sounded like an especially weary sigh. Nick passed him the container of rice, and he busied himself filling Zora's plate. "Somewhere in my head, I can still hear myself screaming."

I looked over at Zora, who had leaned against Nick and buried her face in both hands. Nick dropped a kiss to the top of her head, shaking with silent laughter.

"How scandalous was it?" I was delighted to see Walker grimace into his plate. I poked his side to further antagonize him. My finger hit solid, unyielding muscle.

Damn.

What all was under his nerdy NASA shirt?

"I don't want to talk about it," Walker said darkly. "It was the most horrifying thing I've ever seen. I'm sure I'll have nightmares for the rest of my life just remembering Nick standing there with—" His voice broke. "I can't talk about it."

"Sorry, man," Nick said, looking equally pained. "It's our fault. We meant to call. Coming in for the weekend was a spur of the moment decision. I guess we just got distracted, and before we knew it you were at the back door."

"Alright, Z," I crowed. "Spontaneous, I-gotta-have-it-now sex! On the kitchen table! I'm so proud!"

She took one hand away from her face and leaned forward to slap my waiting hand.

Nick cracked up.

"It's my fault." Walker passed me the rice and got to work on the grape leaves. "I thought Miles and I would have a new house to work on by now. It was wrong for me to stay so long."

"That's bullshit." I looked up at the sharp irritation in Nick's voice. "You're my *brother.* We're happy to have you there, relieved even."

Zora looked appalled. "Of course we want you there. We're leaving again in three days anyway. Nick has work with Rocket, and I'm meeting up with a professor at NYU to talk about a new study we want to bring to KCH. You'll have the place back to yourself. I know it was embarrassing—"

"It was awkward. For all of us," Nick acknowledged. "But that's not a reason for you to leave, unless you want to."

"What happened with the house you and Miles were considering? Did you guys get it during the online bids this morning?" Zora bit her lip as she waited for Walker's answer.

Zora biting her lip? That was her tell. I wondered what she had up her sleeve.

"Nah. Something came up this morning, so we didn't get a chance to connect in time. We figure it was too much of an eyesore in the end anyway."

Something came up this morning. Oh no. I was that something. I'd bum-rushed him into dressing up as Karney the Kangaroo instead of answering his phone.

I jerked around to face Walker head-on. "This is my fault. You were with me this morning when you got the call, weren't you?"

He wouldn't look at me. "No. It's fine, Leigh."

"How can I help? I never meant to be an imposition, let alone—"

"I said it's fine." His voice was gentle as his eyes met mine, but there was no mistaking the finality in his voice. "I'm already looking into executive housing close to the Knoxville bank branch."

"Yes, but—"

"I was there because I wanted to be." His left hand came to a rest on my forearm. The warm pressure of his hand and the heat in his eyes briefly kicked my heart into triple-time. "What we did this morning was incredibly important. There's nothing to regret. I certainly don't."

Our gazes held for another second, and then I was uncomfortably aware of the silence from the other side of the table.

Walker and I both turned to find Nick and Zora watching us with rapt attention.

Walker cleared his throat. "So, like I was saying, it's all taken—"

"What's going on between you two?" Zora interrupted. I caught the subtle jostle Nick gave to the elbow she'd planted on his leg, but she ignored him.

"What do you mean?" The hand Walker had rested on my arm was gone and now clenching his own thigh. Observing the newly rigid set to his jaw, I understood Zora's question had tripped off his own internal alarm. We'd both, individually, without consulting the other, apparently decided to let Zora keep thinking that something had happened between us at the wedding. He wouldn't want to disclose what really happened, I knew, but feeding further into the farce would only make things more complicated.

It would also increase the odds that Zora would sniff out the inconsistencies. She'd spent much of her time in academia studying people—their verbal and nonverbal communication. And I recognized the suspicious squint to her eyes. She was going to keep at this like a pit bull scenting a steak.

As much as Walker and his tomcat ways had annoyed and disgusted me over the years, I felt compelled to help him.

If the tired lines at his eyes were any indication, he'd already had a long and colorful day. And my patient and I had contributed to the strain.

I made a show of narrowing my eyes at Zora. "I know we've compared notes about this kind of thing in the past, but don't you think it'll be a little awkward this time since it's your brother? How much do you wanna know? Like, that he's good with his mouth—"

"Leigh!" Her breath heaved as if I'd kicked her in the chest.

"Or how he's particularly good at standing-up sex? He knows how to rub against all the right spots while still getting the best angles, if you know what I—"

"I forgot to get the wine," Zora announced loudly, noisily pushing back from the table and standing abruptly. She and Nick shared a brief glance before she bolted over to the fridge.

Walker kicked me under the table, and I dug my heel into his instep in retaliation. Glancing up, I made the mistake of letting my gaze wander over to Nick, where it was quickly trapped. He was smirking, arms crossed. *Bullshit,* his expression clearly telegraphed. Clearly, he wasn't buying it.

"You mind helping me open these?" Zora called to Nick from the corner of the kitchen. "My automatic opener isn't charged, and I always have trouble with this tiny manual one."

"Please help her," I said to Nick, "or else we're all having cork in our wine tonight."

Nick shook his head at me once more before standing and ambling over to his wife, who I saw with a quick glance, had already mangled the cork on a bottle of white.

"I'm so happy to hear you're satisfied."

I turned to find Walker close, those full, bite-able lips quivering with laughter. His arm was draped over the back of my chair, his body leaning into mine. I'd never been so physically close to Walker before, close enough that I could kiss him without doing much more than tilting my chin upward. I licked my lips to chase away a bout of dryness, and his gaze darted to my mouth.

"Who said I was satisfied?"

"You just did." His brows climbed his forehead.

"I just attributed a few hypothetical strengths to you, trying to be nice. We both know I have no way of knowing if you can actually validate those claims. And I definitely didn't say anything about being *satisfied.*"

Walker's teasing expression drained from his face, replaced by something infinitely hotter. And dangerous. His foot brushed past mine until it hooked the leg of my chair, jerking me even closer, only centimeters away from him. He leaned toward me, so close our lips almost touched.

"You don't think I can satisfy you?"

The question, spoken at a low pitch only a breath away from my mouth, made my stomach quiver. For a wild second, I wondered if he planned to prove his ability right then and there on the kitchen table.

Yes, God. I'd vote for that.

"Can you?" I gave myself major points for sounding cocky rather than mildly terrified.

He didn't answer for a long moment. The weight of his attention stayed on my mouth as his head tilted, forehead furrowing. I was trapped, suspended in the moment like a tiny insect drowning in the warm amber of our mutual attraction.

"When you get what you asked for," he finally said, his eyes locking on mine, "don't ask for mercy."

My breath caught in my throat.

"Alright!" Zora said sunnily, approaching the table with two bottles in hand. Nick followed with two beers. "We've got Moscato, sangria, and beer for the fellas."

"Thanks, Z." I filled a wineglass with sangria, pretending I didn't feel Walker's heated stare.

Nick pulled out Zora's chair, his eyes moving between Walker and me as he shook his head almost imperceptibly.

Nick was way too sharp for his own good, or mine.

"I had an idea," Zora announced with forced cheer, and inwardly I grinned.

Finally, the sell.

"Walker, you know you're welcome to stay with us as long as you like." She reached across the table to flick her brother's hand companionably, then settled a can of beer across from him.

"Always," Nick said firmly.

"Always," she repeated. "But I know having your own projects is what makes life at the bank bearable. Flipping houses keeps you sane. It's something you get to choose, for yourself."

Some kind of communication seemed to take place between the siblings in the ensuing silence as they stared at each other, motionless.

Walker nodded finally. He sat back in his chair, legs widespread, as he regarded his sister with the slightest smile.

"What do you have in mind, Zozo?"

Zora grinned and made a show of gesturing to the kitchen around us with a flourish. "This place." She glanced back at Nick, and he leaned closer until she relaxed against his broad chest. I smiled at the tiny breath she let out once she was fully within the circle of his arms and his chin rested in her wild curls.

I'd never known that kind of love, never experienced the kind of trust I saw between them. It would be nice to find that, but I'd learned from my mistakes. Nobody was ever going to make a fool of me again.

I shifted my chair away from the temptation of Walker Leffersbee and focused on Zora.

"What, are you ... selling it?" I asked. This was an interesting way of announcing I would soon be homeless.

"No." She looked shocked at the suggestion. "It's half yours! I could never sell it out from under you. It's your home too."

I let out a laugh. "This is *not* my house. I just rent half of it. And I never intended to stay this long, remember?"

"But I'm so glad you did. I'm sorry I've been a bad landlord, and an even worse homeowner."

"Oh, would you stop with the self-flagellation. Save the whips and leather for when you're alone with him," I said, inclining my head in Nick's direction.

Walker kicked me under the table, hard, and Nick coughed.

"You know what I mean," Zora said, resuming her point. "The plan was always for me to rehab the house, to renovate it. I never did that."

"You were working your ass off trying to earn tenure. Besides, my place is fine, and you always got repairs done when I needed them. You just neglected your side because you were never here."

"It's not that bad," she protested, but silence descended as our gazes drifted around the kitchen, taking in the faded wallpaper, the aging wood cabinets, and dull wood floors.

"We're renting the house out on Bandit Lake right now, but we can't buy it because of all the federal land restrictions, and we can't stay there long-term," Nick said, looking at Walker and me. "So if we renovate this house, we'll at least have somewhere to stay while we start new construction somewhere. And I'd like to keep it on hand as a guest house for when our friends, like my partner, Eddie, come through."

"That's where you come in." Zora watched her brother carefully as she moved in for the kill. "The two of you need to agree, of course. That's why I wanted you both here at the same time. I want to renovate the house, restore it to its former glory. It is a beautiful home ... underneath. I'd like to finally do it justice." She zeroed in on Walker. "I want you to do it, big brother. I've seen your work. This would be right up your alley. It's jacked up enough that it's a real challenge, but it's got all the frilly crap you like. Original wood, fancy curlicues, good *bones.*" She sat back, matching her brother's posture as she studied him closely. "So ... what do you think?"

Walker's expression gave nothing away as his regard continued in its unhurried path across the kitchen, assessing the vaulted height of the ceiling, sweeping across the walls. He stood suddenly, stretching as he ambled back to the entrance of the kitchen. Zora, Nick, and I watched as he paced the room, seeming to pay close attention to the windows, the seams where the walls joined the floors. I caught a few snatches of his muttering, something about wainscoting and open concept and other terms I'd assiduously avoided HGTV to escape.

Home renovation? Not my jam.

"Do you have an idea of what you want done to this side?" Walker faced his sister, arms crossed, as he stood in the threshold between the kitchen and formal dining room.

Her grin was smug. She knew she had him. "Nope. I don't care. You can do whatever you want."

At those words, a slow smile slid across Walker's face. A gruff, seemingly involuntary noise issued from the strong column of his throat.

I sat stock still, transfixed. I wondered if he wore that face and made that same noise during sex. When he came.

Good Lord. Look who apparently still hadn't learned her lesson.

I tore my eyes away from Walker, only to have my gaze collide with Nick's. He appeared thoroughly bemused.

"And Leigh's side ... we're just giving her whatever she wants?"

"Exactly." Zora nodded.

"And the exterior?"

"Don't. Care. As long as Leigh doesn't object, have at it."

"Can't believe I still haven't found a way to buy a house out on Bandit Lake," Nick groused.

"Finally, there's something all that money of yours can't buy," I joked.

He gave a self-deprecating laugh, then leaned over to kiss Zora. "I've already got the most important thing money can't buy," he said quietly. "None of the rest matters." They both shared a private smile, then Nick redirected his attention to Walker. "I'll make it worth your while, and then some."

Walker rocked back on his heels, waggled his head from side to side. "I'm in. I've got your back, brother. And you need to lighten up that wallet anyway," he said with a smile, and the two men laughed companionably.

Zora squinted at me. "But are you, Leigh? Is this alright with you? It means you and Walker will be neighbors, and there will be noise and chaos—"

"But only during the day," Walker inserted, "when you're at work, for the most part. And if we start with this side first, you'd be unaffected for a while."

"And I'd feel better about your safety if Walker is around," Nick added.

I held up a hand, wanting to slow the momentum of the decision making. "There is another option."

Everyone stared.

"You could knock down the walls and let Walker renovate the whole thing ... and then sell it."

"And where would you live?" Zora frowned.

I let out a long breath, buying time, trying to figure out how to break the news. "I think I'm going to move back to Jersey. I'm going for a job interview there in two days."

Silence.

"You guys know Visage, that private equity firm, just bought the hospital last month. There's lots of talk of cost-cutting, laying off 'nonessential' staff. They're not filling the three empty positions in our department. I'm the only one left in Child Life, and I'm working in four different departments across the hospital."

Zora frowned. "I didn't realize things had gotten so bad so quickly."

"Two weeks ago my team lead warned me that our department will likely be among the first to go. She recommended I find another job. So," I shrugged, "when I saw the job listing at All Children's in Jersey, I jumped on it. There aren't many good Child Life positions in this area."

We sat in silence for several long moments.

"I'll take care of it," Nick said, sitting up and pulling out his phone. "Child Life is usually funded by private donations anyway, right? I'll—"

"No." I shook my head. "This isn't about just about saving me and my job. I'm not the only one impacted by this."

"But Leigh," Zora said, very quietly. "*Jersey,* of all places? You'd prefer to move back home instead of letting us help?"

"Zora," I snapped, "you were in this same position less than six months ago. Have you forgotten that? Did you let Nick bail you out?"

She screwed her face up at me and let out a noisy exhale. "No. No, I didn't."

"It'd be a superficial solution anyway," I said. "From what I understand, the priorities of the hospital are changing now that it's going to be run as a for-profit."

"There's gotta be something I can do," Nick insisted.

"There isn't," I said.

Nick looked disgruntled. "My business is healthcare innovation, but I may have some contacts—"

"I've got this," I told him. "My coworkers are my family, and we stick together, and you can't fund five different departments. Now that the hospital sale has gone through, I may have to part ways with them."

"And that involves you moving back home? Back to everything you wanted to get away from?" Zora stared me down.

I stared back. "If the job works out, maybe it's meant to be. I've spent six years here hiding out. Maybe it's time for me to face all the things I ran from, so I can move forward. Reclaim who I used to be."

"What, you've been having some kind of identity crisis?" She looked genuinely concerned.

I considered my answer. "I've been wondering what my next steps should be. Could be this situation is nudging me in the direction I need to go."

She didn't look convinced.

"What about this ... thing you have with Walker?" The smile Nick divided between Walker and me had a distinctly mocking edge. "It seems so promising. You're willing to just walk away from that?"

I rolled my eyes. "Nobody ever accused Walker of being a one-woman kind of man. He'll have someone new under him before my U-Haul even pulls out of the driveway." I made the mistake of glancing in Walker's direction and found him strangely expressionless.

Time to move on.

I gave a brisk clap. "Bottom line, I don't have a problem with Walker renovating the house or moving in over here. And I'm not asking for permission from any of you to go on this job interview or to move back home, okay?"

Back to Jersey, I thought, testing out the idea. My gut gave an answering judder of dissent. Damn. I needed a cigarette.

CHAPTER FOUR

Walker

"Damn, she's beautiful."

Miles ran a reverent hand along the stained wood bannister in Zora's foyer. "I can't get over the workmanship in this house. A lot of effort and love went into this place once upon a time. It's a crime to see it in this state."

I gave the foyer and adjacent sitting room an appraising glance, seeing beyond the dark aging wood and dust-filled shadows. Taking on a renovation in this jewel of a home had been a hell of gift from Zora. When I'd hugged her after dinner two nights ago and thanked her, she'd whispered in my ear, *I thought you might like it. I always saw you undressing this place with your eyes.*

She was right, and I shouldn't have been surprised she'd noticed how often I'd eyed these scarred floors and imagined a far grander future for this house. Even now, new ideas and inspiration clambered for space in my mind as I wandered into the sitting area.

"We're going to restore her to her former glory," I said, and turned to see Miles grinning, gripping the newel post as he peered up the curved stairway.

"Yeah we are, Walk. We're gonna have fun and make crazy money, thanks to Nick."

I investigated a deep divot in the floor with my work boot. Miles came to a stop next to me, hands resting on his toolbelt. Glancing at him, I saw the same anticipation, the same glee I felt mirrored on his face.

"It's a hell of a job," he said, going to trace the marbled frame of the ancient fireplace. "But we gotta be realistic. This house looks like it's been left to its own devices for years. That can't be good. She's gorgeous, but my money's on her having a secret. Several." He rubbed at his bald head as he examined the gently sloping floor.

"Mine too."

"And they're prepared for that?"

"They are. The checkbook is open."

"Music to my ears." So saying, Miles executed a sequence of footwork I recognized from a Jackson 5 routine. "Let's get this party started."

"Nick is sending me the inspector's report and an itemized list of what Zora did tackle while she was living here. But I suspect it's not much."

He cocked his head to the side and took in what we could see of the large first floor. "Thing I don't understand is how she ended up with this much house in the first place. Her instincts were right. She can easily triple her investment if the reno is done right. But ..."

I let out an exasperated breath. "Dad. She moved back into town looking for a place, and he guilt-tripped her with one of his 'generational wealth' sermons."

"Oh God," Miles said, making a show of rolling his eyes. "*That* epic speech. 'Build equity, invest in things that appreciate.' I mean, it's not bad advice in general, he's right, but maybe not for her situation at the time. So she folded, huh? Got stuck with this humongous thing when all she needed was a little condo."

"Yep." That's all I said, but I knew there was much more to it. I knew exactly how that conversation would have gone down. Growing up in the same house, I'd watched how my sisters hungered for demonstrations of genuine interest from my father like nest-dwelling baby chicks, their open mouths aimed skyward in hopes of a scrap of undivided attention. Starving for the infrequent, unpredictable moments when his mind wasn't consumed with the running of the bank, or he wasn't gone attending social activities that would cement the bank's standing in the community.

"It'll finally be sorted out now," I said, running an agitated hand over the back of my neck to dispel my unpleasant thoughts. "Both sides might be empty soon. Leigh is talking about potentially moving back home to New Jersey."

Miles's eyes widened. "Really? I hope not. That would be too bad."

Now I was surprised. "You think so?"

"Oh, yeah. That's the first girl I've seen get your number since we were in grade school."

"Shut up, Miles."

"You know I'm right. All the other women around here get a sniff of you, they fall at your feet. 'Oh Walker,'" he said in a simpering falsetto. "'Whatever you want. Whatever you need.' They smile and say, 'Thank you for coming.'"

"Okay, Miles."

"That girl gets in your ass and calls you out on your shit, and it's great fun to watch. I hope she never leaves. 'Cause you two as neighbors? It won't get much better than that."

"You find this entertaining."

I found it somewhat dangerous, like a powder keg sitting a little too close to a trail of explosives.

"Hell yeah, I do. 'Specially when she calls you 'Golden Boy.' You and I both know you're not that guy. But her challenging you has got to make you consider all the ways that mold benefits you. How you lean on it to suit your purposes." He gave me a look rife with meaning. "And all the reasons why you need to break free."

I turned away from my friend's gaze, knowing he saw too much.

Miles and I had known each other for most of our lives as classmates and close friends. He'd provided the respite an older brother of three sisters often needed. Our prepubescent male bonding had often consisted of epic video game tournaments and endless rounds of basketball at his house when we were growing up. We'd taken divergent paths as adults. He entered the Navy right out of high school, and I headed to Duke to study finance.

When Miles came home years later, retired from his last stint with the Navy, I'd been happy to have him back. We'd never lost touch, and I'd been excited to help him finally implement his long-anticipated plans. He now owned several of the most popular spots in the area, including several bowling alleys, a drive-in theatre, and Knoxville Axe.

He'd asked for my advice when he wanted to start investing in real estate. My time at the bank and my background made me knowledgeable about the market. He taught me the engineering and hands-on side of the business. Before long, flipping houses became a hobby, a highly profitable one for both of us.

But the bank would always win its bid for my attention.

In the end, nothing could sever the ties of tradition, of family.

Even when those ties felt like bondage.

"I can't wait to see what happens," Miles repeated, just as the indistinct thump of music sounded from the other side of the house.

Our heads swiveled to the far wall as we strained to listen.

"Is that ... ?" Miles's neck stretched toward the direction of the opposite wall.

His question was answered only a moment later when the decibel level jumped. Missy Elliott's voice came through the wall with remarkable clarity as she assured us that if it was worth it, she would work it.

We stared at each other for several moments as the bass line thumped under our feet. Miles finally dissolved into laughter, planting his hands on his knees as he cracked up.

I shook my head.

"I knew this would be fun," Miles gasped. "Please move in now so I can hear the stories. I wanna laugh."

"As if you need to laugh any more than you already do."

"Life is hard enough, Walker," Miles said, sobering just a bit. "I've seen most of the world, and just about every form of cruelty. Gotta grab joy where you can get it."

"I'll laugh when something's funny."

"I'll tell you what's funny," he said, inclining his head toward the kitchen to indicate I should follow him. "All those years ago when you went to visit Zora at Northwestern and met Leigh for the first time. 'Member that?"

We trudged through the kitchen and down the basement steps. Miles threw a teasing glance over his shoulder.

"I know you remember."

I ignored him, because I did remember. I'd used a bit of my semester break to pop in on Zora, knowing she might have felt a bit out of sorts after transferring to Northwestern. She'd never lived outside Green Valley before and was still completely heartsick over Nick's abrupt disappearance. Privately, I worried the abrupt transition to a big city might have been too jarring for her. But the version of Zora who met me at a popular restaurant on Michigan Avenue was clearly thriving. And as for the roommate she'd dragged along ...

"I was stationed in Iraq at the time," Miles said, ducking his head to avoid a cobweb before we reached the basement floor and total darkness. I groped about for the long string connected to an unseen light bulb. "And I still remember what you wrote me in your letter about Leigh. You said you were expecting someone like Zora."

That was true. Whenever Zora had mentioned her roommate during our weekly calls, my mind unconsciously created a composite of someone like my sister. Young, still more than a little naive, just starting to find her footing in her second year of college.

So I'd been wholly unprepared for Leigh.

My fingers finally brushed against the string, and I yanked it. Weak illumination from the overhead bulb showed boxes stacked against the wall, the indistinct shapes of garbage bags grouped together. I made out the water heater in a corner, eyed the ventilation ducts above. The little tool cubby in the corner was, of course, completely empty.

"You said she looked at you like she wanted to eat you." He chortled again, and I considered tripping him. "And I remember thinking how I was the one sleeping in a tent with one eye open, but it sounded like you were the one being hunted."

I shook my head at the memory of a much younger Leigh, remarkably self-possessed for her age. Shaking my hand, meeting my eyes with surprising boldness, studying me from under heavy-lidded blue eyes while she tossed all that crazy corkscrew midnight-black hair over her shoulder. I'd felt guilty for noticing just how long her legs were in those tiny denim shorts, how smooth the olive skin of her toned midriff was in the halter top.

"Always thought you were a little scared of her, to tell you the truth."

"I wanna check out this foundation wall," I said, also wanting to change the topic. He was right, I'd been a little taken aback, not only by her boldness, but by how attracted I was to her. She wasn't my usual type, with more of a compact, athletic build than the curves I usually preferred. But my gaze kept wandering back to the challenging light in those uncommonly dark blue eyes all throughout dinner. *Get a grip,* I'd lectured myself on the flight home. I was eight years older, in grad school, and way more wise to the ways of the world. That my sister's dorm mate had seriously turned me on was disturbing.

"I left my flashlight." Miles groped at the empty spot on his toolbelt.

"I've got mine in the truck," I said, starting back toward the stairs.

"You mean you've got the exit from this conversation you've been looking for in the back of that truck."

I flipped Miles off behind my back and kept going until I was out the house and back in the sunlight.

I'd made about three steps toward my battered F-250 before I realized the hood was up on the little Honda parked alongside it.

Leigh's head appeared from behind the hood. A dark smudge covered one cheek.

Speak of the devil, and she appears.

Get your stuff and get out of here.

I took a few steps closer. "Cruella."

"Gaston," she returned, her mouth pursing. She aimed a glare down at the car's inner workings.

Go.

"Damn. Gaston? That one cuts deep." I retrieved my toolbox from the bed of the truck and edged closer. "That is one vain, self-absorbed, narcissistic bastard."

"If the shoe fits." She ran the back of her hand against her cheek, further smearing the dark stain.

"Mixing up your Disney now, you must really be off your game. Car trouble?"

"How'd you guess," she said, her voice deliberately deadpan, and I bit back a grin.

"You check your wheel axles for flattened dalmatians?"

She finally cracked a smile. "It won't start. Timing belt's gone bad."

"Guess it pays to be a mechanic's daughter." I leaned against my truck, recklessly ignoring all my instincts for self-preservation.

"Yeah it does," she sighed. "But only if you don't ignore the signs of the timing belt going bad for a month until it gives out right when you're late for the airport."

I straightened. "What time's your flight? You need a ride?"

Her gaze slid to mine, then away as she braced her weight against the car's frame. "I'm fine, Walker. I've got it."

"Does this flight have anything to do with the job interview?"

She closed her eyes. A curl escaped her high bun, brushing her cheekbone before coming to a rest against the graceful slope of her neck. A frantic pulse beat visibly in her throat.

She was so damn pretty.

And clearly stressed about something.

"Look, I know I'm not Zora. I don't know what's wrong. But I can be your friend."

"Aren't you tired of rescuing me yet?" She sounded defeated. "Because I am."

"Maybe it's time for you to acknowledge I'm not always the bad guy in the story. Maybe I'm the good guy in disguise."

She gave me a wry smile. "No. You're the villain. You're just masquerading as the good guy. It's what makes you especially dangerous."

I pulled back, stung.

Well, damn.

"Look, you're busy," she said, casting a pointed glance past me to my truck. "I'm alright here. I appreciate everything you did for my patient the other day, but I'm fine."

I shrugged. "If the job interview's not important, fine."

"Go ahead and take her, Walk."

I looked back and found Miles standing behind me, hands on his hips, wearing a mocking grin. "Hiya, Leigh. Let him take you."

She nodded back at him, her smile strained. "Smiley."

I opened my mouth to respond to Miles, but he had already grabbed the tools from my hand. "You two get a move on. I'll be here when you get back. Might as well bring lunch back while you're at it, Walk."

Leigh's expression was grim as she watched his retreat back into the house.

She did want to make the flight, didn't she?

Didn't she want the job?

"You need to de-grease yourself before you get in my truck," I said, taking pleasure in the way her eyes narrowed to dark blue slits.

"Thank you for taking me," she grumped, brushing past me. I tried not to notice how the leggings and T-shirt she wore clung to her shape as she opened the trunk of her car to retrieve her bags.

"We don't have to go," I said, as she resisted my efforts to help and threw the bags in the bed of my truck before heading back to the house. "Not if you don't want to."

"Of course I want to go," she said, her voice oddly colorless. "Let's get this done so you and Miles can get started with the house."

~

TEN MINUTES later we were on our way to the airport.

Leigh radiated tension from the passenger seat of the cab, her hands tightly clasped in her lap as her foot tapped an anxious rhythm.

"Nervous you'll miss the flight? Or nervous about the job interview?"

She flicked me a sidelong glance before returning her attention to the window and passing greenery.

"Not really worried about the job. My chances of getting it are pretty high. I got a strong recommendation from an old colleague that works there now."

"Alright."

"Think you'll be happy in New Jersey?"

"Yes," she said after several beats, but the hesitation seemed to undercut the truthfulness of her response. "I miss my family. My nieces and nephews are getting older. I miss the culture, the diversity, the faster pace, the rhythm, you know?"

She turned to me at that last, her fists clenched, hips lifting, wrists churning like locomotive wheels to demonstrate *rhythm*. My mind immediately hijacked the innocent word and imputed a much more dangerous meaning. I wondered which of us would set the rhythm if we ever made it into bed, and how well the other would follow.

I cleared my throat. "So. It was just the divorce, then, that brought you to Green Valley. You always meant to go back?"

Zora had consistently lectured that Leigh's divorce, and the Ex-Husband Who Must Not Be Named, should never be brought up. She insisted that it was too hard for Leigh, too devastating to even discuss.

That had never sat quite right with me. Leigh was one of the strongest, ballsiest women I knew. She didn't hesitate to speak her mind and never suffered fools. It was one of the many things I admired about her, even when I was on the other side of her salvos.

"I don't know that I had a long-term plan when I came here," she said, staring out the window again. "I just knew I had to get the hell out."

"And you're excited about starting over again in Jersey?" I couldn't keep the skepticism from my voice.

"*Yes*," she hissed. A sidelong glance showed her gripping the passenger door so tightly that the points of her knuckles were blanched white.

"Okay," I said. I didn't attempt any additional conversation. Meanwhile, she grew increasingly tense the closer we got to the airport. When she finally spoke again, we were almost at the exit for her airline.

"I remember taking that exit to surprise Zora with Nick's proposal. I think that was one of the most romantic things I've ever seen."

I smiled, remembering that day. It had been a touching experience seeing Nick propose to my sister in an airplane hangar full of life-size photos from their past.

"It was pretty incredible," I agreed.

"A fairy-tale ending," she breathed, and I caught her wistful smile from the corner of my eye.

"I don't know about all that."

"Why would you say that?" I was actually relieved to hear that grating tone return to her voice. It showed she had some fight left.

"I don't believe in fairy tales. Nick and Zora are regular people. It's not magic or kismet or fate holding them together. It's their decision to stick together, no matter what stupid crap the other does."

"Maybe *that* is the magic."

"Nah, that's a decision. There's no such thing as 'happily ever after' or 'fairy tales.' I realize that might be a little hard for you to hear, since you're the one with the Hallmark Channel obsession and romance novels all over your place."

"I'm hardly surprised that you don't believe in those things."

I maneuvered the truck toward the exit. "Honestly, I'm surprised you do, as cynical as you are about relationships."

"I'm not cynical about relationships," she said, fighting the seatbelt to face me full-on. "I'm cynical about men like you."

Ouch.

That landed like a blow in the middle of my chest.

"Ah. And now we're at the point in the program where you tell me why I'm Gaston and every other dastardly villain you can think of."

"Really, Walker? You really need me to spell it out after all these years?"

"Please. It's only fair to tell the accused what charges they're facing."

She let out a giant breath. "You're a good guy," she said at last, with less heat. "You've proven that I and just about anybody you care about can depend on you. But you're completely indiscriminate when it comes to women. You have no concept of fidelity. You just bounce from one woman to the next—"

"I have *never* cheated on anyone." If nothing else came across in this conversation, I needed that to ring loud and clear for her. "Never." Reducing my speed, I tore my eyes away from the road to reinforce my words with a direct stare.

"So we're going to hide behind different shades of meaning now?"

"What the hell does that even mean? What are you, the Riddler? If I say I've never cheated, that's what I mean."

"But you don't have much practice at being faithful, do you?" she pressed, and I suddenly hated that we were airing all this out in my truck while I was driving. When I couldn't look at her and clarify her meaning. When I was only minutes away from dropping her off to a fate that had her anxious and tied in knots.

"I have never cheated on a woman, period. I don't know how you can find any uncertainty in that statement."

"Sure, Walker."

"What, you're judging me because I've had sex with different women in my lifetime?"

"It doesn't matter," she sighed, and I gritted my teeth against pointing out that it must have mattered if she'd raised the topic.

"Tell me this," I said instead. "If I'm so terrible, 'the villain masquerading as the good guy,' why did you let Zora think something happened between us at the wedding?"

She took her time answering. "I don't know."

I shook my head, gripping the steering wheel even tighter. "I don't believe that."

"What, did you have a better excuse for how she found us at the reception?"

I considered this. It would have been a pretty incriminating scene to anyone who had walked in on us. Me on the floor, just coming to as Zora opened the door. Leigh straddling me, her face only inches from mine.

"We agreed to keep it between us on the wedding day so we wouldn't worry Nick or Zora," I said evenly. "I'm just surprised you didn't set the record straight with Zora when she came back. Given what you think of me, you should resent any insinuation that we'd been together. In any way."

Silence. "Walker. I'm sorry. I didn't mean to insult you."

"I just want to be clear."

More silence. "I don't feel good about it, for the record. I've misled my best friend, and I don't even know why. If there's something seriously wrong with you, if something happens to you and I was the only one that knew and hid it ..."

"Miles knows. And there's nothing wrong with me," I said, automatically.

"Right. You just passed out and almost smashed your head on the floor for no reason." She sounded exasperated.

"Look, I've had a million tests. Nothing's come back."

Which, strangely, wasn't as reassuring as I would have thought it would be. Of course, I didn't want anything to be wrong. But it would have been nice to have an explanation.

"So I can stop worrying about you, then?"

"Yes, and you never needed to worry about me. My primary care guy ruled out anything potentially serious. We're just waiting for one last test to come back negative, and then I've got a clean bill of health."

"Thank God," she breathed.

"Yes. So we're free to stop the charade."

She was quiet while I guided the truck into the long line for departure drop-offs. Then she took a deep breath and turned to me.

"Look, charade or not, we both know we're attracted to each other. That's real enough."

I cocked a brow in her direction, surprised.

She looked back, undeterred. "I know how good it could be between us, but that's just sex."

"You have no idea what it would be like between us," I said, taking satisfaction in the way her pupils dilated at my words. I leaned forward, and she followed suit, her eyes still on mine.

Behind us, a car horn blasted. We both jumped.

I closed the several car-lengths of space in front of us.

Leigh sounded rattled. "I want you, Walker. I do. I've wanted you since the day I walked into that restaurant and your sister introduced us for the first time. I've always thought you and me, in some form, was an inevitability. But that's the self-destructive part of me. I already made the mistake of trusting a man like you, and I try not to make the same mistake twice."

A space opened ahead of us. I nosed the truck against the curb.

Leigh made no move to get out of the car, but kept her gaze averted from mine. The impact of her words still reverberated through the cabin of the truck.

I weighed my next words carefully. Hearing her describe a liaison between us as "self-destructive" and a mistake? *A man like me?* Couldn't lie, that left a mark. But was I ready to promise her, or any woman, forever? Was I ready to assume the burden of what another man had already done to her?

No. The best I could do was let her know I'd always be there for her. That she'd always be safe if I was around.

"I meant what I said before. I can be your friend. I hope you know I've always been your friend."

"I do know that," she said quietly, finally giving me her eyes again. "I know we'll always care about each other."

A shrill whistle sounded, followed by a yellow-vested traffic attendant rapping on the window. Leigh jumped with a little squeak.

"You can't park here," the attendant yelled through the closed window.

"You've got a plane to catch." I got out of the truck, retrieved her luggage, and rounded the truck to meet her on the sidewalk.

"Safe travels." I handed her the carry-on. My friendly smile tasted sour. "I'll see you when you get back."

I'd started to turn away when she spoke again. "Walker."

"Yeah."

She set down the carry-on and stepped forward, not stopping until she was in my space. Both of her hands rose to grip my arms, and her eyes stayed steady on mine.

"Thank you for the ride. Thank you for helping my patient earlier this week. Thank you for being there so many times when I've been in a tough spot. But, you and me? No good would come of it." Something like regret tightened her mouth. "I hope you understand."

"I do understand," I told her, determined to keep it light, keep it easy. Even if my chest still ached from her verbal punches. "And I hope you find whatever it is you're looking for back home. But it is too bad. 'Cause you know what? You were right that night at Zora's. I am really good with my mouth."

CHAPTER FIVE

Walker

"You bring anything to drink?"

My grandfather studied me from under the wide brim of his fishing hat with half-lidded eyes, a smile creeping across his face.

I suppressed a grin, kept my expression straight. Bandit Lake's current gently lapped at our rowboat, rocking us into an idyllic calm. Behind us, the sun had just barely broken from the horizon, its muted light throwing a prism of pale watercolors across the sky. I straightened my legs as much as I could and returned my grandfather's look.

"What, you thirsty already, Pops? I've got some water."

When his expectant expression dropped, I couldn't contain my laughter. He snatched off his hat and made a show of swatting my foot from his perch.

"It's not nice to play with my emotions like that," he said in that deep, rich voice. When I was a kid, I'd often thought that if I ever heard God's voice, it would have sounded a lot like Pops. "It's not like you to be unkind, grandson."

I fixed him with a stern look. "It's the crack of dawn, Pops, why would I have anything but water?"

He harrumphed, fixing his mouth in that stubborn line I knew all too well. "Wasn't it your idea to go fishing this early in the morning?"

"Miss Collette said I couldn't have you out in the sun when it's hot," I said, explaining what he already knew. "She also said your arthritis is bothering you lately, that's why we're at the house. I didn't want to drive us farther down the lake if it made you uncomfortable."

"Miss Collette needs to mind her own business," he grumbled, and I swallowed another laugh. "Two of you conspiring, making decisions without even asking me. I'm not dead yet, dagnabit. Still got full use of all my mental faculties, thank you very much. Seems like you could ask *me* what I wanted."

I studied the water outside the boat, the shifting pattern of the slow current, the undulating play of light against murky darkness. His uncharacteristic grumpiness, that strain of melancholy in his voice, it saddened me. I knew why he was in this space, and I knew there was nothing I could say to make it better.

"Miss Collette is only trying to help you," I finally offered. "And she's done a great job. You've looked better and seemed happier ever since she moved in." I ran an eye over him. It was clear that someone with an appreciation for color coordination and ironing had a say in his wardrobe now. After my grandmother died, it became painfully clear that Pops didn't have either, and little interest in wearing anything outside of a bathrobe. His socks even had little specks that matched the color of his polo shirt, I noted.

"Miss Collette is supposed to be live-in help, not my mother," he said sullenly.

"I wanted to surprise you, Pops. I needed her help to do that."

He subsided into silence, nodding. Sighing, I reached behind me and fished in the cooler I'd brought along.

His face brightened when I tossed a can of his favorite beer in his lap. "Knew I could count on you, Walk."

"Whatever. Mom finds out I gave you that, she'll skin my hide."

He'd already cracked the top and taken a long swig. "Well, then it's in your best interest to keep that to yourself now, isn't it? How many times did I sneak you Little Debbie cakes as a kid when your mother went on that no-sugar kick? Stayed between us, didn't it?"

"We're even," I agreed, giving him a short nod, which he returned.

We sat in companionable silence for a short while, listening to the birds chattering their early morning news to each other.

"How'd I get lucky enough to get you all to myself on a Saturday?" Pops asked, baiting his line. "You giving the Knoxville ladies a reprieve?"

"Here you go," I snorted, baiting my own line before I cast it out into the water. "I knew it wouldn't be long until you started up with that. I think you lasted a solid hour this time."

He chuckled. "You've got a solid reputation, son. It's not me making it up. Even Miles said he's ready to settle down. But not you. And you've got to be knocking on the door of forty, right?"

"I'm so glad we did this," I said blandly, and he chortled. Hearing this from him only a day after Leigh had similarly characterized me didn't make me feel great. I knew it would've been pointless to defend myself and disclose how long it had been since I'd even been on a date. I'd been too busy and tired and, well, not as interested in playing the usual games for some reason.

"Aren't you dang near forty?"

"I'm thirty-eight, Pops."

He took another swig of beer, squinting at me. "Like I said, almost forty. When I was your age—"

"Here it comes." I grinned. "When you were my age, you'd already conquered the world, founded the bank and your nonprofit—"

"I'm talking about the things that actually matter," he said, and the serious note in his voice made me straighten and look at him more closely. "When I was your age," he continued, gesturing with the pole for emphasis, "I'd already married your grandmother. We both worked two jobs to afford the down payment on our first house. We'd had your father and your aunt was on the way."

I couldn't hide my grimace. "I'm not ready for all that weight right now, Pops."

"*Weight?*" He sounded thoroughly surprised.

I thought of Leigh's face then, standing with me outside the airport, her face drawn with the dread of facing her past. "It's a tremendous responsibility."

"I see." His tone turned thoughtful as he studied the water. "So you avoid all the weight, as you put it, by not committing in the first place."

I shrugged.

For a long while, the only sounds were the wet splash of the water slapping against the boat and the *ticka ticka ticka* of a warbler's call. We both held onto our poles, waiting for a pull, looking everywhere but at each other.

When Pops spoke again, his eyes were still on the water. "It'll never be perfect, Walker. *You'll* never be perfect. No one is."

"I know that, Pops."

He just shook his head. "I know your father was hard on you. I think he'll tell you I was hard on him. One day, you'll understand the baffling blend of pride and fear that comes from raising your own son in this world. Fear because you know what can happen to a young, innocent Black boy in this society. And the pride comes when you see your son, and then your grandson, become an honorable, accomplished young man. We were hard on you because we wanted you to become the best you can be." He took a breath. "But nobody expects perfection. That's not how love works. You've got to let go of the pressure you put on yourself."

I shrugged uncomfortably, studying the unbroken surface of the water. Were the fish still sleeping?

"You think me and your grandmother were perfect?" He relaxed his posture, leaning further back against his makeshift seat. "Half the time I wanted to shake the hell out of her, other half she wanted to shake me." His laugh was colored in wistfulness.

"Y'all seemed pretty perfect to me," I said. Looking out to the shore, I could easily spot where Grandma would have stood after trekking out the back door, waving to us to bring our haul in.

"Hardly. You'd be hard-pressed to find two more imperfect people than the two of us. But we decided we'd stick together no matter what, and that brought our love closer to perfect than it ever would have been otherwise."

I huffed out a laugh, thinking of Leigh. "I had this same conversation with someone yesterday. I don't think there's any magic in love. I think it's a decision, like you just said."

His smile was sly. "Then you weren't listening. Making a decision, that's when the magic happens."

I reeled the line in, cast out again. "That's what she said."

He sat up, looking delighted. "She, as in who?"

I waved a hand at him. "No one. Zora's friend, you know, Leigh."

He grinned openly. "Indeed I do. I like her, she's got spunk. Gives you a run for it every single time. Reminds me of your grandmother."

I gaped at him. "What? She's nothing—"

"Exactly like her. Your grandma was always at least two steps ahead of me. It was good for me," he said, his smile dropping by slow degrees as his eyes found the water again.

I leaned forward and squeezed his puffy ankle. "How many years would it have been today?"

"Sixty." He let out a slow breath. "We got so close, almost made our plans for this milestone. I made it to my eightieth birthday, but ... We only made it to our fifty-seventh year." He lifted his chin at me. "You're a good grandson. You never forget, do you?"

"I'll never forget," I promised.

We allowed the quiet to swell as we both sat with our own thoughts. Darting a few quick glances at Pops, I found him still and unmoving, preoccupied by whatever filled his mind.

"Flipping a new property now," I said, finally.

"Oh, yeah? Whereabouts?"

"It's Zora's. She's finally making the repairs, and I'm going to renovate it in the meantime."

"This flipping thing ..." He looked thoughtful, the gnarled fingers of his free hand tracing the base of the rod. "It's serious, isn't it? Not just a hobby. You'd like it to be more than your side hustle."

I considered, trying to find a response that was both honest and careful. "Could be, Pops."

He seemed to absorb this. I was surprised when he finally said, "I'm glad."

I gaped at him. "Seriously."

He nodded, slowly. "It's the thing that makes you happy. I see that. You talk about the plans, the materials, your eyes light up in a way I've never seen before. You're making a hell of a profit. You're on the way to building something really special." He cut a quick look at me. "You saving what you're making, investing the right proportion of it?"

"Yes, sir."

"That's what I wanna hear. Proud of you, son."

"I love you, too, Pops."

He nodded in acknowledgement of my words, head lowered, throat working. I knew how hard this day was for him now with Grandma gone. I also knew he wouldn't have liked it if I tried to console him. When he looked up again, his eyes were suspiciously bright, but his tone was even and matter of fact.

"Heard things are busy at that bank, changing."

I let his statement just hang there for a few beats, not wanting to touch the topic. "I guess things are always changing, right?"

His face grew impassive as he trained his gaze back out to the water. "Your father there? In the midst of all this change?"

I searched for the right answer, but my hesitation was answer enough.

"Mmmhmmm," he murmured. "And I hear your sister is there, with lots of ideas for modernization."

This here was exactly where I didn't want to be. I didn't want to raise his concern, not after we'd finally just gotten him to fully retire and trust the running of the bank to my father and me. Yet another part of me wished I could unburden myself with him at that moment, share my concerns and ask for advice the way I would have for virtually anything else. But I didn't want to create a schism between my grandfather and my father or sister. The mechanics, the politics, the sensitivities that came with running a family business increasingly presented a Gordian knot of complexities.

"Lately I've realized I should open my mind to new ideas, new ways when it comes to running the bank," I finally said. "It's been pointed out that I need to embrace progress, take risks and try new, unprecedented first steps to make us competitive. There's truth in that."

He was quiet for a long time. "People love that word, 'progress.' And why not? It's the American way, right? Always pushing forward, always searching for what's more effective, new, what's popular. I spent a lot of my life fighting for progress. Marching, boycotting, sitting-in."

I waited, all of my muscles tensed.

"But," he continued, "what's progress to one person, to one side, isn't necessarily progress to all. The thing you always have to ask, when someone's preaching the virtue of progress to you, is who benefits? Who's included in this forward movement, and who's left behind or perhaps further disenfranchised?"

I was silent, remembering Tavia and her "upselling." I couldn't have agreed with him more, but I wanted to be as fair and impartial as possible.

"I hear you. Tavia, she's ..." I rejected the first dozen adjectives that came to mind.

"Octavia's brilliant," Pops said. "Always has been."

"Right. She's ambitious. She wants to be involved. She has an interest and a stake in the business, and those qualities will likely help us."

He took so long to respond, I wondered if he'd heard me. "Ambition's fine, Walker, as long as it's tethered to a strong sense of social responsibility."

I could think of nothing to say to that.

"Do we know what brought her home from New York?" I didn't buy his casually disinterested tone in the least.

"She hasn't been all that forthcoming with those details."

"Uh-huh."

He was silent for another long moment before speaking again. "I need to ask you for a favor, Walk."

I didn't hesitate. "Anything."

His head waggled from side to side, his square jaw set as he seemingly deliberated.

"I don't want to put you in the middle of anything," he said. "I want to be careful not to do that. But I'm hearing some things, and I need you to be my eyes. Keep me updated on what's going on?"

I smirked at him. "Don't you already have Mrs. Watkins doing that?"

"I need you, for *you* to tell me what about any 'progress' you see coming down the line. Just give me a heads-up, that's all I ask."

My gut twisted. "Pops. What's happening? Is something coming?"

He faced me fully then, his gaze shrewd and calculating. "Youngblood, there's *always* something coming." He heaved out a breath. "Just ... keep me apprised, alright?"

"And there's a reason you haven't asked Dad?"

At least a minute passed before he exhaled, "Yes."

I sat back, feeling boneless. Something was afoot. And I would be squarely in the middle of it.

"I'll do it," I said, feeling as if I was sealing my fate.

He nodded wordlessly.

We were quiet for a long time until I felt a tug on my line. "Got something," I said, going about the work of reeling it in. We worked in tandem with the benefit of long experience, getting my haul in the boat, removing the hook, settling it into the prepared cooler of ice.

"Largemouth bass, and it's huge," Pops said, his voice fat with satisfaction, grinning as if it had been his own catch. It'd always been that way. He'd always been king of all grandfathers to me, bursting with pride at my accomplishments.

"Grandma would have said it was a whale of a catch," I agreed, and we both smiled at each other in remembrance. Pops was right—there was nothing more important than family. I just hoped mine could survive what was coming.

~

I RECOGNIZED Miles's truck as soon as I pulled into Zora's driveway later that afternoon, as well as the cars belonging to the plumber and engineer on our renovation team. As I entered the house, Miles's voice drifted up to me up from the basement, and I headed down. I found Miles and the engineer standing in front of the foundation wall, their faces grim.

Miles turned to me. "'Sup, Walk."

I nodded to him and greeted our engineer. "Is it as bad as y'all look?"

Miles hesitated, then nodded. "You know that crack in the foundation wall we found yesterday? It's about what we thought."

"Alright," I said, rocking back on my heels. "We can handle that."

"And," Miles said, drawing the word out, "that wall that we want to knock out upstairs? Load bearing."

I grimaced. "How much is the load-bearing beam down here gonna run us?"

The engineer gave me a speaking glance and melted away, eyebrows raised. Hearing him slinking up the stairs behind me, I groaned. "That bad?"

Miles nodded. "Yep. But here's the great thing, Walk. We've prepared our clients and they're capable of absorbing unexpected costs like these. You're spared from having to give the compassionate undertaker speech this time." He lowered his head, clasping his hands in front of him. "We're gathered here today," he said in a poor imitation of me, "to mourn the death of your budget."

"Shut up, Miles. I don't sound like that."

"You're right, you don't. You're a lot better than I am at breaking at bad news. Speaking of which, what were you already worried about when you came down here?"

I frowned. "I wasn't. I'm not."

He smirked, running a hand over the gleaming surface of his shaved head and the unruly whiskers on his chin. "Please. You looked just like my mother when she thought Denzel Washington died. What happened?"

I turned and headed back up the stairs, only for him to follow right behind me.

"It's some Leffersbee drama, isn't it?" he pressed. "I'm telling you, working with family is like someone pouring itching powder down the deepest crevice of your ass where you can't easily reach or publicly scratch. It always ends in pain and annoyance and everyone looks at you like the bad guy when you finally set limits. I told you I gave my sister three strikes, three strikes mind you, before I fired her from managing the bowling alley. Did she listen? Did she heed my warning? Finally I just said, 'Look, I can show you better than I can tell you.'"

I shook my head to myself, only half-listening to Miles drone on as I passed through the kitchen and headed back out to my truck. I lowered the back of the truck bed and sorted through my toolbox. When Miles finally wound down the story I'd heard at least twice before about his sister threatening to sue him, I asked, "Is the plumber going to be happy when he's done poking around?"

He rubbed his hands against the front of jeans. "Given the size of the new water stains in those three rooms ... I'd say he's no longer worried about how he'll put his kids through college."

"Dang it," I hissed.

"Why are you so upset about this? It's not like Zora and Nick can't afford it, and it's not like they won't make a sick profit if they ever sell it. What happened earlier today when you went fishing with Pops?"

He crossed his arms when I hesitated. "Get it out, Walker. It's always better out than in. Well, unless it's hemorrhoids."

"You've always had a way with words."

"I'm merely a truth teller," he said blithely. "Now, what's going on?"

I headed to the front steps of the porch and sat, happy to be sitting. Miles stood before me, arms folded and frowning while I relayed my earlier conversation with Pops.

When I'd finished, he shook his head. "Tap out, Walker. Regardless of what Pops says, you *will* end up in the middle."

I'd already come to that conclusion. "I already gave him my word."

He scowled at me. "You ever get tired of always taking the honorable route? Ever wanna just get fucked up on bourbon or tequila or, shit, just say 'fuck?'"

"This isn't about me."

"Yeah, but it is. You have the weirdest guidelines for self-regulation. You're always wound up tighter than a tick from trying to be Mr. Perfect, unless you're chasing the scent of new pu—"

"Dear God," I said, unable to keep from scowling at him in distaste. "Listening to you, I'm starting to think Leigh was right about me."

He sucked his teeth, a wide grin spreading across his face. "Oooh. Now I wanna know what Leigh said. Sounds like an interesting ride to the airport."

"You're a worse gossip than my grandmother was."

My phone vibrated in my pocket, and I checked the display. "This is my doctor calling."

Miles's expression instantly sobered. "A doctor calling with test results on a Saturday? That sounds serious. Like 'you've got cancer' serious."

I glared at him. "You always know what to say, don't you?" I realized I was still staring down at the phone as it vibrated.

Miles snatched the phone out of my hand, accepted the call, and shoved it at my ear. I elbowed him back and walked a few feet away.

"Hello?"

"Walker? This is Dr. Gardi. Do you have a second to go over your test results?"

"I do." Behind me, Miles had crept closer and stood at my elbow, straining to hear. Rolling my eyes at us both, I put the call on speakerphone.

"Well, the news is great. Your EKG is good. Taken together with the rest of the test results, I can't find any reason for the syncope."

Beside me, Miles's face fell in relief, and he clapped me on the back.

Relief, warm and immense, unfurled and eased the tension in my chest.

Dr. Gardi had me walk him through exactly what I remembered before losing consciousness, and I supplemented my memory with what Leigh had told me.

"Well," Dr. Gardi said, sounding as if he was gearing down and satisfied he'd cleared his diagnostic hoops, "I can't think of what could have happened. It was a wedding, an exciting day. Did you have enough to drink? Do you think you could have been dehydrated?"

"It's possible," I allowed, unable to recall exactly what my fluid intake had been on a particular day several months ago.

"Have you been under stress, or feeling anxious?" Dr. Gardi pressed, and from beside me Miles stuck an insistent finger in my side.

"Well, no more than—"

"Yes," Miles coughed audibly, and I sighed.

"There's been some stress," I confessed, "but no more than usual."

"Well, that's something for us to work on." Dr. Gardi sounded considerably brighter, and the next five minutes were spent examining my work schedule and exploring my willingness to consider personal counseling or start a meditation practice.

By the time I hung up, I was overwhelmed with relief.

And also worried for another reason entirely. Was I out of my mind ... from stress?

Miles joined me in sitting on the porch in silence as we waited for the plumber to appear with a verdict.

He stretched his legs out over the descending stairs, not quite looking at me. "I've been worried about you."

"Worry about yourself and your apparent aversion to lotion," I joked, inclining my head to indicate the dry white patches around the knuckles of his brown skin.

He narrowed his eyes at me. "Some of this is drywall, for the record. You need some shea butter for your *soul*, brother."

"Yeah, okay."

"With whatever's coming that your grandfather's warning you about, you really need to neutralize Tavia."

Frustration filled me thinking about how much she'd changed since her time in New York. "She's going through something."

"And you still don't know what happened that made her suddenly show up here in Green Valley?"

"I've tried asking." I pulled at a few shoots of grass inexplicably growing through the fractures in the concrete steps. "So has Mom. She's tight-lipped about it."

A memory hit me then, of Tavia and Zora as babies. Almost two years old when I was ten, with chunky baby legs and huge heads. We often played a game in which I'd crouch by a doorway on all fours and pretend to be a snarling, snapping wolf guarding his keep. When either dared to get too close, I'd snatch them up and blow raspberries to their necks and stomachs until they giggled deliriously. We all had fun, but the two of them had very different approaches to playing the game. Zora had simply been delighted by the prospect of getting caught and often ran off shrieking in anticipation before she got very close to the doorway.

Tavia, however, had been a different story. She'd been incredibly bold, brave, often brandishing a weapon if she thought it would help, whether it was a hairbrush or toy. The time she did manage to conk me in the head with a Barbie, she had honestly seemed shocked that she could hurt me.

So many of our current interactions reminded me of that game. Present-day Tavia was still hell-bent but she was also now bitter, charging and uncaring about whatever damage she inflicted.

Pops was right. I did need to find out what was going on.

"And now you've got Leigh," Miles was saying, and I sat up straight at that.

"I don't *have* Leigh."

"What was it she said to you in the car?" His dark eyes were alight with glee. "Are y'all any closer to finally getting it on? She ready to give in to all that horniness dressed up as disdain?"

"Miles."

"This isn't complicated math, Walker. She hates that you're a player, and you hate that she has that impression of you. Why? Because you want each other, and ideally to take out your horniness only with each other."

I rested my forehead against my palms and let out a deep breath. "Well, let me make the math even simpler for you. Yesterday we both acknowledged we're attracted to each other, but we decided it wouldn't be a good idea."

"Who decided? Her or you?"

I cut my eyes at him. "Her."

"Oh." He waved a hand at me. "She just doesn't know you yet, down deep. Won't be long. You'll see. I'd bet on this, but since she'll be your woman soon, I won't. It would make you feel cheap, you know, once you're in a relationship."

"There will be no relationship. It's too much pressure, thinking of starting something up with her."

"What does that mean?" Miles scowled.

"Zora texted me last night, letting me know that Nick somehow figured out nothing really happened between us. Nick convinced Zora to just leave things alone and let nature take its course, but of course she couldn't help herself. She warned me Leigh's already been badly hurt, and Zora's worried about me somehow making it worse."

"Hurt how?" Miles looked interested.

"She was married. I think the guy cheated."

Miles went quiet at that. I snuck a glance at him and saw his jaw working, his gaze downcast. "Hard to come back from that," he finally said, and my heart went out to him. "Not as easy to trust people after that kind of thing. It changes you. Changes how you see the world."

I opened my mouth, wanting to ask about the ex-wife who took off with our mutual friend while Miles was away on active duty, but decided against it. That ice was still too thin, even after seven years.

"So just don't hurt her, Walker," Miles said. When I faced him, his gaze was hard on mine. "Don't start something up until you know you're ready, and see it through when you do."

"Have you been listening at all? I said I don't want that responsibility." I thought of Leigh's face again, coldly beautiful as she said goodbye.

Miles shook his head.

"What?"

"Just ... just grow up, Walker. You only get the payoff if you take the risk. We both know that more than anybody. I'm not busting my ass trying to make things happen just so I can be alone all my life."

"So, that's why you've actually tried it again, right? You're no better than me. Don't preach platitudes you're not living. I don't fault you or her for being stuck in the past where you were hurt, but it's not on me to fix anyone's problems or take the heat for someone else's mistakes."

Miles mirrored my posture, gripping his forehead in his hand. "It's never easy with you. Just like when we were kids, you still have to make a list of why we shouldn't try something."

"If you ever bothered to make a list, maybe you wouldn't have broken Mrs. Babcock's window."

My phone trilled again. I pulled it out and answered when I saw Zora's name on the display.

"What's up, sis?"

"Walker." Her voice was low and urgent. "I need a favor. I know you dropped Leigh off at the airport the other day, but can you do me a favor and pick her up tomorrow? Nick and I left for San Francisco today. Something ... happened with her family, and I don't want her to have to manage on her own."

"Is she okay? Are you going to tell me what happened or keep talking in code?"

She hesitated. "It's her story. Only she should tell it. But if you could—"

"I'm on it, I've got it. Just send me her arrival details, and I'll get her."

"Thank you," Zora said, sounding relieved as she ended the call.

Miles watched me. "Something with Leigh."

"Yeah. I don't know what yet."

"Oh, I do," he said, his smile smug. "Guess you can't run away from your fate after all."

CHAPTER SIX

Leigh

"The job interview went really well yesterday. Really well," I said, feeling equal parts relief and dread.

"Of course it did. That's not what I want to talk about. Rewind back to the part where Walker's moving next door to you."

I rolled my eyes, straightening from my perch at the kitchen's toy-strewn center island. Lucia turned from the stove where she was preparing breakfast to bounce her brows suggestively, pushing scrambled eggs around the skillet with a spatula. She'd scraped all her thick, wavy dark hair into a bun and wore an apron that advised, *No special requests.*

"Focus on the pertinent facts here. I aced my interview. They even asked how soon I can start. I've got one foot practically planted back here in Fairlane again."

"So, you're really ready to move back?" Skepticism hung heavy in her tone. "No second thoughts?"

I hesitated, wanting to iron out any reluctance in my voice. Cia's bull-shit meter was finely tuned, and I was still wondering if it was wrong to leave my KCH co-workers in a lurch.

"I miss you and Paul and the kids," I said, deciding the truth was safer. "And Felicia. You even have my damn dog here now."

She shook her head. "You're the one who gave in to your nephew's tears when we visited last month. And you have to admit that dog is having the time of her life. She's not waiting all day for you to come home from work, and she gets about five walks a day. The kids fight over whose bed she gets to sleep in every night."

"She's living her best life," I agreed. "But I miss her. A lot."

"You know ..." Lucia aimed a sly smile over shoulder, "that could just mean you need companionship of the human variety."

I thought of Simon and his offer for a nightcap, but that was quickly eclipsed by the memory of Walker at the airport, hot and standing only a breath away with a dangerous gleam in his eye.

I'm good with my mouth, he'd said. And damn it, I believed him.

I came back to reality in time to see Lucia watching me with a shit-eating grin.

"Let's review," she said. "Your best friend and the wealthy man she married insist on renovating the duplex for which you pay ridiculously low rent. Her older brother, whom you've been in lust with for as long as you've known him—"

"Inaccurate. I took a shine to him when we first met. I've since learned better. When I moved to Green Valley—"

"When you moved to Green Valley you called me and said, and I quote, 'Walker Leffersbee is still exquisitely fuckable after all these years.'"

"The kids," I hissed under my breath. I craned my neck behind us toward the living room where my niece and nephew had disappeared behind the baby gate only moments before. Beside me, my three-month-old niece slept peacefully in a carrier atop the island, her tiny rosebud mouth working. I couldn't help tracing the translucent, silken skin of her tiny fist with my fingertip while marveling at the perfection of each of her tiny toes. She was so beautiful.

Especially when she was quiet and sleeping.

Since arriving at my sister's house Thursday afternoon, I'd been entertained by the usual child-related cacophony: the bumps of falling objects, squeals, yells, outraged tears. How my sister managed to wrangle three children under the age of five without having a nervous break-down, I'd never know. Then again, all her pre-parenthood experience prosecuting criminals as a district attorney probably provided some parenting hacks. I knew we were both grateful for the rare quiet interlude of the present moment, and I wasn't surprised she'd used the time to start needling me for updates.

Lucia slipped on a pair of oven mitts. "They're glued to the TV in there. They never move when *Kids Hour* is on. And don't try to distract me. You've had a thing for Walker since undergrad. Now you've got him next door. Where he'll be oozing testosterone, swinging tools and jackhammering. Jackhammering," she repeated, bending to open the oven door. "This moment has been fourteen years in the making."

The heat from the oven flushed her face pink and kinked the wisps of hair around her temples. I blinked at her sudden, uncanny resemblance to our mother. We both had our father's pitch-black hair and navy blue eyes, but Lucia's features had been set in a far daintier frame. I'd always joked that God had been bored the day he made Lucia and decided to dally long enough to sculpt the high cheekbones, cupid bow lips, and tip-tilted eyes that made her stunning. Not that there was anything wrong with my looks. But Lucia had the kind of luscious, classical beauty that would have sent Renaissance painters into raptures. It had been one of her most effective weapons in the courtroom, allowing her to bury anyone who underestimated her.

"This is the moment a lifetime of experience has taught me to avoid," I said. "If anyone should know better than to get tangled up with Walker Leffersbee, it's me."

"I've seen you and Walker together." She made quick work of retrieving the bacon and redistributing each strip on a paper-towel-lined plate. "There's serious heat there, and you know it. If you don't believe me, explore it while naked. I have a feeling you'll be delighted with the results."

"Who's getting naked? Hey, Leigh!" My sister's husband, Paul, a red-haired version of Paul Newman, strolled into the kitchen in a ratty Rutgers Law T-shirt and sweats, looking between us with wide eyes. He stepped behind my sister and slipped his arms around her waist, ducking his head to kiss her cheek. "Is it us? Tell me it's us," he murmured against her face.

She attempted to elbow him from behind. "Maybe if you wore your sleep apnea mask and I didn't have to listen to you snoring all night, it could be us. So, no. It's Leigh, if she gives it half a chance." Her tone was acidic as she slapped at his hold around her waist, but I saw the smile pulling at one side of her mouth.

"Leigh?" He turned to me with a grin. "Well, a toast to you." He grabbed the glass pitcher of orange juice from the counter. "This calls for vodka, let me get it. We're celebrating."

I grinned back at him. "No need to celebrate, Cia's mistaken. And wear you sleep apnea mask. It's dangerous to piss off the person sleeping next to you, and Cia's already kinda vengeful," I said, remembering the time I'd snuck her favorite leather skirt out of her closet, only to rip it right before I returned it. She'd absorbed my explanation and apology with relative calm, but I'd woken up the next morning to find she'd cut off my ponytail in my sleep.

"Lucia is merciless," Paul agreed, angling the carrier just a bit so he could check the sleeping baby. "Not that either of us are getting any sleep with this little one." His gaze softened as he took in his daughter. I was certain none of the associates at his firm would have recognized the bemused wonder on his face.

"She's so cute, though," I cooed. The faintest whorl of hair was now barely visible at her crown, hinting she'd have Paul's ginger coloring. "She's worth losing any amount of sleep."

Not all that long ago, I'd planned to have my own sweet-faced baby. Son or daughter, it hadn't mattered, but at least three. Or four. I'd wanted to replicate the brightest spots of my childhood. Popsicle-stained shirts, sprinkler-sodden play clothes, strenuous fights for a turn on the trampoline or for possession of the video game controller. My mother's sisters had followed family tradition and turned out large passels of children. Our ragtag bunch of cousins had been automatic playmates during endless summers as we ran and biked, up and down the street and around the corner, from one aunt's house to the next. Lucia and I had imagined a future in which our own kids would run back and forth between our houses, slamming screen doors, and begging for lemon cookies.

But it just hadn't been in the cards for me. In the end, I'd chosen self-respect over the comfort of self-delusion. I'd had to embrace a different reality.

"She's beautiful," I said again, tracing the curve of my niece's toe as I pushed away the familiar, sneaky grief.

I glanced up just in time to catch Paul and Lucia exchanging an uneasy glance. My sister winced, then cleared her expression.

"Enough baby talk," Paul said, not so subtly changing the subject. He filled both glasses with juice and a liberal splash of vodka and slid one toward me, adopting the air of a sympathetic bartender. "Glad to hear you're living it up, sis. Who's the lucky guy?"

"Walker Leffersbee," my sister said from behind me, and I heard the barely contained glee in her voice. She rounded the island again and leaned against the counter, arms folded, as she watched us.

Paul's face seemed to register shock. "Walker?" He and my sister exchanged another long look. "Really? *Finally?*"

"Nothing's happened," I said, firmly, "and nothing's going to. I'm smarter than that."

"I like Walker," Paul said. "We all do. And you like him, as a person. What's the problem?"

"There isn't a problem," my sister sniffed, pulling salsa from the fridge.

"He's screwed his way through half the female population of Knoxville at this point," I reminded her.

"He's single," Paul said with a shrug.

I scoffed. "I don't want anything to do with a guy that—"

"A guy that what?" Paul narrowed his eyes at me. "That dates? That's not a crime. Why is he the villain just because he's slept with different women? You're all about exploration, as I recall."

"No surprise you're coming to his defense." My sister smirked in his direction.

He gave an aggrieved sigh. "I reformed my ways when I met your sister. I was ready. But no, I wasn't perfect and no man is. Now, I gotta put in a good word for Walker. I never really bought that Southern hospitality thing, all the fake manners and undercover shade hiding behind a 'bless your heart.' Not until I met Walker. That guy's a class act. Disciplined. Kind. Appreciates a good Adam Sandler movie."

"As if such a thing exists," I said.

"And he's down there in that small little town," Lucia said, pulling an innocent face. "What else is there for anybody to do?" She joined Paul in learning against the counter, presenting a united front.

My sister and brother-in-law remained convinced that living in Green Valley was akin to living on the edge of civilization, despite all my arguments to the contrary.

"Hey." Paul visibly brightened as he nudged Lucia. "This could be one of those, which ones do you like, Luce? The small town romances?"

Lucia shouldered him back with a grin. "No, Paul. This would a best friend's brother romance, which, as I think you already know, Leigh, tend to run hot. Although," she drawled, "every time we visit you, I see all kinds of guys I wouldn't mind rescuing me. Those beards, that country twang ..."

Paul's sidelong glance in her direction promised retribution.

"Nothing is going to happen between me and Walker." I stared into my glass of spiked juice. Paul's freckled hand entered my field of vision and clasped my wrist.

"He's not Gio, Leigh. It's not possible for anyone else in the world to be as negligent and careless as that piece of shit."

Gio. Being back in Jersey and hearing my ex's name brought the horrific slide show of memories from my days of being married in Fairlane. When I was in Green Valley, I rarely dwelled on the past and all that had happened. Being back here, it was all so real, the remembered disappointment and humiliation so deep-rooted and visceral.

Leigh, I don't know how to tell you this, I hate to be the person to tell you, but there's a rumor going around about Gio and another woman, and well ...

Steeped in bitter memories, I was glad when Lucia picked up the thread of the conversation. "Leigh applied for a Child Life position All Children's," Lucia told Paul, looking nowhere near as thrilled as I thought she'd be at the news. "She interviewed there yesterday." She went on to explain my imminent unemployment and all the uncertainty surrounding Knoxville Community.

Paul listened closely, nodding.

"But all's well that ends well, maybe," I said. "The chances of me getting the All Saint's job are pretty high. I could be back here eating weekly brunch with you guys in no time."

Paul's smile was weak, and he seemed to struggle for a response.

Lucia traced the gold skeins in the marbled countertop with her fingertip, not meeting my eyes.

"I thought you both would be excited."

"We are," Paul said, slowly. "I guess I'm just surprised. We want you back, Lee-Lee. That goes without saying." He ran a hand through his hair until it stood on end.

"And the kids are getting so big." I smiled at the baby. "Sometimes it sucks being Auntie Leigh from afar. I miss my nieces and my nephew."

"They miss you too." Lucia's gaze hadn't moved from her husband's. "But in the interest of full disclosure, there's something you should know—"

A clatter sounded from the back of the house.

"What was that?" Lucia straightened, her eyes going wide. "Was that in the bathroom? But how? They're behind the baby gate."

"One of them might have snuck down the side hallway," Paul said, hustling out of the kitchen.

"What's going on?" I looked toward the empty kitchen doorway.

"Your nephew," my sister whispered darkly. "I swear, sometimes I wish I still had access to a lockup so I could put these kids in it. He's been playing 'sink or float' in the toilet."

"Paul will handle it," I said, trying to calm her. "I mean, it's a little gross but not the end of the world."

Paul's scream stopped us both in our tracks, and we froze. It was a scream, not a yell, and in a higher register than I would have though him capable of reaching.

Lucia and I both took off for the bathroom at a run.

We found Paul in the bathroom with my adorable eighteen-month-old nephew, his face buried in his hands.

I peered around Lucia's rigid body to get a better view. I couldn't tell if there were any foreign objects in the toilet but ...

It was impossible to miss my nephew gnawing on the toilet brush. Spotting me, he held the brush aloft in my direction, grinning, as if offering me a taste.

"Take it from him, Paul," Lucia gasped, then made a retching noise.

"Oh my God," I breathed, turning back into the hallway, unsure of whether or not I wanted to laugh or hurl. "Was he really just ... ?"

Lucia joined me. I heard Paul inside, his motor functions now unfrozen, calmly explaining that toilet brushes weren't meant to be chewed. Then came the sound of running water.

"That's so disgusting," she breathed. "I can never unsee that. Or not know that he he ... he ate the—"

"Better if you don't think about it," I said, laying a hand on her arm. "That mental image isn't going to get better."

"It's okay," Paul said, walking past us. My nephew was thrown over Paul's shoulder, laughing, head bouncing at each of Paul's jostling steps. "It's a guy thing. We're built tough to survive experimentation like that. And Luce and I aren't gunning for some boring parents of the year award. We want our kids to have interesting lives."

"He'll definitely have a strong immune system," I whispered, and my sister delivered a vicious pinch to my arm as we followed them back into the kitchen.

"Plus," Paul continued, "this is just blackmail for later in his life, when he's an asshole teenager. Any girlfriends of his I don't like, I'm telling them all about the time he ate shit."

"He didn't eat shit—" Lucia began.

Paul grinned at her as he resettled my nephew back behind the baby gate he'd somehow breached. "You sure you wanna split hairs? Or *bristles?*"

"It is kind of funny," I admitted, and she gave me her patented death stare.

"It's probably indicative of his developing personality," Paul added, joining us back at the kitchen island. "He'll probably be a real shit-talker."

"Or a proctologist," I offered.

"Enough with the shit talk," my sister snapped, and from the living room came my nephew's gleeful cry: "*Shit!*"

We all fell silent for a beat, then Paul and I cracked up.

"Don't laugh," my sister snapped. "It encourages him!"

"Which one of you is giving him bedtime kisses tonight?" I choked back laughter.

"*Shit!*" My nephew yelled, doing an admirable job of projecting his voice across the kitchen.

I straightened my expression while Paul retreated to the stove, back turned, shoulders heaving with silent laughter.

My sister yanked off her apron and tossed it on the counter. "We're out of here. Leigh's taking me for a spa treatment today. You've got plenty of pumped milk. Try not to let the kids kill themselves with any more 'experimentation.' Don't call me unless someone's in mortal danger."

Paul executed a snappy salute. "Aye aye, captain! I'm on it."

Lucia didn't even acknowledge him, just grabbed her purse from a stool and headed to the door.

"Shit!" my nephew yelled, his face crumpling when he realized his mother was headed to the door.

Paul called to us as he turned his attention back to the eggs and bacon on the stove. "What? You guys aren't hungry?"

I HAD HARDLY EVER RETURNED HOME to visit after leaving New Jersey, so finding myself in my old neighborhood was uncomfortably discordant, like sliding into a suit of skin two sizes too small. I was different, but it was all the same. Nothing had changed. Same neat row of ranch-style homes fronted by perfectly manicured lawns. Homeowners sat on their porches in white plastic chairs, pretending not to watch their neighbors. A gaggle of kids ran up and down the block on bikes and skateboards, hollering after-dinner plans to each other. I stared out the windshield of my sister's car, eyeing my parents' house. It was a relief to see ours was the only car in the driveway.

"Dad's not home," my sister said, reading my mind. She sounded drugged. Chronic sleep deprivation combined with a ninety-minute massage had rendered her almost catatonic. A quick glance to my left showed her slumped back in the driver's seat, her eyes half-closed and jaw hanging slack.

"I told you to let me drive." I sighed, exasperated with myself for not forcing the issue. But she'd threatened to fight me in the parking lot when I'd tried to take her keys.

If I was anywhere near as difficult and stubborn as she was, my friends all deserved medals.

"I'm fine."

"I'll stay up with the two little ones tonight so you can get some rest."

She shook her head, running a limp hand over her eyes. "No need. It's Paul's turn. It's the weekend, his work is light right now, and I'll cut his balls off if he even tries to skip out." When I laughed, she joined me. "Come to think of it, cutting his balls off isn't the worst idea. I can't take another kid, not right now, not ever."

"Alright. I'll see you back at your place in a few." I unbuckled my seat belt and grabbed the door latch just as she spoke again.

"Wait. How did dinner with the folks go last night?"

I deflated against the seat, letting my hand fall from the door. "About the same. What it always is."

She smiled, her eyes still closed. "Let me guess. TV blaring loud as hell, Dad mostly grunting, Ma talking for the both of you?"

I let out a humorless laugh. "You know it. One day she's gonna stick her hand up our asses and work our mouths like puppets." I closed my eyes. "God, will it ever get any easier?"

"Nah. They're old, set in their ways. You never were any good at playing the denial game with them anyway."

"And who does that serve?" I demanded, angry at myself for even posing the question for the millionth time, much less to my exhausted sister. "Certainly not Ma. It just makes it easier for Dad to do whatever he wants with impunity."

"It's her decision," Lucia said, sounding exasperated. "You think you're frustrated? I still live here. I spend most of my time with them biting my damn tongue. But I've always admired you speaking your mind. It's cost you, I know. But I respect the hell out of you for it."

I opened my eyes, sighted the house again. "If I'm so much more enlightened, how the hell did I manage to marry Dad? No, actually a slightly worse version of Dad?"

Lucia sucked her teeth. "That wasn't your fault. Gio—"

"It was my fault. I should have known better. How frustrated can I get with our mother if I made the same bad decisions?"

"You're nothing like her." I turned to find Lucia watching me, her expression fierce. "You're the anti-Ma, and I can say that because we both love the hell out of her reality-avoidant ass. I can't ever see you hiding your head in the sand. If anything, you've swung all the way to the other side of the spectrum. But, sis, I hope you give love a try again. For real."

That, I thought, was no different from hoping I'd shove my head in a pre-heated oven.

"You know I love Walker, and I think the two of you would be perfect together. But if not him, somebody. I see the way you look at my kids. I know you want that for yourself."

I sat up, reached up the latch again. "I hear you, Cia."

"One more thing," she said, and I looked back. "There's something I need to tell you when you get back to my house. Tonight, before you fly back tomorrow." She turned her attention to the windshield as I watched her warily.

"Why can't you just tell me now?" *Good Lord.* D'Alessandro secrets always came with a hell of stinger. Might as well rip off the Band-Aid.

"When you get to my place," Lucia insisted. "It requires explanation."

"Dysfunction usually does," I sighed. "I'm not gonna like it, am I?"

Her gaze slid away from mine. "No. You're not."

We sat in silence, staring at our childhood home.

"Alright," I said, opening the car door and sliding out. "I'll head back to your place after this."

"Have fun." She snickered, waving goodbye. I couldn't help noticing her worried expression as she watched me slam the SUV's door shut.

I headed down the driveway, past the colorful flowerbeds my mother carefully tended, and went through the squeaky side gate to the back of the house. I immediately recognized the shape of my mother's upturned, paisley-covered bottom amid the flowerbeds adjacent to the back porch.

"Hey, sexy," I said, giving a long wolf whistle.

From the time we were teenagers, Lucia and I had loved to keep our mother off-balance with our off-color, flirty commentary. On one level, earning our mother's exasperation brought us great joy. On another level, we always sought to compliment her, to bolster her confidence, to remind her of how beautiful she was inside and out.

After all she'd been through with our father, we figured it couldn't hurt.

She jumped, startled, and briefly stumbled forward.

I rushed forward to help her, pulling her upright before she crashed into the brick wall of the house. Her face was still red when she turned to face me, but we were both laughing. *She never ages*, I thought, taking in her wide smile, her big dark eyes, and wavy dark hair.

"Leigh! I wasn't expecting you to come by today. I thought you and Lucia were going to spend the day getting massages and shopping."

"Sorry, Ma. I couldn't help myself," I said with a grin. "Since I'm leaving tomorrow, I thought it might not hurt to spend a little more time with you. Lucia's tired anyway. She went home to take a nap."

"I'm making you sauce to take home, but it won't be ready until tomorrow," she said. Her smile faded as she began pulling at the hem of her gardening shirt. "I thought we said I'd pack it up and have it ready before you leave for your flight."

I peered at her. "We did. You alright, Ma? You seem nervous. You don't have to make any sauce."

Her eyes darted to the side of the house, then back to me.

"I'm fine. So ..." She slid her gloves off and knocked them together to shake off the excess dirt, then checked the delicate gold watch on her wrist. "What, uh—"

Footsteps sounded at the side of the house, followed by the rusty whine of the side gate opening.

"Shit!" my mother said under her breath, and before I could recover from the shock of my mother cursing, a voice sounded from the back gate.

A very familiar voice.

"Sorry I'm late, Mom, traffic on the GW was at a standstill—"

My breath caught.

My mother's face fell, her eyes briefly closing.

"Leigh," she said to me, quietly, urgently, her eyes holding mine. "Listen to me—"

I let out a disbelieving breath, and turned to face my ex-husband.

Gionni Bernardini stood only a few feet away, surprise all over his deceivingly handsome face. I ran a dispassionate eye over his immaculate dark suit, the crisp white shirt, the perfectly shined shoes. He was just beginning to show traces of his age with a growing proportion of salt to pepper in his beard and at his temples, but it would only make him look distinguished, more seasoned with time. The perfectly engineered weapon, ridiculously effective at assailing a woman's common sense. I shook my head at myself, at the fool I'd been. Devilishly handsome, well put together, with a perfect smile to hide all those miles of forked tongue.

"Leigh." He nodded, reaching for a buddy-buddy tone all while he swallowed nervously.

I studied him, curious yet unnerved as some instinct screamed that this was wrong, something was off.

Run. But my instinct for self-preservation lost out to the conviction that I wasn't going to be intimidated by him at my own parents' house.

I'd done enough running. It was time to stand still, to reclaim my ground, to recover what I used to be. I'd left so much *me* behind in the wake of all that had happened.

"Gio," I said, evenly. I heard my mother clearing her throat behind me, but I kept my focus on him, trying to ferret out what exactly was going on.

Before I'd left Fairlane I'd had to stomach his presence at almost all our family functions and social gatherings. Our families had been braided together since before we were born, and I soon learned it was impossible to cut him off, to amputate him from my life like the gangrenous limb he was. After we'd separated, being in the same room with him had always invited the same chatter, the uninvited commentary from all the different corners of our friends and families. What I could have done differently to "keep him in the house," how it was or wasn't my responsibility to forgive him yet one more time, to give him another chance. And Gio had always been there at the center of everything, gaslighting on the sly, playing the injured party, doing nothing to discourage the talk.

"I didn't expect to see you here," he said, although talk of my visit would have gotten to him soon enough. His mother lived at the end of the block, and my sister's family was right around the corner.

"To what do we owe the pleasure?" I asked.

The back screen door exploded open, and the blur of a small child clambered down the back steps and shot over to Gio, burying his face between Gio's legs.

Gio let out a happy exclamation and caught the child up, effortlessly tossing him up in the air. He managed to deliver a raspberry to the child's stomach before settling him on his hip.

"Who's that?" The little boy twisted in my direction and gestured to me, and I felt my heart drop. Behind me, I heard my mother's inarticulate murmur of dismay.

It was Gio as a child, but, that couldn't be right. I shook my head, confused, as my brain tried to sort out how the miniature version of Gio, who looked just like the boy I saw in old family pictures throwing Cheerios with me in the nearby highchair, was now somehow perched on Gio's hip in some bizarre time hop.

When it hit me, when reason finally kicked its way through to the front of my brain, I went cold all over.

It was the baby. Gio's baby. The baby he'd conceived with some other woman, all while I'd been struggling to recover from his *last* indiscretion.

He was beautiful, this child. Fashioned from a template of Gio, yes, but with enough distinctions for me to wonder who his mother had been, what she looked like, how she'd contributed to this child's adorable, smiling face.

Gio opened his mouth to answer his son, but whatever answer he'd prepared stalled out, and he closed it again.

"This is my daughter," my mother said, stepping beside me. "Her name is Leigh." She used the same gentle, matter-of-fact tone she'd used with me a child. "You know Lucia. She's my daughter too. This is the other daughter we talked about, who lives far away in another town."

Her explanation sliced me open. So this child knew my sister, knew of me—the daughter who lived *far away.* Well, my mother must have been right. I lived very far away for all of this to be happening with me totally clueless.

The little boy held out one hand in my direction, fingers spread wide. "How do you do," he said, enunciating slowly, and despite myself, I smiled at his careful manners.

He was just a child, not a ghost, an innocent child with an adorably gap-toothed smile, I reminded myself. That gave me the strength to cover the twenty feet between us to shake the tiny hand, to withstand being in such close proximity to his father.

"It's nice to meet you," I said past the shards of glass in my throat.

"Tell her your name," Gio said quietly, his face averted from mine.

"My name is Matteo," he said proudly, giving my hand a little up and down shake. "And I'm five years old. I can count to a hundred! Wanna see?"

I worked up a smile, kept it on my face even as I felt something vital splinter and break inside me.

"You're such a smart boy," I managed, giving the little hand one more squeeze before I released it. "One day I'd like to hear you count, but I have to leave right now. It was nice meeting you, okay?"

"Okay," Matteo said, giving me Gio's old smile, and I managed to return it.

"Goodbye," I said, and Matteo returned the greeting just as I turned on my heel to leave, stalking through the gate and around to the front of the house.

Behind me, Gio apologized to my mother in a hushed voice. I thought I heard genuine regret in his voice.

"Leigh!"

Putting her mall walker speed to good use, my mother caught up with me halfway down the driveway and clamped a hand around my arm until I stopped in front of the Range Rover now parked there.

"Leigh. I'm sorry."

"What was *that*?"

She wrung her hands together, her brow creasing. "I watch Matteo sometimes for Gio—"

I let out the breath I was holding. "When were you going to tell me about this? Wasn't it enough that you insisted on keeping Gio around after I finally divorced him? You had to take his kid in too?"

"Listen to me." She shook her head, her eyes on the pavement. "I can't imagine how you feel, walking into that with no warning."

Now it all made sense. Lucia wanting to talk to me, why she couldn't quite look at me. "Lucia knows about this, doesn't she? That's what she wanted to tell me."

Her eyes met mine briefly before she looked away. "Yes, she knows. I mean, she knows that your father and I have been spending a lot of time with Matteo. She wouldn't have known he was here today. This was a last minute request."

"Last minute. So you do this, watch the kid, on a regular basis."

Until that moment, I hadn't known there was anything left of my heart to break, not when it came to all the ways Gio had broken my confidence and stolen my trust. But a sudden, crushing pain assured me that yes, grief still occupied a shadowy corner of my heart.

"Of all people," I said, regarding her steadily, "I would think you'd understand how I feel right now."

Her face flushed to the roots of her graying dark hair and she looked around nervously. "We're outside. The neighbors."

"You're worried about the neighbors right now? What could they possibly not know about Dad's exploits at this point?"

"You know we don't talk about that."

"You never let us," I snapped. "It was all about keeping a smile on our faces while our lives were falling down around us."

"Well, you didn't make it any easier, Leigh," my mother snapped, and I took a step back, away from her. I looked at my mother, really looked at her, and wondered about the woman she used to be before her life was consumed by a relentless cycle of disappointments. I wished I hadn't spent so much of my life trying so hard not to be her that now I was just as numb to disappointment as she was.

I shook my head at the absurdity of it all. Why had I expected things to be any different?

"Bye, Ma." I turned and headed to the end of the driveway.

"Leigh." Her voice was tight and low as she followed me. "Don't you dare turn your back on me. Tell me, what do you want me to do, huh?" I glanced back to find her hands clenched into fists at her side. "He's my best friend's son. My best friend, who has breast cancer right now and can't look after her grandson when she gets radiation on Tuesday and Thursday afternoons. So I stepped in. And then as time went on, we grew attached."

"I would ask you to vote for me. For once."

"He's a child, an innocent child."

I kept walking, trying not to feel my heart breaking. "I get that, Ma. I used to be one too."

That silenced her.

I made it to the end of the driveway, calculated the distance to the nearest gas station and how soon I could coax a calming cloud of nicotine into my lungs.

"I can't believe I thought I could do this," I said out loud, laughing at my own stupidity.

"So, what? You're not moving back home now?" My mother's voice from behind me was thin and defeated.

I turned back to face her, beyond caring, beyond worried about what the neighbors would hear. "I don't know where home is anymore. But it's for damn sure not here."

CHAPTER SEVEN

Walker

"The roads are pretty bad this afternoon."

I glanced over at Leigh in the passenger seat. It was the first thing she'd said in the half hour since I'd picked her up from the airport. Before she spoke, she'd been sitting with an unnatural stillness that worried me, eyes staring forward, limbs stiffened, shoulders hunched upwards as if she longed to transition to the fetal position. In profile, her jaw was tightly set, lips compressed into a thin line, temple working spasmodically.

She was struggling to hold herself together.

I adjusted the speed of the windshield wipers as the downpour intensified. From outside came the sounds of tires sluicing through standing water and the steady drumbeat of raindrops pelting the car.

"Should've driven my truck," I said, easing off the accelerator as the car fishtailed slightly.

Leigh nodded meditatively, took a breath, let it out. Working herself up to talking, I surmised.

"I like your car," she said, glancing at the digital display. "It's fancy. Electric, right?"

"Ah, now, I don't know about all that. Teslas are good for the environment, and there's an ever-changing suite of toys with the updates.

Although I guess you'd think any car that's running is fancy compared to yours."

I was gratified to hear her tiny huff of amusement. "True. I need to run it by the Winston's garage tomorrow before work."

"I already took it in," I said, taking the exit for Green Valley. "Didn't know when you'd need it, so I thought I'd get it to the top of their queue. Your extra set of keys are still at Zora's. Hope you don't mind."

She went quiet then, turning to face the window and the slender rivulets of rain racing down it. I contented myself with listening to the plaintive tones of Chet Baker's trumpet while my mind worked at unknotting the problems of the bank and the woman beside me.

When she spoke again, I almost didn't hear her. I turned down the volume.

"Thank you," she said again.

"For what?"

"For everything," she said, sounding spent. "And I want to apologize. For what I said when you dropped me off at the airport."

I lifted a shoulder. "I don't know that you need to apologize. What you said didn't make me feel very good, if I'm honest, but maybe it was something I needed to hear. And you should always tell your truth, no matter what."

Her head snapped around to me at that.

"What?" I risked a quick glance in her direction.

"Nothing," she said, sounding confused.

We rode in silence for a while longer.

"We're almost home." I glanced over at her. "You hungry? Want to grab something?"

"No, I don't have an appetite."

"When's the last time you ate?"

She appeared to consider it. "Well, I guess I didn't today. I skipped breakfast, and then my mom came by my sister's ..." There was a tiny catch in her breath. "And then I just headed to the airport."

Ah. So something went wrong with her mom.

"I've got some vittles at Zora's. I don't mind sharing."

I turned the last corner, feeling the weight of her stare. "What?"

"Why are you so good to me, Walker? So nice? Even though I give you a hard time?"

The questions, and their whispered delivery, gave me pause. She was facing me, head tilted in my direction, waiting for my answer.

I pulled into the driveway directly behind my truck and parked before I turned to face her, giving her my full attention.

"What else would I be but good to you, Leigh?"

Her mouth worked, eyes downcast.

I leaned toward her, slowly, so she could take in my approach and object if need be. Gently, I lifted her chin until her eyes met mine. Her gaze was soft and uncertain, the usual cynicism nowhere to be found.

"I don't know what happened this weekend, but you're safe with me. I don't want to take anything from you. I'm not that kind of man."

Our gazes held as the rain persisted in battering the car. Concern and anger mounted as I watched her bite her lip, her breath hitching.

"Alright," I said briskly, reluctantly pulling my hand from the silken underside of her chin and sitting back. I knew she'd never forgive herself if she broke down right now. "I need you to meet me on Zora's side in twenty minutes. Wear something you don't care about, long pants, closed shoes. I'm putting you to work."

She blinked. "Are you serious?"

"Very serious. Come prepared to work." She sat looking at me for several beats.

"Whatever happened today, it won't help you to go home and obsess over it. Give me a hand with getting started with the reno. It'll take your mind off things and give you some ideas about what to expect for your place."

"Uh, okay. I guess."

I swallowed back a smile at her vaguely startled expression, then worked to coordinate her bags and walk her to her front door under my golf umbrella. Letting myself into Zora's side, I wondered if she'd be a no-show.

I shouldn't have been surprised when she showed up as requested twenty minutes later. I was glad to see she'd worn an old pair of jeans and shoes, paired with a form-fitting, bleach-spotted T-shirt. All that soft dark hair was wound into a bun high on her head, showcasing the graceful column of her neck. I wondered how the sensitive spot behind her ear would taste, how it would feel to sink my teeth into that smooth skin, to lick away the sting of the imprint left behind.

"I don't know what I'm doing here," she said, looking around the kitchen.

I reached inside the pantry and pulled out the pair of sledgehammers I'd stashed there. "We're finally doing something about these cabinets," I said, nodding behind me.

Her jaw dropped as her eyes moved to the cabinets. "I've always hated those ugly-ass cabinets." Her voice was hushed. "You mean I actually get to help tear them down?"

"You do. Right after you eat this." I put a plate in her hand.

"What is this?"

I went to the fridge, pulled out a bottle of water. "That's ham and cheese on rye. I guessed at your condiments. You can put the chips on the sandwich or eat them alone."

One of those thick dark brows went up, and her lips twisted in a smirk. "You put chips in your sandwich? What are you, a sociopath?"

"Thank God. I wondered how long it would take before you finally said something biting or sarcastic."

She smiled then, wide and unrestrained, and I felt like I'd won something. "Thank you, Walker."

I waved that away and went to the corner of the kitchen to retrieve my toolbox. "Call me Voldemort or something before I get confused. Friendly's never been our schtick."

She took a bite of her sandwich and watched quietly as I went to work with the drill, fitting the bit and removing the anchoring screws from the cabinets. She'd gotten about half of the sandwich down when she asked, "Will I get time and a half? Since I'm working on this two-person demolition crew on a Sunday?"

"I'll put in a good word for you with the contractor," I said. "He's notoriously frugal though, so don't get your hopes up. An argument can be made that *you* should pay for this free anger management."

When she didn't respond, I looked back at her.

She'd put the empty plate in the sink and now stood studying her sneaker-clad feet. "Did Zora tell you what happened?" she finally asked.

I pulled out the drawers in the lower cabinets and started stacking them by the back door. "No. Only that something happened. Here." I handed her a sledgehammer, showed her how to grip it, to lock her stance and manage the momentum of her swing. She put on the protective eyewear I handed her. "Go ahead. Take a swing."

She looked to the cabinets and back to me, eyes bright as her hands tensed about the hammer's handle. "Really? Anywhere?"

"Anywhere."

She started toward the cabinets, then stopped. "You're not going to ask?" She didn't look back at me.

I leaned back against the kitchen counter, prepared to enjoy the show. "I figure you know you can trust me. If you want to talk, I'm here to listen. If not, we'll just have fun taking those cabinets down."

She sidled up to the end of the cabinets and held the sledgehammer upright like I'd showed her, arms tensed, stance wide. I felt a moment of guilt for appreciating her form in profile, her high upthrust breasts, how snugly her shirt hugged her slender waist.

I averted my eyes when she suddenly spun back around to me. "I might as well tell you."

"Alright."

Lowering the sledgehammer so it rested between her feet and shoving the glasses on top of her head, she straightened. "The Cliffs-Notes version is that I got married too young to a guy who never had any intention of being faithful, although I should have expected that." Her gaze went to the kitchen floor and grew unfocused. "He, Gio, we grew up together. So did our mothers. They went to the same school and they've been best friends their whole lives. So when Gio cheated the first time I knew about, I tried to get over it. I tried to move past it."

I struggled to hide my surprise. She caught my expression.

"I know," she acknowledged. "Not very smart of me."

"No," I fumbled, but I was taken aback. The Leigh I knew would have yanked off his nuts and hung them from her rearview mirror. "It's not a judgment at all. Relationships can overcome infidelity. I just—"

"I was young. Gio had a reputation as a playboy, a fast mover, but he was ridiculously handsome. When he showed interest in me all of sudden, I was shocked. Flattered." She shook her head, mouth pursed.

"Why?" I asked, aghast. "You're gorgeous."

She flushed. "I don't need that, Walker."

I took a step closer to where she stood, then another, keeping my eyes on hers. "The first time I saw you," I said, not stopping until I was directly in front of her, "I couldn't stop thinking about you, not for a long time." *I never stopped.* "He was the lucky one, not you. You've got to know that."

A flush had spread from her cheeks to her neck. "I appreciate that, Walker, but it doesn't matter anymore."

"It does," I insisted.

"I'm not the same young girl I was when I married Gio." Her gaze dropped to our feet again. "Back then, I was ashamed to admit that maybe my marriage needed to fail. When I said yes to his proposal, I wanted him. I wanted the marriage, I wanted kids and happily ever after." Her eyes closed. "So when I found out about the first girl, we went to counseling. He swore he'd never do it again. I got a lot of unsolicited advice about what I needed to be doing to 'keep him satisfied.'"

I thought of all the ways I'd like to dismember Gio and took a deep breath, swallowing my growing fury.

"Let me guess." I knew where this story was likely headed. "It wasn't the last time he cheated."

She gave a mirthless laugh, her gaze briefly touching mine before it lowered again. "How'd you know?"

"I've seen it. I've known those kinds of guys, the ones who'll cheat and find a way to blame someone else. Cowards."

"Yes," she agreed.

"Tell me the rest."

Her exhalation was bone-deep. "He went back to cheating, probably never stopped. I found out for sure when he had to tell me he had a baby on the way. 'It was just a quick fuck at the club.' That's what he told me, as if it made it more excusable somehow. 'Just a little fun with a bottle girl in a back room.' And just like that, there was a baby."

"Is that when you moved here?"

"Yeah. Zora knew what was happening, so she scouted the Child Life job and gave me the other side of this house. I had to force rent money on her. I'm still so grateful for her. There was no escaping it in New Jersey. The only way I could get away from it was by leaving the state."

She looked so alone in that moment.

"What happened on the trip?" I prompted.

The heels of her palms rose and briefly ground into her eyes, smearing her eye makeup. "Yesterday I went to visit my mother. Gio was there."

I groaned. Surely she wasn't about to say—

"He was picking up his son. My mother was babysitting, apparently." She went quiet for a while before she added, "His name is Matteo. I'd heard that, secondhand, but it was different actually seeing him there, a living, breathing child." Her grip on the handle tightened. "Matteo," she said, absently.

Her eyes rose to meet mine. She looked so lost, so uncertain.

"Leigh—"

"It doesn't hurt anymore, not in the same way. I guess I was just ... surprised by the whole situation, and so disappointed by my mother's unflagging support of my adulterous ex-husband. I really shouldn't have been surprised by that, but I still was."

She was more than surprised, I thought. More like bruised, tender, aching from a newly awakened wound.

Held captive by the rage she refused to acknowledge.

"Anyway, I got the hell out of there. Went back to my sister's. She and Paul had been trying to tell me what was going on. Lucia was pretty horrified at how I found out. They gave me all the details about how my folks got entangled with Gio's kid, but it doesn't really matter. It's not Lucia's fault, or Paul's."

I glanced down, noting how her thumb and fingertips rubbed compulsively.

"I used to smoke," she said, seeing the direction of my gaze. "Terrible habit. I'm glad I quit, but I'd give anything for a cigarette right now."

"Let's take it out on these cabinets instead." I reached out, slid her protective eyewear back over her eyes and smoothed a wisp of hair back from her temple.

She turned her face into my hand. My thumb instinctively skimmed the surface of all that rose petal softness. Her lids closed against the brilliance of her eyes and I stood stock-still, savoring the moment, taking in the loveliness of her face in repose.

Then she pulled away, opening her eyes and looking away. "Alright," she ground out, "I'm taking it out on the cabinets."

She pivoted back, lifted the sledgehammer, and rammed it into the corner cabinet. The wood, soft with age, easily gave way and cratered inward with a resounding BOOM. She kept at it, demonstrating surprising strength as she raised and lowered the sledgehammer. Wood splintered, ricocheted, fell around her feet. I stayed back and merely watched. When her careful, methodical movements gave way to wild swings, I stepped a little closer, checking to make sure she didn't hurt herself. I made myself hold still when I heard her heavy breathing become gasps that finally gave way to tears as her arms visibly trembled with each impact. I didn't interfere even as she swiped intermittently at her eyes in between each of her desperate lunges and then finally stood whimpering after clearing out an entire row of upper cabinets.

But when she turned to me, her face full of tears, shoulders shaking, I opened my arms to her.

And she came.

I hadn't imagined the first time I held her she'd be quaking from sorrow and anger, not passion. I gathered her up, guided her legs around my waist, whispered comfort into her ear as her arms twined about my back and neck.

"I'm sorry," she whispered thickly. Warm tears splashed onto my neck.

I turned us and headed to the kitchen table and settled into a chair. "I'm proud of you," I told her, rubbing a circle into her back. "Sometimes feeling is harder than not feeling."

She sat up, hiccupping, swiping at the remaining moisture under her eyes. "I'm so embarrassed," she whispered.

I smiled, watching her swirl makeup around her eyes until she resembled a raccoon. "There's nothing for you to be embarrassed about. Absolutely nothing. I'm glad you got all of that out."

Her laugh rattled in her chest as she threw a look at the remaining carcass of cabinets in the kitchen. "Yeah, I guess I was holding a lot in. Years' worth of rage."

I studied her silently, taking in all the new little details now visible with her so close. How the thickness of her dark brows, the length of her long lashes made her eyes ridiculously blue in contrast. The trio of freckles at the edge of her jaw was almost lost to the dark olive cast of her skin. The mole at the base of her neck.

What was wrong with me? Hadn't she just gotten done crying?

Slow down, Walker.

"That felt good," she said on a shuddery breath. She looked at me as if seeing me for the first time, as if becoming newly aware of the fact that we were only inches apart with her legs still straddling my waist in the narrow kitchen chair. "I needed that."

"I could tell. Listen," I said, slipping one my hands under one of hers. "I'm sure this isn't your first time hearing this, but I want to tell you again. It's not your fault, what he did. Even if you were young and didn't know any better, that doesn't make what he did right."

She let out a breath then, looking more tired than sad. "I do know that. I do. I hate that I allowed so much to happen, but I'm smarter now. I grew from the experience. I don't know why I just lost it like that yesterday. I mean, I knew he had a kid—"

"It's different seeing it. Different knowing a thing in the abstract than actually seeing it." I swallowed.

She leaned forward on my lap, her small hands on my legs as she narrowed her eyes at me. "You sound like you know about this."

I nodded reluctantly. "I do. Grad school. I'll tell you all about it one day."

"I'll ask." She nodded slowly, her gaze going drowsy as she watched me.

"Walker ..." Her breath caught. "Thank you."

"Please stop saying that."

"No, I mean it, I'm so grateful for all you've done."

"It was nothing."

She bit her lip then, those crazy blue eyes settling on mine in a way that made my pulse quicken. "Can I ask you for one more thing then?"

I couldn't look away as she canted forward, inch by inch, biting her lip again in the way that made my thoughts go wild.

"Anything." It came out scratchy.

"Well, it feels like more of a *big* thing." She smirked, just as the heat of her moved suggestively over the part of me that was rapidly growing.

Her arms went around my neck. The last thing I saw was her gaze dipping to my mouth right before she closed the distance, pressing her lips against mine.

I straightened, electrified, as her tongue followed, breaching the seam of my lips, sliding in, tangling with mine. One of her hands rose to cradle the back of my head as she leaned into me, her breasts pressing sweetly against my chest. Below, her hips were rocking, rolling, undulating until I was painfully hard.

My hands had already risen, intent on exploring, claiming, before I yanked the chain on my control.

I framed her face with my hands and very gently pulled back, as much as it killed me.

"Leigh." I was surprised to realize I was out of breath. "What is this? What are we doing?"

She blinked. "It's you and me, Walker. It's what's always been between us, waiting."

I shook my head, trying to clear it. "Not like this. Not while you're upset."

Her grip around my neck tightened. "I'm clear, Walker, not confused, and my judgment isn't compromised. I want this."

Her head lowered again, but I shook mine. "Not while you still think I'm just like him. It matters to me that you know we're different."

Her shoulders fell, and her hands unwound and rested on my shoulders. "I could never confuse you with him. Not anymore. I see you, Walker. You've always been there for me, always wanted the best for me. Those things I said before, when you dropped me off—" She closed her eyes, shaking her head. "I was scared."

That worried me. "Scared?" She looked away and I captured her chin, steering it back to me. "Scared of what?"

She gave me that wry smile I knew so well, and I relaxed a bit. "You won't be satisfied until you drag it out of me, will you? Can't you just leave me with my dignity?"

I shook my head, ghosting a finger over her bottom lip. "Why should you be allowed to have any dignity? Why shouldn't you be every bit as off-balance as I am right now?"

Her chest lifted with an inhalation. "I was scared that what I felt for you would destroy me. Again."

I couldn't help the skepticism that colored my voice. "And all it took was a weekend at home to make you think differently? Your trash ex-husband following his usual script suddenly convinced you that we aren't the same person?"

Her lips firmed. "You were never the same. I know that."

I shook my head. This wouldn't work. "I can't be what you need, Leigh. I can't give you the hero, the perfect guy, that knight in shining armor that heals your wounds. I'm not your second chance."

Something briefly flickered in her eyes, and her jaw pulled taut. "I'm not asking you to fix me, Walker, and I damn sure don't expect you to be my second chance. You don't need to worry about my foolish female mind imagining marriage or doodling your name in my journal. All I want is one night."

I opened my mouth, closed it, started to explain that I thought she deserved those things, needed those things after all she'd been through. I just wasn't the guy to take on that burden, and she deserved my honesty.

But one night? My blood warmed at the thought.

"One night," she said, echoing my thoughts, her eyes boring into mine. "We get whatever this is between us out of our systems. No more wondering. No more wanting. One time."

Time slowed, stopped, balanced on the edge of a knife. Everything hinged on this moment, I knew.

"Fine," I said, sealing my fate. "One night."

~

Her eyes went wide. "'Fine?'" She repeated.

There was no need to repeat my response, not with the flare of heat that turned my thighs to steel beneath hers. Not with the way my blood already simmered in anticipation.

She gave a startled squeak when I stood from the chair with her in my arms and strode to the kitchen counter.

"So," I began, checking the countertop for debris before I lowered her onto it, "you think it'll be awkward between us tomorrow after I turn you out? You gonna be speechless after you find out what it's like with a Southern gentleman?" I grinned to show I was teasing.

Her eyes narrowed to familiar, battle-ready slits. "You sound ridiculous right now. 'Southern gentleman.'"

"We do it different," I informed her, already half-distracted as my palms settled on her denim-covered thighs. Heat from the friction of my hands' restless back and forth slide burned me.

She smirked. "What, does your dick wear a monocle like Mr. Peanut and talk like Deputy Dawg?"

I choked back a laugh. Then all the air in my lungs evaporated as she whipped her T-shirt over her head with a shocking economy of movement. Her hands disappeared behind her back while I still gaped at the sudden expanse of all that olive skin, at the sudden revelation of her sheer black bra and shadowed nipples.

"Hold up," I said, still struggling to force air back into my chest even as the straps of her bra slackened and fell down her arms. The cups of her bra inched down, tortuously slow, revealing the plump, taut shapes of her breasts before snagging on her nipples. "Slow down." I pulled her into me, adhering her chest to mine, trapping her arms against her sides. "We Southern gentleman like to go slow."

She pulled back just enough to meet my eyes. "We Jersey girls are impatient. We like talk backed up by action."

I made a disappointed sound. "That's sad. Means you've been missing out."

I bent and took her mouth before she could say anything else. She responded immediately, her tongue meeting mine in sinuous strokes, her teeth catching my bottom lip. Her arms slid from under mine as she gripped the back of my head to bring me in closer while seeking the waistband of my sweats.

"Nuh uh," I said, trapping her wandering hand and holding it captive. It was all too much. We were in an alternate reality where the only thing that mattered was the way her hips rhythmically churned upwards into my torso and threatened to ignite the fuse of my self-control. I wouldn't survive long in the clasp of her hand, and I wanted to make this last for her. To prove something after all she'd been through that day.

I endured another of her biting kisses before I turned to explore the sweet curves I'd long admired. "You smell so good," I managed, inhaling the sharp tang of sweat and vanilla. I nosed the strong column of her neck, groaning at the salty tinge of her skin and the wispy tickle of hair at her temples. I didn't miss her sharp intake of breath or the way her hips circled more tightly. "I'm guessing you don't mind it slow, then?"

"Shut up and keep doing that," she said, her moist breath collecting in my ear, and I took a moment to get my own arousal back under control.

Time crawled by, slowed, stopped, as I gloried in every centimeter of her smooth skin. When I loosened her hair and watched the dark tangled curls settle around her shoulders, I felt the moment that my heart stuttered and stopped.

Dear God. She was so beautiful.

I took my time, tasting as much of that candy-cotton soft skin as I could reach, letting my tongue trace the all peaks and slopes from her shoulders, to her throat, to her full breasts, exploiting each of her gasps and shivers and sighs with more. And more. Meanwhile, she never stopped moving, never stopped with the throaty groans that drove me crazy and further tightened my groin.

"Walker," she moaned from above. I gave her hardened nipple one last suck, one last lick, my hand tightening around the deep curve of her hip before I met her gaze.

"Please," she breathed. I took in her lust-hazed expression, how the blue of her eyes had grown impossibly dark as to be almost indistinguishable from the iris. I'd never wanted a woman like this before. Never felt pulled by the contradictory desires of wringing more pleasure from our foreplay or finally relenting to her need for completion.

"Yeah," I breathed, filling my hands with her breasts, circling the nipples and loving how her body responded in kind.

"Please. I'm ready. I'm so wet." Her words almost broke me. I let out a ragged breath, my grip on her tightening. *Stay focused.*

Tonight was about her.

Her hands were already at the fly of her jeans, her hips lifting in an attempt to pull them down.

I couldn't help my chuckle. "Seems like slow worked for you after all."

"Don't gloat, just get inside me. I think I have condoms in my wallet.

Oh, damn, my wallet is next door," she said, her voice so forlorn I couldn't help wheezing with laughter.

"We aren't going to need those tonight anyway." I lifted her hips to assist her now frantic efforts to free her waist from the jeans.

"What do you mean?" Her eyes went wide. "We're not going to—"

"You're going to," I told her, then stole another kiss from her mouth while it hung open in outrage. "Tonight is about you. That's enough for me."

Sensing the denial on her lips, I shucked the jeans from her legs and stepped closer beneath her thighs. Her breath caught when I ran a finger along the dampened seam of her underwear. Hooking a finger around the fabric, I let my fingers slip into all that melting softness. I couldn't help groaning as I petted all along the lips, then gave her clit the barest caress.

She jolted, her thighs widening even more in invitation.

"I can't believe I'm actually naked on a kitchen counter with Walker Leffersbee right now." She sounded bemused but looked anything but shy as she shoved her hips at me. "I can't say I saw this coming."

My grin felt depraved. "I predict we'll both see you coming very soon."

I watched her face as I slowly slid two fingers into her. The immediate, greedy grasp of her inner muscles was almost my undoing.

"I can't believe I have Leigh D'Alessandro naked and spread out in front me," I said, bending to take her mouth again, letting my tongue provide accompaniment to my fingers below. "And I can't wait to see all of her. To taste all of her."

So saying, I pulled back and settled to into a crouch between her legs.

Her hand appeared out of nowhere, almost dislodging my exploring fingers. "Walker!"

"What?"

"I, I hadn't planned on that. I thought we—it's been a long day. I haven't showered since this morning."

I pulled up enough to meet her eyes and lift a disbelieving brow. "Since when have you ever been shy?"

She actually blushed. "I'm not, I just—"

"I want you. Just like this. Just the way you are right now."

Our gazes met and held.

"You're perfect," I told her. "And I've wanted this for a long time. I wouldn't change anything about this moment."

She looked as if she wasn't breathing. "Not even the kitchen counter?"

"Especially not the kitchen counter. This feels like our speed, Cruella," I joked, letting my fingers burrow even more deeply inside of her, enjoying the reflexive flutter of her eyelashes. I used my free hand to guide her open palm against the curve of her breast. "Doesn't it?"

"Yes," she breathed, eyes closing.

It wasn't supposed to be *this* good, I thought. Drugging and instantly addictive.

I lowered, braced one hand against the counter and guided her hips closer to the edge. Counseling myself to go slowly, to savor, I allowed myself a slow lick that delved the depths of her honeyed center and ended with persistent flicking against that knot of nerves above. Her shriek from overhead only further emboldened me, and I committed to learning every inch of her. I took my time, worshipping the creases of her legs, the outer petals of her sex, the delightfully wet furrow that led to her luscious grip on my fingers.

I wanted to be inside her. I wanted to know the feel of her clamping around me.

But nothing in all my experience had yet come close to the satisfaction of seeing this woman, always so self-possessed, now coming apart on a silent cry. Nothing would match the triumph I felt as her reaching fingers seized my shoulders, the nails painfully indenting my skin.

And nothing worried me as much as the sight of those blue eyes slowly opening to meet mine as I stood and regarded her, just before she pulled me in for a deep, searching kiss.

Yes, I'd wanted to show her how beautiful she was, to convey what I felt every time I saw her. I'd *needed* to finally free myself from more than a decade of unexplored desire.

Now I wondered if I'd only managed to work myself deeper into a snare. Now, with the taste of her still in my mouth and that final gasp of pleasure still trapped in my memory, there was no mistaking the fact that I wanted more of her.

CHAPTER EIGHT

Leigh

I jerked awake at the sound of something crashing against the front door below. Pushing up from the bed on one arm, I squinted at the clock on my bedside table.

6:04 a.m.

Who the hell was hammering on my door like that at six in the morning?

"Somebody's about to die," I muttered, stretching my arms overhead and feeling the satisfying pull of muscles in my limbs ... and other interesting places.

Ah. That's right.

Walker Leffersbee had gone down on me in Zora's kitchen. The details of the previous night rushed back in merciless detail. Had I really cried in his arms after sledgehammering cabinets? Had he really given me the best orgasm of my entire life with just his fingers and tongue?

One night, I remembered. That's what we'd said. One night.

But how would *that* work, now that I knew exactly what Walker's facial hair felt like against all my softest places?

The knocking resumed.

"Coming!" I yelled, throwing back the covers and shoving my feet into the house shoes beside my bed. "I'm coming! Stop banging like that!"

The pounding persisted even as I stumbled, half-fell, down the stairs, yelling.

"*Goddamnit,*" I shrieked, so incensed I threw open the door without bothering to check the peephole first.

Walker Leffersbee towered over me on the porch, eyes wide and fist still raised in the act of knocking. He wore the same gray sweats and T-shirt from the previous night. I didn't miss the way the shirt stretched enticingly across his pecs. He returned my regard, his gaze traveling over my body in slow perusal as one side of his mouth kicked up in that trademark smirk.

"You always answer the door like this?"

I looked down. I was in my underwear and a camisole, my usual sleep uniform. Seeing his eyes catch on the pert protrusions of my nipples, I straightened my spine. He'd already seen everything I had. No point in playing shy now.

"Fuck is wrong with you, knocking like that?" I hissed. "What do you want?"

"So much for the afterglow."

"Don't flatter yourself," I said, but I couldn't deny the fact that my labia were applauding at the mere sight of him. "Especially if your so-called Southern charm comes with an early wake-up call."

He took a step closer, almost crossing into the threshold of the foyer. "No," he said, those dark eyes settling on my mine with unnerving intensity. "That Southern charm is what had you up there sleeping so hard you haven't heard me knocking for the last ten minutes."

Well, damn. That was ... accurate. Not that I'd ever let him know that. The last thing I needed was Walker Leffersbee feeling smug.

I made myself meet his eyes. "Come in."

He ducked his head, but I caught the flash of his grin as he stepped into the space I vacated, closing the door behind him.

"What brings you over here, neighbor? What do you need, a cup of sugar?" I folded my arms and tried not to notice how the morning growth of his beard intruded on even more of that smooth mahogany skin.

He averted his gaze, seeming to smother a laugh.

"Go ahead. Say it. Get it out of your system."

"No, no," he said, openly cracking up as he waved a hand at me.

"Go ahead," I insisted. "We agreed it wouldn't be weird. You wouldn't hold back under any other circumstance. Let it fly."

"Alright," he drawled, rocking back on his heels with a silly grin. "I was just gonna say, I thought I got all your sugar last night."

I stared at him for a beat, then we both burst out laughing.

"*Dun dun dun dun,*" I sang, mimicking the loser horn sound effect from *The Price is Right*.

He nodded in easy acknowledgement. "Going for the easy laugh's always taking a risk."

"And to think, all this time I thought you had a little finesse with your philandering."

"Oh, I think you'd agree I have more than a little finesse where it counts." His smile was sly, but his eyes held a heat that compelled me to step closer into his warmth, to trace the contours of his finely molded chest.

"Why are you here, Walker?" I ignored the steadily accelerating drumbeat of my heart. I would *not* let my imagination run wild with every lurid possibility for his sudden appearance.

"I need a shower." He lifted the garment bag I hadn't even noticed he was carrying.

I blinked against the sudden visual of Walker's fine, densely muscled body covered with suds behind my Captain Marvel shower curtain. Damn shame I hadn't gotten to see more of him last night to fill in crucial blanks. "Is there something wrong with your shower?"

He let out a breath. "Yeah, actually. A pipe in the bathroom finally busted."

"Oh, God. You can't use the water in the bathroom?"

"Nope. So I was hoping," he jiggled the garment bag from his finger, "that my neighbor could do me a favor and let me shower at her place."

I made a show of shrugging. "I guess I could. I won't charge you if it's this one time."

His brows went up. "I would hope not. Especially since I'm your only way to work this morning."

That's right. I didn't have a car. "We're even," I agreed. "Go ahead, you can have the bathroom first. Upstairs, second door on the left." I gestured behind me to the staircase.

He didn't move, just stood there watching me, his expression suddenly serious.

"You sure you're alright?" he asked. I realized then that he'd made a concerted effort to keep it easy, keep it light and funny, to make sure I was comfortable with all that had happened between us.

That he was capable of such caring and sensitivity should not have been surprising, but it was.

But even if he wasn't Gio, he was still Walker. A first-class player who'd explicitly warned me against catching any feelings for him.

I gave him an easy smile. "Don't worry, Jafar. It was fun, but I'm not looking for a repeat performance. We Jersey girls are built tough, and we do our best ass-kicking after temporary setbacks. But," I delivered a friendly punch to the arm, "I'll never forget how kind you were to me when I was feeling so low. It was very generous of you."

His forehead lowered into a creased frown. "Kind? You think I was being kind? Generous? It wasn't about—"

I smiled gently. "It was a friend helping a friend, I know that. I'm honestly grateful. I appreciate how you've had my back so many times. I'll always be there for you too."

His expression was inscrutable, his body noticeably stiffening as he stared down at me.

"What?" I asked, confused by his reaction. I thought he'd be relieved to have me define our present circumstances in such a bald, no-frills manner.

He took a while responding. The light in his eyes had gone somewhat flat by the time he did speak. "I'll be quick in the shower. Meet me at my car in the next hour to hit the road?"

"Sounds good," I responded as he headed up to the bathroom.

And yes, I did stand and watch the muscled bulk of his ass as it went up the stairs.

That's what friends do, after all.

~

"HOLD UP, let me make sure I understand this." I craned my neck to face Walker fully as he drove. "After you nearly crack your head open from passing out, the leading theory is that you've been what, stressed?"

Walker's sigh was edged in exasperation. "This is actually good news."

"Maybe I'd feel that way if it felt like a decent explanation."

"It's not like I really passed out. I got dizzy for a second. I probably hadn't eaten."

"You ended up on the floor."

"Technically, I didn't fall, and I didn't completely lose consciousness."

"You kind of did," I persisted.

"It was more like a ... slow topple."

I took a breath, stepped on my gathering impatience. "What, you think you folded into yourself like a Transformer? I think you should get a second opinion."

He kept his eyes on the road, silent, while I stared at his profile. "It's fine," he said. "I've been checked from 'the rooter to the tooter.' I'm going to work on my stress, and I'm going to do a better job of eating."

What the what?

"Do you not eat every day?"

He shrugged. "Sometimes I get distracted when I'm working. I get to work early and I leave late, and whatever happens between is a blur. If I need to, I grab a protein bar before I go to the gym."

He fell quiet. The indistinct murmuring of the radio was the only sound in the car.

"Tell me what's been going on." I turned just in time to see his mouth and shoulders tighten. "What's been going on that you've been stressed?"

I could almost see him physically shutting down at the question. "I'm not stressed."

I closed my eyes. "Yet you accept that as a viable diagnosis from your doctor. There has to be a reason why."

He flicked a sidelong glance at me. "Is there a reason you want to talk about this?"

I raised a brow. "What, do I need to go down on you to get you to talk? Is giving head your love language?"

He let out a strange hybrid of a laugh and a cough. "I, uh ..."

"Although I could easily give you some tips on de-stressing."

His head turned on an eerily slow swivel to meet my gaze. "I think I might be interested in hearing your tips."

I smothered a grin. "Keep your eyes on the road, psycho. And no, my tips don't have anything to do with any of your tip getting in me. I'm not offering right now."

He grinned in profile, and I spotted the brief appearance of his tongue between his teeth. Good Lord, the things he could do with his—

"Music," I said, redirecting my traitorous thoughts. "Or the lack thereof." I plucked his phone from the center console. He didn't have it locked and I easily navigated to his music application. "No more Ira Glass and NPR when you're heading into work in the morning, especially when you're dreading some part of your day."

"I can't wait to hear what this has to do with helping me."

"As hot as I find your nerdiness, I very much doubt that hearing droll commentary on the fucked-up state of the world is going to improve your stress levels."

He gave me a flat look, then returned his attention to the road.

I executed a search for the song I wanted, hit play, and Ira Glass's tepid voice gave way to the upbeat syncopation of André 3000 singing "Hey Ya!"

Walker sent me a brief dirty look I ignored as I turned up the volume and rocked out to the beat. It was almost a welcome treat to have him driving. Body rolls were easier to execute when you weren't holding the steering wheel.

He shot me a few incredulous glances, but less than a minute later he joined me in grooving to the chorus, even working his shoulders in his suit jacket as we shook it like a Polaroid picture. By the time we grooved into "The Way You Move," he looked far more relaxed and had even turned up the volume further. We'd made decent progress to Knoxville and covered a fair amount of Outkast's catalog by the time the playlist ended.

"See?" I turned down the volume. "Wasn't that better than dry-ass Ira Glass? Did you wish you were listening to a summary of all of the world's horrors while you were instead of dancing?"

He shot me a reluctant smile. "Aren't you a little young to be bumping Outkast?"

"You forget, Lucia is your age. I was forced to listen to whatever she was listening to because she drove me everywhere. But these are classics, everyone knows them. And this isn't my morning drive playlist, I'm just trying to ease you in slowly."

"You think I can't hang? You think just because I rock with *This American Life* I can't keep up with your busted morning playlist?"

"I accept your dare," I said solemnly, switching the song to one of my favorite Jay-Z songs, rapping along with Jay and Kid Cudi about already being home. Walker listened for a minute, and then he groaned.

"You've got half the lyrics wrong," he protested, laughing. "I've got this." He took over then, his flow and timing startlingly impeccable, and suddenly I wanted to revisit my stipulations about his tip and where I'd allow it.

"That's how it's done," he gloated when the song finally ended and I gave him applause. "Don't test me when it comes to Jay or Kendrick."

"I shouldn't be surprised," I admitted. "But I never even hear you listening to music. You're always closed up somewhere with podcasts and stacks of paper. You don't seem to have any other forms of non-vagina related entertainment."

His eyes narrowed. "Thank you for offering your professional opinion."

"I wanna see you cut loose and have fun, Walker! Be a little careless for once. You're so damn *cautious*."

"You're telling me, a Black man living in America, to be 'careless'?" he scoffed. "You sure it wasn't you that hit your head at the wedding?" He snorted, half-joking, but I sobered.

His words easily summoned my memories of all the injustices, the unfairness I'd watched Walker endure since I'd met him in undergrad. The cop in downtown Manhattan who pulled us over on the pretense of a broken taillight after we left a club, then held Walker at gunpoint when he merely asked why he was pulled over, then threw him against the hood of the car in a fruitless search for drugs, all while the cop's partner screamed at Zora and me to stop yelling.

I remembered the salesclerks who followed him through stores, until either me, Zora, or Walker lost our shit. The cold resignation on Walker's face when he'd silently hand the car rental keys over so Zora or I could drive in certain cities after repeated, unjustified traffic stops.

And that was just what I'd witnessed. I knew Walker had to move through life with a different, parallel set of rules governing his survival and success.

"Touché," I said, intent on letting him know I understood, as much as I could, but his big hand covered mine as he spoke.

"It's okay."

"But I—"

"I get your point. You think I could do with loosening up from time to time. You're probably not wrong. Miles has said something similar. But some of the stuff with the business and my family can't be shaken off with a good Outkast song."

I nodded. "You're right, about all of it. But I do care about you, Walker. I know how unsafe it can be out in the world. But maybe there could be, with me and you. As friends," I hastily added when something in his expression changed. "I just wish there was a way for you to lighten some of your load."

Walker was quiet for a while, then a reluctant smile pulled at the corner of his mouth. "I'll give Outkast a little of my morning."

"That's all I'm asking."

"We're here," he announced.

I looked up, startled to realize he'd steered us into the parking lot of Leffersbee Savings & Loan and slid into his reserved spot by the front entrance. "Damn. That was fast."

He put the car in park and faced me. "I guess time does fly when you're having fun." The tiniest of smiles sat on his lips, and a voice in my head advised me to hurry up and throw myself out of the car before I embarrassed myself.

"I thought you were going to drop me off at the hospital." I looked around at the mostly empty parking lot.

He pulled the keys from the ignition and handed them to me. "I could, but I don't want you stranded at work if you want to go somewhere for lunch. I know from Zora that you all have your hen meetings over lunch."

I mock-glared. "Somehow, I don't think your use of 'hen' is a quaint regionalism. But thank you. I do like to escape the hospital on break when I can, just to get some air."

He nodded. "What part of your day are you dreading?"

"Huh?"

"Earlier," he said, jerking his head to the left as if indicating the past. "You said, 'especially when you're dreading some part of your day.' I didn't say I was dreading any part of my day."

"But you are," I said, guessing.

"Come on. What made you say that?" He settled back into the seat, waiting for my answer.

I turned to look out the windshield. "Parents of a Peds patient who died are coming in today to say goodbye to all of us who worked with them. It's nice to have closure, we all get attached. And then there's the stuff with the hospital being sold."

"Yeah, that can't be easy," he said, his eyes softening. "I'm sorry, you know. Sorry that it's happening at all, and especially to you. I know how much you love your job, and those kids." He smiled, and the words felt like a hug, an unexpected balm to the constant buzz of anxiety I felt nowadays.

I needed to get away from him.

"Thanks. It sucks. But," I said, running a covetous hand along the steering wheel, "opening this baby up is going to make me feel a lot better."

"Uh, you better go easy on my baby," he said, caressing the dash as he got out of the car. I snickered as I opened my door. I walked around the car and slid into the driver's seat, luxuriating in the sumptuous leather as I watched Walker's progress into the bank. The glass exterior of the building gave easy visibility to the interior of the bank, allowing me to follow his route to the back offices. With each step he took, it seemed his shoulders went higher and higher.

Not stressed, my ass.

An idea bloomed to life in my mind. It would likely irritate Walker, but after all he'd done for me, the least I could do was return the favor. I knew exactly which like-minded woman to consult.

When I pulled into the bank's drive-through, I wasn't surprised to see Mrs. Watkins's round, petite figure bustling by the front window.

"We're not open yet," she said through the speaker automatically, then paused when she straightened and actually looked out the window. "Is that ... Walker, is that you out there?"

"No. It's just Walker's car. It's Leigh, you know, Zora's friend?"

She let out a laugh. "I remember you, baby! Zora's friend, the pretty one with a boy's name. What can I do for you?"

I shook my head. No matter how many times I'd met Mrs. Watkins and spent time with her, it seemed there was no erasing the peculiar descriptor she'd filed away for me in her mental Rolodex.

"Yep, that's me. Listen, I don't need to access my account today. I just wanted to put a bug in your ear."

~

"WHAT HAPPENED IN THE MEETING?" I poked my head in the doorway to the shared conference room that connected our office suites, quickly zeroing in on Aaron, Layla, and Ebony among the potluck participants.

Everyone looked up at my question. The room went dead silent.

Uh-oh. Not a good sign. I didn't know what I'd been hoping for, but it wasn't winces and grimaces. Apparently the rumors were true. The hospital I knew and loved was about to undergo a dramatic transformation.

"Didn't make it to the meeting after all?" Layla swiped at the corners of her mouth with a balled-up napkin, then threw it into her mostly full plate of sandwich, chips, and dip.

Dread gnawed at my gut. "Had to show a kid what to expect for his surgery tomorrow. What, you don't have an appetite? Was it that bad?"

She let out an unsteady sigh, shoving a hand through the short mop of her new haircut. "You want the good news or the bad news?"

Why did she even ask?

"Tell me the truth."

"Good news it is," Aaron interjected smoothly, yanking on his beard. He'd attempted to sound upbeat, but he only pulled on his beard when he was extremely worried or disturbed. "Deborah sent along her garlic challah knots." He flicked a glance to the end of the table where an empty platter sat and let out a groan. "Never mind. They're all gone. I thought we put some aside for you."

"Oops," Ebony said through a mouthful, her eyes widened, one cheek comically protruding. She looked like a guilty squirrel. "I think these were yours."

"Ebony!" I groaned. Aaron chuckled as I narrowed my eyes at her. "You know I don't mess around when it comes to Deborah's garlic challah knots. She hardly ever makes them!"

Ebony made a contrite noise, still chewing. "They were good, too, I'm sorry. I'd wanna fight me right now if I were you."

I rolled my eyes at the absurdity of all of it all. Damn, I was going to miss this ragtag, offbeat bunch. We had to figure out a way to keep the hospital going in its present form. "What was said at the meeting?" I hated to be a killjoy, but I'd been wrestling back worry about the meeting all morning.

The social workers at the opposite end of the table exchanged glances and silently rose to leave, as if tacitly agreeing to escape our little tableau of tragedy. Now, with only the four of us remaining, no one would look me in the eye.

I pulled a folding chair from under the table and sank into it. "Did they say how long we have?"

Aaron leaned back in his chair and fisted his hands on the table. "No. It was all cleverly done, acknowledging all the lay-off rumors while doing nothing to assuage our worries. Strongly hinting that hard decisions have to be made 'in the near future.' Confirming none of the current open positions will be filled, lots of talk of realigning under the new model to eliminate redundancy."

I let out a groan, and Layla nodded in commiseration.

"About what I expected," I sighed, feeling my gut turn on itself. "So they'll play coy for what, another month, before they let us go?"

Layla slid her cardigan off, revealing tattooed sleeves that started just above her wrists. "My guess? They're already working out how to replace us." She and Aaron exchanged glances. "There was lots of talk of partnering with the university to 'augment our staffing' by training volunteers for certain positions."

"They can't do that." Ebony looked thunderstruck.

"Plenty of hospitals use volunteer chaplains," Layla said gently. "It's not such a huge leap. Leigh would be a bigger loss, for sure. As it is, there's only one of her right now."

"One Child Life Specialist for an entire hospital of this size." Ebony shook her head. "It's absurd. What'll our kids do, especially our long-term frequent fliers?"

"There was mention," Layla said, closely studying the table's surface, "of focusing on what we're good at, providing basic services to the local community and letting other metro hospitals shine at their respective specialties."

"I knew that would happen." Rage nearly blinded me. "They can't cut the Peds programming here. We can't expect people to trek over to Nashville. Do they realize St. Jude is over five hours away? What, they don't think our community members deserve to have a decent program here for their kids?"

We were all silent for a beat before Aaron ventured, "Losing our jobs isn't the worst thing, I'm afraid."

I covered my eyes. "How do you mean?"

His voice lowered. "Deborah's been doing some research on Visage, the corporation that acquired us. Seems they've developed a reputation."

Ebony's voice was wry. "I'm guessing this is worse than a 'rounding the bases in the back of a Pinto after prom' kind of reputation." I lowered my fingers in time to see her crack up at her own joke, then blanch with realization. "Sorry, Reverend. Rabbi."

Aaron cracked up and Layla joined in. "Our underpants haven't been set on fire. No, the reputation I'm speaking of is the fact that they've been sued by surgeons at two different hospitals for serious breaches in patient safety. They were also heavily fined by a state board or two for the same thing. It seems our new employer is chiefly concerned with maintaining a bottom line and doesn't mind cutting corners to do so."

We all sat in defeated silence for several moments, then briefly greeted the music therapist who came in and began filling a plate.

"We're never helpless," Layla said, finally. "We've been praying for the hospital and everyone who works in it. We will continue to pray."

"And we'll fight." I nodded at each of them in turn, buoyed by a new grim resolve. "I don't know how yet, but we'll fight this."

"Speaking of prayers," Aaron said, his tight expression easing, "you were on our minds this weekend. I know it's too early to know for certain, but how do you think the job interview went last Friday?"

Ebony's eyebrows shot up. "You had a job interview? You're leaving us?"

I let out a bitter cackle that seemed to startle all of them. God, it felt like an entire year had passed since that interview in Jersey. "Not anytime soon. I went, but ... it's not gonna work out."

"They called you already?" Layla looked profoundly disappointed. "But you just got back, I would think—"

I shook my head. "It's just not gonna work out. The situation wasn't right for me. Don't look so sad. The hospital will have me out of your hair soon enough."

"Oh no," a familiar voice said from the doorway. "Why the long faces?"

Aaron looked to the doorway, and a huge grin split his face. "Uh-oh. Here comes trouble. Time to clear out."

Adesola Rojas propped one arm up against the opposite surface of the doorframe and treated us to one of her most beguiling smiles. I was certain she knew exactly how fetching she looked, all five feet of her, framed like a picture in her tangerine A-line dress.

I lifted a brow at her outfit. "Where have you been?" This wasn't the white-coated OB/GYN version of Adesola, nor was it the professorial, researcher version. This was a modified version of "on the town" Adesola that most often accompanied me on beer crawls and shopping trips.

"It's not where I've been, it's where I'm going." She only smiled, raising her brows as I squinted at her suspiciously. Pivoting on gorgeous peacock blue heels, she advanced toward us and came to a fashionable lean against the conference table.

"I'm not going with you." We all turned to find the music therapist shaking her head resolutely at Adesola. "I'm not doing any more role-plays for your videos. You'll have to find some other victim."

Layla coughed out a laugh behind her fist. "Stop complaining. I played 'Supportive Parent' last month."

"What was the topic?" Aaron asked, attempting to hide his smile.

"Fertility preservation and sperm cryopreservation," Layla said, drawing the words out in mock indignation. I snorted back a laugh. Leave it to Adesola to assign Layla to the sperm banking video. "And to be clear, the lesson included information on how to collect the sample."

Adesola hid her smile, but I couldn't help the full laugh that escaped me. Prior to Zora's departure, she and Adesola had partnered to create a curriculum intended to better educate adolescent and young adult cancer patients about their sexuality and reproductive health. Their efforts included an expansive library of instructional videos meant to coach clinicians through discussing difficult topics while simultaneously educating patients. On more than one occasion, Adesola had dashed over to our suite, desperate for an "actor" to play a patient's parent during the professional filming of re-enacted clinic visits. Most of us were accommodating if time permitted, and she often managed to snag volunteers from among the social workers and chaplains. I secretly suspected she got a perverse pleasure out of getting our chaplains to sit through the subject material. Aaron and Layla, however, were hardly shrinking violets, and we all knew they secretly enjoyed their star turns.

Damn, I was going to miss these people.

"I don't need any actors this time," Adesola said, her dark eyes full of laughter. "I just need Leigh. She owes me lunch."

I shook my head. "Since when, exactly?"

"Since *now*," she said, already kicking impatiently at the leg of my chair. "Let's go."

"Take her," Ebony said, waving a hand in my direction. "I already ate the challah knots Aaron's wife brought, and she hasn't had lunch yet."

Adesola smirked. "You ate her food and lived to tell about it?"

I aimed a death glare at Ebony as I pushed to my feet. "Whether she'll be permitted to live remains to be seen."

"Sounds like a Thai food kind of afternoon," Adesola suggested, and as I nodded my agreement, inspiration struck. I knew just who I needed to invite along with us.

"Take a load off, general." Layla executed a snappy salute with a quiet smile. "Your troops will still be here. When you get back, we'll draw up a battle plan."

~

"WELL, well, well. When the cat's away the mice diddle each other."

"Adesola!"

Adesola threw back her head and cackled. I sent a furtive glance around the Thai restaurant where we'd settled for lunch. It was my favorite off-campus spot for lunch: far enough from the hospital to reliably avoid employees and patients' family members, and soothing with its low lighting, dark wooden furniture, and eclectic decor. The place was packed with the lunch crowd, with all available seating occupied. I hadn't imagined the snort of laughter that erupted from the booth behind us immediately after Adesola's pronouncement.

Leaning forward across the table, I swatted her arm with the phone book of a menu. "There was no diddling!"

She continued to gasp with laughter, holding a white cloth napkin to her mouth with her trademark short red fingernails. "That is the absolute definition of diddling! What, you're going to tell me Walker didn't crack your papaya open on the kitchen counter and—"

"I'm going to kill you." My cheeks burned, but it was almost a relief to unburden myself to her. Talking to Adesola was like talking to myself, and thank God for it. I much preferred her bluntness over time-wasting diplomacy. She'd been in Knoxville for at least six years, but her speech was still flavored with familiar East Coast badassery. Her clipped way of talking, almost impatient in its rate and liberally peppered with coarse words, reminded me of home. It was a relief to talk with someone who spoke my language and wasn't put off by my rough, unvarnished conversational edges.

"Okay, okay," she said, adopting a sober expression. "I'll be good."

I shook my head at her. "Is that the clinical term you use with all your patients when you're wearing your gynecologist hat?"

"For patients? No, of course not. During this kind of girl talk? Absolutely."

"That's regrettable." The waitress approached to take our order. Only after we'd requested our usual selections and the waitress cleared the menus away did I kick her shoe under the table.

"Hey," she protested. "These are my Blahniks!"

"Why are you even wearing those in clinic?"

"I only came in to collar you for lunch. I don't have clinic today, and I have a date later this afternoon."

I groaned. "Oh no. Zora put you on Leigh Watch."

She tossed her dark mane of TV-worthy hair over one shoulder as she sat forward, her red lips twisted in annoyance. "Trust me, Zora and I know you're tough. I know the drill. You're a soldier and you've disavowed any emotions or feelings."

"I don't deny my feelings."

"You've got so many suppressed emotions, I'm amazed your head hasn't exploded. I was sure this little visit home would finally do it. If I'd gotten the kind of surprise you did this weekend, I would most definitely not be okay."

"I didn't say I was okay." I sat back and folded my arms, trying not to think about the fact that Adesola might have been right, given how easily I'd come apart with Walker. My normally air-tight inhibitions had dissolved at his first touch.

"Well then, how are you?"

The answer was a lot more complicated than I'd expected. "Well, kind of like the wind was knocked out of me. But I'm nowhere near as hurt as I would have been four years ago."

"But it still hurt."

I studied the framed artwork of a lazy river hanging over our booth, thinking. "The initial shock of seeing Gio's son, that was like a lance through the heart. Wasn't like I didn't already know. But it hurt."

"And how much of your current recovery has to do with the healing properties of Walker Leffersbee's mouth?"

I felt certain my face was now bright red. "Why did I even tell you?"

"Don't pretend this isn't what we would do under normal circumstances if we were talking about any other guy. But something's different this time, huh?"

I took a sip of water, then nodded in reluctant agreement. It was true. Certainly we'd dissected my relationship with Simon down to the cellular level. But somehow it was different when it was Walker.

Her gaze was sharp and assessing. "Back up and tell me everything. Start with seeing the love child and Walker picking you up from the airport."

I told her everything over pad thai and herbal tea. She listened, saying very little. By the time I described my drive to work with Walker, she was beaming.

"This thing with you and Walker has been brewing for a while now. The two of you, you're like two pieces of flint. There's no mistaking the sparks."

"You're talking out of your ass."

"Nope, I'm not." She looked unbearably smug. "That whole sniping thing, it's your foreplay. And now you've finally had real foreplay." She took a delicate sip of tea, then slid me a sly look over the little cup. "Speaking of which, how was it?"

"Adesola!"

"Oh, save the fake embarrassment for someone else. I'm hoping for your sake all Walker's experience means he knows his way around a clitoris."

I broke then, covering my face with my hands as I let out a thready sigh. "It was sublime."

She let out a loud whoop that silenced the conversation at several nearby tables and pumped her fist in the air. "Alright, Walker!"

"Home run," I agreed.

"That's what I want to hear!"

"Daze, I swear, I think I lost consciousness at some point."

She held up her hand and we slapped palms, giggling.

"I don't know why I even considered going home," I said after a while.

"I do," Adesola said. "I'm a city girl by design. I need noise, air pollution—"

"Decent Chinese food—"

"How about Chinese food delivered at two in the morning," Adesola said. "Decent bagels, pizza that's worth a damn, being back in your old neighborhood and hearing different languages coming from every doorway."

"Yes!" I exclaimed, slapping the table. Three women at a nearby table threw startled glances our way, and I realized we'd both gotten loud. "Well, I've got to go back in a month. My niece is getting baptized."

"Oh boy," Adesola said, raising an eyebrow.

"Well, it sounds like you two are having fun," a new voice said at my elbow. I glanced over and let out a whoop of excitement.

Loretta Clemons, an old friend of mine, returned my whoop. I hadn't seen her in almost a year, but she was still the same: dark-haired, beautifully round, with a winning smile. I slid out of the booth to hug her while Adesola watched us with a bemused smile. After introducing the two women, Loretta slid into the booth next to me.

"So you provide support to all the executives," Adesola said, watching us both with outright curiosity.

"Yep," I confirmed. "She's upstairs breathing that rarified air, supporting all the head honchos."

"How did you two meet?" Adesola asked.

Loretta and I exchanged grins. "We're both members of the Sacred Order of Smokers," I said. "Although I'm a former member."

"But she still smoked when she moved here," Loretta put in. "Often."

"My nerves were bad."

She nodded. "We'd see each other outside all the time. Smokers talk. We know everything. It's the most effective information network, whether in rain, snow, sleet—"

"Winters standing outside are a bitch, though," I said.

Adesola's eyebrows went up. "You should really try to quit," she told Loretta, and I recognized her Counseling Physician tone. "It raises the risks for all kinds of—"

"Adesola," I said, just as Loretta leveled her with a severe look. "Are we going to allocate equal time to discuss your compulsive shoe shopping?" I raised a brow at her silence. "Well, then, let's stick to the topic at hand."

"What do you need to know?" Loretta asked, sending Adesola one last wary look.

"We've all heard about the changes Visage is planning for the hospital. I just wanted to know if you had any idea of what's coming down the pipeline? Any proposed changes?"

Loretta's gaze thoroughly swept the room before she replied. "And what do you plan to do with this information?"

"I need to know if the things we're hearing about Visage's business practices are true. If they are, we have to find a way to save the hospital from their clutches."

Loretta sat quietly, seeming to absorb my response.

"I know it's a lot to spring on you at once, and dangerous in your position, and it's probably unfair for me to even assume you even know anything—"

"No, I know more than I want to." She looked ill at ease.

Adesola scooted forward in the booth. "Like what?"

Loretta looked around the restaurant again before answering. "I'm never named as a source, do you both understand?"

"Got it," I said, and Adesola responded in kind.

"What are your questions?" Loretta was practically whispering.

"Is it true that they're planning to let several departments go?" I asked.

"Yes," Loretta said, and went on to outline a gutting that far outstripped anything I'd expected.

I blinked in disbelief. Adesola looked shell-shocked.

"There's more," Loretta said. "The goal right now is to 'increase the odds of KCH's economic viability' by shedding as many liabilities as possible. One strategy they plan on putting into place rather soon is suing patients for uncollected balances."

My mouth dropped open. "What? Are you serious? I'd say about eighty percent of my patients have an ongoing balance! How can they do that?"

"The powers that be feel it's fair game if the patient doesn't have an up-to-date, approved payment plan on file."

My mind whirred with names, faces of family members who struggled to balance their lives, employment, and emotional health to meet the needs of their loved ones. "Some people don't have the money, period."

"More people than you think," Adesola said, looking sickened. "Lots of people have high deductible plans that cover only a small percentage of their medical expenses. Punitive methods like this are what keep people from going to the doctor when they need help."

Loretta nodded in agreement. "The system is broken. Period. But Visage doesn't care about that, they want their money. They bought us to cut what little fat we have, strip us down to the bones, and turn the hospital into a money-making, for-profit enterprise."

I sat, sickened, overwhelmed by what Loretta described.

"But there is one thing," Loretta said, rousing me out of my stupor with an elbow to the ribs. "When Visage bought Knoxville Community, they insisted on a ninety-day escape clause. They can back out of this deal up to ninety days in, no questions asked. We're in the test period right now. They're trying to figure out if KCH is worth their while."

Understanding dawned. "So we need to do our best to make it not worth their while," I said.

Loretta nodded, her eyes never leaving mine. "Exactly."

"Loretta." Adesola squinted down at her red nails. "Any chance you have any documentation of this just, I don't know, lying around?"

Silence descended. Loretta studied her clasped hands for several long moments. "Could be," she said, finally. "But it can't ever be traced back to me."

Adesola and I exchanged glances. "Of course," we chorused.

"Alright," Loretta said, sliding out of the booth. "I gotta get back. I spent half my lunch hour driving here. Leigh, I'll be in touch once I figure out how to get the docs out."

"Thank you," I said.

"You're welcome," she said, but she looked grim. "Normally I wouldn't risk my job. I need it. But I think what they're doing is terrible, and I haven't worked at the hospital this long to see it go out this way. You're right. People should know what's going on."

"It was a pleasure to meet you," Adesola said as Loretta and I hugged.

"Likewise," Loretta said. "And now I'm going to my car. To *smoke*."

Adesola shook her head as she watched Loretta's departure. "Your friend is a trip."

"Trust me, you both are."

"Looks like you've got your smoking gun," she said, brows raised. "So, where are you going to point it?"

CHAPTER NINE

Walker

Trouble had a physical presence.

I sensed the finger of it ghosting up my spine just before I crossed the threshold into the bank. Some preternatural instinct hitched my stride, stiffened my reach for the familiar brass handle to the door of the bank.

"What?" Mrs. Watkins asked from beside me, her dark brows knitting in suspicion as she stared up at me. We'd just walked back from lunch at the taco joint around the corner. She'd insisted that we have lunch that afternoon, and I'd humored her.

Honestly, it hadn't been all that hard to convince me to go along. I'd been feeling strangely relaxed after my night and morning with Leigh. Errant Kendrick Lamar lyrics wove in and out of my mind and fueled my morning work routine.

I'd gotten too complacent.

I'd let my guard down.

Upon throwing open the door, nothing seemed amiss. At first. Everyone was in place, all three tellers at their respective stations. Our security guard, an older man in his sixties whose role was more symbolic than functional, gave me a chin check when we made eye contact. Then his gaze darted away, toward the reception area, before it returned to mine. A quick glance showed two of the available tellers sneaking furtive glances in my direction as they made a show of being wholly absorbed with shuffling papers.

"What's going on over there with Mrs. Baker?" Mrs. Watkins frowned over at reception. Our positioning in the lobby allowed us to just make out the shadowed figures of one of our regulars, Mrs. Baker, and our loan officer, Jamal, behind the textured cubicle glass. I followed her gaze and sighted the details that had likely raised her concern.

Jamal, whose relentless cheer and uncanny perceptiveness made him the ideal loan officer, now looked stricken as he stared at his computer screen. His ran an agitated hand along his jawline and patchy goatee. Mrs. Baker, to be fair, always looked harried and disheveled when running errands at the bank. On an average day, she'd bleat exasperatedly at the one or two of six children that typically tagged along. But she was alone today and seemed distressed, balancing her weight at the very edge of her seat. Even across the lobby, I saw how tightly both of her hands gripped the edge of the desk, how the tips of her knuckles had gone white and her shoulders had risen to her ears.

"You mind taking this back for me?" I cut a quick look at Mrs. Watkins as I nudged my Styrofoam container of leftovers in her direction. "I'd be grateful."

I'd be especially grateful if I could divert her, redirect her while I looked into this. Her eyes were already narrowing, nostrils quivering as if literally scenting out the brewing conflict.

She squinted up at me, her lips drawing together. "I'm *gonna* find out, Walker. But go on ahead. You know where I'll be."

She snatched the container from my hand and turned toward the administrative offices, muttering to herself the entire way. I looked up to find the gazes of all three tellers now glued to me.

What have you done now, Tavia?

I worked on smoothing the grimness out of my face as I made my way over to the reception area on leaden feet. My smile felt patently false, overly wide, when I greeted Jamal and Mrs. Baker. Both looked relieved to see me.

"Mr. Leffersbee, sir!" Jamal bolted upright from his chair, his face brightening.

"Mrs. Baker." I dipped my head in her direction, noting her red-rimmed brown eyes. Tufts of graying blonde hair stood up from the crown of her head where she'd apparently yanked at it.

"Mr. Leffersbee," she began unsteadily. "Good to see you."

"Walker," I reminded her. "Pleasure. Saw you were in and couldn't walk by without saying howdy. We treating you alright, everything's okay?"

Her smile was tremulous. "Jamal is, as always, a huge help. But ..." She looked to Jamal, shoulders going tighter.

He stepped closer to me, his voice dropping. "It's about the loan she applied for."

I nodded. I'd seen the application, signed off on it when it came across my desk.

"Well ..." He gave a tiny nod toward the screen and I moved forward, switching places with him so I could read the record he'd pulled up.

After several beats of silence Mrs. Baker ventured, "I thought, after I got notification from you all, that we were all set. Then I went to my account this morning thinking I could transfer funds from the line of credit, and it wasn't there. Not like before when we've gotten the loan."

Her voice faltered and she looked away while she swallowed. When she met my gaze again, she lifted her chin, expression stoic. "Mr. Baker hasn't been able to work, not with—"

"It's okay," I said. I knew how it cost her, how it hurt her pride to be in this position. I also knew what was unsaid. I didn't need her to tell me about her husband's multiple sclerosis, or how hard Mr. Baker worked to get up every day, no matter how poorly he felt, to work at the mill every day to support his family. Reviewing the record, I noted the relatively small amount of the requested loan and instantly recognized the pattern. This was for groceries, gas, the essentials that would keep her household going while Mr. Baker drew a reduced salary from the mill. Seeing the last note on the file from my sister, my teeth clenched against rising anger.

"There's been a mistake," I announced, and both Jamal and Mrs. Baker seemed to wilt with relief.

"So it's gonna be okay?" she asked. She swiped at her eyes with the sleeve of her jacket.

"It's gonna be fine." I stood. "If you don't mind waiting right here, give me a little bit of time to update a few things. But the funds'll be available before you leave. Jamal can give you cash before you go. Sound alright?"

She pushed up from the chair and circled the desk to hug me. I patted her back awkwardly and met Jamal's steady gaze over her head. "We're family here," I said into her nest of hair. "And family takes care of each other. I'm sorry for the confusion. From now on, you can call me direct. You have my number right?"

"I do." She pulled back from the embrace and smiled shyly before returning to her seat.

"Alright. Jamal'll be right back." I headed out of the cubicle, and Jamal followed me back to the administrative suite.

By the time we arrived at the open doorway to Tavia's office, fury rode heavily on my shoulders, burned in my fists, buzzed in my blood.

Tavia looked up, sensing our presence. Her eyes went wide at whatever she saw on my face, then briefly moved behind me to Jamal.

"Walker. What's wrong?"

"You tell me," I said, advancing into her office with slow, measured steps. *Take it easy. Deep breaths.* "Delores Baker came in here last week, applied for a line of credit. Has to be the fifth or sixth time she's done so."

"Sixth," Tavia said, crisply.

"Sounds about right. Now, I signed that paperwork when it came across my desk. Just like I've done five times prior. So imagine my surprise when I come in today and find you've taken it upon yourself to overturn my decision and deny that woman her funds. After Jamal already called to notify her the application was approved."

From the corner of my eye, I caught Jamal's emphatic nod and hard expression.

Her jaw jutted forward and she sat back in her chair, folding her arms.

I'd just taken a step in her direction when a hand closed on the inside of my elbow. I looked back to find Mrs. Watkins behind me, her eyes intent on mine. She tugged me back until I was abreast with her.

"Walker," she said, so quietly it felt as if we were the only people in the room, "take a deep breath." She took in a noisy breath that lifted her bosom as if demonstrating, her eyes never leaving mine. "This has to be done. But if you're angry when you do it, it's you who'll hurt worse, you who'll be disappointed with yourself tomorrow. And this here? Nothing to feel any regret about. So take that breath."

Silence swelled for several beats as she nodded slowly, her dark eyes never leaving mine. Her small hand didn't leave the crook of my arm until I felt the tension in my neck and shoulders seeping away.

"Alright," I said to her, quietly, and she gave an infinitesimal nod before stepping back.

Jamal stood in the hallway, his gaze bouncing between all of us, eyes wide.

I took another breath, squared my shoulders. I looked at my baby sister, really looked at her, trying to remember the younger, softer versions of her. Skinned knees, missing teeth, Froot Loops milk dribbling down her bib from her perch in the high chair. I reminded myself of the love, the reluctant admiration I'd felt even as a kid, watching her hurl herself at me in a desperate bid to reach her goal. And I let the truth of what had to be done settle.

"Mrs. Watkins. Jamal." I didn't look back at them, kept Tavia under my gaze as I spoke. "I want to apologize to you both. This bank, this business, it's family owned. But us letting our family dysfunction affect business and intrude on your ability to help customers, well, there's no excuse for that. It's inappropriate. Please accept an apology on behalf of my sister and me—"

Tavia's mouth fell open. "Walker."

"For the recent lack of clarity regarding chain of command."

Tavia's expression darkened. "Listen—"

"I take responsibility for this," I said, turning to see Mrs. Watkins and Jamal gaping at me. "So I want to be clear today, right now. My sister is family, that will obviously never change. She is using an office here to pursue her own business, which, when established, will likely have an affiliation with Leffersbee Savings & Loan. But she has no authority here, was never appointed in a supervisory capacity, and has no say in the daily running of this bank or loan decisions."

I let the words hang there, gave it a moment to sink in as I surveyed their expressions. Jamal looked giddy. Mrs. Watkins wore a small smile. "If you see something is wrong, if you see that we're not treating a member as we should, I want you to tell me. No matter who's behind it, even if it's a member of my family. I promise I'll back you up." I held Jamal's gaze, and he nodded. "I hope that's clear," I said, turning back and taking in Tavia's now strangely blank expression.

Mrs. Watkins nodded, her smile threatening to grow across her face. "Crystal. I'll write up a memo and we'll discuss it in our next employee meeting."

"Understood, sir," Jamal said, a grin briefly eclipsing his face before he regained control of his expression.

"Mrs. Watkins, would you be so kind as to help Jamal finish the transaction for Mrs. Baker? I'll take care of the paperwork here." I gave Mrs. Watkins a meaningful look, and she immediately nodded in understanding.

I didn't move my eyes from Tavia until I heard the office door close behind them.

"Don't look at me like that," she said, looking away.

"Like what?" I moved to the desk and unbuttoned my jacket, settled in the seat across from her.

"You and Mama, you're both exactly the same with that slow simmer temper. Steadily bubbling until you go off like a solar flare and singe everyone around you. You've got the same look she'd always get, like she wanted to pitch a fit. Same 'I'm so disappointed' look. Do you have her speech down too? Is this the part where you tell me I should be more like Zora?"

"Has nothing to do with Zora or who she is and who you are, and you know it. First off, I'm not our parents. I don't want to be in this position. You'd be the first person to characterize this moment right here as me being controlling and paternalistic, when God knows I've done everything I can think of to try to make you feel welcome, wanted, with your own autonomy."

Her brow went up. "Oh, really?"

I ignored the bait. "Second, I'm not disappointed. I'm mad as hell."

Her eyes dropped to the cluttered surface of her desk, and she blinked rapidly. When her gaze met mine again, I felt a measure of relief as something like contrition flitted across her expression. "Finally too far, huh?" she asked on a low laugh.

"I can't allow it. You're not gonna come in here and start making changes that hurt our members."

She nodded slowly. "Did you even look at her most recent credit report? She filed for bankruptcy less than six months ago, you know."

"I know it."

Her mouth jaw dropped. "How could you think that was an acceptable risk?"

I leaned forward. "How could you come back into town after all these years and overrule the decision I made based on all the years I've known that family and their history? Of all the loans they've taken out, they have never been late. Not once. Besides the fact that there are special circumstances, they're a part of our community, a part of this bank's family."

"It's not a family, Walker," she spat, and I was momentarily taken aback by her sudden vehemence. "It's a business. And that is the problem, why we never agree. Running a business means you make decisions based on logic, reason, hard facts. You want to run this place like some kind of hippy dippy—"

"What are you doing here?"

That brought her up short. She even blinked a few times, as if attempting to reorient herself to the conversation. "What does that mean?"

"You understood the question. What are you doing, here? In Green Valley, back in this bank?"

I watched her collect herself, stall for time as she sat back and deliberately crossed her arms. "I didn't know I needed a reason to come back home."

I closed my eyes. God, I'd been dumb. Miles was right. Pops was trying to get me to see the obvious, what had been staring me in the face the whole time.

"I'm tired, sis. I don't have much more in me to keep doing this, and I don't know how much more our relationship can take. Now, you showed up here almost a year ago out of thin air and informed us you suddenly had an interest in the bank." I opened my eyes and found her studying her hands, her face set. "And I bought that, then. For that, I ask you to forgive me."

She fixed me with a sharp look. "Forgive you? For what?"

"For forgetting who you are, not taking into account how smart and determined you are. The other day Pops called you 'brilliant,' you know that?"

Her smile was thin. "I've been meaning to stop by, visit."

"Yeah, well, he'd be the first one to tell you he ain't going nowhere. Said his ass is growing into the chair. It'd be nice for you to show your face, convince him to stop making his companion's life hell 'cause he misses Grandma." *Let him interrogate you about whatever the hell you've got up your sleeve.*

She winced. "I said I'll go, okay? What's your point, Walker?"

"You wanted nothing more than to get out of this town, you and cousin Dani. You finally got your bite of the Big Apple and, what? You suddenly just had enough?" I sat back in the chair, stretched my arms, laced my fingers behind my head. "Nah. I don't buy that. Not you. If you came back here, you had a reason. Your plan, building your consultancy for corporations ... What's come of it? What progress have you made in a year?"

She looked wary now, and uneasy.

"See?" I gestured to her, indicating the empty silence. "That's not the sister I know. The Tavia I know managed to undercut the church bake sale revenue with her underground candy business when she was twelve."

A wry smile curved her lips. "Daddy thought it was hilarious."

I nodded. "And Mama almost took your ear off when she found out."

She gave a shrug, her expression opaque. "Guess I've always had an entrepreneurial spirit."

"Yeah." My gaze fell on her desk, and the assortment of opened correspondence. I returned my eyes to her face as I dropped my hands from my head and leaned forward, the better to glimpse the title of the brightly colored charts. "That's what I'm worried about."

"Walker, what the hell is that supposed to mean?"

"You keep saying, thinking, we want you to be like Zora. That's never been true. Zora is passionate about people. You're passionate about ideas."

Her mouth drew tight as her shoulders caved inward. "And what exactly does that mean?"

"It's what makes you formidable, your passion for pushing innovation forward. But somehow your calibration's gotten off since the time you left and came back. I could lecture you, tell you all the things you already know. The stuff Pops drilled into us when we were kids, the same stories he told us over and over again when he took us fishing. The stories people tell us in town about how much the bank's meant to them."

"Neither of us need that, Walker. I was right there with you."

"You sure? You don't want me to remind you of how hard Pops worked in the 60s for this bank to help Black people get home loans in the midst of racial discrimination and redlining? Don't want to hear about that again?"

She heaved a sigh and glared down at her lap. I leaned closer, took advantage of her misdirected attention, and peered more closely at the bold title straddling the top of the charts and figures.

Focus Group Results.

Huh.

"You don't want to hear about how Pops is responsible for the higher-than-average rate of home ownership among Black and Brown people in this area, as compared to the rest of the country?"

"Walker—"

"Don't lie to me." It came out lower and harsher than I intended, and her head reared back. "Not to my face. Not as if I'm not the same brother who watched you take your first steps and held your hand when I walked you into elementary school every morning. Do me that courtesy, at least."

Our eyes held for a long moment before she looked away, her hands clenching into fists on the desk.

"Whatever it is, Dad is in on it too," I said, not asking. "Has to be. Makes sense why I haven't seen much of him around here."

She kept her face averted from mine, seemingly studying a spot on the opposite wall. "Walker," she began, her voice breaking, "I—"

"No." I shook my head. "We're not gonna do this. When you're ready to talk about this, let it be because you're ready to tell the truth. Or, we could just wait until it comes out. One way or the other, I guess I'll know soon."

I pushed the chair back and stood. She stayed still in the same position, not looking at me, but I couldn't help noticing her quickened breathing.

"You're my sister and I'm always gonna love you. I'll love you no matter what you've done. But make no mistake, if what you've started is something that will undermine the integrity of this bank or hurt our members, I will stand against you. Sister or no sister."

Leaving, I couldn't help but reflect that the bang of the door closing resembled the sharp crack of a starter's pistol.

"SEE THAT RIGHT THERE?" The plumber's voice was bright with glee as he aimed his flashlight at the exposed piping in the bathroom ceiling. "That's where this morning's leak came from. But that's not all." He gestured to the section of wall adjacent to the tub where drywall had been cut away. "You can get a closer glimpse. Leaking over here, too. But more than that ... brother, you are looking at *lead pipes.*"

His grin grew so wide I almost expected to glimpse his tonsils. I rubbed at the dull spasm at the back of my neck. "This is like Christmas for you, isn't it?"

"This is Christmas, Kwanzaa, Thanksgiving, and Easter all rolled in one. Few things make me happier than running new pipe. Expensive, but it can't be helped. Lead is unsafe."

"I know it." I gave up on trying to unknot the muscles and let my arms fall to my sides. "So this means I can't use the water over here 'til you're done. Which means I need to look into that corporate housing after all." Figured, after this day. All I wanted was to collapse on a soft surface and surrender to sleep. Instead, I had a drive back to Knoxville ahead of me.

"There you are."

We turned to see Miles standing in the hallway, thumbs tucked into his toolbelt. "We were wondering where you were."

"We?"

He gestured to something unseen in the hallway. Leigh's head suddenly appeared in the doorframe, followed by the rest of her. My eyes automatically took a trip down her body and back up again, noting she'd changed into a pair of soft-looking shorts and a tank top. Her dark hair was piled up in a messy knot at the top of her head.

I wanted to run my hand along the sinuous curves of her waist, revisit that tantalizing dip between her ass and lower back. Trace the flare of her hips, taste the smooth olive-tinged skin all along her legs.

That's what I got for playing with danger. I'd gotten a taste of her and now she was in my blood.

"This looks serious," she said, her eyes widening as she took in the powdered disaster of the bathroom. "Any progress with the leak?"

Behind her, Miles grimaced. "I don't need to ask if you told him," Miles said to the plumber. "Not with you standing there grinning like an accountant on tax day."

The plumber ran a hand over the lower half of his face, making a comical attempt to smooth out his smile. "Why don't I just give y'all a little space to grieve and reflect? I'll be back with a crew tomorrow morning, early." He slid past Leigh and made his way down the stairs.

"Well," Miles began, his eyes bright with laughter, "this isn't totally bad. We were gonna change the walls anyway. And if the drywall's already down ..."

"Did she know about this?" I squinted at Leigh.

"Who?" She blinked in surprise.

"Zora. She would have to be blind not to see the massive water stains gathering on the ceiling in her bedroom."

"She was never here," Leigh said in clipped tones, automatically defending her best friend. She folded her arms, shoving her breasts higher in the process. I turned away from the sight. "She was always working her ass off, trying to get tenure."

"Alright, alright." Miles held up a placating hand and sent me a censuring look. "Walk, you look and sound tired. You know there's no point in haranguing anybody about this plumbing mess. Leigh's not responsible for Zora letting things get out of control, and it's all a moot point anyway. These are lead pipes. They have to be replaced for safety reasons, whether they were leaking or not. We'll do Zora's side first, then Leigh's side."

I sat on the lip of the tub, for once not caring about what the drywall dust would do to my suit. "You're right, Miles. I apologize, Leigh. It's just been a long day."

She studied me for a moment, her head tilted. "Well, I came over to ask if you and Miles wanted to take a break for dinner."

Miles immediately perked up, pushing off the hallway wall to stand. "Hell yes! Where'd you order from? I can pick it up."

"I cooked," she said, throwing a smile back to him. "Spaghetti, but with my ma's sauce I brought home. That stuff is like gold."

My stomach sat up and begged at the mention of food. "You brought back your mother's sauce yesterday?"

"Yeah."

"Music to my ears," I said, thinking of the wild, raucous weekends when Leigh's family visited and took over both sides of the house. It seemed her mother always had a huge stockpot of something delicious-smelling simmering on the stove when she was here. I loved her mother's cooking.

Spaghetti. God, I was hungry.

"I'm going to pop the garlic bread in the oven now," she said, turning to head out the doorway. "There's more than enough for you both, if you're interested."

I opened my mouth to heartily accept, then remembered. I had to check into a hotel and find housing tomorrow. Still ... "I'll take mine to go, if you don't mind. I've got to head out."

She stopped and glanced back. "Oh. Okay."

Miles stood behind her, glancing between us with a stupid smirk on his face.

"Where ya going, Walker?" he asked, with all the avidity of a small child asking how to get to Sesame Street.

What was he up to?

Then I saw that Leigh also seemed keenly interested in my answer, having gone still.

"There's no water here," I explained. "So I need to get a hotel."

"But," Miles said with sham concern, "that would mean you'd have to drive all the way back to Knoxville, unless you want to go home to continue your conversation with Tavia at your parents' house."

"I'm going to Knoxville," I said.

"That's a long drive," Leigh said. She looked thoughtful, but I also thought I detected a trace of relief in her expression. Where had she thought I was going? "And it has been a long day already."

"I would offer up my place," Miles said, making a great show of conveying deep regret, "but you'd still be heading all the way back to Knoxville."

His eyes slid to Leigh just as she said, seemingly on impulse, "Well. I have a guest room. Two of them actually." She looked to Miles, and he managed to smooth out his lizard smile just in time. "How long before the pipes are in and the water's working?"

He gave a casual shrug. "Not long. I'd say a week, week and a half at most. And hey, if you all were still roomies, it would make your morning commute easier, right?"

I shook my head. This felt a lot like trouble, and trouble was the last thing I needed right now. I'd never done any drugs, not even weed. But watching Leigh in that moment, I suddenly comprehended how a powerful want, a seductive longing could leave a man weakened and desperate yet completely accepting of his own demise.

"I can get a hotel," I said, my throat suddenly dry as I recalled those lust-crazed moments from the previous night when I'd stood between her thighs and sampled her sweetest bits. "You can take my car. I'll drive my truck to work."

She waved that away, looking even more determined.

Jesus, I thought. *Please help me.*

"That's a waste of time and money. I have guest rooms. Take your pick of one. I can survive sharing space with a man for a week, I think. You *do* know you should put the toilet seat down?"

"I have a mother and three sisters."

"And you've mastered the art of peeing inside the bowl? We don't need to throw a few Cheerios in the toilet for target practice first?"

"I can't stand you," I said on a reluctant laugh, somewhat relieved to feel a trace of the old, residual rancor that powered our previous exchanges. But my relief was somewhat short-lived by the new urge to wipe that smirk off her face in a very un-friendly, non-platonic way.

"Walker's housebroken, so I'm sure it will be fine," Miles said, looking way too pleased with himself. "And yes, I would love some dinner. Walker, would you like some help getting your stuff over to Leigh's?"

CHAPTER TEN

Leigh

"That was amazing. I'm tight as a tick." Walker fell back against the chair with a theatrical groan, making a show of rubbing a nonexistent paunch.

I swallowed back a smile. "I'm not surprised. You put down a lot of spaghetti. And garlic bread. And chocolate cake."

He grinned at the empty serving dishes on the table between us, then frowned briefly when his gaze settled on the empty place setting I'd laid out for Miles. "He never made it over. I'm sure they're still working. I should get changed and head on over."

"He sent me a text, while we were eating. Someone on the crew came by with fried chicken from The Front Porch, so they had that."

His frown deepened as he dug in his pocket and pulled out his phone. "I didn't get any message from him. Why didn't he say anything to me?"

I shrugged. There was no way I'd let Walker in on the rest of the message from Miles: *Walker really needs some rest. I'm hoping he just takes the night off for once.*

"Maybe he got busy," I said off-handedly. Walker nodded, looking distracted as his hand rose to briefly press the back of his neck for what had to be the hundredth time that night. I peered at him over my water glass, noting the tight pull of his jaw and the awkward tilt to his head. Probably a pulled muscle, I surmised.

He rose, towering over the table as he briefly adjusted his belted trousers and loosened the knot of his tie. "Well, I'm in your debt tonight. That was an extraordinarily good dinner. Send my thanks to your mother." He began stacking plates and platters, and when he glanced up at me briefly and smirked, I knew something smart-ass was coming. "You did a great job boiling the water to make the noodles, so shout out to you too."

"You ungrateful bastard." I laughed, and was rewarded with the briefest flash of his smile before he turned to deposit the towering stack of dishes into the sink. "I'll have you know, those were *my* meatballs. Not my mother's."

He shot a teasing look over his shoulder. "Yeah. I could tell."

I grabbed the roll of paper towels from the middle of the table and tossed it in his direction. He jumped a bit when it connected with the center of his back.

"I'm kidding, Leigh. It was wonderful, all of it." He started the water running in the sink, then turned back to face me, arms folded. "In all seriousness, thank you for everything. Taking me on as a guest, feeding me. I'm grateful. It's been a hell of a day today," he said, his expression sobering before he turned back to the sink.

"Leave those alone, I'm just going to stack them in the dishwasher."

"But they've gotta pre-soak."

I lifted a brow, impressed. "You just might be a decent houseguest after all."

He turned back to face me with a frown. "What's that supposed to mean? Just because I'm a man I'd expect you to look after me?"

I blinked at the edge in his tone. "I'm not typecasting here. I know a lot of guys who wouldn't have bothered to clear the table, much less run water over the dishes. I'm not giving any man an award for cleaning up after himself, just to be clear. But I appreciate it."

"I'm not most guys." Silence fell as he regarded me steadily, his lips twisted. Between us sat a whole carcass of meaning, and its name was Gio.

"I know you're not," I said, finally. "I'm learning that more and more every day. The more I spend time with you, the more I'm pleasantly surprised. Intrigued."

His eyes widened briefly at that last bit, and he pulled himself up to his full height, his gaze boring into mine with unnerving intensity. I wanted to kick myself.

Intrigued? Why the hell did I say that?

"In a friendly kind of way," I added hastily.

Several beats passed. "I'm finding you pretty intriguing too," he said, his voice heavy with what sounded like dread.

Why had I insisted he stay over?

"Listen, I'm going to get changed," he said, tugging at his tucked-in dress shirt as if he planned to disrobe in the middle of the kitchen.

Take it off! my brain cheered.

"I'm going to go for a run, then head over to do my part next door."

I considered my response carefully, sensing that I was walking a very fine line between persuading him and provoking male pride. "You seem tired and uncomfortable." *And worried.* "You sure a run is really what you need right now?"

He was already heading toward the doorway. "Running always helps me process things. So does tearing stuff up in a reno."

"Okay." He needed to change anyway, I figured.

"I'll start the dishwasher when I get back." With that, he disappeared, and I heard his heavy tread on the stairs shortly thereafter.

I sat in the comforting silence of the kitchen, weighing approaches, considering. It was time to bring my figurative Child Life kit home to help Walker.

For his own sake.

By the time he returned to the kitchen in athletic shorts and a T-shirt beautifully exploiting the muscled contours of his biceps and waist, I was ready.

He paused, one brow raised as he noted the deck of cards and the bottle on the table.

"What is that? Scotch? Is that a deck of UNO cards?"

"You can read," I said, as he glowered down at me. "Have a seat. This week's rent is a round of cards and a shot."

He stared at the cards and Scotch bottle for several moments before his gaze rose to meet mine and sharpened. "So I'm supposed to go along with this plan to skip my run, huh?"

I made my expression innocent. "What makes you say that?"

He chuckled as he pulled out the opposite chair and sat. "Please. Save that 'little ole me' act for someone who doesn't already know you're the wolf masquerading as Little Red Riding Hood. That's how you fool those poor little kids, isn't it? They never see you coming. You're lucky I'm in the mood to give in to your evil plans."

I slid the bottle and glasses in his direction. "Just pour."

He turned the bottle to read the label and let out a low whistle. "Macallan? Scotch? I was expecting a poisoned apple or whatever gruel Hansel and Gretel got fattened off of. You do realize we still have work in the morning, don't you?"

"This is a cease fire. My broom's parked in the garage and you could do with a little letting go," I told him, sliding his cards across the table as I dealt to us both.

He seemed to consider that for several moments as he fanned out his cards and rearranged their order. "I asked you to trust me and do that very same thing yesterday. I guess I can take a chance on you."

"You can," I said, holding his gaze. He nodded and gathered his cards.

As it turned out, Walker Leffersbee was a fierce opponent at UNO and unrelenting in his shit-talk. Draw 4s were thrown down with taunts and threats. He gloated every time he changed the color of play. By our third hand, Walker didn't need much coaxing to unburden himself of the tale of Tavia's treachery at the bank. I asked a few questions but mostly listened as he outlined his concerns for the employees, his grandfather, and the growing potential for conflict within the family. It was the kind of family drama that had made my mother a die-hard fan of *The Young and The Restless* for the last thirty years. I hated the weight and toll it was taking on Walker.

"Sounds like quite a mess," I said, noting he looked considerably more relaxed once he'd finished talking.

"I don't even have the full picture yet," he said, sounding exhausted. "I don't know what she's planning, and now I'm no longer sure I wanna know."

"You tell Pops yet?"

"Haven't had a chance," he said, his hand rising once again to dig into the back of his neck for several seconds before it lowered. "But I will. Soon. I promised him I would."

"Well, there's nothing else you can do about it tonight. I propose you take a night off from worrying and let your mind rest so you can be ready for tomorrow."

"I shouldn't have told you all this," he said with a rueful smile after we'd sat in companionable silence for several moments.

"Why?" I asked, surprised.

"I know you don't like her very much. Tavia."

I shrugged. "I'm not fond of her, no."

Our eyes met, and Walker cracked up. "You never pull any punches."

"Why lie? I can be uncomfortable with your sister's behavior and still support you as a friend."

He absorbed that with a quiet smile. "Let's talk about you and what's going on at the hospital. Something happened. Still looking for that cigarette, I see," he said, nodding to where my thumb and fingers twitched together on the table.

"Nope. Not tonight. Another day. And that's all I'm going to say about that."

"So, what's next on the agenda then? Now that you've extracted all my deepest secrets with play therapy?"

I told myself it was the Scotch swimming in my bloodstream that made Relaxed Walker with the hooded eyes and rakish grin somehow even more irresistible.

"What?" he asked at my continued silence. "You've got me loose and pliant. What's the next step of your diabolical plan, Bellatrix?"

I inclined my head toward the living room. "We're going to sit and watch one of those stupid movies you love."

"Really?" He looked up sharply, with such naked hope that my heart broke a little for him. I wanted to find Tavia and kick her conniving ass for all the times she'd made Zora miserable, and now Walker. He was a much better man than I'd realized, and loyal to a fault. The concern, the deep and abiding love he felt for his family, his naive insistence on seeing the best in his manipulative-ass sister ... lothario or not, he needed a friend. I could be his soft place to land. Just for one night.

"Let's do it," he pronounced, standing abruptly. "That sounds perfect."

"I'll do the dishes," I protested when he advanced to the sink, but he waved me off.

"I've got it. I'll be quick."

Minutes later, I was settled comfortably on the couch. "Sit here, please," I said, directing Walker to sit in front of me on the floor when he emerged from the kitchen.

There was a noticeable hitch in his stride. His eyes went wide. "So, uh, what kind of viewing is this? Are—"

"This isn't Netflix and chill," I told him dryly. "It's me offering to help you with whatever's wrong with your neck."

Something like understanding relaxed his features, and he quickly lowered himself to the floor. Such was the breadth of his shoulders that I had to crank my knees open as far as my hipbones would allow. He settled against the couch within the cage of my legs with a noisy exhale. Tentatively, I explored the tightly bunched muscles at the base of his strong neck, the unyielding tautness of his jaw. He gasped as I began kneading at the unyielding flesh, his hands rising to grip my calves on either side of him. On the television, Adam Sandler gave a cringe-worthy performance in *The Waterboy*.

Soon, I was just as caught up in the movie as he was, laughing at Kathy Bates despite myself as I massaged the stiff planes behind his ears. His hands on my calves began to move, sliding up and down, back and forth across the surface of my sensitized skin. I swallowed, trying not to acknowledge how good it felt, those huge, rough-palmed hands tracing an enticingly slow, warm winding path from my ankles to the backs of my knees.

"That feels really good," he said, his grip on my ankles tightening as I manipulated a particularly stubborn knot at the apex of his spine. His near growl of approval provoked an answering tingle of electricity down low, and my knees closed reflexively against the width of his shoulders.

"I'm glad. Probably doesn't compare to what you did for me yesterday," I joked. "But I'm glad it's hitting the spot for you." I let my fingers ease past the silky coarseness of his hairline and delve into his scalp. He nearly purred, resembling a big cat as he lowered his head to one of my thighs.

A chill ran up my back at the imprint of his soft lips and scratchy beard against the thin skin of my inner thigh.

"Thank you," he said. "And to be clear, I'm pretty sure nothing could be better than what I'm feeling right now."

"I'm glad." Slow breaths, Leigh. *Try not to think about where his head and mouth are right now.*

"And as for last night," he continued, his eyes still closed, "that wasn't charity. I think I enjoyed it even more than you did."

I opened my mouth, closed it. Was he? Were we—

"But what I'd love right now," he began, opening his eyes and suddenly lifting the pleasant weight of his head from my thigh, "is to finish the movie from the comfort of the couch." He stood suddenly, and I barely had time to register his change in position before he turned and plucked me up, pressing me against his hard chest. In no time, he'd resettled us on the couch, him with his back against the cushion, me in front of him as the little spoon. I stretched out my legs and they automatically threaded through his. Walker inched a throw pillow under my head and over his arm, then wound the other arm around my waist. I was caged in, trapped, manacled to the searing warmth of his solid form.

And I loved every minute of it.

"I thought I should pick the next activity," he said into my hair. "It *is* my therapy session, you know."

I couldn't work up my usual biting remark, not with the heady scent of his cologne and the musky spice of his skin enveloping me. His strong limbs tightened around me, and I had to suppress a sigh of contentment. So I gave in. I settled back against his chest and took the same advice I'd given him, watching Bobby Boucher lead the Mud Dogs to victory, all while worries about my growing attraction to Walker scuttled through my overactive brain.

~

I AWOKE ABRUPTLY, jerking into a disoriented awareness. I didn't remember falling asleep, much less turning and burrowing into the shelter of Walker's granite chest. Our legs were still entwined. At some point, I'd hitched my leg higher over his hip and slid a hand under his T-shirt, high enough that my fingers were nested in the crisp hair of an apparent happy trail.

Gingerly, I withdrew my hand and tried not to think about how I already missed the warmth of him. A long sigh rattled in his chest, his arm around my back reflexively tightening before his sleep-roughened voice spoke my name.

"Leigh."

"Yeah," I said past the sand in my throat.

"We fell asleep. What time is it?"

"I'm not sure." I half-turned, craning my neck to see the time display on the television's screen saver. "Three forty-two."

The warm exhalation of his breath skimmed the top of my forehead. He stretched all of those magnificently wrought limbs before his arms wrapped around me again. "We need to get in bed."

"We do," I agreed, sliding up the couch with the intention of clambering off. But suddenly Walker's face was right in front of mine, and any motivation to move evaporated. After all, when would I have another opportunity to take in that sinfully handsome face when it was slack with this drowsy contentedness? It must have been that same hazy veil of dream-like consciousness that prompted me to reach out, to follow the lines of his full lips. My fingertip took off on its own odyssey, savoring the curves of his nose, the sharp-edged planes of his cheekbones.

He blinked once, twice, those dark eyes fixed on mine. Then his hands came up and bracketed the sides of my face just as his mouth settled on mine.

In the ensuing silence, when the only sound in the room was the articulation of our mouths, I came to an unsettling realization. I'd always been bewildered by women who made questionable and downright dangerous decisions while dickmatized. How, I'd always wondered, were women rendered senseless by an erect penis? Even in my dumbest days with Gio, it hadn't been the sex that kept me in my wreck of a marriage. Hardly. It was the fear of failure and defeat, a desperate bid to somehow rationalize what was an appalling lapse in my judgment. Yet right now, Walker's player ways were far from my mind as my hips canted against his, seeking, searching, desperate for more. Even the smell of his freaking deodorant was turning me on.

"You're a face holder. I love that," I said, taking advantage of his preoccupied hands to snake my own below the waistbands of his shorts and boxers until I gripped the heat of him.

"Oh, God," he panted, resting his forehead against mine.

"'Oh God' is about right," I breathed, stunned at the length and breadth of him. I snagged the waistbands of his shorts and boxers until they cleared the delicious roundness of his ass.

"Flatterer," he said on a noisy exhale, laughter coloring his voice. His chest lifted and fell rapidly against mine as I thumbed the tip of him, working and squeezing him until he groaned loudly.

"Turnabout's fair play," he said, his face briefly reappearing in my vision before he threw up my shirt and peeled my bra upwards until my breasts sprang free. "And I was so hoping I'd be reunited with these again sometime soon."

"I thought we said one night only." I tightened my hold on him as I stroked all that satin encased steel. The throbbing between my legs only intensified when I felt the slick of his moisture in my palm.

Walker's eyes closed, his breath catching as he drew circles around my breasts, pinching and teasing my nipples until they tightened almost painfully. I couldn't help the throaty cry that ripped from my throat when he finally lowered his head to take a nipple in his mouth.

In less than a minute, we were both breathing harshly and groaning. Just as Walker grew impossibly thick and hard in my hand, his long fingers slid into my underwear and dipped into my wetness before joining my grip on his straining cock.

"I want you inside me," I managed, inflamed by the raw carnality of his hand moving with my mine, spreading our arousal on his cock.

"Not tonight, not like that," he ground out. The cords of his neck were straining, I saw. His breathing was rough and labored as his hand left mine and returned to plumb the entrance to my body.

I opened my mouth to protest, and suddenly his mouth was on mine again, swallowing my protests. The world narrowed down to the faintest pinprick of awareness as his thrusting tongue and pelvis worked in tandem, his rhythm uneven and desperate. His fingers played over my clit with diabolical skill, teasing my hips into a fever even as I frantically worked him in my tight grip.

We came together, him groaning and me shrieking as he erupted in my hand with spreading warmth. We laid together for several long moments, our hands still affixed to the other. Walker moved first, sitting upright and stripping off his shirt.

"I think I died and came back to life," I murmured, feeling wrung out. He chuckled darkly, using his shirt to clean his orgasm from my hands and his belly.

"Well," he said, shaking his head ruefully, "I think your therapy worked. I'm a lot more relaxed now."

I let my eyelids fall closed, too weary to keep them propped open. "Good. This'll be the last time. For real." I'd decided not to recall the moments when I'd begged him for more, when I'd have been willing to trade anything in my possession to feel him moving inside me. I was back in my right frame of mind. Immune to smooth gamesters once again. "This was the last time," I repeated to the silence. Behind the darkness of my lids, I waited to hear some sign of Walker's agreement.

It never came.

CHAPTER ELEVEN

Leigh

"Mind if we make a quick stop before heading home?"

I turned in the passenger seat to meet Walker's inquiring gaze. Moments before, his car's AI had read aloud an incoming text message from his phone: *I've got cinnamon rolls.*

I swallowed back a knowing smile. "You really are ridiculously predictable. Your whole family says those cinnamon rolls work on you like a homing device."

"What can I say?" His smile was wide and unabashed. "I'm a mama's boy. That's the real driver for me, not the cinnamon rolls. Knowing she wants to see me is enough."

"Sure it is," I scoffed. "Prove it. Decline the rolls when you see her. Then I'll buy that."

He was silent for nearly a mile before he spoke up again. "I don't feel a need to prove anything, thank you very much."

I couldn't help laughing then, and his cheek bunched up in a grin.

I turned back to the lush, verdant scenery passing outside my window. Walker and I had settled into a strangely comfortable camaraderie since our, er, interaction the previous night. We'd each stumbled off the couch, taken turns in the shower, and retired to our respective bedrooms. Nary a reference or allusion was made to our couch make-out session during our shared commute to and from work. But there was no mistaking the new comfort and ease I felt with him. This must be what the short road to hell felt like. Cozy and pleasant enough that you don't care about the hot flames licking at your feet.

"So?"

I turned back to find him glancing back at me. "So, what?"

"You okay coming with me to Mama's house? Or would you prefer that I drop you off first?"

I shrugged. "I'll go with you. I love your mom."

"Alright. But no ganging up on me with her."

"You're asking for too much."

When we entered the Leffersbees' stately home, Ellie Leffersbee's eyes widened in excitement when she saw me.

"My Leigh girl! It's so good to see you. I didn't know you were coming. This is a wonderful surprise!"

"It's good to see you too," I said, stooping to hug Walker's petite mother. She was the spitting image of Zora, but that's where the resemblance stopped. Where my best friend was shy about discussing potentially sensitive matters, Ellie had an old school "gives no fucks" attitude that made her wry commentary and uncomfortably direct way of speaking hugely entertaining.

She was exactly what I wanted to be when I grew up.

Ellie waved me into the house. I glanced back in time to see Walker lift his mother off her feet in a hug while blowing a noisy raspberry on her cheek.

"Stop that, boy," she said, slapping at his arm once she was on her feet. But I heard the undercurrent of joy in her voice, and I smiled.

She got us settled in her bee-themed kitchen, automatically seating us at the kitchen table with sweet tea, as was her custom. I glanced around, reflecting for the hundredth time how neither Zora nor Walker blinked twice at their family's means, yet they were both so well adjusted. Ellie's home hinted at their wealth but also conveyed how deeply she cared about their family. The kitchen had been renovated, again, but they'd kept the scarred kitchen table the same. It reflected the family. On trend, while prioritizing tradition. Walker waited until she joined us with her own glass of water before he pointed out the obvious.

"So, uh, Mama, there's no cinnamon rolls?"

I shook my head at him from across the table. "I thought all you wanted was to see your mama, Walker. You don't care about those cinnamon rolls."

Walker turned his head, pointedly ignoring me as Ellie broke into laughter. "Now, I know you knew better than that, Leigh. You've never been one to fall for his okey-doke."

"Never," I confirmed, while a voice at the back of my head whispered, *Liar.*

His eyes met mine across the table, and I easily read the dark promise of retribution in them. "No one would ever expect that of you," he said, his voice fat with irony.

"There's turkey meatloaf," Ellie said, giving a backwards nod at the stove, "with hot water cornbread and green beans. You're both welcome to it."

"Yes, thank you," I said automatically, and both Ellie and Walker laughed.

Walker continued his line of cinnamon roll-related questioning once we'd gotten our plates and sat back down. "Mama, were there ever cinnamon rolls?"

"You should be ashamed," I told him, and Ellie laughed again.

"Technically, yes. I just haven't put them in the oven yet."

His eyes widened. "Since when do you tell 'technical' truths?"

She sat back and took her time studying him before she answered. "I guess I'm just keeping up with my family. You know, with the technical half-truths. The *secrets*."

Walker went still mid-chew. Only then did I realize how neatly we'd been trapped. She'd known exactly how to lure Walker in, and the rolls were still held hostage, unbaked, in the fridge. Plenty of time to turn him on the spit over the roasting fire of her interrogation.

Genius. I fucking loved her.

Walker recommenced chewing, very slowly, as his mother watched with an unblinking stare. "Whatcha talking 'bout, Mama?"

"There's so many things to choose from. Let's start with the topics that affect you."

He took his time sipping from his water glass. "I don't know what you mean."

Just tell her, I thought, taking care to stay quiet and out of the way. I shoveled green beans in my mouth, watching as Ellie folded her arms and fixed her son with a classic "you're not fooling me" look.

"Well let me help you," she said, examining her unpainted nails. "Tell me what's going on at the bank. And don't you dare try to skirt around the truth. Mrs. Watkins and I already had quite the conversation."

Walker set down his fork, looking grim. "I've got it, Mama. I don't want you to worry about it."

She leaned forward then, laying her hand atop one of his clenched fists. "Baby, that's never been in question. Never. I know your heart for that bank and this town. I just don't want you knee deep in Leffersbee bullcrap."

The smile Walker gave his mother was wry. "That's not your last name too?"

She harrumphed, folding her hands together on the table. "That nonsense comes from your father's side of the family, you know that. Us Jacksons, we use the common sense God gave us. We're a peaceful lot."

Walker shook his head when I caught his eye. *Tell her,* I mouthed. I had a feeling Ellie knew a lot more about what was going on than she'd admit, and I didn't want him to struggle alone with someone else's burden anymore. He didn't deserve it. He had enough on his plate.

He shook his head slightly, and I widened my eyes at him insistently.

Ellie looked between us, her brows raised.

"Fine," Walker said, and Ellie and I both listened as Walker recounted Pops's warning, his power struggle with Tavia at the bank, and his suspicions about her future plans. Ellie bit her lip as she listened, one of her fingertips tracing a whorl in the table's woodgrain pattern.

"I was afraid of this," she said when Walker finished. "Your father's been out a lot, God knows where. Mrs. Watkins says he's never at the bank anymore. I haven't seen a great deal of Octavia either. I thought something like this might be afoot."

"I don't want Walker stuck in the middle of all this," I surprised myself by saying. Both Leffersbees looked up at me with obvious surprise. "Not that I should have a strong opinion about what is obviously a highly personal family matter," I hastily amended. "But it's not fair to Walker. Especially because he ..." I cast around for the right words.

"He cares," Ellie said, her gaze sharp and assessing as she watched me. "Deeply."

"Yes," I acknowledged, now uncomfortably aware that she saw a little too much. She didn't move her probing stare from mine for several prickly moments.

"Here's what we're going to do," she said briskly, wiping her hands. "We're having Sunday dinner in two weeks. *Everyone.*"

"Oh, Lord." Walker covered his eyes.

"That includes you, missy." I looked up to find Ellie nodding at me. "Yes, you. You're family too."

Since when? I almost said, but managed to stop myself in time. I hadn't been to the Leffersbees' home in quite some time, and I'd always been accompanied by Zora when I did go. But Ellie's gaze on me was altogether too uncompromising and knowing.

"I really don't think it's appropriate," I tried.

"I'm making oxtail stew," she said.

"I'll take my plate to the family room while you all talk out here," I said, and she gave a brief snort of laughter.

"Alright," she said, refocusing her attention on Walker. "Next. How's your health been? Did you take ill recently? You look tired, peaked. Is it this bank mess that's got you looking worn out?"

Walker's gaze shot to mine, and I took care to lower my own to the table before Ellie intercepted any nonverbal communication between us.

"I'm just tired. Probably too many hours working at the bank, then on the house. I'm going to take a few days off, get some rest soon."

Silence swelled within the kitchen. "So," Ellie said, her voice deceptively sweet as she rose and headed to the fridge. "How's your love life, Walker?"

Walker sighed in defeat, and I cracked up. Ellie busied herself at the stove, arranging the dough onto a baking sheet.

"Those cinnamon rolls cost you today, huh?" I whispered under my breath. Walker shot me a glare.

"It's fine," Walker called to his mother, and I laughed again.

"I don't know what 'fine' means," Ellie said from the stove, her back still turned to us. "But I know your father and I have been talking about how you need to settle down. You're getting older, you know, and these streets are nothing to play with nowadays. You never know what's going on with somebody. Just the other day, I read this news article about how there's a *super* gonorrhea now—"

"Mama." He shook his head, long since accustomed to Ellie's candor. I melted into hysterical silent laughter. "There's no reason for us to discuss—"

"Well, I hope you're careful. I'll tell you this much, I know everyone talks about variety being the spice of life and all, but there's nothing so comforting as having sexual relations within a monogamous relationship, preferably marriage, if you know what I'm saying?"

He closed his eyes and didn't answer. His lips twitched faintly.

"Because then," she continued, opening the oven door and sliding the baking sheet in, "you get to really learn what you partner likes. Everyone knows life's a lot easier when you know how a thing works, as opposed to having to fumble through the orientation."

"Everyone knows," he echoed, shaking his head at me in quiet exasperation.

"Those'll just be twenty minutes or so," she said, rejoining us at the table.

"Great. I wonder what other fascinating subjects we can cover in the next twenty minutes or so," Walker said, narrowing his eyes at her.

I sent him a bland look. "Not that you care about the rolls or anything."

"And you're a good man," Ellie continued as if we hadn't said anything. "An incredibly kind, caring, compassionate young man. I just know, if you applied yourself to a relationship with the same energy you do everything else, you'd be an outstanding husband."

"Alright," Walker said.

"Now, what about you, Leigh?"

My heart just about stopped when I realized Ellie's predatory gaze was on me now. "Uh, me?"

"Yes, you," Walker said, his smile taunting. "I believe she asked you a question."

"How's your love life? You still dating that young man at the hospital, the nurse?"

Walker propped his chin on his fist, looking between me and his mother, clearly enjoying himself.

I cleared my throat. "Uh, no. Simon and I aren't seeing each other anymore."

She made a dismayed clucking sound. "That's too bad. I thought Zora said you two liked each other, that things were maybe even heating up."

"We broke up," I said, clearing my throat again. "A while ago, before Nick even came back in town. Simon, uh, asked me to move in with him, and I didn't think it was a good idea, so we parted ways."

"I should say so," Ellie said staunchly. "As if you'd want to shack up with a man when you deserve a marriage proposal, as young and beautiful as you are."

I kept my eyes trained on Ellie. "No, Mrs. Leffersbee. I'm not the marrying kind."

Her brows shot up. "What does *that* mean, exactly?"

A gurgle came from Walker's end of the table. "Been there, did that, got the T-shirt," I informed her.

Ellie watched me for several moments. "You know," she ventured finally, "bad times, hard times, they're not always a loss because they often teach us a lesson." Her eyes narrowed. "What lesson did you learn from your previous marriage?"

I blinked a few times, taken aback.

"I hope it's not too personal a question," Ellie said with a little smile that didn't fool me in the slightest. "I was just curious, and you *are* family, you know?"

I stretched my lips over my teeth in a poor imitation of a smile. "Yeah, I'm certainly feeling like family at the moment," I chortled. "I guess my marriage taught me I should always listen to my instincts. To hold myself responsible for what I allow, and not repeat the same mistakes."

Ellie seemed to absorb my response. "Sometimes," she said finally, very quietly, "when you make a mistake, there's a natural inclination to hide your heart away to protect it from being hurt again. But that's the real tragedy, baby. Love, real love, requires you to have both hands open so you can receive it. It's surrender, not control that opens us up to all the possibilities of what could be."

"Okay," I said, wanting to end the conversation as soon as possible.

"Leigh." She patted my forearm. "You need to hope again. It's okay to hope for all the wonderful things that are still waiting for you."

"Mom. Enough." Walker's expression was full of warning as he watched his mother.

"Fine, I won't keep at her." Ellie rolled her eyes, and I sent him a grateful look he acknowledged with a nod. The moment with Ellie was getting, well ... touchy. I didn't want to think about all the things I'd left behind.

The diddling with Walker probably wasn't helping to clarify my state of mind either.

"Tell me about the hospital. How's work, baby?" Ellie said, and a light bulb went on in my head. Who better to consult about my work dilemma? The Leffersbees were well-connected and active in the state's political circles. Even if they didn't know anything about KCH's recent sale, Ellie still might have some tips for mobilizing the community to fight with us.

"Actually, I could use your help," I told her, and inwardly grinned at the way her eyes darkened with pleasure. "I need to take down the hospital's new administration, and I have an idea that you might know just where to start."

CHAPTER TWELVE

Walker

"Slow down, Speed Racer." I looked back and forth between the digital speedometer and Leigh in the driver's seat of my car. She was biting her lip, grinning, as we hurtled along at better than ninety-five miles an hour down one of Green Valley's back roads.

"C'mon, Walker. Hardly anybody uses this road."

"You're about to talk your way out of the driver's seat," I said. The car hit a dip in the road and went airborne for the space of a heartbeat.

"I'm telling you, I never see anyone back here."

"That's what the sheriff would like you to believe. Jackson James is a little too quick to write a ticket under normal circumstances, let alone when you're going fifty miles over the speed limit."

"Fine. You're right." She eased off the gas and snuck a sidelong look at me. "It's such a cool car. My dad would love this." The thought seemed to amuse her for a moment. Then the smile drained from her face.

"Where are you taking me?" I wanted to distract her from thoughts of home that might spoil her good mood. "Must be somewhere good since you conspired with Miles to pull me off the reno."

"You've done enough work on the house this week. The crew will survive without you just this once."

"That's what you decided?"

"Yes. And where we're going is a surprise."

I bit back a smile at the determined lift of her chin. In the two weeks since we'd joined my meddlesome mother for dinner, we'd settled into a comfortable rhythm. The Winston brothers still hadn't fixed her car for some reason, but I'd come to relish our commute to and from work. We previewed dueling playlists and Leigh would sing out of tune at the top of her lungs when the spirit really moved her. We took turns cooking dinner and washing dishes, and always ate together at her kitchen table as we dissected our day and strategized next steps. Hands down, though, my favorite part of the night was always the moment when we retired to the couch, or her bed, or mine in the guest room, to watch the shows we took turns choosing. Only recently had I acknowledged to myself that *MythBusters* or even an Adam Sandler movie wasn't why I looked forward to this time so much. Increasingly, I enjoyed just drifting off next to her, relishing the warm weight of her head on my chest, the playful tickle of her hair under my nose, the vanilla scent of her all around beckoning me to a deep, dreamless sleep. Spending time with her had become addictive.

Which was why I'd put the brakes on our physical relationship. Once acknowledged, our attraction had all the potential of a wildfire: limitless energy, with a ferocious appetite for *more.* But I didn't want to give in to the inevitable. I wanted to access all the parts she'd walled off in the name of protecting herself. I needed to discover who she was when she wasn't hiding behind that wall. Why she insisted on making me a lunch every day, but appeared fearful and apprehensive when I went out of my way to do anything for her. Sex would come easily, once we finally got around to it. But it would take much longer to penetrate the calcification around her heart. So, I'd kept things PG between us, slowed down the momentum toward sex, while I chiseled my way through her seemingly tough exterior.

It seemed to be working. She now looked entirely at ease, open and warm in a way I wouldn't have imagined possible months ago.

"Green Valley is only a minute big," I said. "Can't be too much of a surprise."

She slowed, took a familiar turn-off, then steered us into the parking lot of The Front Porch, the town's fancier restaurant. Before I could comment on the unremarkable nature of the location, I noticed the balloons, signs, and banners lending the building's exterior an uncharacteristically festive appearance.

I squinted at the banner draped over the doorway and the illegible words painted in a childish hand. "What's that say?"

"I'll use my young eyes to help you, old man," she said, elbowing me in the side. "It says, 'Welcome to Maddie's Fundraising Dinner.' A few of the letters are backwards, so it's a little like reading the Greek alphabet."

"Alright! Is Maddie home from the hospital yet? Is she here?"

She shook her head. "No, far from it. But the expenses are piling up for her family, so we convinced them to do a fundraiser. The owner agreed to host it here with a special menu. Half the proceeds go to the family."

I was already unbuckling my seatbelt. "Well, let's go. I brought my appetite."

I'd barely made it three steps in before Leigh announced, "He's here!" and a vaguely familiar woman launched herself at me.

"Karney," she yelled into my ear at full volume, and I resisted the instinct to recoil from the aural assault as she hugged me.

"Hey," I said, and then it clicked. Maddie's mom. "It's good to see you," I told her, returning the hug.

Maddie's father suddenly materialized and gave me a few hearty thumps on the back. "Good to see you out of the kangaroo suit, man. Thanks so much for what you did for our little girl."

Maddie's mother pulled back and framed my face in her hands. "You are the kindest, most generous man."

Leigh watched it all with a quiet smile. "I told you I'd get him here. He gave me some resistance, but I persevered."

Maddie's mother reached back to squeeze Leigh's arm. "You always do. Come with me, Walker. I want you to meet all our family."

For the next half hour, Maddie's parents escorted me through a crowd of grandparents, cousins, aunts, uncles, and friends, all of whom expressed unwarranted thanks for my brief stint as Karney the Kangaroo. I was helping Maddie's younger brother shape toy soldiers out of Play-Doh at the makeshift activity table in the corner when I felt a hand settle on my shoulder.

"Walker Leffersbee," Drew Runous said, smiling broadly. He inclined his head to his smiling wife, Ashley. "We saw you over here and just had to head over and say hello, especially after hearing about your gig as Karney. Anybody get any pictures of that?"

"I didn't realize the word had gotten around. And heck no, there's no pictures for you to blackmail me with."

"We'll get you on something else eventually," Ashley said. "You know there's no secrets in Green Valley." She opened her arms for a hug and I obliged. "But I'm hardly surprised," she said, planting a kiss on my cheek before she sidled back up to her husband's side. "You've always been one of the best guys I've ever known. Mama used to always point you out to my brothers when we were growing up and tell them what a perfect little gentleman you were."

I groaned. "Yeah, we all enjoyed that. Where's your little one?"

"Roscoe is watching her. We were just about heading out. Didn't plan to stay all that long, but we had to come and show our support for the family, you know?"

"I do know," I said, studying the blown-up picture of Maddie that graced the hostess stand. "Terrible thing, what this family is going through."

"Well, that's why they've got us. Family, community, it's the best thing to get you through hard times."

"Speaking of family," Ashley said, craning her neck as she looked around the restaurant, "You here with yours? Mrs. Leffersbee with you?"

"No. I'm here with Leigh," I said, realizing after a brief search that Maddie's mother had corralled Leigh to a table at the back of the room.

Ashley followed my gaze and her eyes went wide. "Good Lord. Why, Walker Leffersbee. I do declare that is the first time I've seen you look at a woman like that."

"Here you go," I sighed, and she squealed under her breath like a schoolgirl.

"Not denying it, I see. What's going on between you two?" she whispered, and Drew gave me a look of shared commiseration.

"Would y'all excuse me for a moment? As much as I would have enjoyed the interrogation to come—"

"Escape while you can," Drew advised me, nodding.

Ashley was smiling so widely, I felt certain I could see her back teeth if I applied myself. "I'm gonna find out anyway, Walker. Might as well—"

"Alright, I'll see you later," I said, laughing, as I veered around them and headed to the back table. A quick check of my watch showed more than an hour had passed since we'd arrived. I knew Leigh didn't need me to check on her, necessarily.

But I wanted to.

Both women looked up at my approach, their expressions taut, and I questioned my timing. "Everything okay?" I asked, immediately realizing the underlying stupidity of the question.

Of course everything wasn't okay.

Maddie's mother worked up an unconvincing smile. "Leigh and I were just talking about the usual. Maddie's upcoming surgeries, new behavioral issues with the other kids because her father and I are spending so much time away from them at the hospital. Hours being cut at the mill, bills from the hospital piling up 'cause we can't ever get ahead of the out-of-pocket portions." She gave a tired shrug, exhaustion lining her face. "You know. The usual. If you've got an appetite for all the misery I'm dishing out, please, have a seat."

I pulled out a chair and sat beside her. "Sounds like you have a lot on your plate."

Her answering smile was thin. "I'm not handling it well, apparently. One of my girlfriends just gave me a lecture about how I need to write in my gratitude journal instead of complaining. Said it would be the right example to set for my kids and help me put things in perspective." She shrugged. "I'm sure she's right, but lately, I just feel like I'm going to explode."

"Do the 'right thing' some other day." Leigh's face was twisted with scorn. "Walker and I are the only ones here right now," she said, lowering her voice. "Just us. Not your family, friends, kids. Not even your husband. Get it out."

Maddie's mother was silent for a long moment. I realized she was choking back tears and placed a hand at her back.

Leigh reached across the table and captured the other woman's clenched fist. "One of my favorite Rumi poems tells us not to deny the emotions and feelings passing through us, but to invite them in, welcome them, and remain open for all they have to teach us." She leaned in even further, her eyes never moving away from Maddie's mother. "You've fought so hard and so long, and there's still some road ahead of you. It might be more helpful right now for you to acknowledge your feelings and heal so you have strength to continue."

I stared at Leigh, struck by the fierceness of her affection for Maddie's mother and the force of her words.

Maddie's mother knuckled the tears at her eyes and gave a rueful laugh. "What you must think of me, Walker. I'm a mess every time I see you."

"I think you and your family are remarkably strong. Even kangaroos know everyone needs a shoulder to cry on sometimes," I said, and she gave a tearful shudder. "You're safe here with us."

"Thank you," she managed, and Leigh gave me a small smile.

Maddie's mother seemed better after a short crying jag, at the end of which one of her children arrived and dragged her back to the family. Leigh and I sat quietly after she left.

"I hate that this is happening to them," I said. "It's incredibly unfair."

"It is what it is," Leigh said in the prosaic manner that often accompanied her blunt observations. "For her and a lot of other families I see every day. Though I wish like hell it wasn't."

I watched her downcast expression. "Can't be easy, seeing so much heartbreak every day. Are you this close to all your patients? Should I be prepared for another turn as Karney?"

"Nah. I have a good relationship with all my patients, but Maddie and her family are special."

"They are."

"Y'all ready to order?" We both looked up at the arrival of Hannah Townsen, the hostess. "We've got a special menu today," she said, laying two small laminated sheets on the table. "Half the proceeds go to Maddie's medical expenses."

"I'm ready," Leigh said. "I'm starving and everything on here looks good."

"Better get your own fries," I teased. "Don't say you don't want any and then end up eating all mine. I'm not gonna be a gentleman about this. I want my fries."

"I don't know those games," Leigh said over her menu, "and I can assure you I have no intention of pretending I don't like food for you or any other man." Hannah, who had been waiting with a distinctly bored air, looked startled then shot Leigh a grin.

"I'll take the mozzarella sticks, a bacon cheeseburger, and onion rings," Leigh said, then turned an accusatory eye on me. "You better not ask for any of my onion rings." I thought I heard Hannah snicker as she walked away.

"No danger of that. I don't want to lose a finger."

"Smart man."

"Sometimes."

"So," she said, drawing out the word as I met her teasing regard, "where are all your women, Walker? I've never known any of your droughts to last this long."

I sat back and studied her. She toyed with the wrapper from her straw, looking uncharacteristically nervous.

"Why are you looking at me like that?"

I shrugged. "I guess I'm just trying to understand your question. You're with me every morning on our drive to work. You eat dinner with me every night. We dang near sleep together every night, whether it's in your bed or mine. And yet you're asking me, what? Where my other women are?"

It's time, I thought. Time to put our cards on the table. I was beyond ready, and apparently, so was she. Even if she didn't realize it yet.

Across from me she was silent, ostensibly searching for an answer. I waited a beat, inspected the folded placard on the table advertising Maddie's GoFundMe information, while I figured out how I wanted to approach this. I looked at her over the placard, not raising my head.

"You think I have that little respect for you? You think what's been happening between us means that little to me?"

She squirmed. "As long as I've known you, there's always been a woman in the wind. Now all of a sudden, it's quiet." She squinted at me. "Are you not feeling well still? Are you tired?"

I took out my phone and took a picture of the placard's info. "So, my not dating anyone right now has to be the result of me being physically incapacitated, is that it? I have that little self-control?"

She double-blinked, and I realized some of my annoyance had leached into my voice.

"I didn't mean to insult you, Walker. I just thought it was curious."

"Curious. Okay." I nodded. Outside the window next to us in the parking lot, an old clunker parked perilously close to my car. I kept an eye on the window, waited until the driver and a gaggle of kids got out and walked away with my paint still intact before I looked back at her.

"Seriously, I didn't mean to offend you," she said, wincing. "I know things have gotten ... weird between us since you moved in—"

"Define 'weird.'"

She bit her lip, studying the table.

I waited, watching her struggle. She needed a nudge, but she wouldn't go easily. Approaching this head-on wouldn't work, not while she was so clearly caught between her head and her heart. Hope and fear.

Keeping my eyes on hers, I sat back against the red vinyl booth and stretched my legs out in front of me. "I have a question for you," I said, just as Hannah arrived in a blur of movement to deposit the plate of cheese sticks and disappear again.

"Shoot." Leigh opened her napkin, spread it in her lap, and immediately grabbed one of the cheese sticks. Dark grease bled a trail across the table as she rushed it to her mouth, blowing on it to cool it off.

"No point in waiting, huh?"

"Nah. Ask your question." She stabbed the cheese stick into the soufflé cup of marinara sauce several times before popping the remainder in her mouth.

"I know your ex-husband cheated on you. Did Simon?"

She paused as she reached for another cheese stick. "No."

"Why'd you break up with him?"

"He, uh ..." She shifted uncomfortably in the booth and studied the white tablecloth. "He wanted me to move in with him. We'd dated for almost a year, so he felt like it was time."

"And you didn't?"

"No."

"Why?"

She let out a breath. "Because I knew he was getting serious and that moving in with him was incremental progress in his long-term plan."

I watched her closely. "And you didn't want what, him or his plan?"

"Neither. I don't know ... I want a family one day, but in the end, I guess he wasn't the right guy."

"Did someone else, besides your ex-husband, cheat on you?"

She frowned as she chewed. "Why would you ask that?"

I shrugged, not wanting to give voice to my suspicion or comment on how easily she'd believed I was capable of betraying her. "I'm just curious. Asking is my way of getting to know you."

"Fine. No. No one else cheated on me."

I took a shot in the dark. "Was it your dad?"

She went still. I dove in deeper.

"It's pretty clear you have a complicated relationship with your father," I said, piecing together what Zora had told me over the years, and remembering the way the light died from Leigh's eyes when she'd mentioned her father in the car earlier. "Did he cheat on your mom?" I braced myself for the pushback, but it didn't come.

"Over and over again. And then I kept the pattern going with Gio, you know, because I learned so much from watching them." Her mouth quirked downwards at the corners.

I studied the way she unconsciously wrapped her arms around herself in a self-soothing gesture. I hated that she'd experienced that as a kid, and that the pain of it still reverberated in the present.

"When all that was happening when you were a kid, who did you talk to about it?"

She took a while to respond, her grip on her arms tightening. "No one. We weren't allowed to talk about it. Lucia and I had to pretend nothing was wrong. Even when we had to leave our house and stay with my aunts. Oh, but I did tell my entire fifth-grade class about it during a presentation."

I whistled. "That couldn't have gone over well."

She shook her head, smearing a trail of mozzarella sauce around her plate with a cheese stick. "I got in a ton of trouble. Looking back, I think I just needed the release of saying it out loud."

"And with Gio? Who helped you then?"

Her eyes closed briefly. "I didn't let anyone in on what was happening, not at first. I was embarrassed and ashamed, and I kept thinking I could fix it, so I kept it all in. Learned behavior, I guess. And then it got to the point I couldn't hide it anymore." She let out a harsh laugh.

"And then?"

She shrugged. "I ended up here."

That explained a lot. It also meant I might have a steeper hill to climb than I'd anticipated.

But she was worth it.

Hannah returned, sliding our plates and condiments in front of us before moving on to her next table. Leigh dressed her burger with mayo, ketchup, and mustard before she spoke. "Why are you asking me all this?"

I paused to swallow a bite of my grilled chicken pita. "'A joy, a depression, a meanness, some momentary awareness comes as an unexpected visitor.'"

Her eyes went wide. "You know 'The Guest House'? You have it *memorized?* I can't believe this."

"What," I said, affecting mock offense. "I can't have layers?"

"I just wasn't expecting that."

"Let's talk about the unexpected," I began, and Leigh's eyes narrowed.

"What's unexpected?"

"You. Me and you."

She stared at me fixedly. "What the hell are you talking about, Walker?"

I took another bite of my sandwich, chewed, swallowed. "I like you."

Several long moments passed.

"What did you say?"

"I said, I like you. After these last few weeks, that shouldn't surprise you at all."

"What are we, in third grade?"

"I feel like I'm in third grade right now," I admitted. "Been a minute since I told someone I have a crush on her, but ... here we are." Taking in her deadpan expression, I decided to further extrapolate. "I like—"

"Pussy. You like pussy, Walker." Her face had gone tight, the way it often did when I surprised her with her favorite donut from Daisy's or replaced the flowers in her vase. She was afraid.

"Oh, for sure. No denying that." I nodded. "But it's easier to tell yourself that's all I care about, isn't it?"

"Easier than what, exactly?"

I shook my head, pushing my plate back. "The way I see it, we both have the same problem you so sagely counseled Maddie's mother through."

"And that is?" Her brow went up.

"Neither of us have been willing to face what we're feeling, so we've been telling ourselves whatever stories keep us comfortable."

"Walker, I haven't been telling myself any story."

"You have. It's a story you know really well. It starts with 'Once upon a time' and it ends with Gio."

She ducked her head. "Walker. I don't know what you want from me."

"You. Everything."

"There's no 'me' left to give you," she said, sounding despairing. "Maybe it's better if we put some space between us, spent less time together. You need a woman who's ready for a new journey, without all the baggage from the past still on her back. Someone looking forward, not back. I'm pretty risk-averse now. I don't have it in me to start over again."

I considered my response, groping for a way to push her past her fear before that familiar wall rose up between us again.

"You know I had to watch just about every fairy tale movie that existed with my sisters when we were growing up," I said, injecting subtle humor in my voice. "That's the cost of having three younger sisters, I guess. But now, as a grown man, I can't help but think those stories aren't all that triumphant. Cinderella meeting the prince at a ball and finding her happily ever after? That's easy. Lazy."

She didn't look at me.

"What happens when the prince turns out be a monster? How does Cinderella move on? How does she find love again?"

I waited until her eyes met mine. "There's the real triumph. That's the story I want for you. A new story."

"I don't know if I'm capable of that story." Her voice was low. "I've gotten to know you a lot better, Walker. I know you're not the man I thought you were. But the part of me that believes in happy endings? She's gone. I'm not naive and hopeful anymore."

I smiled. "It pains me to quote my interfering mother, but here we are. It's okay to hope again, Leigh. You know I'm not Gio, so I hope you'd know by now that I'd never want to hurt you."

Her smile was sad. "It never starts out the way it ends. It didn't with Gio. And you might not mean to hurt me, and I might not mean to hurt you. But sometimes it happens all the same."

I leaned forward, capturing her reluctant gaze. "You're not the only needing to learn a new story. I've been telling myself I'm not ready to stare down the barrel of anything long term or permanent. But I've realized how untrue that is, the more I spend time with you."

"Okay, Walker," she said with a disbelieving snort.

"I won't bother to argue with you. I know I've been secretly hoping the Winstons take forever to fix your car and the plumber never replaces those pipes."

"I can admit that I've loved spending time with you. Far more than I ever would have expected. But we've always liked spending time together. Doesn't mean we're cut out for a relationship."

"I'm a little scared, too, you know. I know I'm not Gio and I'd never do anything that bastard did. But I do worry about overcoming your past—"

"My past is for me to overcome, not you, damn it," she said, sounding tired. "If you were paying attention, you'd realize I'm already doing my best to protect you from it."

"I don't want to be protected from anything. What we have, what we're becoming? It's not nothing. It's not casual. I want more. I want to get to know you even more. I don't want to play games."

"I ..." She looked flummoxed.

"And I need you to be brave. Brave enough to believe in what we could be if you gave it a chance."

"You're delusional." She shook her head at me.

"Maybe. Let's find out. "

CHAPTER THIRTEEN

Walker

"Y'all made it!" My mother gave an excited squeal and whacked me with the dish towel over her shoulder when Leigh and I arrived for Sunday dinner at the kitchen's back door.

"Did we have a choice?" I sent her a narrow look as I slid the pressure cooker from the hands of our family's long-time cook and emptied oxtail stew into the waiting serving bowl. "Hey, Ms. Davis."

My mother pretended she hadn't heard me, returning the dish towel to her shoulder as she refocused on Leigh. "Don't you look pretty, baby! Just a vision of loveliness. Isn't she, Walker?"

I nodded, not bothering to look back as the two exclaimed over each other's dresses. My mother may have had all the subtlety of a pickax, but she was right. The air had grown thin when we'd met me in the foyer right before we left for dinner. She'd left her hair in a cloud of loose, untamed curls and wore a dark blue dress that showcased the dark blue of her eyes. The nervous way she'd eyed me heated my blood. Since our discussion at the fundraiser yesterday, she'd been quiet and contemplative but had avoided talking about what I'd said to her. There was no denying, though, that things were different between us now. We both felt it. I couldn't wait until she allowed herself to fall into all I felt for her. As I briefly caught her eye, my chest constricted at the sight of her unrelenting prettiness. I wondered what it would be like to make love to her with all that wild hair everywhere.

"Well, we're all here now," my mother chirped in an overbright voice, interrupting my reverie and tripping off several internal alarms. "Why don't you two help Dorothy get all the food to the table while I get the others."

Leigh and I exchanged glances as she hustled out of the kitchen, yelling for my father and Tavia.

Working together with Ms. Davis, Leigh and I transferred the remaining serving platters from the stove to the table. We'd just finished when Tavia sailed in, with my father cutting a slower, reluctant path behind her.

"Son. Leigh." My father ambled over, still in his Sunday best, his arms open for hugs. He'd grown a goatee during his absence, and maintained his trademark baldness to hide the thinning spot at his crown. I looked him over, returned his hug and the strong clap of his hand on my back. I wondered where he'd been and what he'd done in all the time he'd been gone from the bank, and what it meant that he hadn't seen fit to tell me.

"Mr. Leffersbee." Leigh smiled, but her eyes on him were sharp and watchful as we made small talk about the weather, goings on in town and at the hospital. Tavia claimed a place across from us with a brief greeting, her gaze moving between Leigh and me. Ms. Davis left with a wave, she and my mother quickly embracing before she quietly slipped out the back door.

Something was off. This wasn't a typical Sunday dinner, infrequent as they were now. Uneasiness hung over the table, pulled my sister's face into a sober expression, sent my mother's gaze darting anxiously around the table, straightened my own spine. I glanced beside me and found Leigh's eyes on me as she bit her lip. I squeezed her elbow twice.

She gave an almost imperceptible nod.

"Bless the food, Ezra," my mother said, and we all stood behind our chairs as my father launched the kind of never-ending prayer that had always made us kids groan in exasperation. I cracked open one eye after my father took in more air and found Tavia's eyes on mine from across the table. We exchanged a knowing grin, and I felt the briefest moment of relief knowing we could still share a genuine moment not fueled by suspicion and resentment.

Then Tavia's gaze settled on Leigh beside me, and she lost her smile.

"Food's getting cold, Ezra," my mother said, right on schedule, as my father launched into act three of his prayer.

My father acknowledged her with a smirk as he finally brought it home. We all murmured our amens, sat, and tucked into the food as we passed serving platters around the table.

"*Hell yes*," Leigh murmured under her breath when I served her a generous portion of oxtail stew.

"You're about to earn it," I murmured back.

"I've got you," she said quietly, her steady gaze lifting to mine and startling me with its fierceness. "Whatever happens, I got you."

I found the wherewithal to tear my eyes away from her. My mother, who'd kept up a steady prattle about everything and nothing and was now watching me with a smug expression.

I shook my head at my mother, and she shifted her gaze back to the table at large, that same little smile still curving her lips. "Did Audre tell y'all about her latest major change?" she asked, her tone deliberately offhanded and upbeat with forced cheer. I realized she planned to ease us into choppy waters with small talk about my youngest sister.

"Again?" Tavia rolled her eyes.

"Film. She wants to make documentaries," my mother said, buttering a roll.

Dad looked up, his forehead creased in annoyance. "Another major change? Does she have 'major change' money? Does she think UCLA is giving tuition away for free? She better ask Spike Lee to send a donation for this latest pipe dream."

As conversational devices went, this one was usually pretty successful at getting us talking and laughing over my youngest sister's flighty, indecisive ways. But we were all too tense, too on guard to relax into any topic, and I saw my mother realize it as the dense weight of silence returned to the table.

It was almost a relief when a knock sounded on the back door.

"I'll get that." My mother rose, smoothed a hand down her dress, and crossed the kitchen.

"You want anything else?" I turned to Leigh, prepared to hand her any of the serving dishes from the middle of the table, just as I saw her face split with a smile.

"Pops!" she said, grinning, and we all looked up in disbelief at the sight of my grandfather and his companion coming into the kitchen.

I glanced around the table. I'd had no idea he was coming, and there were no unclaimed place settings at the table, though there was one empty chair.

This was Ellie Leffersbee at her craftiest.

I swallowed back a laugh at the stunned expressions on my sister's and father's faces.

Things were about to get interesting.

"You can start the party now," Pops boomed. Behind me, my mother averted her face to hide her smile, and his companion rolled her eyes good-naturedly.

"Did we get here in time?" he asked, his gaze moving over the contents of the table as he came closer.

My mother produced a place setting, complete with utensils, that she'd obviously hidden away in advance. "I'd say you got here just in time," she said, directing him to the seat next to Tavia while situating his plate on a charger.

"You missed Dad blessing the food," I said with a straight face, and Pops laughed, the tip of his tongue caught between his teeth.

"Thank God for that," he said, sending my father a look full of *something*. "Son, I keep telling you, Jesus already has His hands full. Don't tie Him up all day listening to you bless the food."

"Good to see you too, Dad." My father's smile was thin. "I didn't know you were coming." My mother returned my father's pointed stare with a look that clearly telegraphed, *Checkmate*.

"It's your lucky day," Pops returned. "Food still warm after all that praying?"

"Still warm," Leigh reported, smiling at him unreservedly. I chuckled, waiting for them to revive their usual routine. The two of them always found each other during family events and gossiped in a corner like the Muppets Statler and Waldorf.

My mother got Pops's companion settled in the family room after

Pops advised us he didn't need anyone's help pre-chewing his food, and then we were all settled again.

"So," Pops said to Leigh, leaning across the table with one ear cocked in her direction, "shit go left yet?"

Leigh let out a gasp of laughter, and I joined her.

Tavia glared at us both.

"Not yet," Leigh said in the same stage whisper.

"Ah. That's my cue, then." He made a show of jumping in his chair, as if seeing Tavia seated next to him for the first time. "Octavia! Long time since I've seen you, Little Bit! Thought you'd have made your way to see me by now, long as you've been home."

Tavia wilted under his suddenly sharp gaze. "I'm sorry, Pops. I should have come to see you long before now."

"Uh-huh. And what was it, again, that brought you from New York to share all those business smarts with us?"

She hesitated. "I just wanted a change of pace, that's all."

"Mmhmm." Pops caught my father's eyes. "And how about you, son? Seems you've been MIA as well?"

"Business," my father said, squaring his shoulders.

"Uh-huh," Pops said again, taking up a platter of collard greens and filling his plate. "That business have anything to do with the deal you and Octavia put together to sell my bank to Consolidated?"

Silence blanketed the table. Disbelief stalled the breath in my lungs. "*What* did you just say?"

"Ezra," my mother hissed, fire in her eyes as she glared at my father. She clenched her fork in a bloodless grip. "Tell me that's not true."

Leigh's hand settled on my knee and squeezed.

"Ah. I see they didn't tell you." Pops's expression was serene as he peered at the various dishes and settled for the platter of fried catfish. "They didn't tell me either. Which is damned inconvenient given it's *my* bank, don't you think?"

"Nothing's decided," my father said, his temple working.

"You're damn right it's not decided," Pops said, abandoning his nonchalance to glower at my father. "I made damn sure it got to the right ears that I'm not about to let my bank go to those opportunistic buzzards."

That woke Tavia up. "Pops, *why* did you do that? Dad and I were going to bring it to you. We were. We were just working out the details—"

"Do you *hear* yourself? What you're saying?" Pops's tone was frightening in its quiet intensity. "I built that bank from nothing. From the ground up, me and my wife, scratching the foundation in the dirt with our bare hands, sweat stinging our eyes, fighting to make something in a world that begrudged us *anything,* including our dignity. I raised you all, fed you all from that bank. I did it *for* you all, before I ever knew you, before you were more than a thought," he said, his eyes hard as they settled on my father. "I planted a seed and tended it in the hopes of leaving a legacy you would grow beyond my wildest dreams long after I was gone. But I turn my back for one minute, and you two are busy trading it all away."

The two men, my father and grandfather, locked eyes. Hurt and pain were palpable in their charged silence.

My father rose, his throat working. "Dad. We should talk."

Pops watched him, his face giving away nothing. "Aren't we talking now?"

Dad swallowed. In that moment he was as uncomfortable as I'd ever seen him. "Please. Let's go to my study so we can talk."

Pops made a sound of disgust and eventually acquiesced, taking his glass of water with him as they shuffled out.

The rest of us sat in shocked silence for several long moments as the gravity of what Pops had just disclosed imposed on our reality.

Leigh's hand had settled at my lower back, a warm comforting weight.

My mother sat back with her head cradled in one hand, her eyes closed.

Tavia looked vaguely sick and kept casting anxious glances at the doorway our father and Pops had just gone through.

I watched her, battling my rising anger. It was a unique experience, feeling like the disappointed parent to my wayward father and sister.

"Consolidated, Tavia?" I shook my head, let my hand fall to the table with a slap that made her jump. "How do you square that? They are the lowest of the low; bottom-feeders preying on vulnerable customers with no options."

"They're turning over a new leaf, they're rehabbing their image—"

"That tends to happen after Federal Reserve sanctions."

"We're coming to the table as equals, Walker. They want to know and learn from us, what our ways are, how we treat customers."

I couldn't help a snort of disgust. "You believe that? You believe a national behemoth that's made billions of dollars from abusing their own staff and defrauding their customers is interested in our little Smalltown, USA branches and how we operate them?"

"Yes."

"Well, then, who's teaching them? 'Cause warm and fuzzy isn't your brand. I'd expect to see you on the other side of the table with them."

"You may be too noble to care about money, but it *is* the whole point of our being in business."

"Money is *not* why we're in business."

"That's nice, Walker," Tavia said, "and convenient for you. Now I'm the heartless bitch because I want to make something more of this business, help Dad take it leaps and bounds above where we started. "

"Language," my mother ground out.

"Sorry, Mama." Tavia barely spared her a glance before refocusing on me. "This is why we knew we couldn't say anything to you. You're completely unreasonable when you—"

"'We.' I used to be part of 'we.' Mrs. Watkins is going to set on the both of you like a pit bull when she finds out."

"Mrs. Watkins is gonna dance a jig when she realizes how much money her shares are going to be worth," Tavia said, crossing her arms and looking smug. "Enough money for her to retire, travel the world, build a new house in Nashville to be with her daughter and grandkids if she wants."

I ran a hand over my chin, praying for patience. Leigh's hand tightened on my knee. "Tavia, did you see Pops's face just now? Did you hear how devastated he is? Regardless of how much money's on the table, all he sees is the betrayal. It's all I can see."

"Betrayal," she sniffed.

"We're a family business. Forgive me for operating under the assumption that working together means we disclose something like an attempt to sell the business. Just like we owe it to the community we serve to let them we know plan to pull the rug out from under them."

From the end of the table, my mother murmured in assent.

Tavia's expression hardened. "We're doing this to better position ourselves and our members."

I let out a bitter laugh. "Pops made a name for himself by educating folks about the importance of home ownership and investments, providing guidance and giving them an opportunity when no one else did. He's always found a way to say 'yes,' always invested in others' empowerment. Why the hell would the two of you want to sell out the people we serve to line your pockets with money?"

Her face twisted. "You may be the one sitting behind that big desk at the bank now, Walker, but that doesn't mean you know best. I don't need you to lecture me about *our* history. You seem to forget Pops taught me too."

"Coulda fooled me."

"I'm not you. I'm not waiting for the Sweet Bye and Bye. I know just as well as you do how Black folks have been systematically held back from building wealth over the years. The game is as old as time, and it doesn't change, whether it goes back as far back as the Tulsa massacre, racial discrimination in the GI Bill, de-valued and under-appraised homes, hell, even those predatory-ass payday loans. It's always us getting played, and I'm tired of fighting a giant system with nothing more than a few pebbles in hand. I'm ready to pull ahead in this race, after years of others having a head start. I'm getting mine. I'm going to play their game and change it from the inside. That kind of money, real money, will put us in a position to help people far more than we can even imagine."

I cocked my head, staring at her in disbelief. "You think your plan is worth sacrificing the bank? That the solution to years of systemic discrimination will be solved by you, and you alone, by giving our bank to the very people who contributed to the discrimination?"

"We can't give what we don't have. If you're not motivated to get yours, that's on you. But it's not fair of you to hold the rest of us back because of some bleeding heart, savior complex."

Tavia sat back and folded her arms, her expression fierce.

"What do you think?" my mother said. I glanced over to find her watching Leigh. "What's your take on all this?"

Leigh froze like a possum confronted by a pair of headlights on a dark country road. "I don't know if it's appropriate for me to share my opinion," she said.

"I don't know that it is either," Tavia said.

"She's family," my mother countered, her icy gaze warning Tavia not to cross her. Satisfied Tavia would not interfere, she turned her attention back to Leigh. "You've got an opinion. As long as I've known you, you've never been afraid to speak your mind. Don't start holding back now."

Leigh was quiet for a long moment. I knew she was considering and ultimately discarding the idea of blunting her trademark honesty.

"One thing I know for sure, Tavia," she said, splitting her gaze between Tavia and me, "you never sacrifice your community and its well-being for your own profit."

"Wait a minute," Tavia said.

Leigh held up a hand to halt Tavia's interruption. "In the last few weeks, my hospital has been hijacked by mercenary suits who don't know or care anything about us. They sleep just fine at night after implementing cost-cutting measures that'll make it even harder for people to get quality care. I'm gearing up to fight like hell to stop KCH from being gobbled up by a heartless, merciless profit-hungry machine. And here you are, fighting like hell to turn what you hold dear over to one. It'd be one thing if Consolidated had a decent reputation, but it sounds like you already know what they're capable of," Leigh said, shaking her head.

"Anything else?" my mother asked before Tavia could butt in again.

Leigh hesitated, then said, "Secrets. They're not a business you want to get into, and if today isn't proof of that, I hate to see what it'll take for you to learn that."

Tavia opened her mouth again, but Leigh plowed ahead. "I've known you all since I met Zora in undergrad. I've always loved this family, how you all talk to each other, how you work out your disagreements, even when it isn't easy or simple. I don't come from a family like that." Her face fell a bit. I knew she was thinking of her parents, of Gio, and I covered her clenched fist on the table with my own hand.

Tavia's brows shot up at the gesture. My mother smiled.

"In my family when I was growing up, we lied to each other for a lot of reasons. For survival, a lot of the time. We lied and told each other everything would be fine. We lied to everyone around us about what was or wasn't happening at home, even though anybody with eyes knew we were barely limping along after each of my father's affairs. We told ourselves we were protecting each other, or being hopeful about the future." Leigh let out a sigh. "And the only thing that came out of it was that we got really good at lying to ourselves."

"I didn't lie," Tavia said, but she looked and sounded chagrined. "It was business, I—"

"You lied." Leigh's gaze on Tavia was unflinching. "Lies don't bring you closer. They just widen the space between you. I will never understand why you're so hell-bent on pushing your brother away."

Tavia's eyes met mine, and we regarded each other in painful silence.

"You don't know him," Leigh said, shaking her head. "I didn't either. I thought he was just Zora's whorish older brother—" She swore, flicking a glance at my mother. "Sorry, Mrs. Leffersbee."

"Don't be," my mother said, waving away her concern. "I told him he was gonna get worms if he kept going the way he was."

Mom shrugged when I glared at her.

"But now I have a much better idea of who he is. And I like him." I turned to find Leigh looking at me. "I like him a lot, and I love what's in his heart. He thinks about other's people needs before he thinks about himself. If you saw how much he gets done, no matter how tired he is. If you knew how important it is to him that you, his baby sister, always feel his love, that he never lose his temper with you no matter how much you provoke him ..."

Tavia looked away, her restless fingers tracing the pearls of her charging dish.

"He may be your brother, but he's not required to shovel your shit," Leigh said. Then her eyes widened and she darted a glance at my mother. "I'm sorry for swearing—"

"You're fine," my mother said blithely, looking unconcerned.

"Well said," a deep voice grated, and we jumped, surprised to see Pops and our father standing at the end of the table. "It's a good reminder for all of us." Pops sent a pointed glare at both my father and sister. "No more secrets. I'll just find out anyway and straighten you all out, so just save yourselves the effort. We've come to an agreement," he announced, nodding at Dad.

"The deal hasn't been completed," Dad said. "We were never going to finalize it without everyone's buy-in. We're still in the exploratory phase at this point, weighing our options, testing concepts."

Testing concepts. I thought of the focus group results on Tavia's desk and shook my head. This barn door had been standing open for a while, then.

"Dad has graciously agreed to hear us out," my father said. "To at least hear the terms of the deal and review what we've negotiated so far. We'd like to have Walker, Mrs. Watkins, and Pops there for our next meetings with Consolidated. Nothing will be decided until all the information is presented, and then we'll take a vote." He rocked on his heels, hands in his pockets, while Pops watched with narrowed eyes. "And let me just say that, after hearing Leigh and talking with my father, I'm not proud of how we handled this. We *are* a family, and that should imply transparency in all we do. I didn't model that behavior. For that, I ask all of you to forgive me."

I acknowledged his words with a curt nod. I appreciated the apology, but it did little to soothe the sting of their actions.

I stood. "Appreciate that, Dad. Mom, thanks for dinner. It was delicious, as usual. I need some time to digest all that's been said today. I'll be in touch soon with my thoughts. Leigh and I, we're gonna head out now."

Leigh popped up beside me, weaving her hand through the crook of my arm. "Yes, uh, thanks for everything," she said, nodding to each of my family members in turn. "We got dinner and a show."

CHAPTER FOURTEEN

Leigh

Walker didn't say much on the way home, and I left him to his thoughts. I was still absorbing all that had transpired during dinner and reeling from what I'd said.

Dear Lord. What all had I said, and *why* had I said it?

Maybe it was the colossal unfairness of it all, and the shock of seeing the normally well-behaved Leffersbees descend into D'Alessandro-grade dysfunction that got me spiling my guts. Whatever it was, I'd said way more than I intended and Walker was now curiously nonreactive.

"We're here," I said brightly, and unnecessarily, when we pulled into the driveway behind his truck. I popped out of the passenger side as soon as he killed the engine, brimming with nervous energy.

Walker, meanwhile, said nothing as he followed me to the door, but his eyes were disturbingly intent on mine as he watched me fumble with the key in the lock. When I dropped the keys and bent to retrieve them, he gently slid them from my hands and inserted the key in the lock himself, pushing the door open.

"I'll just—" I began, but the next words were forever lost as Walker's big body urged me against the foyer wall, his mouth descending to mine in a delicious assault of wetness and heat. I moaned, dropping my purse at our feet as my hands went coasting around the cobbled surface of his back and gripped the hard terrain of his shoulders. We stayed that way for endless moments, with him wringing pleasure from every cell of my body with the urgent clasp of his hands around my waist and at my breast. Just when I reached the point of dissolving into a liquid state, he pulled back to look at me with an expression so tender my heart seized.

"Finally admitted you liked me," he said, smoothing my hair back with the roughened surface of his thumb. "In front of witnesses." His grin had a distinctly teasing edge to it.

"I meant it," I admitted, throwing all caution and self-preservation to the wind as I looked into his gentle dark eyes. I knew what was going to happen next was inevitable, but I was also afraid of how things would change. I believed I could possibly trust him, and I wanted him so much I could barely stand.

It was a potent combination.

"I know you did, sugar," he said, running a thumb over the surface of my bottom lip as his eyes darkened. "That's why it meant so much. It's what's going to make everything that comes next so much easier."

My breath caught. "And why's that?"

His head bent to my neck, his teeth and tongue catching delightfully on the sensitive skin. The prickle of his goatee awakened all my nerves, and I clenched the muscled expanse of his arms. "Because now," he said, his voice almost lost to the delightful torment of his tongue against my collarbone, "now when you have doubts you can remember this isn't just physical. You see me, and I see you. I'd never intentionally hurt you. Not if I can help it."

"I don't know," I said. My stomach was quaking with sudden nerves. "Doesn't have to be intentional. Still happens."

He cradled my face in those huge hands until my vision was filled with just him, only him. "A few people have been reminding me that nothing ventured is nothing gained. You won't know how much better it could be unless you try. How 'bout we make an agreement?"

"Tell me what you're proposing," I said, squinting at him cautiously.

He laughed. "That we give each other the benefit of the doubt. That when we feel uncertain we'll have the courage to admit it, and not lean into our assumptions or fears."

"I think I can do that."

"Good," he said, his thumb stroking the underside of my chin as he straightened. I barely had time to reflect on what I'd agreed to before his arm swept my legs out from under me. In less than a second I was hanging over his back, gripping the back of his thighs as he stalked down the hallway.

"Walker," I said, spitting out unruly strands of my hair as I bounced from the momentum of his steps. "What are you doing?"

"You know what I'm doing." He sounded alarmingly calm. Hardwood flooring passed under my gaze until it gave way to the carpeting in my bedroom.

Suddenly I was airborne and landing on my back on the bed. I barely had time to register my new location before Walker was over me, everywhere, the enticing musk of him filling my senses, his mouth sliding hotly over mine, the coarse hairs of his beard branding my neck, his hard cock against me making explicit his desire to be inside me. Before I could blink, he'd pulled my dress over my head and worked the bra strap under my back free.

"Thank God," I breathed, yanking impatiently at the buttons on his shirtfront until I finally gave up and snatched his shirt open, scattering buttons everywhere.

"Impatient, huh?" Walker grinned, his eyes wicked. His thumbs slid against my hipbones, hooking under the waistband of my underwear.

"This has taken way too long." My breath caught at his fierce expression when he snatched my underwear from around my feet and pushed my thighs open.

"I guess so." His fingers delved through my wetness, ghosting over my clit. I bucked under him, unable to suppress my needy groan. Walker smirked. "Huh. You ready, sugar?"

"Beyond ready." I wrestled at his belt, fighting to clear it from the belt loops. The momentum sent my naked breasts into motion and trapped Walker's gaze.

"You sure?" His brows went up, his grin cocky.

"Walker!"

"I know the last thing you want is for me to slow things down." His long fingers tortured me as they traced the rise and slope of my breasts before moving to tease my nipples. "But we gotta cover some administrative details before I turn you inside out."

"Get to it. *Please*," I said, on the verge of begging. I finally figured out that I could simply unzip his pants to coax all that glorious, warm heat into my hands. "I'm on birth control," I said, sweeping my thumb across the wet tip of his cock and enjoying the way his eyes closed in response. "But we have to use condoms, too."

Walker didn't respond for several moments, the only sound in the room the harsh exhalations of his breath as I gripped him, using my own wetness to lubricate my exploration of his hard length. "Exactly." He pried his eyes open and reached for the wallet in his back pocket.

"I have some." He pulled out a long foil strip and laid it alongside us.

I tightened my grip on him until the cords of his neck tightened. "That's all you've got on hand? We have a long night ahead of us."

"Big talk," he ground out, his hips moving ever so subtly to work himself inside the circle of my fist. "You didn't think I could satisfy you, remember? Now, don't go begging for mercy when you can't hang."

"Let's see who wins," I said, and we both laughed.

"Another thing," he said, reaching for his wallet again.

"What's that?" I asked, already ripping a condom packet open.

I was *done* talking.

"Up-to-date STD results." He dropped a folded sheet of paper by my head. "I'm clean, always have been. I've never had unprotected sex with anyone, ever. And for the record, I'm nowhere near as prolific as you seem to believe."

"That's wonderful, all of it," I said, working at smoothing the condom along his impressive length. "And I have an item of my own. We keep this between us, as much as possible. I don't want outside interference and 'help.' We wait to see how this thing naturally develops."

Walker stilled, his head tilting to the side as he considered me. "So, I'm your little dirty secret, huh?"

"Not hardly, you know that." I paused in rolling the condom to give him my full attention. "We just need a safe place between two of us. No other voices. Just you and me."

He nodded, but his lips thinned as he watched me. "Fine. We'll keep it undercover. For now."

"Okay. Great," I said. "Have we covered all the necessary points? Can you please hurry up and get inside me?"

"I have one more condition," he said, blinking as I used him to pleasure myself. "This here? It's exclusive. Just me and you. No one else."

"Fine, fine," I said, waving him along impatiently. But my heart gave a thump at the significance of his request, and the speed with which I'd so easily granted it.

"Sure you're ready?" His gaze was riveted between my legs, his cock stabbing against my clit in little teasing thrusts that had me jolting off the bed.

"Walker, I swear, if you don't fuc—"

"Like that?" I lost my breath as he thrust forward, filling me so thoroughly and completely I arched off the bed.

"Oh shit," I cried, dimly aware of him rearranging my legs until they were folded against my chest as he leaned in, his cock reaching the very end of me.

"Oh, my God," I stuttered, and his face broke out in a beautiful smile.

And then he surged forward, his hips moving slowly as I acclimated to him, then faster as I clutched desperately at him.

I hardly recognized my own voice, shrieking and shouting and swearing as Walker's hips powered into me. His fingers never stopped in their artful torture of my clit. I combusted around him in record time, squeezing him for dear life.

Walker watched me from above, ducking his head to laugh. "Got that out your system?"

I came to, blinking blearily at him, realizing—

"You're *still* hard?"

"You ready to beg for mercy yet?" Walker pulled his hard length out of me and flipped me over. "Or are you ready for more?"

I pushed to my hands and knees and met his challenging gaze over my shoulder. "Show me what you got."

CHAPTER FIFTEEN

Leigh

"Why do you smell like cigarettes?" Layla squinted at me suspiciously, her mouth turned down in obvious disapproval.

I rolled my eyes as I flipped down the base of a seat and sat. We were settled in the very back of an auditorium tucked away in the hospital's basement. Ebony had assured us it was rarely used, with the exception of a biweekly Tumor Board meeting. I checked my watch again, hoping she would join us soon so we could begin and end our covert meeting as quickly as possible.

Friday afternoons usually made me giddy for the weekend, but not today. Today I was a knotted mess of anxious nerves.

For many reasons.

"I'm pretty sure you're mistaken," I said, taking perverse pleasure in the way Layla's eyes narrowed even further to slits.

"That's cigarette smoke I smell," she said, pointing a finger at me, and beside her, Aaron cracked up.

"I don't think you have to worry about her smoking right now." Aaron studied me closely. "Last week, maybe—"

"Last week she was twitching, doing that thing with her fingers, just like when she first quit," Layla said, doing an impressive imitation of me. "And she definitely looks twitchy right now."

"I actually thought she seemed a little calmer," Aaron said. "Also, I heard a rumor about a certain young man."

They both studied me in silence, as if I were a museum display. Unbidden, I remembered Walker wishing me good morning in the most delicious manner. Heat burned my cheeks.

"Well," Aaron said, "the plot thickens. If you turn the 'bad cop' thing down, Layla, I just might be able to get us more details."

"My money's on the dinosaur," Layla said.

"Let's just get started," I said, and Aaron snickered when Layla said, "Told you."

"Loretta gave me the documents." I stood and reached under my scrub top to produce a manila folder bulging with documents.

They both gaped at me, and I laughed. "Give me a break. I met Loretta in her car for her smoke break so she could slip me the documents. There's cameras all around the outside of the hospital, and I couldn't just walk in with this in my hand."

Layla stared at the file in my hands. "What are you going to do with it while you're still on your shift? There's no way you can let that thing out of your sight, not for a single second."

"Nope, you're right." I shook my head. "And I gotta get back on the floor in the next twenty minutes to help prep a kid for testing. He's been giving his nurse trouble. It's been nonstop, now that I'm the only one left in Child Life. I don't even get a chance to eat anymore."

"The file stays in your pants until you get home then," Layla said, and I nodded in agreement.

Aaron cleared his throat delicately. "So you haven't had a chance to look at the contents yet?"

"No. I barely managed to slip out in time for her smoke break." I sat again and flipped open the folder. "She says there's good stuff here, clearly outlined plans for what they aim to implement over the next few weeks and months. I'm going to take it home and sort through it. I'll bring a summary to our next meeting."

"Quite a risk Loretta's taking," Aaron said, stroking his beard. "Admirable, but it has to worry her a bit."

I let out a long breath. "She's pissed enough at what she's hearing and seeing every day from the new administration that she feels justified. But we're both getting a little paranoid. She pointed out they could subpoena our phone records and link us if we're caught. I can accept the risk to my own job. I'd never forgive myself if she got fired for this."

Layla sat back and folded her arms. "It's not too late to quit, you know. Buyouts and transitions happen all the time. We could easily accept the inevitable and refocus our attention on finding new opportunities."

"I'm paranoid, but I'm not a coward." I rubbed at my brow. "When I was a kid, something similar happened to my dad and the other mechanics he worked with. He was eventually let go. It was what finally made him open his own garage. But he fought it all the way because it was the right thing to do."

"So that's where you get it from," Layla said.

"This fight isn't just about our jobs," I said. "It's about the community and all the people who will be impacted when these changes take place. Publicizing what's happening almost feels like a moral obligation."

Aaron nodded. "I agree."

"Speaking of those changes," Layla said, "this whole thing has given me a new appreciation for the snooping, intrusive investigative reporter I married."

"I'm telling Carla you said that," Aaron said, and Layla laughed.

"Tell her. She does snoop, that's not news to her. And I did just say I have a new appreciation for it."

"What'd she find out?" I asked.

Layla sat forward, looking excited. "She started keeping a log of hospitals Visage acquired and what usually happened shortly thereafter."

We all looked at her expectantly during her long pause.

Aaron rolled his eyes. "Oh, drag it out, why don't you? What did she find?"

"Tons of malpractice and whistleblower suits, sanctions. A clear pattern of Visage's attempts to cut costs at the expense of patient safety, whether in staffing, inadequate supervision of inexperienced clinicians, delays in lab tests, shortcuts in safety protocols, all kinds of stuff."

"At least they're consistent in their negligence," Aaron said, resting his forehead against his palm.

"And they're crooks," Layla said. "Several of their hospitals lost their Medicare-compliant status at some point for fraudulent billing."

I stared down at the folder on my lap. God, the stakes were so high. I could *not* mess this up.

"So we need to make a case. I need to find something in here that's predictive of that pattern," I said, thumping the folder against my thigh. "And soon."

"Before the ninety days are up," Aaron said. "Well before that, really, if we want the community activated."

"Agreed," I said. "We're already running out of time. Have you guys learned anything on your own reconnaissance?"

Aaron shook his head, lacing his fingers behind his head. "Hearsay for now, rumors about what's possibly coming. Nothing solid."

The door banged open and rebounded against the wall as Ebony burst in the front of the auditorium and ran up the steps to meet us at the back. "Sorry I'm late. We've been slammed with patients and I couldn't get away until lunch."

Lunch, I thought, and my stomach cramped at the reminder that I hadn't eaten all day.

"What'd I miss," she asked, breathless, and we all exchanged amused glances.

"Well, Leigh just pulled a rabbit out of her pants." Layla smiled. "And Aaron was just saying we don't have much in the way of updates."

"I do," Ebony said. She pulled a folded slip of paper from her pocket. "Scheduling for our floor, for the last two weeks and the next two weeks. You'll see the nurse-patient ratio has gone up, and there aren't as many of us scheduled for each shift."

"That is gold!" Surprising us both, I stood and pulled her into a hug, briefly twirling her on the short landing. "Thank you, Ebony!"

"Does this make up for eating your garlic challah?"

"Not quite," I said, and Aaron laughed.

"I gotta go." I turned my back to tuck the file back in my pants. "If that kid is still giving his nurse the blues, I'm hoping a little Nintendo will help. See you guys later."

"Uh uh uh," Aaron said, a twinkle in his eye. "I was hoping we could get a follow up on Karney."

Ebony immediately perked up. "Yeah, this is just as important as our spy work. You can spare a second for an update."

"There is no update," I said, smoothing my scrubs top over my waistband and checking to make sure the folder was unseen from the outside. "Listen, we've gotta stop meeting in the hospital. It's too risky."

"I agree." Layla nodded. "So, how well did you already know this guy? Y'all an item yet?"

"I'm leaving now," I said, starting down the steps.

"Monday at the Chinese restaurant," Layla called after me. "We'll have lunch there and talk next steps."

"I can't," I said over my shoulder. "I'm off."

"Oh?" Ebony said, and I looked back at the doorway to find all three of my colleagues closely following behind me.

"My niece is getting baptized this weekend. I'll be back Tuesday."

Such a simple statement. What I wanted to say was, *This is bound to be a shitty, drama-filled weekend.*

"Always nice to see family, isn't it?" Aaron said.

"Sure," I said.

Suddenly I felt too tired to continue through the motions that would end the workday and find me in New Jersey over the weekend. The file seemed to acquire extra weight as I thought about all that was ahead of me. The baptism was going to be its own special hell, and then after my return, I'd still have to summon the courage to open the pandora's box of this file and make a decision. How far was I willing to go to "out" Visage? And how the hell did *I*, a Child Life Specialist, find myself in this position? Surely there was someone more qualified, or with more experience in overthrowing evil corporate entities.

"Leigh."

I pulled up short, turning to see Layla frowning at me. She drew even and locked arms with me. "Are you alright?"

I tried a smile. "Yeah, of course.

She frowned. "You don't look or sound it. Listen, if all of this is starting to get to you, if the pressure—"

"It's not any of that," I said, projecting my voice to Aaron and Ebony, who were a few steps behind us, pretending not to listen. "I guess I'm just tired, probably a little hangry. I'll be alright."

Layla looked unconvinced. "It's Friday. You live for Fridays. Promise me you'll take some time for yourself. Go eat at that rib shack you love, get a pedicure, watch a movie, and eat some ice cream. I'm worried about you."

"You're ridiculous to worry," I said, pulling her along with me as we made progress back to the elevator. "I'm The General, remember? Impervious to pain or any of the messy emotions that plague mere mortals. I get stuff *done*, I get it over with, I don't whine."

"I don't buy it," Ebony said from behind us, and I briefly considered ducking into the elevator and closing the doors before they could follow and needle me anymore.

The four of us made lunch plans for the following Tuesday while we rode the elevator back up to our floor. Aaron alternated between sneaking watchful looks at me and contributing to Layla and Ebony's fierce debate over ice cream flavors.

"Try to enjoy your weekend," Layla called to me when I bounded out of the elevator. I waved goodbye without looking back.

Please, God, I thought. *Let this file stay hidden in my pants.* I flicked another surreptitious glance over my shirtfront, checking for any visible indentation.

Back on the floor, I was immediately waylaid by Ruth at the nurses' desk.

"Somebody's here to see you," she said, her lips twitching.

"Who?" My heart immediately burst into a frantic rhythm. Did Visage already know what I was up to? I sucked in my stomach to better hide the file and rearranged my face into a pleasant expression. "What's going on?"

"I think you're gonna like this surprise." She inclined her head to indicate I should follow her. "This gentleman has been looking for you."

I didn't have a second to ask more before we bent the corner. But I recognized that tall, broad figure almost immediately.

Walker.

His head was down, his attention wholly absorbed in the phone he held in his huge hand. But my heart gave an altogether different kind of leap at the sight of him and his perfectly shaped goatee, the fresh fade, the superb fit of his perfectly tailored suit. The deep sense of foreboding lifted, and suddenly I was excited to see him, as if I hadn't spent that very morning with him moving ever so slowly inside me, his strokes painfully disciplined as he whispered filthy words in my ear.

"Hey," he said, glancing up suddenly and smiling a smile so intimate and *mine* that I thought, *Maybe this time. Maybe,* and gulped back the reflexive fear. I drew closer, smiling despite myself, and his grin grew. Then his gaze settled on Ruth, and his expression became inscrutable.

Right. We were keeping our sleeping arrangements secret.

"Maleficent."

"Golden Boy." I just managed to stop my mouth from tugging up in a dopey grin.

Get it together, D'Alessandro. He's just a man.

Ruth's eyes moved between us. "Alright, glad I found her for you, Mr. Leffersbee. Let me know if either of you need anything." She gave us one last teasing, speculative glance before she walked off, her clogs slapping against the floor.

I peered through the glass pane of the inpatient room behind Walker and found it empty. "Wanna pop in here for a sec to talk?"

"I'd say that's a good idea," Walker said, nodding at something behind me. I turned to find all activity at the mammoth nurses' desk had gone still as everyone openly gaped at us.

I slid past him and opened the door, beckoning him in. "Yeah, a little privacy wouldn't hurt."

Once inside, Walker closed the door, settled a brown paper bag on the counter, and faced me. "What's wrong, sugar?"

I blinked. Since when did I like pet names?

Wake up. You're slipping, D'Alessandro.

"Nothing. Nothing's wrong."

He smirked, his eyes never leaving mine as he took slow, measured steps toward me. "I'll get it out of you. One way of the other."

"I'd like to see that," I said. He was so close now his fingers dipped into the reef of my spine as he pulled me into him.

"I know you would," he said, laughing quietly. And damn it all, he was right. The fear and anxiety crowding my throat began to dissipate. I gave in and took the comfort he offered, letting my head lower to his chest, sliding my arms around his waist, past his suit jacket, around his broad back. He smelled like expensive musk and spearmint. I wanted to burrow into him and never leave. "What happened today?" he asked, his voice reverberating in a deep rumble against my ear.

I sighed, closing my eyes. "Loretta gave me the documents today. The file's in my pants."

"Why is it in your pants?"

"There's no safe place to put it, not while I'm here. I can't be caught with it, but I also can't let it out of my sight."

"And?"

"And I'm worried I'll get Loretta fired doing this."

"But you're not worried about you getting fired?"

I tightened my grip around his lean waist. "If I'm fired, it's my choice. She's more of an innocent bystander."

"Give me the file."

"Huh?"

He stepped back just enough to meet my eyes. "Do you trust me?"

Our gazes held. "Yes," I said.

I pulled up my scrub shirt, casting an anxious glance behind him out of the narrow glass pane. The hallway was clear.

Walker's warm fingers slid along the skin of my belly, gently pulling the file from my scrubs before he tucked it in the small of his back, behind his sports coat. "I'll give this back to you when you get home," he said.

I swallowed back the frisson of panic I felt at the realization that we both now routinely referred to my place as "home."

"Alright."

"What else?"

I hesitated, debating internally as Walker's fingers returned to slowly glide across the skin covered by my scrub top.

"Just tell me," he coaxed. "You'll feel better."

I hesitated, trapped by his dark-eyed gaze. The urge, the instinct, to unburden myself intensified. Within the protective cage of his arms, it was somehow perfectly natural to give voice to the agitation once again threatening to claw at my chest.

"I'm fine," I lied, and his brows lowered.

"Alright," he said, sounding resigned. "I'll wait until you're ready." Abruptly, he shifted his weight, holding me tight as he upset my balance, swaying us in a slow tight circle, away from the view of the doorway. I scrambled to catch his rhythm.

"What are you doing?"

He reached back to capture one of my hands from his waist and interlaced his long fingers with mine, keeping our joined hands tight to our bodies. "What does it look like?"

"Like you've lost your mind and forgotten our agreement to keep this whole ... thing a secret."

"'Thing?'" His voice was tinged with amusement as one of his dark brows lifted. "I'm so flattered."

"You know what I mean. Walker—"

"Two minutes," he said, his voice low. "No one's coming in here in the next two minutes. Not when they're all out there taking bets on how much of a 'thing' there might be between us. You're allowed a two-minute break."

I swallowed my rebuttals, torn between saying the right thing and acute regret at the idea of leaving his arms. "You're a terrible dancer."

"I'm a great dancer. Nobody hustles, ballrooms, or electric slides better than me. You just refuse to follow."

"There's no music."

"That's the beauty of it. It's whatever we want. In my mind, we're currently grooving to 'In A Sentimental Mood,'" he said, turning us on another revolution. "You tell me what you hear. And if you relax, close your eyes, and follow my lead you'll find the steps. 'Cause, sugar, you still ain't found them yet," he huffed, and despite myself, I laughed and tried to relax.

"Give me my two minutes," he said. The low tenor of his voice, his assured grip at my waist, all of it liquefied the tension straining my limbs. I let out a contented sigh of defeat and lowered my head to his chest once again. His hold tightened. Before long, I forgot where I was and all that had preoccupied my thoughts. After several silent revolutions, the jukebox in my head supplied its own soundtrack, Van Morrison crooning, "Someone Like You."

I'm fucked.

"We're going to get away from all this foolishness," Walker said, turning us. "Once the dust settles. You need a break."

"So do you. Where do you wanna go?" I didn't open my eyes, now pleasantly entranced as I followed his lead and fell into the rhythm of the steps.

"Where have you always wanted to go?"

"I'd be happy with an undisturbed weekend on the couch for now," I said.

"That's it?"

"With an inexhaustible supply of brownies, coconut rum, romance novels, and trash television."

"Any room for me?"

I pulled away, pausing our momentum so I could meet his gaze. "Your presence is required. We'll take turns picking what we watch. I'd even watch SportsCenter or one of those space shows you like. If you threw in a foot rub, I'd bet you could talk me into anything."

Heat flared in his eyes. I took a step toward him, already craving the heat of his body and feeling reckless enough to kiss the hell out of him, potential observers be damned.

But Walker took a step back. Followed by another step, and another, until he'd retreated nearly to the door.

"That's two minutes," he said, and his smug smile told me he knew I'd wanted more of him. "Don't want anyone to get suspicious."

"Walker," I said, going to him, wanting to tell him everyone else could just fuck right off, I wanted him—

A brisk knock sounded and the door swung open. "Sorry to interrupt, Leigh," Ruth said, her gaze moving between Walker and me with open interest. "Radiology wants to know if you can help room 918 bed one drink the barium he needs. He's not playing nice with the nurses."

"Oh my God." I'd completely forgotten. "Thanks, Ruth, I'm on my way. Walker—"

He was already nodding as Ruth left the room and closed the door. He retrieved the brown paper bag with the name of a local BBQ joint emblazoned on the side from the counter. "Take this," he said, putting it in my hands. "You said you hadn't had lunch when I texted you earlier this afternoon. Have this eaten before I pick you up today."

I swallowed past a sudden thickness in my throat. "Thank you."

"No more thanking me," he said, dropping a brief kiss on my forehead before heading back to the doorway. "I've gotta run too, I need to get back to the bank. I'll see you tonight."

"Yes." I followed him out into the hallway, hating the stupid agreement that wouldn't allow me to hug or kiss him goodbye under the interested eyes of my colleagues. Instead, I stood watching his impressive figure retreating down the hallway while I clutched the bag of food.

"You are *gone* over that guy," Ebony said at my elbow. "Karney's got you whipped."

CHAPTER SIXTEEN

Walker

"Shit, shit, shit!"

I came awake in the darkened bedroom, blinking through my initial disorientation. Sitting up, I finally spotted Leigh's shadow bent over at the foot of the bed.

"What's up?" I turned on the bedside lamp, squinting so I could make her out in the low, warm light. "What time is it?"

She glanced up at me. Her hair trailed over her shoulders in unusually tame, wet ropes as she pulled her bath towel more tightly around herself. "Shit. I woke you up."

I moved to my knees, inched to the end of the bed. "Why didn't you turn on the light?"

"I was trying to let you sleep," she hissed.

"Uh-huh." I reached out and stealthily captured her arm, pulling her close enough to haul her entire body onto the bed with me.

"Walker! Let me go! I've gotta be at the airport," she sputtered as I pulled her damp, wriggling body under mine.

"Your flight leaves at nine a.m. It is now ..." I squinted at the display of the digital alarm clock at the bedside, "4:07. You're in no danger of missing your flight."

"I have to pack."

"I thought you were doing that last night."

"I didn't get to it," she said, sounding petulant.

Why was it so hard for her to say it? Why couldn't she just admit she didn't want to go?

Would she ever really let me past the brick wall of her defenses?

I don't want you to go either.

I maneuvered her under the covers, ignoring her squeaks as I turned the problem around in my mind. She couldn't bring herself to admit her dread over the trip, but she couldn't very well skip out on her niece's christening, could she?

"What were you cussing about down there? What happened?"

"I smashed my ankle against the bed frame."

I shucked the bath towel off, trying not to get distracted by all that soft, fragrant olive skin as I brought her leg over my hip. "Was it this one?" I asked, gingerly running a thumb over her ankle.

"Yes."

"Let me make it better."

"No," she said, pulling her foot from my grasp and scooting in even closer until her damp head was against my chest. "It's fine."

We laid there, huddled together under the covers. I gathered the weight of her wet hair away from her neck. "You'll be home Monday, back home with me, and you won't have to go back there again until your sister has another baby to baptize."

"Cia said she'll chop Paul's nuts off before she has any more kids," she said, and I grimaced.

"Alright. So you won't have to go back for any more baptisms. They'll visit you here in Green Valley."

"I'm not worried about going back home," she said, and I smiled into her hair, deciding to wait, to give her another opportunity to confess before I called her on her bluff.

"Well, what's on your mind?"

She shivered. I tucked the comforter tighter around us. "Maddie's dad got laid off at the mill. He carries the family's insurance."

"That's terrible. I'm sorry, baby."

"And we're going public with the information we got on Visage next week. We're meeting next Tuesday," she continued, growing more and more tense in my arms. "And I don't know what's going to happen when we do, and if Loretta loses her job over this it'll be all my fault—"

"Take a deep breath, sugar." I pulled the towel from under the comforter and tossed it across the room.

"And I haven't checked on my car at the Winston's garage because I've been so distracted, and weirdly enough, they've never called me."

"I'll take care of that today."

"No, I don't need *you* to take care of it, I'll—"

"What if I want to take care of you?" I countered. I leaned in, nosed the vanilla scent in the crease of her neck, and reminded myself to go slow. "What if you finally accepted that I'm your man? And that I'm gonna be there for you because you're my woman?"

Even in the darkened shadows, I glimpsed the trace of fear on her face. "I can take care of myself."

"Let me in, sugar," I whispered, bracketing her face in my hands. "I'm not gonna hurt you."

"I'm more than happy to let you in," she said, her voice taking on a distinctly lurid tone as she guided my hand under the covers. "I'll never complain about that."

I swallowed back my disappointment. If that was all she could bring herself to offer, who was I to complain? Hadn't I resisted the idea of a relationship mere weeks ago? She'd catch up, I told myself.

"Relax." I let my hands coast along the surface of her back, the front of her thighs, ending at her slick heat. "I've got you."

And then I went about the business of proving it to her.

Fifteen minutes later, we were sweating and still intertwined.

"You know," she said, sounding thoughtful. "None of my problems have changed, but I do feel a lot calmer."

"I'm glad."

A long silence.

"Walker?"

"Yeah."

"I don't want to go home for the baptism. I love my niece, but I don't want to go."

Finally.

"I know, sugar. What'll happen there, do you think?"

"It's just," she shook her head, her expression drawn as she stared at the ceiling, "it's never easy. Every time I go back, the past is right there, like no time ever passed. The longer I'm there, the less 'me' there is. And everybody's got a goddamn opinion about what I should or shouldn't have done. It's only going to get worse, because now I know about Gio's little boy and how everyone's gotten attached to him. So they won't even bother to hide it or avoid the topic. Do you know what that feels like, knowing your whole family's been keeping a secret from you?"

She turned her head to look at me, and we both burst out laughing.

"I have some idea," I said, using the corner of the sheet to wipe the sweat-slicked hair from her brow. "But nowhere near on the same scale that you do."

As pissed as I might have been with my family at times, I'd never experienced genuine dread at the idea of spending time with them.

"I'm done whining," she said, affecting a neutral tone that didn't fool me in the least.

"Leigh—"

"What do you have up for the weekend?"

I closed my eyes, suddenly bone tired. "Consolidated is flying me, Dad, and Pops out for deepwater fishing Sunday. Somewhere in Florida. Then there's a meeting at their headquarters Monday."

"Sounds like fun?"

"I couldn't care less about some stupid fishing trip, or whatever stops they pull out. They're not getting my bank if I can help it. But Pops and I told Tavia we would try, hear them out."

"Do me a favor."

"What?"

"Rest tomorrow. No working on the house, no gym. You rest up for Sunday all day, okay?"

"I'm fine."

"You're not. You're stressed and tired and you need a break."

"Let's just stay here together." I pulled the covers back over the both of as she snuggled against my shoulder. "We'll go back to sleep, we'll let those flights take off without us, and we'll keep each other safe here. We'll even work in the couch time. Deal?"

"You have no idea how much I would love that," she said. I felt the press of her lips against my collarbone and something inside my chest came loose.

"Then we'll make it happen."

She laughed. "No, but I've done enough hiding. I'll deal with whatever comes my way." Her voice was strained with false bravado.

But I didn't want her to handle it alone. She needed me, even if she'd never bring herself to say it, and I needed to be with her, watch over her, and break someone's face if necessary.

"I'll follow your instructions and take it easy if you promise to call me when you get to your sister's house. And you call me, immediately, if anything pops off with your family."

"I'll handle it." She sounded drowsy.

"I know you can. But I'm asking. For me," I said, kissing her shoulder.

There was no way I could let her go alone.

~

"GOT A MINUTE?"

I looked up from my computer screen to see Tavia in my doorway, one hand poised to knock.

"What do you want?" I rubbed at my brow, fighting a wave of fatigue. Maybe Leigh was right. I *was* tired. Why had I pushed myself to come in on a Saturday? Especially when, after a week's merciful reprieve from her presence, Tavia had apparently picked this day to show up at the office again.

"Can I come in?"

"Do I have a choice?"

Her face fell. "I know—"

"What business do you want to discuss?"

Something like shock flitted across her face. "Walker."

"If you don't have business to discuss, something that concerns this bank and the running of it, just go."

"So much for you being understanding."

"We all have our limits. I hit mine when I found out you've been looking me in the face and lying for the last year."

She took several steps into my office and stopped, biting her lip as she studied her feet. "I knew you'd be mad."

I returned my attention to the monitor, finalizing my transaction on the travel website.

"So, you're just going to what? Not speak to me? We can't talk this out?"

"Not today."

She stalked forward and dropped in one of the office chairs opposite my desk. "It's not a crime for me to look out for my own interests, Walker. If I waited around for Dad or Pops to even consider giving me a say in what goes on at this bank, I'd still be waiting. I don't apologize for taking what I need. If I were a man, you'd say it was an admirable trait."

"Don't do that," I said, disgusted. "Don't try to make this about anything more than you lying to your family."

"I didn't have any other choice, Walker. They handed this place to you on a platter before you could even tie your shoes. How sexist and antiquated is that?"

"Not my doing," I said, but my belly twisted at the truth of her words. Put like that, it *wasn't* fair.

She sat back and watched me, her gaze calculating. "You're right. It's not your doing. Hell, if anything, you're just as much a victim as I am. I always wanted the bank, to prove how much farther I could take it, even when no one believed in me. And all you've ever wanted was to get out from under it."

I went still, struck by her words.

I'd come to accept my role. I still loved and respected the tradition my grandfather had built, enough to serve as a guardian to that legacy. Even if it was a reluctant watch.

"Dad's stuck too," she said, her eyes still on mine. "His whole life has been this bank, what Pops built. Dad wants to take a risk, make a move that he can claim as his own victory."

I ran a hand over my eyes. "And here I am, standing in y'all's way. Doing my best to keep this thing standing while you both do your best to dismantle it."

"Should you get participation points for that? Can you say you ever put in any real effort to grow it beyond what it already is? If anything, you're more concerned with fitting in your hobbies, like the house renovations. You're not really driving this thing, Walker. You're asleep at the wheel and content to let it just roll on."

I met her gaze, considering her words. "Maybe you're right."

Her eyes widened. "What?"

"Maybe I need to get out of the way." I executed the print function on my computer and stood to gather my things as the printer on the corner of my desk came alive, spewing pages.

"Where are you going?" Tavia asked, looking up at me.

"I'm going home for the day. I'm tired, and I'm going to take someone's excellent advice to rest up for my flight Sunday."

Tavia watched me, seeming uncertain. "So ... can I count on you to give the folks at Consolidated a chance tomorrow? To really hear them out, to not give them a hard time?"

I buttoned my suit jacket and grabbed the papers off the printer tray. "You won't hear a peep of dissent from me."

"Thank you."

"Because I won't be there."

"*What?*"

"I won't be there," I repeated. "I'm needed elsewhere. And you need a chance at the wheel, since I've apparently been derelict in my duties."

"Where else are you needed?" She stood to meet my gaze, her fists clenched.

"Have a good day, and a good weekend. I'll see you when you get back."

"Walker," she shrieked as I turned off the light to my office and headed down the corridor, "what are we supposed to do without you there? This was your opportunity to get the details you said you wanted, to see them lay out their presentation."

We reached Mrs. Watkins's doorway, and I paused. Mrs. Watkins sat at her desk, one ear cocked in our direction as she listened, grinning at Tavia's ire. "See you later, Mrs. Watkins." I gave her a nod and salute. "I hope you enjoy your time fishing in Florida this weekend."

Tavia's head swiveled between Mrs. Watkins and me. "What are you talking about?"

"Well, I can't go, so I'm sending Mrs. Watkins and Jamal as my proxies."

"The loan officer?" She scrunched her face in an expression of distaste so vile, I was glad Jamal wasn't there to see it.

"Yes. The loan officer, who is quite capable. They're both going to give me a report when they return. I figure this works for everyone. I get the briefing I need, you don't have to worry about me being well-behaved in front of your corporate puppets, and Mrs. Watkins gets a little sun."

"I could always use a little sun," Mrs. Watkins said, her eyes flat as she stared Tavia down.

"See? Everyone's happy."

I'd made it to the end of the hallway when Tavia's bitter snicker made me pause in reaching for the door handle.

"This is about her, isn't it? That's where you're going. To be with her."

I looked back over my shoulder at her. "Yes."

"And you would pick her over your own family right now. Over your own blood."

"Blood isn't what makes a family."

Her chin went up and her eyes went suspiciously bright. "You're saying we don't have that anymore? That I'm not still your sister?"

"Leigh needs me, and what she needs is my business. I'm going to be there for her."

Tavia looked away, then back to me. "So this is serious."

I nodded. "Very."

We regarded each other in silence.

In that moment, we'd never been further apart.

~

"So, the meeting is Florida is a big deal. It could potentially determine the entire future of the bank. The bank you live for. And you won't be there?"

Miles turned from the road, brow raised.

"I knew I'd regret this."

"Why? I'm already heading toward the airport at the crack of dawn on a Sunday. I can't think of anything I'd enjoy more than seeing my brother and discussing his recent domestication."

"Let me out here," I said, watching Green Valley's landscape go by in a blur of spring greenery.

"What, you ashamed? Or is it that you just don't want to admit I was right. 'Cause I was right."

"Miles. I'd have happily driven myself if I'd known I was going to have to listen to your mouth the whole way."

"But you wouldn't have had the benefit of coffee and Daisy's donuts," he said, gesturing to the grease-spotted bag between us. "Now, tell me. When did you know you were in deep with Leigh?"

That was actually a very good question. I couldn't quite identify a specific event or moment. Our attachment had built stealthily, quietly eroding my worries and objections until I found myself hungering for the next time I would see her.

How *had* I gotten here? And so quickly?

"I'll tell you when I knew," Miles said, sounding entirely too pleased with himself. "When you two were hugged up on the couch together, all twisted up together like a pretzel, watching some stupid reality show."

I laughed. "*The Real Housewives of New Jersey*."

He aimed a comical squint at me. "Since when do you watch that?"

"I'm usually reading *Forbes* or *Sky & Telescope*, but it's actually pretty entertaining. I prefer the one set in Atlanta, but New Jersey will do in a pinch." I laughed. "She watches Adam Sandler with me, and she's agreed to be fully indoctrinated into *Star Wars* next month. It's a fair trade."

"You made your mother's chicken and broccoli for her."

"Still mad I didn't save you any?"

"You picked her over the bank," he said, and I went still as I considered the significance of that.

Neither of us said anything for a while. I relished the quiet as I considered the magnitude of what my decision to join her for the christening meant. I'd known, when I heard the distress in her voice, that I couldn't leave her to go alone.

But more than wanting to protect her, I genuinely liked her. I admired her internal strength and her commitment to all the people she held dear. And I loved the way we were together. All my thoughts went mercifully quiet when she was in my arms and we were watching some inane bit of television or listening to the radio. She was my peace, all while pushing and harassing me to reconsider life in a way I never had before.

I'd never be able to get enough of her.

This wasn't temporary.

"You know her people? This isn't a *Guess Who's Coming to Dinner*? situation, right? You call if you need me. 'Cause you know I'll be on standby." Miles's gaze cut from the road to meet mine. "Be careful while you're up there."

"I will. I know some of them, her sister's family and her mom."

"Just call if you need me," Miles repeated.

"I will."

"We'll have the pipes fixed in the next week or so," Miles said, and I didn't have to look to know his expression would be mocking. "Think you'll be relieved to get back over to Zora's side so you can have some privacy?"

"Enough," I said, only mildly alarmed by the prick of unease I felt at the idea of sleeping without Leigh. "I know it's serious."

"I'd say it's a little more than that." Miles lifted his coffee cup and took a long draw. "You want me to take you by the jewelers before you get on the plane? Make it official?"

"I want you to stop flapping your gums and leave me in peace," I said.

"You're not even scared," Miles laughed. "I mention the jeweler and you sit there cool as a cucumber. I'm happy for you, Walker. Really."

He jawed on for the rest of the ride, something about the duplex's roof needing work. I didn't even hear him, not as I sat with the dawning realization.

When the hell had I fallen in love with her?

CHAPTER SEVENTEEN

Leigh

"Jesus, there's shit all over the baptism thingy." Paul held my niece aloft to show us the viscous smear of dark poop staining the delicate lace trim of the baptismal gown.

Behind him, a stout woman with faintly orange hair stood and smacked him on the back of his head with a program booklet. "Your *mouth*. We're in a church."

"What did I say?" he asked, looking genuinely bewildered as he handed my niece off to a harried Lucia.

"'Shit,'" my nephew supplied gleefully at top volume, and the heads of other early arriving parishioners all over the church turned in our direction as Lucia glared at Paul.

I closed my eyes, torn between exhaustion and amusement. Today was shaping up to be the circus all our family events were. My nieces and nephew had kept me up all night, unable to contain their excitement about the party their parents were hosting after the baptism.

"Come with me, young man." Paul's mother grabbed my nephew's hand and whipcracked him over to her. "We're going to take a walk and have a talk about your language."

I bit my lip, torn between rescuing him and risking a beating of my own from Paul's mother. She taught third grade English at the nearby

Catholic school, still wielded a disciplinary ruler at misbehaving students, and was, in general, no joke. Besides, there was still a horde of remaining children to be wrangled. I had no idea how any sane adult expected all those restless, wriggling bodies to somehow sit still for an hour.

"Makes you want to have a few of your own, doesn't it?"

And then there were the asshole adults.

I pasted on a plasticine smile for my annoying, pushy shrew of an aunt and moved aside to let her into the pew where I stood.

"Not particularly, Aunt Marie. I'm pretty happy with what I've got."

She raised one of the poorly drawn-on eyebrows that resembled umbrellas shading her eyes from inclement weather. "And what exactly do you 'got?'"

Whatever happened to "hello?"

"The joy of the Lord in my heart," I said, inclining my head to remind her of our setting and hopefully delay the typical flood of harassment. "Isn't it a beautiful Sunday morning?"

She harrumphed, taking her time easing down on the pew. "Last I heard, what you've 'got' consists of a silly job playing with children in a backwards town that doesn't even have a Target. You don't think it's time to stop hiding under a rock, get married again, and settle down, old as you are? Or have you not had any decent offers?"

I was saved from having to answer when a cheer went up at a new arrival.

Gio, followed by his mother in a sharp designer suit. She spared me the barest wave, not even attempting to make eye contact, before she greeted our collective family in the pews ahead of us.

Matteo tugged free of his father's hand and ran to join the other children.

I looked away and found Aunt Marie watching me. "Heard you finally met the kid."

I didn't attempt a response.

"Nowadays nobody takes marriage seriously anymore," she opined. We both watched as Gio made the rounds, weaving through people and pews, hugging everyone, joking, making merry.

That motherfucker had successfully co-opted my entire family.

"It's true, he shouldn't have brought trouble home," she continued, and I just barely managed not to scream at her oversimplification of Matteo's conception and birth as mere "trouble" in my marriage. "But grace, mercy, and forgiveness have their place, do they not?"

"Leigh. You're here."

I turned to find my mother next to me, flanked by my father. She was beautifully turned out in a sky-blue suit, her hair pinned into an elaborate updo. Beside her, my father was already pulling at the collar of his button-down shirt, looking pained. Even after all these years, he'd retained the rocker-chic thinness that made him impervious to middle age bloat and rendered the blades of his cheekbones *objets d'art*. I knew he'd remove the tie as soon as they found a seat.

"Hey," he grunted, nodding at me.

"Hey, Dad," I said, and he gave another nod as he ambled up the aisle, already sliding off his sports jacket as he waved away the loud greetings from my family members.

"Your father's in fine form, as usual," my mother said. She watched me closely, worrying the small gold crucifix at her neck. "He asked how many children your sister had to have before we could stop going to all their events." Her weak attempt at a smile was strained.

I swallowed a sigh, knowing I'd have to give her the response she wanted. It was the easiest thing to do, and probably the best course of action in our present setting. I could accept this moment as a bridge, knowing we'd never openly acknowledge or resolve the conflict, as usual. As much as my mother frustrated me, she wasn't changing anytime soon.

"Sounds like Dad," I said, giving her a half-hearted smile.

"I'm glad you came, Leigh." She reached out and grasped my arm. "I—I didn't —"

"Okay, Ma," I said nodding, and her face cleared in relief.

"Momo!" A child cried. A few pews ahead of us, Matteo had sighted my mother and came running toward us. She scooped him up, laughing as he planted kisses on her cheeks. Acid seared my chest as the two of them did a little dance in the aisle. My mother shot me a brief look, winced, and continued up the aisle, bouncing Matteo on her hip.

"You're getting too big for me to pick you up," she told him in an artificially bright voice as they joined Gio's mother, and Matteo's disbelieving chortle carried back to me.

I lowered myself onto the pew, gripping it for dear life in both fists.

Beside me, Aunt Marie made a clucking noise. "Might as well get it over it, girl. Family's family in the end."

Ain't that the fucking truth, I thought, swallowing against the heat of rising bile.

I don't belong here. Maybe I never did. I need to go back home.

I opened my mouth to say exactly that, gathering my belongs, just as a familiar deep voice rumbled to my left.

"Is this seat taken?"

I looked up. My mouth fell open at the sight of a beautifully suited Walker Leffersbee smiling down at me.

Time stood still as my mind struggled to acclimate to the reality that Walker, *my* Walker, was somehow standing next to me in Fairlane, New Jersey.

One of his big hands descended to settle on my shoulder. "Would it be alright if I sat here?" he asked very quietly, and I was mortified to find my vision suddenly distorted with tears. I only nodded, surreptitiously swiping at my eyes. Walker squeezed my shoulder in response.

"Aunt Marie," I managed to say. I dared not risk a glance at her for fear she would sense my moment of weakness and devour me whole. "Could you please move down?"

"Who is *this?*" Her voice was razor sharp and loud enough to radiate several feet around us. All other movement ceased as dozens of eyes landed on us.

"I'm Walker Leffersbee, ma'am. I'm a friend of Leigh's. It's very nice to meet you." Walker gave her a congenial smile, extending his hand.

She stared at it for several long moments before limply gripping the very tips of his fingers. "I'm her aunt," she said, without any warmth. Then she sat back and folded her thin arms in defiant silence.

"Aunt Marie." I turned to look at her full on. "If you don't move your ass down this pew, I swear to God I'll move it for you."

Her eyes bugged under her umbrella brows. I stared back, prepared to polish the pew with her old, mean ass if it came down to it.

She finally ended the standoff and moved down the pew in short, stiff jerks as I followed behind her.

Walker settled next to me, an immense, calm presence smelling of clean skin and home. His forever-long leg adhered to mine, his knee trapped by the pew in front of us. Blindly, I reached for the long-fingered hand he'd rested on his thigh, interlocking his fingers with mine. He squeezed back.

"Everyone's staring at us," he said out of the side of his mouth, chuckling.

"Yes. It's what they do. We're a rude lot."

"I don't know about all that," Walker said, and I turned to see him smiling at me. "But if that's true, it's charming on you."

"Why aren't you in Florida?" I asked, still gripping his hand like a lifeline and not caring Aunt Marie was watching and listening with avid interest.

"I'm exactly where I need to be today," he said, "and I'm not going anywhere until we fly home together tomorrow."

"Really?"

"Really," he said, turning our interlaced fingers so his thumb swept across the back of my hand in comforting strokes.

"Thank you, Walker."

"Don't thank me. Although, your family might start getting ideas, seeing you holding my hand," he warned. One side of his mouth curled up in a teasing smile, and I barely suppressed the urge to kiss him, this beautiful, kind man who'd gone out of his way to rescue me.

"I don't care what they think," I said, and Walker's brows lifted.

"Alright," he said, lifting our joined hands to press a kiss against my fingers. "We'll face whatever comes, together."

THE RECEPTION at Lucia and Paul's house was an ambitious effort, given the exhausted state of the proud parents and the overwhelming volume of people packed into every nook and cranny of their two-story home. Luckily, one of my aunts volunteered to watch all the small children at her house nearby, and that helped keep the noise and general chaos under slightly better control.

Slightly.

I divided my time between helping Lucia replenish platters of catered food and keeping a wary eye on Walker as he sat with Paul's brothers and talked sports.

Paul and his brothers, I didn't have to worry about. My family, on the other hand, was always the wild card. And there was the looming issue of Gio, who kept shooting glares in Walker's direction from the adjacent den where he pretended to play cards with his asshole friends.

"Stop babysitting him," my sister hissed at me as we worked side by side at the center island to refill a platter of cold cuts. Supplies were running low and someone would need to make a run to the store soon.

"I'm not," I said, elbowing her.

"You are. Walker's a grown ass man. A real one. Nothing will happen today that he can't handle. So, relax. That was the point of his coming in the first place."

"I can't believe you knew he was coming and didn't tell me."

"He knew you'd try to be brave and stop him. He made the right call. Hey," she called to Paul as he passed by, "I'm about to head out. We're out of a few things."

"I'll go," Paul and I said at the same time.

Lucia glared at us both. "Neither of you are going. *I'm* getting the hell out of here."

Paul looked as if he wanted to cry. "I need a break from your wild ass family, Cia," he said under his breath.

"And I need a break from your overbearing Doberman of a mother," she whispered back.

"Sounds like everybody needs a break," a new voice said, and the three of us jumped. Walker stood on the other side of the island. Judging from his wry smile, he'd obviously heard our whispered conversation.

"I don't know about everyone," Lucia told him, "but I'm getting one. And since I'm the one still healing from the fourth degree tear I got giving birth to the guest of honor, no one gets to ask me when I'm coming back."

Walker nodded, grimacing. "Understood."

"But I'll be back before you leave," she told Walker. "Because I love you, and I want to see you off."

"Understood," Walker said again, trying to hide his smile.

"Keep the baby alive while I'm gone." Lucia grabbed her purse and keys from the counter before she disappeared out the back door without a backwards glance.

Walker's eyes settled on mine, and I smiled, suddenly feeling shy. It was disorienting seeing him there, so solid and dependable, in my sister's kitchen.

"Oh, you two have got it bad," Paul said, looking between the two of us with a sly grin. "I'm really glad to see it."

I rolled my eyes. "Walker, do you want me to take you around, introduce you—"

"Don't you dare," Paul interjected. "I like Walker. I want him as a brother-in-law, and the chances of that happening will decline precipitously once you clue him in to just how wild this family is."

Suddenly, from the unseen family room, a shout: "For the love of God, somebody shut that baby up! We can't hear the game!"

Paul looked at Walker. "See?"

Seconds later, one of my cousins scurried over with my screaming, hiccupping niece in tow. Paul's efforts to calm her were unsuccessful as he walked the kitchen floor. His aggravation grew as several people shouted unsolicited suggestions into the kitchen.

"How many kids did you say you wanted?" Walker asked me, his eyes on Paul and my niece as they made another loud circuit around the kitchen.

As we watched, my niece gurgled pale vomit down Paul's back.

"Ask me some other time."

"Can one of you take her while I get cleaned up?" Paul asked.

To my surprise, Walker took her, settling my niece on the broad expanse of his crisp white shirt under his neck.

"You've had a hard day, haven't you," Walker crooned to her in that deep voice, and the engines to my nether regions roared to life.

He'd be a great dad. Way more patient than me. Calmer.

Girl. What are you *thinking*?

"All this excitement, all these people in your house. You haven't even had a nap. Poor

thing." Walker's huge hand easily dwarfed the baby's back as he patted it.

Paul and I watched in astonishment as my niece's crying gradually subsided. She gave a few drowsy blinks, residual tears clinging to her long lashes.

"Well, isn't this a cozy picture." Turning, I found Gio standing in the archway to the kitchen. He was attempting to affect a casual pose, but I glimpsed the telltale signs that presaged some display of his temper: the clenched fists thrust deeply into his pockets, the tight clench of his jaw.

Paul's face twisted, likely with the same annoyance I felt. "Gio," he said, his tone one shade south of civil as he ripped a paper towel off the nearby roll and began swiping at the vomit down his neck.

I didn't bother to respond, just returned Gio's flat gaze.

Walker broke the tense silence.

"I'm Walker," he said, lazily ambling over to Gio and offering his hand. My niece, secure in the grip of Walker's other arm, gave a contented smack of her lips as she burrowed farther into Walker's neck.

Gio stared at Walker's proffered hand for several lagging moments before he finally pulled a hand from his pocket and shook it.

"Gio, Leigh's husband. I'm sure she's told you about me."

The statement was loaded with enough arrogance and presumption that both Paul and I bristled, but Walker sounded amused when he responded.

"Ah. Her *ex*-husband. That's right."

It was jarring seeing them together in the same space, my former and current lovers. Taking in Walker's tall, commanding presence, the ease with which he comforted a sleeping baby while staring down my fungus of an ex-husband, I could only shake my head at myself.

God, I'd been stupid. What the hell had I ever seen in Gio?

"So, you two are ..." Gio waved his hand in the air, looking between Walker and me.

"Walker came with Leigh," Paul said, with a distinct edge to his voice. "Was there something you needed from back here, Gio? Drink? Something to eat?"

"I came to talk to Leigh," Gio said, his temple working as his gaze settled on me. "Last time we saw each other, it wasn't on the best of terms."

"Those terms will be different today?" Walker sounded pleasant. Curious.

Gio looked past Walker and turned an appealing gaze on me. "Leigh, your mother's been upset. I was hoping we could clear the air between us, try to make things right for everyone."

Walker looked back at me, one brow raised as he waited for my response.

Paul caught my eye, shook his head.

"Fine," I said. I wasn't coming back to Fairlane for the foreseeable future if I could help it. This was potentially a watershed moment, the perfect opportunity to finally stop reacting to Gio's behavior, to stop running. I could stand in my truth, stand up for myself, and reclaim the pieces of myself that I'd left here almost six years ago.

I wanted *me* back.

Walker watched my face for a long moment before he spoke. "Alright. I'll be right here if you need anything, sugar."

Gio's shoulders drew up and stiffened at that.

"Outside." I inclined my head to the kitchen's back door. Gio's mouth tightened at the directive but he followed me, past Paul and Walker's glowers, to the manicured courtyard outside.

"Thanks for agreeing to talk with me," Gio said, pulling the door closed behind us. He gestured to the patio seating nearby. "You wanna sit?"

"No." I shook my head, not moving from my spot near the back wall of the house. "I'm fine standing."

Gio opened his mouth, closed it. Tried again. "I'd hoped we could have a civil conversation, as friends, after all these years."

"We didn't end on friendly terms."

He shoved a hand through the salt and pepper wave of his hair in a gesture I remembered all too well. "Well, whose fault was that?"

"Look in the mirror."

"You're the one who went haring off, running to some hick town. I was your *husband*, Goddamnit, and we never got a chance—"

"In name only. You never took our vows seriously. You were never faithful to me, were you?"

"You needed to grow up and realize you weren't some precious little Disney princess. Life *happens*."

"You're right, I'm not. Villains have more fun, anyway. And you sure as hell weren't a prince."

"I was young, *we* were young. I made a mistake, and instead of you standing by me you ran."

"It wasn't just one mistake, Gio! I stood by you the first time it happened, like a dumbass. You have no idea what that cost me. The humiliation, the insecurity, even though I knew better. And then you did it yet again, all while blaming me. And you're still doing it now."

"I made a mistake," he repeated stubbornly, and I shook my head at us both.

"I know. It's never your fault."

"You're unforgiving," he spat. "Some things have been going on between men and women, husbands and wives, since the beginning of time."

I shook my head, crossing my arms. "Not for me. Not my husband. Unacceptable."

"So self-righteous," he sneered. "And yet you're mad your family picked me after you made them choose."

"It should never have been a choice," I said. My heart hammered in my ears, and I realized my hands were shaking. I was unraveling. But I couldn't stop myself. "Me finally standing up for myself and leaving you and your bullshit should never have made my family feel as if they had to choose between us."

"Did you think they wouldn't choose me?" Gio's voice was fat with satisfaction. "My mother's been your mother's best friend since they were in elementary school. My mother is your sister's godmother. My mother spent many a day and night during our childhood listening to your mother complain about your father. If anyone could understand what we were going through, it would be your mother," he said, and I had to hold myself still.

I'm going to kill this fucker.

"Your mother and my mother have been inseparable since grade school. They wouldn't know what to do without each other. There's shared history there, roots, that nobody's about to just snatch up because you had a temper tantrum."

And there it was. He'd so neatly laid out the reasons why it had taken me too long to leave him. Because I had known deep down that leaving him also meant leaving my family.

"You're right, Gio. You won. You got everything and everyone. Happy?"

A dark expression briefly eclipsed his features.

Trying to talk to him was a mistake. I'd hoped we could forge some semblance of a reconciliation that would help me make peace with the past.

But he was still the same selfish asshole.

"Yeah, I am happy," he said, his voice low and scathing. "Though you're asking seven years too late. If you'd been a better wife and tried a little harder, you'd be Matteo's mother and home where you belong. But you've always been a lazy bitch, especially when it comes to pleasing your man."

That salvo hit its mark, even though objectively, I knew it had no basis. But that had always been Gio's talent, sniffing out old wounds and exploiting them. He of all people knew how earnestly I questioned what I should have done differently after he cheated the first time.

But I wasn't that woman anymore. Thank God.

"I please myself now, and I'm not young and dumb and flailing through the insecurities of my early twenties anymore. I was never responsible for your personal happiness. Wherever or into whoever you stuck that filthy dick of yours? That was on you."

He watched me closely, his temple working. Rethinking his approach, I knew.

"Look," he said, impersonating a false calm I didn't trust for one second. "This isn't helping anyone. I asked to talk with you because your mother was upset by your reaction when you saw Matteo. We need to fix this. It's not good for the family."

Good for the family, I thought bitterly. How many times had I heard that one?

He gave me an expectant look.

I said nothing.

"Your mother feels like she owes you something, that she shouldn't have helped with Matteo."

"My mother has my phone number. She knows how to use it."

"It could have been handled better, you not knowing. I admit that," he said with a self-deprecating shrug.

"No shit."

"It's in the past now, Leigh. I can't change it."

That was Gio for you. *I fucked you over, but it's in the past. You're the one who has to deal with it.*

"This is between my mother and me. The last thing this situation needs is you playing peacemaker when you're the root of all the dysfunction."

"It affects me, okay? Your mother being upset is something me and my mother have to hear about."

I laughed despite myself, and his expression grew dark. "Oh, I get it. My mother having feelings threatens your childcare options. God forbid you're inconvenienced."

"Those other women, all that was years ago. If you're not over it by now ..." He spread his arms, palms up as he aimed an infuriating smirk at me. "Sounds like it's more of your issue."

"Poor little man-boy Gio. For once, all the women in our family aren't jumping to do your bidding and reassure you of how precious you are."

His fists clenched. "Just tell your mother we've talked and you're fine. Matteo loves her, he depends on her. So do I. The least you could do is make things right before you leave. I have to live with the trouble you've stirred up after you go back to Mayberry."

"I'm not on your cleanup crew anymore. Bye, Gio," I said, moving to go past him.

He stepped into my path, blocking me.

"I'm not asking you for a lot."

"It's more than I'm willing to give. Move."

"Matteo's the innocent one, Leigh."

"He is, and he's beautiful. He seems like a great kid, and I wish him all the best. He'll need it, with you as his father." I sidestepped and attempted to move around him.

"Don't just walk away from me." His hand settled around my upper arm in an iron grip as he yanked me back in front of him.

"Gio, let me—"

"Get your hands off of her. Right now."

We both turned around to see Walker standing at the back door, his expression forbidding.

"I'm not asking again," Walker said as he made his way over to us, his gaze never leaving Gio's.

Gio's glare deepened, his nostrils flaring as he eyed Walker's approach.

"Now. Before I put hands on *you*." I was taken aback by the malevolence on Walker's face as he came to stand next to me.

Gio let go of my arm, giving me a little shove in the process that caused me to stumble. Walker righted my balance and gently steered me off to the side.

"Sugar," he said, not looking at me, "would you do me favor? You mind giving me and Gio a little privacy so we can talk? We need to get on the same page about a few things."

"No," I said from behind him, gripping the waistband of his dress pants in a futile bid to tug him back toward me. "Come inside with me. Don't waste your time on him. It's exactly what he wants. After you kick his ass, he'll just play the victim."

My words seemed to incense Gio. He drew himself up to his still shorter than Walker height, his chest puffing out ridiculously. "If anybody's ass is getting kicked, it's not gonna be mine. But listen to your mama."

I saw Walker's back stiffen. "He's small and pathetic," I said, gripping Walker's arm in a desperate attempt to pull him away from the fight Gio was spoiling for. "Let's just go. Please?"

I couldn't see Walker's expression from behind him, but he must have come to a decision, because I felt the gradual relaxation of the muscles in his back and arm. "If you ever touch her again, I promise you'll regret it," Walker said, his voice low and threatening. "You won't get another warning."

I managed to ease Walker back a foot and gave a sigh of relief. *Thank*

God. We needed to get out of this house, away from Gio and the potential for an ugly confrontation.

I barely registered what happened next. It all happened so *fast.*

"Fuck you and your warning," Gio roared, throwing a wild punch at Walker.

Walker feinted to one side, easily evading the blow. Gio went off-balance, stumbled, backed up, and came again. Walker shook his head even as Gio regrouped and launched another blow, Gio's forward movement working against him as Walker maneuvered, lowering his shoulder and gripping Gio's shirtfront as he sent Gio sailing into the pavement face-first with a sickening crunch.

I gawked at Gio. He didn't even attempt to gather himself up. Blood bloomed on the pavement with each of his exhalations.

Walker stood looking down at him, his gaze dispassionate.

"This day just got even better. That was epic," Paul crowed, coming from the kitchen doorway to join our study of Gio on the pavement. "I saw it all. Walker, what was that? Jiujitsu or something?"

Humor briefly lit Walker's features. He and Paul exchanged grins. "No, man. I just let his momentum work against him, just kept it going 'til he was where he so badly wanted to be. On the ground."

"Police," Gio ground out, gagging on blood and spittle.

My eyes met Paul's in a moment of shared horror. I couldn't help my loud groan of distress. *Why* hadn't I listened to Paul and stayed inside? If the police came, what were the chances we'd would have a moment to explain that Gio had initiated the fight? What if I'd allowed Gio's stupidity to cost Walker his freedom or his life?

Paul shook his head, holding up his palms to calm me.

"Gio," Paul said with studied nonchalance, lowering himself to his haunches besides Gio's prone body while ignoring the hand Gio held up for assistance. "Go ahead and call the police. I'm sure they'll want to hear from the attorney who witnessed the entire thing. I'd love to help them with the charges against you, Gio. You assaulted Walker. I saw it with my own eyes."

Gio ignored us all, blood dripping from his fingers as he went through the kitchen door and slammed it behind him.

"Welcome to the family," Paul said, still grinning broadly as he clapped Walker on the back. "I'm requiring Leigh to bring you to all the family events from now on. I've been needing a partner in crime."

I finally found my voice to speak. "Good luck with that, Paul. He's not coming back and neither am I. You'll have to make your way down to Green Valley. No one deserves this shit show."

"Nah, I think you both managed to vanquish evil on this trip. You gotta come back."

Walker offered Paul a quiet smile. "It's up to her, man." Then he turned to me. "Sugar," he said, his eyes softening as he looked me over, "let's get your stuff. We're staying in the city tonight."

CHAPTER EIGHTEEN

Leigh

"This is absolutely decadent." I slipped out of my heels at the door and my feet immediately sank into the dense white carpeting. "I still can't believe you got a suite at The Pierre."

Walker followed behind me, shrugging out of his suit coat. "I thought you might enjoy it."

I padded further into the suite, charmed by the elegantly appointed sitting room, the strategic pops of color against the stark white solemnity of the décor. Heavy textured curtains were pulled back to reveal a jaw-dropping view of the city. "It's like a fairy tale," I said. "You shouldn't have done this. It must cost a fortune."

The Victorian era mirror in the hallway leading to the bedroom reflected his easy shrug as he loosened his tie. "I can afford it. I like staying here when I come to the city. It's close to most things."

I rounded the corner and gave a contented sigh. "The bed," I marveled, taking in its mammoth size and the ornate curves of the upholstered headboard. I rushed forward and flung myself backwards across the bed, arms spread like a starfish, feeling like a small child again.

And then, as I studied the ceiling, I went silent remembering the scene we'd just left at my sister's house. Gio, the idiot, trailing blood across my sister's floors, Paul and his brothers congratulating Walker as we left. I even thought I glimpsed something like respect in several family members' eyes.

The weekend with my family had not followed its usual soul-crushing script, thanks to Walker.

So much had changed.

"You alright?" Walker stood in the doorway, shirt partly unbuttoned, tie in hand as he watched me with cautious eyes. Below us, traffic noises drifted up to the otherwise silent room.

I sat up and met his steady gaze. "I'm better than alright. Come here. Please."

He made his way over, eyes never leaving mine. I captured his hand and stared down at it, tracing a path along the wide span of his palm, the long reach of his fingers.

The callused surface of Walker's other hand slid along the side of my face, cupped the back of my neck, and slid into the thicket of my dense curls.

"You sure you're okay?" he asked, easing my head forward until his lips pressed a cool kiss against my forehead. "I'm not sorry for what happened. He's lucky I didn't do more, with the way he put his hands on you. But I'd never want you to feel embarrassed or frightened of me."

I shook my head immediately, struggling against the emotion clogging my throat. "I'm feeling a lot of things right now," I told him, "but none of it comes anywhere close to embarrassment. And I could never be afraid of you." I knew what I was feeling for him, and I knew there was no escaping it.

Please, God. Don't let it hurt so much this time.

Walker gently disentangled his hand from my grip, grabbed my hips and boosted me farther back on the bed until I was flat on my back again and facing the ornate chandelier above. He crawled on the bed, laying on his side next to me as he ran a possessive hand all along my chest, up between my breasts, down my belly and back again.

"Tell me," he said quietly. "Tell me about these feelings."

I closed my eyes, loving the warm weight of his hand against my heart, the comforting wall of his body against my side, the tenderness in his eyes that conveyed all he felt for me.

"I've never had anyone stand up for me like that before," I said, not daring to look at him, not when my heart was already overflowing with those three little words, when they wanted to escape from my mouth and fly to him. I closed my eyes, overwhelmed by all that I felt for him. "I've never felt so safe with anyone. I've never felt as much for anyone as I feel for you."

Walker hooked a finger under my chin and turned my head until I was facing him. "I know, baby. You're scared, aren't you?"

"Yeah," I said, and to my eternal horror, my eyes filled with tears.

"It's okay," he said, lowering his head to give me the gentlest of kisses all while my tears escaped and leaked trails down my face. "It is scary, I know. I was scared for a while too." He chased the tears away with the rough surface of his thumb, then outlined the shape of my lips.

The seal to the tomb of my heart cracked open. I hid my face behind my hands, mortified that he would see me this way. Defenseless, consumed with emotion, unable to summon enough strength to mount my usual facade.

"You don't have to hide from me," he said, his voice silk-soft in my ear. "You can trust me with the hard stuff, remember?"

I nodded from behind my hands.

"You want me to tell you what I'm feeling? So you don't feel like you're out on this ledge alone?"

I nodded and heard his dark chuckle. "You gotta look at me, sugar."

I moved my hands and faced him, well aware that I probably looked like a tear-stained mess.

"You should be looking at me when I tell you I love you," he said, and I lost my breath.

He moved from my lips to caress the curve of my jaw with the lightest touch, as if I were something precious. "I love you," he repeated, smiling down at me. "And I'll take apart anybody who even thinks of hurting you in any way. You know what else?"

"What?" I croaked.

"I know you love me too," he said, very quietly, with that same small smile. "But I don't expect you to say it just yet. I know you need a little more time to trust what all of this is between us, and to trust this new you that loves me."

I do love you. I ached to say it, but the last remaining vestiges of that old fear kept me mute.

"And that's okay," Walker said. "You take all the time you need. You lean on my faith in our love until you've got as much faith in it as I have. 'Cause I know what's going to happen."

I sniffled. "What? What's going to happen?"

"One day soon," he said, dropping a kiss on my forehead, "you're going to throw open the door to your heart and let out all the hurt and betrayal that's been keeping you company for so long." He delivered the gentlest of kisses to each of my closed eyelids, then the tip of my nose. "And then do you know what'll happen?"

"What," I asked, breathless as he stroked the bare skin of my thigh and began a tortuous, slow journey coaxing the hem of my dress upwards.

"You'll let in all the things I feel for you. You'll welcome my admiration and adoration and devotion. You'll let yourself sit with the knowledge that nobody will ever love you the way I love you, with the same absorption and intensity and surety. You'll just let me love you. And then one day you'll look around," he continued, tracing the whorl of my navel, "and realize there are no more shadows, no more ghosts from the past. Just you and me. And all the wonderful things in store for us in the future."

I pulled him down to kiss me, utterly wrecked by his words and the truth I saw in his eyes. He cupped my face, gentling my wild kisses, resisting my frantic efforts to urge him over and on top of me.

"Slow down," he breathed, laughing into our kiss. He returned to the slow exploration of my leg, awakening sensation all along the sensitive skin of my inner thigh.

"I don't want to go slow," I huffed, frustrated, held captive by the sly circling against the dampness of my underwear.

He laughed again as he pressed a whisker-roughened kiss against my neck and then moved gently to my mouth. I groaned, my hips lifting as the wicked play of his tongue against my tongue and the indolent swirl of his fingers against my clit wrung me tight.

"I want us to take our time. I want you to feel this. Feel everything I feel for you," he rasped, sitting up as his thumbs slid to my hipbones and hooked into my underwear. Slowly, slowly, he eased them down my legs and past my clenching toes. "We don't take our time nearly enough." His hands returned, warming the insides of my thighs with sure, soothing strokes until I was restless, nearly begging for his touch.

"You're cruel," I gasped, "to make me suffer like this."

"You think so?" He seemed to consider that as he finally went right where I wanted him. We both groaned as his clever fingers slid slickly through me as he alternated between working my clit and feeding me his long fingers.

"I want you," I said, my hips lifting and churning against the heel of his hand, my hands gripping his shirt in desperate handfuls.

"I want you too. I want all of you." His dark eyes were intent on mine as he used one hand to shuck my dress over my head and unhook and discard my bra. I shivered at the onslaught of fresh air.

"Cold?" Concern creased his brow.

"I'll survive," I said, sliding a hand down to where he still played my softness with devastating skill. "Your cock can keep me warm."

He gave a short, surprised laugh, then pulled his fingers from me. "Not yet, no skipping ahead."

"Walker," I protested, then gasped when he moved down my body, captured my hips with both hands and took a long, lewd lick down my center.

"Yeah. What were you saying?" he said, looking up with an impish smile, running his tongue along his upper lip as if savoring the taste of me. He pinched and flicked at my nipple.

"Nothing," I panted. "Don't let me stop you."

The sensual onslaught of his mouth against my melting wetness, my inner muscles squeezing against the width of those thick fingers, him pulling and tugging at my nipple, all of it fed the climbing heat in my veins. When I finally came, my screams echoing off the hollow walls, my blood evaporating into dense fog, Walker's eyes were on mine.

And I fell.

My want for him went beyond rational thought. My love for him was forever.

"No," I said, stilling his shaking hands as he fumbled for a condom in his wallet. "I just want it to be us. I know we're safe. Just you, only you."

His eyes widened, and he visibly swallowed. "Are you sure?"

I smiled, my fingers working at his remaining buttons before I pushed his dress shirt off his broad shoulders and bit the taut skin there. "I've never been surer of anything," I said, vaulting up further to run my tongue through the dip of his collarbones. I tasted the sweat of his neck, bit his ear, filled my lungs with the musk of him and clenched against the anticipation of having him inside me soon, skin on skin.

"Leigh," Walker ground out, his voice even more gravelly than usual.

"Yes?" I made quick work of unbuckling his belt and unzipping his pants until he sprang into my hands like a gift.

"I'm—" He shook his head as if to clear it.

"I know," I said. I guided him down over me, reached between our bodies to run the head of his cock against me in slow agonizing circles. "I feel it, too. It's a lot."

"It's always been you, you know," he said, framing my face. His hips moved, circling his cock more explicitly against me, teasing, kissing where I wanted him. I gripped his back and rubbed circles into his overheated, sweat-beaded skin, trying to coax him further against me, into me.

"Always you," he said again, and his eyelids fell as his cock tentatively breached me, retreated, and then, on a sharp intake of breath, he slid all the way home.

I gasped at the sheer magnitude of him filling every part of me.

"Fuck," he breathed on a fervent exhale, his entire body going stiff, the tendons in his neck straining.

"Just let go," I whispered, licking the shell of his ear as I rocked up into him. I couldn't stop the tight circling of my hips, not while I was so incredibly full of him. "Let go," I said, unable to stop my compulsive squeezing and gripping his thick cock.

"*Fuck*," he hissed, his head lowering to his chest, his arms shaking in the cage he'd made around me.

"It's everything. It's so, so much. It's too much. Let go," I whispered, scoring my fingernails along the roundness of his ass, and he finally lost it then, his hips jetting like quicksilver as he stoked the flames in me higher and higher until we both combusted and held on to each other for dear life as he came.

"I love you so much," he said weakly, his heavy body going slack over mine, and I clutched him, all of him, wanting to bind him to me for eternity.

CHAPTER NINETEEN

Walker

"Your brother-in-law proposed to me."

Leigh barked out a laugh, hunching over the cutting board in front of her. Cantaloupe rinds were scattered all over her kitchen counter.

"I heard. Cia said she helped him stage the picture. What was in the ring box?"

"Bacon." I retrieved my phone and navigated to Paul's text while stirring the pot of grits on the stove. Leigh drew closer to peer at the picture of Paul on bended knee. The jewelry box he extended toward the camera held a single piece of bacon standing upright. The index card in his other hand read, *Will you be my brother-in-law?*

"He's an idiot," Leigh said, but she was smiling.

"Well, he got my attention with the bacon." Leigh mock glared, planting a hand on her hip.

"I'm glad you all are taking it upon yourselves to make these decisions. You don't even need me, do you?"

I shrugged, covering the pot with its lid and turning the flame low. I knocked the rinds into the sink before I scooped her up and settled her on the counter next to me. "We're all just waiting for you to catch up, sugar."

"Who said I needed to catch up?" She pulled me between her legs, her grin sly as she slid her arms around my neck. "You're not going anywhere, not if I can help it."

"What, we're not undercover anymore?" I teased, loving the way her eyes darkened. "I don't know how I feel—"

She silenced me with a kiss, pulling me into her heat and vanilla-scented softness. I grasped the supple curves of her hips, lightheaded with the perfection of the moment. Stevie Wonder provided the accompaniment to our kisses, singing about "Rocket Love" as my heart turned over.

This. Her.

Forever didn't seem nearly as frightening anymore.

I was relaxed, loose-limbed, and happy. We'd both played hooky from work on Monday to recover and refuel after the high drama of our visit to New Jersey over the weekend. Today, and all the challenges that awaited us, would have to be faced. But in this moment, with her in my arms, I knew all would be well.

"You ready for today?" I pulled back to study her, tucking a curl behind her ear. "You ready to pull the trigger?"

"Doesn't matter if I'm ready, we have to ride into battle. Layla's bringing her wife, Carla, to lunch today. Carla used her reporter credentials to pull some strings with a major news affiliate. The story should run all over the state as part of an exposé."

"That's amazing. I'm so proud of you, sugar."

"Well, your mom helped a ton. She swayed all the wealthy ladies who lunch over to our side and mobilized some of the nonprofits in town. Plus, we're going to have a huge protest at the hospital after the story airs."

I squeezed her hand. "You did this. *You*."

"Well, we have to see if it works." She swallowed hard. "I hope I won't get Loretta fired for leaking the documents, and that no one else gets blamed—"

"Right now," I drew her close and pressed a gentle kiss against her head, "we celebrate all you and your friends accomplished. Whatever happens after this, we'll handle it together. Your strength, it's one of the things I love most about you. But you're not alone anymore. You don't have to be strong all by yourself. We'll keep building together no matter what happens. Alright?"

"Yes. Speaking of building." She inclined her head to indicate the other side of the duplex. "Miles says they're making progress and I need to start thinking about what I want, design-wise, for my side. Fixtures and flooring and layout ..."

I nodded. "He's right. Now's around the time we start ordering and pricing the materials."

She let out a long sigh. "I appreciate your sister doing all this, and paying for it, just so I have the house of my dreams. But I hate thinking about that stuff. I've never been the kind of woman who delighted in design or even thumbed through an issue of *Homes & Gardens.* I don't have a lot of strong opinions about how the place should look. It's not like I own it, anyway. I don't know how long I'll still be living here, especially if I get fired—"

"One step at a time."

"I knew you'd say that." She raised a brow. "We're sticking together, right? Even for the move next door, when they start renovating this side?"

I eyed her, wondering how to ease her into my thoughts of late. "Of course."

She visibly relaxed. "Alright."

"You and me, that's not a question. I know the renovation details may seem overwhelming with everything else you have on your plate. But I want you to try to come at it another way."

"Like cancelling it?"

"No. Like I always tell clients: a home should be a shelter, an oasis. A refuge from the harshness of the world. A space that reflects who you are." I bit back a smile at her growing scowl. "Close your eyes."

"Why?"

"Just do it."

"Fine." She huffed a little, closing her eyes, briefly cracking one open to peer at me in suspicion before closing it again.

"Keep them closed. All right. I want you to take a deep breath. Clear you mind. And imagine. Imagine what this place would look like if it was all up to you, if you could wave a wand and make it reflect everything you care about. Start with the kitchen."

"Bigger," she said immediately. Her eyes stayed closed this time.

"Bigger how?"

"Way bigger than what I've got. I'd want more space to move around, more cabinet and storage space. Maybe a center island, a big one. A casual seating area and a TV. And a really big table with room enough for everyone."

"That might require both sides of the duplex," I mused, mentally calculating the dimensions.

She shrugged. "You asked me to dream."

"What if ..." I hesitated, wondering if she'd bolt at the next line of questioning. "What if I asked you to dream about a different space altogether? Not here. Someplace we'd get for the both of us. Something with enough room for both sides of our families and even all the neighbors to gather for the holidays. Something big enough for us to ... grow into. What would you say?"

Her breath caught. Her arms lowered from around my neck and she grabbed my arms. "What, are you asking me if we should get our own place together somewhere else?"

"No, sugar. I play for keeps. This is me wanting to know what *our* house should look like. Where I'd carry you over the threshold, where our kids will crawl and fall and learn to walk. Where we'll grow old."

She wasn't breathing. She'd gone absolutely still, her nails digging into my arms.

I kept going. "I'm not too particular. The most important thing is having you in there with me. Although, I'm not opposed to a vaulted ceiling in the entryway. And we'd need a decent backyard with a deck. Room for me to grill, plenty of square footage room for a Soul Train Line—"

"A screened-in sunroom. A swing set and slide. An area for our kids to skate and write their names with sidewalk chalk."

"How many?" I grinned. "Kids?"

"No fewer than two and no more than four."

I considered that. "Four? You *were* at Lucia's house this weekend, right?"

She laughed.

"They'll have to be evenly spaced out, if we go that high," I said. "We'll need a few years of decent sleep in between."

"Agreed," she said promptly. Her eyes flew open. "Oh my God. Did we just—"

"Plan our family?" Delight was a pleasant ache in my chest. "Yes, we did. And you pulled off a little home design along the way."

Her gaze bore into mine. "I want it all, with you. But I'm worried it's too good to be true. What if I have to find another job? What if—"

"We've figured out the most important things. You and I can build our world anywhere."

"But I might have to move for another job, and you can't leave the bank."

"Well ..."

"What haven't you told me?"

I leaned to the side to give the grits one last stir before I extinguished the flame. "Tavia said something Saturday, and I've been thinking about it ever since."

"What?" Her voice went stiff.

"She raised the point that the bank was always considered mine, that it was a foregone conclusion that I would run it. She never had a chance at it."

"So that makes up for her lying to you all this time?"

"No, but maybe it explains why she went about it the way she did. It was deceitful, but maybe she thought the back door was the only way to get in."

"Walker." She shook her head. "Your sister is not the victim here. She could have talked to you—"

I held up both hands in an attempt to quell the rising tide of her temper. "I know, sugar. You're right on all counts."

"The bank is not safe with her," Leigh pronounced, echoing my own internal struggle.

"No, I don't think it is either. But I'm also starting to question if I'm what's best for it."

She went silent, her gaze steady on mine as she chewed her lower lip.

"What?"

"Your turn," she said, sliding from the counter and capturing my hand. She pulled a chair from the kitchen table and turned it. "Would you have a seat, please?"

"Only because you asked so nicely." I sat and was immediately rewarded when she lowered herself onto my lap, facing me.

"I'm loving this so far." I traced the round protrusions of her knees, coasted down the lean lines of her legs to other delicious places.

"Be serious," she said, covering my eyes with her hands. "It's your turn to dream."

"That's easy. You're already in my arms."

"Alright, sweet-talker. Keep your eyes closed," she said, as the weight of her hands left my face. "I want you to imagine yourself in a world free of obligations and duty. A world where no one expects you to do any particular thing just because you should or because your last name is Leffersbee. If you were free to walk away from whatever or whoever you wanted—"

That didn't sit right with me. "Leigh, I can't —"

"Walker. I'm asking you to imagine what it would look like if you could cut loose from the bullshit that's been holding you back. What would you do? Where would you go? Who would you be?"

From behind the darkness of my lids, I considered her questions. Some answers came with immediate, startling clarity.

Others were surprising.

"You don't have to tell me now," she said. I opened my eyes find her studying me with surprising solemnity. "Just be honest with yourself. Whatever it is, I promise I'll walk through it with you until we get it done. No matter what."

I pulled back to look at her, sighing in contentment. Who'd have ever guessed that we'd end up this way, and that it'd feel so good? "How did I get so lucky," I said, brushing a wild, errant curl back from her bun.

She grinned. "I don't know, but I would not be opposed to you showing me your appreciation. In this chair to start, then in the shower."

~

LEIGH LEFT in considerably improved spirits after we took a long, highly collaborative shower together. I watched her climb into her newly rehabbed Honda and said a prayer that all would go well when she met her friends for lunch. Then I changed into my running gear, intent on finally getting back to the gym now that I felt human again for the first time in weeks.

But first, I needed to check in on Miles.

"'Sup, chief!"

Miles grinned when I walked in. Zora's side of the house was a beehive of activity. The kitchen and living room floors had been taken up, and all the counters and fixtures were removed. Loud voices echoed from the basement stairs. I recognized the plumber's rumbling bass as he lectured his apprentice downstairs.

Things were progressing, and right on schedule. They'd be done in a few more weeks, and Leigh and I would move in while they renovated her side.

It was heaven, pure heaven to be standing here. I didn't get this same raw satisfaction from my work at the bank. Never had. It was time to face that fact.

"What are you doing over here?" Miles took off his hard hat and met me in the kitchen doorway. "Don't come too much further with those athletic shoes on. Still got some nails in the floor here."

"I can't check on my partner? Thanks for bringing Leigh's car home while we were gone, by the way."

He smirked. "Finally tore yourself away from your woman's side, I see." He hesitated, brows bouncing as he waited for my response. "She *is* your woman now, isn't she?"

"That sounds so proprietary—"

"Oh, get the hell out of here." He laughed, and looked back at the plumber who was now headed toward the back door. "Mack. What did we say when we saw him out in the driveway a few minutes ago telling Leigh goodbye?"

Mack gave a short laugh. "That he was officially gone. She's got your nose wide open, Walker." Then he smiled. "Happy to see it. You both look good on each other."

I watched Mack leave while Miles gave a self-satisfied chortle. "It's alright, you don't have to acknowledge I was right. When y'all have your first kid, I'll tell you about the gymnastics I had to go through to keep her car at the Winston's garage all this time. I think I had them fix just about every possible thing they could find." He laughed. "You'll probably get her another car soon, but I'm here to tell you, that one should run 'til the end of time."

I shook my head. "You did that? That level of interference—"

"Is what kept you both together until you realized you needed to stay together," he said. "Good Lord, you were skittish. I paid for it all, so you should have no complaints. And it's my business 'cause you're my brother, always have been."

I let out an exasperated breath and gave him a companionable punch in the arm. "Thank you."

"You're welcome."

"New pipes'll be in by the end of the week, but I don't expect you're worried about moving back in," he said, a knowing grin playing around his lips. "Not alone at least."

I shook my head. "No, not alone."

"Ready for us to find your forever home? Know how many kids you want?" Miles teased, and I let out a rueful laugh.

"Yes, as a matter of fact. I came over here to tell you we need to start looking. Far as the kids go, we're thinking no fewer than two and no more than four at the moment. But—" I paused, wincing as I remembered Paul's infant daughter vomiting down his back. "We'll probably need to do a reassessment after the first two."

Miles gaped at me. "You're serious."

"Yep. I got some loose threads I gotta tie up in the meantime, though." I laid out my dilemma, getting him up to speed with all that had happened with Consolidated, my new reservations about my future with the bank, and Leigh's efforts to overthrow the hospital's new administration.

Miles listened to it all, his expression growing increasingly tense. "I can't lie, Walk," he said finally. "I'd love to see what you come up with if you do end up stepping away. We could make some serious moves if you weren't distracted with the bank, you know? But the thought of your sister behind the wheel, aided and abetted by Consolidated ... Whoo.

Makes me queasy, for me and everyone who counts on the bank in this community."

"Me too," I admitted. "But maybe it's time for a little risk and ambitious growth down there. I haven't done that. I've just been keeping watch. I haven't planted any new flags."

"So what are you thinking?"

"I don't know," I admitted. "Figured I'd go to the gym, run a few miles. That always helps me think."

"You sure you're up to all that?" he asked, watching me closely.

"Yeah. Why?"

"No reason," he said quickly, shrugging. "You'd been looking tired before you left, that's all. Do me a favor and take it slow. Tell your woman I'm in for whatever she needs help with when it comes to the hospital. Marching, protesting, renovating your new five-bedroom Tudor, you name it."

"Love you, man."

"Love you too," Miles said, returning my one-armed hug with his trademark smile.

I drove to the gym, marveling at my sudden and dramatic reordering of priorities. Leigh was now the most important thing. But something had to be done about the bank, and quickly. I owed it to my family to make a decision sooner rather than later.

But what, exactly, did I want? And what was the best way to put it all in motion in the midst of all that was going on?

I considered and discarded various solutions during my warm-up and workout with free weights. By the time I stepped on the treadmill, I'd made some headway.

The answers, murky as they were, had just emerged, half-formed, as I transitioned into the most taxing stretch of my run. But my breathing stalled as my heartrate accelerated, my heart slamming against my chest as a strange opacity chewed at the edges of my vision. I slapped at the emergency stop button, feeling as if I was moving underwater as all light and sound receded.

Then everything went black.

CHAPTER TWENTY

Leigh

"So, it's decided." Carla gave the file in her hand a decisive thump, briefly upsetting a soufflé cup of sweet and sour sauce. "The news report is going to air statewide in a little over a week. The protest will take place the following day. We're all systems go."

"Yay," I said, feeling my forehead break out into a sweat.

"Let's pray," Layla said, and we all joined hands at the table in the private dining room of the Chinese restaurant. Aaron, Ebony, Layla, Carla, and I asked for guidance, courage and conviction, peace.

And less sweating.

"Alright," I said, feeling somewhat calmer as I sat back in my chair. "I think we're ready."

Aaron, who'd been staring at the display of his phone and frowning, wordlessly passed it to Layla for her review.

"Everything alright?" Carla looked between the two of them.

"Yes," Layla said slowly, her eyes going to Aaron's and holding for several beats. "But still, we really should get back to the hospital."

"It's only been twenty minutes. Our food hasn't even come yet," Carla said, gesturing to the remaining eggroll carcasses from our shared appetizer.

"How about if I go," Layla said, once again speaking at half-speed as she watched Aaron, who nodded in slow motion. Staring at them, I couldn't help but wonder at the secret subtext I was clearly missing.

Aaron nodded. "That sounds great. Carla and I will finish up here, and I'll bring your food back to the hospital with me."

"Perfect." Layla rose and shrugged on her thin windbreaker. "Leigh, I might be able to use you on this one. You mind coming?"

I frowned at her strained attempt to affect an offhand tone. "It's serious, isn't it? There's an accident with kids involved?"

"Tell you when we get there." She pushed her chair in as she nodded at me to get up. "But we'd better get a move on."

Layla said very little as we drove. I left her to the tense silence, trying not to dwell on her white-knuckled grip on the steering wheel or the fact that she'd sped through three yellow lights.

After we parked in one of the designated chaplain parking spots outside the ER, she seemed to slow and collect herself as we headed toward the emergency entrance.

I glanced at the empty ambulance bay. "Well, I guess they got everyone in."

"Leigh."

"Yeah?"

"Listen to me." Layla grabbed my arm after we both flashed our employee badges and bypassed the metal detector. She steered me opposite the direction I'd expected, toward a suite of private waiting rooms.

"You're scaring me."

"I'm not trying to," she said, pulling me into a family consultation room and closing the door. "But we need to talk."

"Now I'm officially freaking out. What's happened?" My mind immediately filled with all the possible scenarios that might have landed us in this tiny, windowless room with her staring at me with a pale, pinched expression.

She nodded at the chair behind me. I lowered myself into a nearby chair. She retained her grasp on my arm. "Ruth sent me a text." Her eyes were steady on mine, her grip unyielding. "Walker was exercising this afternoon, and he had some kind of medical emergency. He's here in the ER."

The memory of Walker suddenly unstable on his feet and nearly falling at Zora's wedding slammed into me. Panic unfurled in my chest as I pushed to my feet. "Where is he?"

She urged me back down into the chair.

"Last update I got said he's stable now and they're running tests. But apparently he lost consciousness for a bit at the gym before he woke up in the ambulance."

"I have to see him." My lungs had lost all elasticity. I couldn't force air through the petrified stone of my chest.

"Breathe, Leigh. I'm going back to see where they are with testing and if you can see him. You should call his parents, make sure they know and they're coming."

The door flew open and Ellie, accompanied by a nurse I didn't know, stumbled into the room.

"Leigh!" Ellie cried, and I jumped up to meet her open embrace.

"I'm so glad you're here," I said, finally unthawing from my shock.

"I'm glad you're here too," she said. Her voice was unsteady as she ran a wild hand through her hair.

"Is Mr. Leffersbee coming?" I offered her the seat I'd abandoned, and she sat, nervously tracing the stitching of her purse.

"Ezra's out of town, but flying back as soon as he can. Nick and Zora are here, though. They flew in earlier today and drove me here as soon as we heard. They're just looking for a parking spot."

"Good. I'm glad," I said.

Then suddenly Nick and Zora were there, filling the tiny room and asking rapid-fire questions of Layla and the nurse.

"I know it's hard not knowing more right now," Layla said, and we all quieted to hear her. "But I promise, we will do our best to get you some information as soon as we can. Let's all have a seat and try to take a deep breath."

She and the nurse left as Zora sat across from Ellie and me, all of us asking questions of each other in a desperate bid to piece together what might have happened. Nick paced, his color high.

"This is my fault," I said finally, and they all zeroed in on me.

"Don't be ridiculous, baby." Ellie shook her head emphatically. "There's no way—"

"It is. Walker got lightheaded and kind of passed out at Zora's wedding reception. But when I checked on him—"

"So that's what happened in the storeroom," Zora breathed, closing her eyes as she put it together. "I thought you two were making out."

Secrets, I thought. They never ended well.

"We didn't want to ruin the honeymoon and Walker didn't think it was serious, so we decided to let you think that," I said. "And he did get checked out. They told him it was nothing, probably stress, and that honestly fit. I should have done more, I should have made him get that second opinion, I should have told you all—"

"Not your fault," Nick said firmly, pausing in his pacing to look at me. "And Walker wouldn't want you thinking that way. He'd hate it if he knew you were in here blaming yourself."

Zora got up, sat next to me, and held my hand. "We're family, Leigh. I know you did what you thought was right. No one's blaming you for anything. You hear me?"

"Yeah," I managed, squeezing her hand back. Rising terror made it difficult to say any more.

"Tavia's on her way," Nick said, resuming his pacing. "My partner Eddie's picking her up. I'm going to go see if I can get us an update a little faster." He left abruptly.

Ellie gave a rueful huff at Nick's departure. "What, does he think he's going to go intimidate the doctors?"

"He's going to throw his weight around," Zora said. "And for once, I'm not even going to complain about it. I'm grateful for whatever results he can get."

The door opened again, and we all jerked upright, hopeful that it was a health care professional with some clue as to what was going on.

But it was just Tavia and Eddie.

"What happened?" Tavia's eyes were wide as she scurried in. "Eddie wouldn't tell me anything, only that we had to get to the hospital."

"Hey, Eddie," I said weakly. It felt like an entire lifetime had passed since I'd harmlessly flirted with him at Zora's wedding. He looked as relaxed as I'd ever seen him in a T-shirt and jeans. He'd grown his hair out into a perfectly edged nimbus of kinky curls, with a full dark beard now complementing his deep brown complexion.

"Hey, Leigh," Eddie said, folding his height to crouch in front of Ellie and me. "Good to see you again, though I wish it were under better circumstances."

Even in the midst of turmoil, Eddie was still even-tempered and calm. I took a deep breath, drawing comfort from those affable brown eyes and his soothing voice. He took my hand in his own huge hands, giving it a brief squeeze.

"Same," I said, just as the door opened again. I nearly wilted with relief when a tall, scrub-clad man came into the room, closely followed by Nick. He was one of my favorite ER docs, very patient and thorough.

"Leffersbee family?" he asked, and we yelled in the affirmative, jumping up and crowding closer to him.

"I'm his mother," Ellie said. She hooked her arm into mine and pushed me forward. "And this is his girlfriend. What can you tell us?"

"Hello. I'm Dr. Lyons." He took a moment to nod at each of us. "Hi, Leigh. Walker came in today after a syncope episode during exercise. He regained consciousness while en route here. We've run a number of tests since his arrival, and he'll need more for an official diagnosis, but we believe we have an idea of what caused this."

"What is it?" Ellie asked, her hand squeezing the life out of mine. It was the first time I'd ever seen her looking close to her age.

"We think it's a heart condition called hypertrophic cardiomyopathy. It's a congenital condition where the heart muscle is abnormally thick. It fits the symptoms he's described to us, especially the fatigue. He mentioned he was diagnosed with exercise-induced asthma in his youth, which also fits the pattern."

"You mean he's had a heart condition since he was a child? Why didn't anybody ever tell us?" Ellie asked, wrapping her arms around herself. I pulled her into my side and she relaxed against me with a long exhalation.

"This condition can take decades to show consistent symptoms. I'm not surprised no one ever thought to look for it if there's no known family history."

"But he had an episode recently, and lots of tests," I said. "I know he did."

Dr. Lyons nodded. "Luckily, we have a new cardiology fellow here from the Mayo Clinic who specializes in these kinds of congenital heart conditions. We're giving our fellow a lot of credit for correctly following a hunch, and it also helped that Walker had an episode during exercise. That gave us one more piece to the diagnostic puzzle. We were also able to pick up abnormal activity in his heart rhythm since we got him in here so quickly after the incident."

"He thought it was stress," I said, running a restless hand through my hair.

"Yeah," Dr. Lyons said, wincing slightly. "It's often misdiagnosed as that, or anxiety, or a number of different things. We're fortunate we caught it this time."

"And I was trying to think of ways to help him relax, all while his heart—" I broke off, unable to continue.

"Listen, he's in very stable condition," Dr. Lyons said, lifting both hands in a staying gesture. "He does need surgery to remove the overgrown portion of muscle in his heart. That will likely help significantly with some of the symptoms he's having, although results are always variable. Our fellow has advised us that the best surgical outcomes are achieved by surgeons who've done a lot of these, so we'll refer you to a surgeon who's qualified. It's not the most common procedure at a small hospital like ours, but I'd like to see surgery happen sooner rather than later. Keep in mind, this is a chronic condition. Even after the surgery, he may still experience some symptoms, though we hope they'll be reduced. But he'll learn how to make adjustments over time."

"What kind of adjustments?" Nick asked, his jaw working.

"The surgery, called a myectomy, will likely help with the severity of his symptoms, but it won't fix the underlying condition. His cardiologist will talk about modifications he may need to make regarding exercise and prescribe a medication regimen that helps with symptom management. In a small percentage of cases, because this is progressive, patients may go on to develop heart failure and worsening of their condition."

"Oh God," I said.

"But that may not be Walker's trajectory," Dr. Lyons hastened to add. "Only time will tell. He's young and in excellent shape otherwise. I can't make any promises about long-term prognosis. He'll need to follow up with a cardiologist for a full work-up. But from where I'm standing right now, I think his prognosis is pretty good."

"Oh, thank God," Ellie said, sagging against me. "Can I see him now?"

"Yes, I'll take you," Dr. Lyons said, and we all let out a collective breath as Ellie turned to retrieve her purse from the chairs behind us.

"One more question, if you don't mind," Tavia asked, holding up a finger.

"Yes?" Dr. Lyons seemed distracted as he peered at the pager clipped to his waist before silencing the shrill ring.

"You said he needed surgery and you'd prefer for that to happen soon. But how soon does it have to be?"

We all went silent. Tavia fidgeted under the weight of our collective scrutiny.

"I guess I'm just asking if it could wait, say, a week or two? We have an important vote coming up for our business, and if it's not an emergency—"

I couldn't see the look Ellie sent Tavia, but whatever it was, it made Tavia freeze in place.

"I'll take you back now," Dr. Lyons said, not bothering to address the question. Ellie followed behind him, shooting one last tight look at Tavia.

"I'd like to talk to you a little more about the surgery referral, I've got a few questions, if you don't mind," Nick said to the doctor, following them out.

The door closed with a definitive click, and I let out a whoosh of breath, suddenly overcome with residual nerves as and I stared at Tavia.

If she hadn't been Walker's sister, I'd have already been dragging her down the hallway by her hair.

But Walker was okay for now. I wasn't going to lose him.

That news was enough to restart the stalled beat of my heart, and I fell into a chair, relieved I'd have a chance to see him soon. I could probably make it out of the room without engaging in assault on Walker's sister if she didn't say anything ...

And then Tavia's sister said something.

"What *are* you?" Zora asked, her face frightening with rage. Internally, I groaned. Zora seldom got angry, much less furious, but it appeared she about to make up for lost time.

And I was cheering her on.

Tavia threw up her hands. "Zora. Asking for a time frame doesn't make me the villain."

Zora's breathing had quickened, her chest lifting at a rapid rate. "Fifteen minutes ago, we all broke our necks getting here, not knowing how serious Walker's condition was or wasn't, or if we'd even see him alive again. That doctor just walked in here and announced that our brother, our *brother*, has a serious heart condition. For which he will require surgery. That he'll have to live with this thing for the rest of his life. And the first thing you can think to ask is if his surgery can be delayed for the goddamn *bank*?" Her volume had steadily increased until she was dangerously close to shouting.

I winced. Zora rarely shouted.

Eddie pushed off the nearby wall, looking alarmed. "We're all a little worked up right now. This was a scary situation, and now might not be the best time to have this conversation. Everyone reacts to stress in different ways," he said, projecting his usual California cool as he tried to interject a note of calm. Zora fixed him with a censoring glare that immediately silenced him.

"Tavia's pretty predictable." Zora's tone was bitter as she eyed her twin sister. "She's always been really good at calculating what's best for her."

"You have no idea what's at stake," Tavia said, glaring at her twin. "You've never given a damn about the bank."

"Out," Zora said, looking as cold as I'd ever seen her. "Get out. Get the hell out of here."

Tavia blanched. "Zora. You don't mean—"

"Get. Out. *Now*." Zora actually took a step forward, and Eddie subtly pulled Tavia back a foot. "Leave those of us who actually care what happens to Walker here to think about how we're going to take care of our friend and brother. Go be with your precious bank. You clearly don't need any family, so I think you should have it all to yourself. After all, isn't that what you've been angling for ever since you came back here?"

Tavia swallowed. Her head went back as if she'd been hit.

And then she turned and left without another word.

"Can't believe her," Zora sniffed, wiping at her eyes.

"Me neither," I said.

"I'm going to go check on her," Eddie said, quietly slipping out.

I sank into a chair. My nerves were still thrumming from all the fear, anxiety, and rage of the past hour. To my eternal mortification, I started to cry.

"Poor baby. This has been terrifying. Just get it out," Zora said, wrapping her arms around me. I was completely undone by the tender gesture from my best friend, and I completely lost it, weeping into her shoulder.

She rested her chin on my head as she rocked me in her arms like a small child. "I know, he scared me, too. I kept thinking there was so much I wanted to tell him, and so many more things I wanted to do with him."

"Me too. There's things I need to tell him."

"Like the fact that you love him," Zora said, and I pulled away to meet her all-knowing expression. "Oh, don't look so surprised. You just snotted both my shirt and yours. The last time I saw you cry was six years ago. You love my brother." She slung an arm around my shoulders and squeezed me into her side. "I'm so grateful for it. He's incredibly lucky to have you."

"Fuck," I breathed, wiping at the tears snaking down my face with sniper-stealth. "I fucking hate crying. And lately that's all I do because of your fucking brother."

She laughed then, and I closed my eyes at the beauty of the sound. For far too many moments, I'd wondered if I'd ever breathe again, let alone appreciate laughter.

"He got under your skin, then. Good."

"I never even saw him coming," I sniffed.

"He's the best person I know. My first best friend, from birth. And now I get to tell him he's gonna be an uncle," she said, and I gawked at her in shock. "What? Are you *pregnant*?"

"I can't believe it myself," she said, shaking her head with a stunned expression. "But yeah, I am."

I'd barely had time to absorb the news when the door opened and Ellie came in, looking far more relaxed.

"Leigh, I've seen that big-headed boy, and I'm happy to report he's fine. And he'll *be* fine, too, just you wait and see. Right now all he wants is to see you," she said, bending to give me a hug.

"Zora should go first, she's his sister," I said politely, but they both laughed.

"Go on now and see him," Ellie said. "Neither of you will feel any better until you put eyes on the other."

She didn't need to tell me twice.

Minutes later I stood at the foot of the curtained bay in the ER, overcome at the sight of Walker, alive, in bed and talking. He was banged up from his fall on the treadmill, sporting a growing lump on his forehead and a nasty cut to his lip and cheek. Half a dozen machines parked nearby kept close watch of his vitals, but he was alert and active enough to engage Nick in a spirited debate at his bedside.

Thank you, God. I love him so.

"Let me do it," Nick said, sounding frustrated.

"I don't need all that, man," Walker said, shaking his head on the pillow, then grimacing.

"I just talked to the doctor. Yeah, you do. Listen." Nick ran a rough hand through his hair with obvious frustration and looked away, his throat working. "Do you remember when my mother got in that car accident, and I stayed with you guys? I was in elementary school and you were in high school. But you turned your room into a planetarium and read me Carl Sagan books every night until I fell asleep. 'Cause you knew how scared I was that my mother would die. You did so much for me growing up, when my mother wasn't there because of her addiction. You taught me how to drive, how to tie a tie. You always said you were my big brother, no matter what. So it works both ways. Let me help, man. Let me be your brother."

The two said nothing for several long minutes as they held each other's gaze.

"Alright, brother," Walker said finally, and Nick gave a nod, wiping at his face as he turned to leave.

"Leigh." Nick pulled up short at the sight of me, then gave me a gentle smile as he steered me closer to Walker. "You're just what the doctor ordered. Get in here. You're all he's been talking about."

"Sugar," Walker rasped, his face lighting up at the sight of me. "Come sit by me. I've been asking for you for a while now. Hey, don't cry. I'm alright."

I rushed forward, gingerly placing a kiss on his forehead. His hand rose, cupping my face as he pulled me down to him. "I'm sorry I worried you, I—"

"Shhh," I said, lacing my fingers through his as I sat beside him. "You don't have to apologize or explain. I'm just so glad you're still here with me."

"Where would I go?" he asked, sounding perplexed.

"That's not funny," I said, using my free hand to swipe at the tears running down my face. He used his grip to tug my closer.

"Hey, don't cry," he said. "I'm okay."

"I love you, you know," I said, finally finding the bravery to look him in the eye. His expression softened as one of his callused fingers wiped my tears away.

"If passing out is what it takes to get you say that out loud, I'll do it again tomorrow," he said, and then we were both laughing.

"I'm serious, Walker. I love you. I've wanted to say it for a while."

"I know, sugar," he said. "I know."

HALF THE TOWN commandeered the hospital's two waiting rooms for Walker's surgery two days later. I shouldn't have been surprised at the overwhelming turnout. Ellie certainly wasn't. Walker's cousin, Daisy Payton, sent employees from her restaurant to set up a makeshift donut stand in the corner of the waiting room. When she arrived in person she immediately sought me out to give me a care package with a thick ham sandwich, bottled lemonade, snacks, and puzzles. Jennifer Sylvester, the reigning queen of all confections, brought enough compassion cakes to feed half the hospital.

Layla, Carla, Ebony, and Aaron sat nearby playing cards. They took turns joining Ezra, Ellie, and me during our tense watch, not saying much, just being there. Miles sat alone, attempting to read a book he kept setting down to sneak glances at his watch. Things went on that way for the first few hours, with me trying my damnedest to quell the gnawing knot of terror in my gut. I couldn't help watching the clock and begging God to guide the surgeon's hand, to help them excise the overgrown heart muscle and leave everything else vital behind. I couldn't imagine a future without him now.

Who else would make sure he got his vaulted ceiling and big back yard?

Nick looked much calmer, and by now I knew that had everything to do with the fact that he'd gotten the situation sufficiently under control, as much as he could. He'd pulled strings to have a world-renowned surgeon fly in for Walker's surgery, and ensured Walker would be comfortably ensconced in the VIP suite. Nick and Zora planned to stick around for a few weeks during Walker's recovery, and I was glad to hear it.

More hours passed uneventfully. Several of the Winston brothers came by and kept me entertained with jokes, riddles, and saucy talk of sausage. Only after a nurse came with an update that the surgery was still progressing well did I realize Tavia was missing.

Not that I particularly wanted to see her. Still, her absence was curious.

I decided to take a walk and get some air since the surgery was expected to last a few more hours. Ellie nodded when I informed her of my plans and promised to text me if she heard anything. I grabbed my jacket and headed out the front door, nodding to the staff I knew.

Once outside, I let out a sigh of contentment as the sun warmed my face. It felt good to be up and walking and stretching my legs. Greedily, I filled my lungs as I walked past a knot of smokers and turned the corner past the ambulance bay. The faint crying I heard didn't capture my attention at first. Years of working in a hospital had taught me some of the most distraught cries and fervent prayers took place outside an emergency room. But the familiar flash of dark, curly hair made me pause and look twice. Sure enough, I recognized the two people huddled together.

Eddie sat on the ground, his back against the building and his long legs spread ahead of him as he cradled a weeping Tavia across his lap. She clung to him, her head buried against his chest. He held her close, pinning her to him. She gripped his lightweight jacket in both fists, digging desperate crescents in the light cotton fabric. I couldn't help but stare at the arresting scene. The obvious grief, yes, but also the intimacy in their positioning.

What was going on between Tavia and Eddie? And how long had it been going on?

I ducked around the corner before they could see me, then debated the ethics of eavesdropping.

Fuck it, I decided. I was staying to listen.

"I know I messed up. I usually do in these situations." She was weeping, hiccupping periodically. "It was the wrong thing to say, the question about Walker's surgery."

Eddie's voice was low and comforting, but when I snuck another look around the corner, I caught his wince. "It was extraordinarily bad timing."

"That wasn't how I meant it," she sniffled.

"How did you mean it?" he asked, sounding genuinely interested.

"Does it matter? Once again, I've proven I don't know how to relate to regular people."

"Regular's overrated," he said. "And slightly boring. Your family loves you. Talk to them when things calm down a bit."

Her breath hitched. "I can't. There's things they don't know. Stuff that happened with my old job. They wouldn't understand."

Who was this Tavia? I shook my head in bewilderment. Suddenly it felt wrong to eavesdrop while she battled her way through her own heartbreak, whatever it was.

I turned on my heel and left, heading back to the waiting room.

"He's out!" Ellie clapped her hands like a small child, bouncing on her heels as she greeted me outside the waiting room. "The surgeon just came and told us. It all went perfectly. We can see him in recovery in about an hour."

"Oh good," I said, letting out a breath I hadn't even realized I'd been holding. "Thank God. Thank God."

"I know," she said, pulling me down for a hug. "I know."

True relief didn't come until I finally saw Walker in recovery. He was still intubated and more than a little swollen, but he was alive and beautiful and mine.

"I love you," I told him, not caring that he was still unconscious as I held his hand. "I love you, and whatever comes next, we'll get through it together."

CHAPTER TWENTY-ONE

Walker

Ten Days Later

"Summer's coming." Zora slouched down in an Adirondack chair, hooking her bare feet on the porch railing of her lake house rental. "You can almost smell it."

"Getting warmer." I frowned as I attempted to adjust my position in a matching chair.

She bolted upright. "Oh no. That's chair's uncomfortable."

"It's fine, Zora." But she'd already disappeared into the house where I could vaguely make out Nick and Pops responding to her shouted question. Less than a minute later, the three of them appeared on the front porch, Zora and Pops carrying pillows of varying sizes and Nick dragging a different chair.

I swallowed a tired sigh. It was unreasonable to expect everyone to forget what had happened over a week ago. They'd all told me, in their own ways, that I'd scared the hell out of them and they needed time for equilibrium to be restored.

"I know you all love me," I said, "and I'm grateful. But you gotta relax. I won't die from being a little uncomfortable."

Nick eyed the chair I sat in, then studied the cushioned, high-backed chair he'd dragged in from the living room. "This one will be a lot better. You're down way too low in that one, and leaning back like that must be hell on your chest."

It was, but I'd never admit that. It had hurt a lot more than I expected getting into it, and I'd need help to get out of it. But I'd wanted a minute, just one minute where things were normal and I didn't need special accommodations or to be fussed over by someone I loved.

"That chair is probably better," I conceded.

Nick got to work settling it next to me, then leaned forward and grasped both my elbows.

"I've got it," I groused, and Nick closed his eyes briefly.

"You can't pull yourself up, Walk, it'll strain your chest muscles. Just let me do this. Jesus, it's not like I'm wiping your ass," he said, and Pops cracked up.

"Fine," I said, and Nick managed to lever me up to a standing position with no effort required on my part.

"Take this and put it behind his back." Pops handed Nick the long pillow in his hands. "I'm going to get his pain meds and some water. Must be hurting, the way he's frowning so hard."

"Just the Motrin 800s," I said as Pops headed back into the house. "Nothing stronger. Please."

I lowered myself into the new chair and looked up to find Zora and Nick scowling down at me. "What?"

"Little early to wean yourself off the painkillers," Nick said, raising one brow at me as if I were a wayward child. "Even the nurse said so. Six to eight weeks to heal, that's what they said. Six to eight weeks. You're only at the start of that, and you're not allowed to drive yet anyway."

"Maybe if you were in less pain you'd be taking your daily walks the way you're supposed to," my sister said, folding her arms as she stood next to Nick, the two of them a united parental front.

"Why am I starting to regret this visit?" I asked.

"Leigh was right, he is cranky," Zora said to Nick, as if I wasn't sitting right there. "Walker, if you don't do right, I'm gonna unleash

Mama on you. If you thought she was already a lot, just know it can get worse. She will move in with you and Leigh and put an end to field trips like this."

"Leigh is still at work and you could do with getting out of the house while she's gone and breathing in some fresh lake air," Pops said as he returned with a glass of water in hand and two prescription bottles. "We are your keepers while you're in our care. Your wife gave us strict instructions."

"We're not married yet, Pops."

"I'm just speaking it into existence," he said, winking at me. "And it's working. See how you said 'yet?' Now, I brought the good stuff and the Motrin. You can pick which one you want, but know this: your ass is taking me on a walk around this lake before you leave here today. I told Leigh I'd get you straight, and you're getting both your recommended walks in today. You're doing those breathing exercises, too. You wanna be comfortable when that happens or not?"

"Just consider it," my sister said. "Please. I can tell you're in a lot of pain right now, and there's no need to white-knuckle it. The nurse said—"

"Fine." I just wanted to end the conversation and ease the strained looks on their faces. Pops unscrewed the cap to the "good stuff," dropped the prescribed dosage in my hand, then stood watching as I downed the pills with water.

"I know this isn't easy," Zora said after Pops and Nick disappeared inside and she was back in her chair. "I know we're all getting on your nerves. But we want the best for you."

"I know, Z. I love you all for it. So many important things are passing me by while I'm out of it. I need to be alert."

"Rest and heal," she said. "That's the best thing you can do for any of us. Nothing else is more important than that."

We subsided into silence for a while, watching the lake lap at the shoreline as birds skimmed along its surface, searching for their prey. Gradually, I felt the iron grip of my jaw loosen and the tension drain from all my muscles as the medication kicked in.

"Pain's better?" She watched me closely.

"Got way less of a grip now, yeah. You heard from Tavia?"

"Now, that's playing dirty," she said, smirking. "If you wanted to talk about something else, you could have just said so."

"Have you?"

"No, and I'm not looking for her."

"You can't stay angry at her forever, she's your sister. Your twin. Don't you miss her?"

"No," she said so resolutely I cringed. "And you wouldn't be asking me that if you'd been there in the waiting room when she asked that question."

"Don't you wanna tell her about the ..." I leaned my whole body to the side carefully, checking to make sure no one was standing at the screen door as I mimed a baby bump.

She flicked an anxious look behind us. "No. The only people that know right now are you and Leigh. Mama's hands are full micromanaging *your* life right now, thank you very much, and I'm fine leaving it that way. Especially with the news we got yesterday."

"What news did you get yesterday? Give up the goods. I need something to liven things up."

She closed her eyes, then covered her face with her hands. "You won't believe it."

"Try me."

"Two heartbeats," she hissed.

My jaw dropped. "Are you serious?"

She nodded her head, still hiding her face.

"Twins again," I said, shaking my head with a grin. "Mama is going to lose her mind. This is like a miracle. What are the odds?"

"Pretty good, actually." She dropped her hands in her lap as she faced the lake with a tight expression. "I'm thirty-one. My body is basically having a two-for-one fire sale on eggs every month. Multiples are common when you get older."

"You're going to be a mom," I whispered to her. "Twice over."

God, the pills improved one's outlook *and* pain threshold.

"Yeah," she said, sounding disconcerted. "Fucking Nick."

"That is how it happened. Probably on the kitchen table." I laughed, then instantly regretted it as the laugh morphed into a coughing spell that incinerated my chest like hot lava.

"That's what you get, smart-ass," she said, and got up to press another pillow in my hands. "Hold this against your chest when you cough, like they told you to."

"Yes, Mother. See, you're ready for the job."

"I'm far from ready." She wore an expression I hadn't seen since I'd taken her to a haunted house when she was still knee-high. "Let this be a lesson to you and Leigh. We didn't plan this, but it's happening. We've been married less than year. It's going to change everything."

I tensed, wincing at the thought of Leigh, pregnant, with all the unknowns we were facing.

"What?" Zora peered over at me. "What did I say?"

"Nothing."

"Walker, stop. It's something. What is it?"

"Your echo came back clear, right?" I kept my gaze on the water.

She turned to face me head on. "Walker, we have talked about this. We have all been screened, Mama, Daddy, Tavia, and even Audre at school. None of us have signs of any heart problem."

"But that could change."

"You did the genetic testing. We'll see if they identify one of the known genes that causes it, and if they do, we'll all do the cascade screening to see if we have the same gene, just like the genetic counselor said. And even then, having the gene doesn't mean it'll turn on."

I ran an agitated hand along my brow. "What if you have it too? You're already pregnant. Your babies—"

"Walker."

She got up and came over to me, kneeling at my feet as she clasped my hands. "Walker, stop. There are so many unknowns right now. It could be that you're the first in our family to have this mutation. Or it could be that this gene has been lurking in our family tree for years, just waiting to jump down a couple branches and play peek-a-boo with one of us. Whatever it is, we don't have any control over it. All you can do is take it as it comes."

I shook my head. "I don't want to take the chance of passing this on to a kid I would have with Leigh. And it's not fair for her to have to worry about that when she wouldn't have to if it weren't for me. "

She went still. "I really hope that's the painkillers talking. Maybe we should talk about this later."

"Painkillers aren't doing anything more than making it easier for me to say what I've already been thinking. She didn't sign up for this. And she's been holding out for her second chance for a long time until now. I don't know that I'd like these odds, if I were her."

"Leigh loves you, Walker. Loves you. Now, *that* is the real miracle, her being able to love again after all her ex-husband and family put her through. She doesn't care about anything else."

I closed my eyes. "The day I passed out at the gym, Leigh and I spent the morning planning our future. Planning for the median two and a half kids we wanted."

"Well, then, have them." Zora sounded frustrated. "And if you're so worried about maybe passing on a gene, remember what the genetic counselor said. There are assisted reproductive therapies that can significantly reduce that chance."

"I'm not putting her through that."

"Walker. You're not going to do anything stupid, are you? Not over children you don't even have yet."

"It's not just the kids. Everything has changed."

She closed her eyes. "I know. All of this has been a big shock and adjustment for us, so I can't imagine how you're feeling."

I shook my head, wrestling against the dark thoughts that had plagued me for the last week. "I know this is the part where I'm supposed to be grateful for being alive, for having it caught in time and not sharing the fate of so many people who've died while running or swimming or playing football or basketball. I'm lucky, I know that."

"That's not the question," Zora said. "I thank God every day that I still have you here. And I know you're grateful too. But I don't want to engage in toxic positivity. I want you to feel comfortable venting about however you're feeling. How are you dealing with it all, Walker?"

I started to shrug then and stopped before I provoked a flare of pain. "I'm working on accepting that the surgery didn't make this magically go away. I still have a stiff, oversized heart. I'll always have to take medication. I have to accept that I'll likely have good days and bad days, forever.

In spite of that, I know I'll likely live with this and have a good life. Other people do."

"That's right," Zora said.

"But I love Leigh enough that I don't want her to have to live with this hanging over our heads. I can't avoid it, but she can."

"Walker, if you could have seen her in that waiting room, if you saw how distraught she was when we didn't know what would happen ... I don't think you understand how much she loves you."

Maybe not, but I knew how much I loved her, and it was enough to want to spare her from the constant worry about my health that I could tell was already taking hold in her mind. The last week had shown me that she'd sacrifice herself and her comfort for my benefit.

I didn't want that for her.

"Did you know she sleeps in the living room with me?" I asked. Nick had bought a recliner for Leigh's living room so I could sleep comfortably sitting up. I'd spent a good deal of my time parked in it, passing through varying stages of consciousness.

Zora looked as if she wanted to cry. "Does she really?"

"Yes. She sleeps on the couch, next to my chair. She keeps me on schedule with my pain meds, even as tired and anxious as she is with all that's going on with the hospital. Even though I tell her I'm more than capable of setting the alarm and doing it myself. She's spent all of her time taking care of me when she's not at work."

"That's how people behave when they love you. You'd do the same for her. I know you would. Before this happened, you could see forever with her, couldn't you? I bet you were going to propose at some point."

"Yes," I said, with no hesitation. "I already had a ring in mind. I figured I'd need to slow walk her a bit, give her time for the jitters to calm down long enough so she'd be receptive to the idea. But she's more receptive to the idea than I expected."

"So what's stopping you?"

I hesitated, unable to speak past the dual assault of physical and emotional pain. "Now I understand what love truly is."

"Meaning?"

"Meaning it's selfless enough to deny yourself so your partner still has a chance to fly."

"Walker," she whispered, "please don't do anything, don't make any big decisions while all of this is still so new. Now isn't the time to be noble."

I closed my eyes and looked away from her beseeching expression.

There was no point in arguing over what was already inevitable.

~

"You guys wore him out today, huh?"

I started, opening my eyes to find Leigh looking down at me, her blue eyes directly over mine.

"Sugar. You're off work." The pull of pleasure I felt at the sight of her was immediate, involuntary. I pulled her in for a kiss, unaccountably glad to see her. "I think I missed you."

"I know I missed you," she said, easing to sit beside me on the oversized, padded armchair. I leaned into her softness and gripped her knee.

"I never thought I'd see this day," Zora said. "They're so cute, aren't they?" Nick, Zora, and Pops watched us from the couch with rapt expressions.

"I told you it would happen if you left them alone," Nick said, and Zora rolled her eyes.

"I'm just glad I have new contenders in the race to give me great-grandchildren," Pops said, looking mighty pleased with himself. "Hurry up and make this thing official. I'm not getting any younger, and I've got money to give away."

Zora's eyes shot to mine and widened briefly before she looked away.

"Don't be greedy, Pops. You've got your hands full with the grandkids you've got." I made my voice light, not wanting to hear Leigh's appreciative laugh or see the worry growing on my sister's face.

"I don't know," Pops said, his gaze speculative as it settled on my sister. "Zora here is eating a lot more than usual. Could be I might not have to wait that long."

Silence.

"How are you feeling, Walker?" Nick stood abruptly and headed over to Leigh and me, while Zora did a very poor job of trying to pull a straight face. "Comfortable? Would you be alright staying here another hour or two?"

"Dinner's ready," Zora said, "and we thought we'd have it while we watch the report about KCH and Visage tonight."

"I was starting to think they'd never air it," Leigh said.

"Of course we can stay," I said.

Leigh looked to Pops. "Is he on schedule with his pain meds?"

"Yes," Pops reported. "He's been walked twice and we made sure he ate lunch."

"I've also been diapered in preparation for pickup," I joked, and we all laughed. "No seriously, I'm fine. I'm comfortable. Let's do it."

Thirty minutes later we were all settled around the big screen television with TV trays, eagerly anticipating the start of the evening broadcast.

"Make sure you eat that," Zora said, eyeing the plate of salmon and mixed vegetables the housekeeper had set on the tray beside me. "You can't take your next round of pain meds on an empty stomach."

"It's starting," Pops said, and they all shushed each other as the commercial ended and the camera panned to a sober-faced news anchor.

"Tonight's story," the anchor intoned, "shines the light on a larger conversation taking place all over the nation as private equity firms gain an increasing foothold in the health care landscape. Critics say this shift is especially troublesome for rural hospitals, where patient safety may be compromised to optimize profit." The screen filled with a shot of KCH's exterior. Everyone cheered.

I tried to stay awake, but I couldn't resist the weight of my eyelids for long. I caught snatches of dialogue and brief glimpses of white-coated people being interviewed.

When I finally surfaced back to the world, the television was off. Pops, Nick, and Leigh were conferring in a tight knot around the coffee table, their voices low.

"Gotta be someone with skin in the game," Pops was saying, nodding at Leigh. "I know this is scary, but you've brought this thing to this point. No matter what happens next, you're not alone. You've got all of us behind you."

"I just hope we're not alone out there tomorrow during the protest,"

Leigh said, one hand gripping the wild mane of her hair while the fingers of her other hand twitched.

"You won't be alone," I said, my voice scratchy. Their heads all swiveled in my direction.

"Hey, you," she said, getting up and coming over to me. I frowned at the dark shadows under her eyes and the tense set to her mouth. "You're awake. You didn't eat. Does your stomach hurt?"

"I'm okay," I croaked. I gestured for her hand and she gave it to me. "But you're not. You're stressed and jonesing for a cigarette. That's never a good sign. Please don't worry. You won't be alone tomorrow. I've got it."

"I'm fine," she said, her hand closing around mine. "And you are not coming tomorrow. You're resting. You ready to go home?" She ran a cool hand across my brow. "Or are you too comfortable to move?"

"You guys can stay here tonight," Nick said, rising to stand beside Leigh. "We've got plenty of room and your meds are here, Walk."

I studied Leigh. "Do you feel up to driving home?"

She nodded immediately. "I'm fine, and it's not that late. Plus, we're all wearing pink shirts tomorrow, and mine's at home."

"Then I'm going home with you."

"Alright."

We all headed to the door. Leigh went to get the car from the back of the house while Pops stood with me on the porch.

"What's going on with Consolidated, Pops? What am I missing while I'm vacationing in Narcotics Land?"

He faced me, running a hand over the gray bramble of his beard. I raised a brow as a sly smile grew across his face. "Absolutely nothing, as far as anyone else is concerned. We're giving you time to recover before any decisions are made."

"But what are *you* up to?"

He only stared at me. "You'll see," he said finally, his rich laughter rolling through the dark night. "Just wait. You'll see."

CHAPTER TWENTY-TWO

Leigh

The knot of anxiety in my gut grew tighter and tighter the closer I drove to KCH. It was barely dawn, with the sun still hiding behind the horizon, but I needed to get out in front of the hospital early to pass out signs and organize whoever showed up. I'd signed up for the early shift so I could still round on Peds patients with procedures scheduled that day. Layla and Carla were going to relieve me, followed by Aaron and his wife.

All we could hope was that we wouldn't be marching alone, that our careful communication about the protest had reached the right ears. But even if we did stand alone, we'd committed to standing firm.

There was so much to hope for, while so much was still unknown. I didn't even know if I'd still have a job by the end of the day, or if all my efforts would be for nothing. Visage could very likely sink their tentacles further into the hospital and opt to ride out the contingency period, leaving us with nothing.

It was terrifying.

I *was* terrified.

But then my eyes fell to the two sticky notes Walker had stuck to my dashboard, who knew when. Had to have been past zero dark thirty, since I had no memory of him ever leaving the house. He'd insisted that

I sleep in my own bed to get the best possible rest, but I'd resisted his efforts and slept on the couch in the living room beside his recliner.

I didn't know how to make him understand that I didn't care about being woken up by the alarm for his medication, and I didn't mind sleeping on the couch. I couldn't sleep in my own bed without him now anyway.

And sometimes, when I woke up in the middle of the night with my heart still hammering from the remembered fear of that day in the ER, I just needed the reassurance of seeing him next to me, alive and sleeping.

My nerves were drawn tighter than violin strings. I was reaching the end of my emotional reserves.

Courage, dear heart, Walker's sticky read, and I smiled and let out the breath I'd been holding, recognizing the C.S. Lewis quote that hung in my bathroom at home. Beside it, another note written in his bold, slanted handwriting: *I got your back.*

I couldn't count the number of times my eyes flicked to those sticky notes as I drove. They held me up, kept me steady and buoyant all the way during my drive, even as I turned down the long road leading to the main campus of the hospital.

I didn't see them, not at first. I was already scanning for an available parking spot on both sides of the lane. But the sea of pink shirts finally caught my eye, and I suddenly realized they were everywhere. Pink-shirted people cut in between cars in the parking lot, marched toward the entrance in small groups, streamed down the side of the road single file.

I squinted through the early morning gloom, trying to make out the dark lettering on the back of an older woman's shirt.

Get Out, Visage! it read.

My mouth fell open. I realized my car was standing still in the middle of the road when a horn sounded behind me.

By the time I parked and started walking toward the front of the hospital, I was overwhelmed.

A multitude of pink shirts, hundreds of them, swarmed the front entrance. As I got closer to the bank of doors, I spotted two pink-shirted volunteers handing out signs with pithy protest slogans.

"Leigh!" A smiling woman I didn't recognize, with laughing eyes, a flawless brown complexion, and cowry shell-accented dreadlocks, grabbed my elbow. "Welcome to the resistance!"

I gaped at her, frantically rifling through my mental Rolodex. Had we ever met before? "Hi. Yes, I'm Leigh."

"I know," she laughed. "I'm Melora. My colleagues and I are here representing the local chapter of a national association of Black nurses," she said, raising her voice to a shout at the end of the statement. Nearby, dozens of women let out a loud cheer. "I went to school with Walker Leffersbee. He reached out a week ago to let me know what was going on."

"Wait, he—what? He just had—"

"Heart surgery, I know. But he wanted me to make sure you had backup today, and we were more than happy to answer the call. Many of us work in this hospital, and we know patients are a lot safer when we can provide the best possible care. This is our fight too. We're prepared to stand with you as long as this takes."

Before I could throw my arms around her in gratitude, another familiar voice spoke up. "You nurses are always trying to show us up," Adesola teased. She carried a sign that read, *I'm Fighting for My Patients!* "Don't forget about us docs. I'm representing clinicians of varying specialties who are here for our patients and want to protect our ability to provide the best care." She turned to the men and women behind her, arms raised, and another cheer went up from the crowd. "We're here for as long as it takes too."

"Who ... how?" I stared at her and the press of bodies behind her in shock.

"Layla and Aaron. They spread the word and got us going," Adesola said, squeezing my hands.

Behind me, someone cleared her throat. I turned to find Mrs. Bowers, Maddie's mother, behind me.

"Leigh!" she exclaimed, and we hugged each other while doing an awkward sideways shuffle dance. "You did it! How did you manage to pull this off? I'm so proud of you!"

I looked around at the crowd, swallowing past the burn in my throat. "This isn't my doing. This is all of us."

"That's right," she said, "it's all of us, but we're blessed to have you leading this. I'm here representing Parents in Peds. We all know what's at stake here, and we don't want to see the pediatric programming we depend on fall by the wayside." Turning back to the crowd, she shouted, "Where are my mommies and daddies?"

The crowd erupted into a deafening roar. My jaw fell open.

"Get us moving. We've got marching to do." Melora handed me a bullhorn and gestured for me to step up on the stacked milk crates behind me. "We're ready."

"Come on, chica," Adesola said, her eyes shining. "This is the moment you fought for. Take it."

I stepped up on the crates with a hand from Mrs. Bowers and looked out over the growing pink-shirted crowd in the parking lot. *We did this,* I thought. What had started with four frightened employees had grown into a legitimate movement.

It meant so much to me that Walker had had a huge hand in assembling the crowd, and I couldn't help but feel his presence.

Cheers went up at the sight of me. "Thank you for coming," I said into the megaphone, and the crowd roared back in response. "Starting today, we're reclaiming our hospital for this community and everyone it serves!" I yelled, and another cheer went up.

Melora, Adesola, and Mrs. Bowers nodded approvingly as I outlined our demands, including Visage's retreat from the sale. Marchers worked among themselves to quickly disseminate signs, and I led the march around the building with hundreds of voices chanting, demanding that Visage abandon the sale. "Hey hey, ho ho! Visage Corp. has got to go!"

In the space of four hours I gave three interviews to local news stations during which I reiterated the concerns as reviewed in the news program the previous night and successfully dodged any questions probing the source of the leaked documents Carla had turned over to the press. Familiar faces from all over Green Valley were peppered throughout the crowd, including Daisy Payton and her children, several Winston brothers and their spouses, and at one point I thought I even saw Pops. By the time my shift ended and it was time to report to work, I was overjoyed. The massive turnout, the media response, the genuine concern expressed by community leaders ... it was more than I ever could have hoped for, a real public statement. So when a wide-eyed Carla and Layla showed up to relieve me and I headed into the hospital to report for work, I really should have anticipated what was waiting for me.

I was pinning my badge to my scrub top as I passed through the front entrance when a deep voice spoke up from the side.

"Uh, Leigh? Ms. D'Alessandro?" The guard who usually kept watch at the entryway and occasionally flashed me a friendly smile now fidgeted nervously as he watched my approach.

"Hey, Mark. What's up?"

His eyes darted over his shoulder as his mouth tightened. *I'm sorry,* he mouthed, before saying out loud, "There's some people who'd like to speak with you."

Looking beyond him into the hospital's expansive foyer, I zeroed in on the polished, officious-looking woman in a gray suit flanked by several other suits I'd never seen before.

"Oh no," I said under my breath, and Mark nodded significantly, his back still to them.

Walk toward your future, Leigh. No more running.

I squared my shoulders and held my head high as they approached.

"So, what'd they say? Who all was in the meeting?"

Carla and Layla sat in the back seat of my car at a nearby gas station, casting surreptitious glances out the windows. We'd agreed to rendezvous there to compare notes after I was done with work and after they were relieved by Aaron and his wife at the protest.

Never had there been a moment when I'd craved a cigarette more.

I closed my eyes against the memory of the firing squad I'd faced earlier that day. "The better question is, who wasn't there? Five HR reps, three attorneys, a publicist, and a crisis consultant."

Layla whistled. "Sounds scary."

"It was. All of them sitting across from me, glaring."

"What'd they say?" Layla asked.

"They wanted to confirm I'm leading the protests and clarify what our demands are. They were also very interested in how we came by certain knowledge. Like, the details of the sale and other things disclosed in the documents Loretta gave us."

"What did you say?" Carla's voice was hushed. "You could always blame it on me, say I dug it up—"

"I told them nothing. Nothing. I let them know we had no intention of backing down from our demands, and that I needed to get to my kids. Then they offered to let me keep my job if I told them everything. Where we got the documents, who all was involved in planning everything. They said it was my last chance to save myself. That they'd already accessed all my emails, anything I touched while at the hospital. Then they let me leave and said they'd keep an eye on me."

I closed my eyes.

"You did good," Carla said, and Layla murmured in agreement.

"Yeah, this time." I ran a hand over my eyes, struggling against the weight of encroaching fear and uncertainty. "What am I even doing right now? I'm a Child Life Specialist. I love those kids and their parents, I love all our patients. But I'm not qualified to do this. We should have someone that's, I don't know, a lawyer or something. Or someone who's done this before."

Layla spoke after several long moments. "You know, this seems like an opportune time to remind you how Moses told God—"

I groaned. "No, Layla, please, it's not. There's no comparison. I'm not equipped, there should be someone else."

"That's what Moses said," Layla said, sounding smug. From behind me where she sat, she placed a hand on my shoulder. "I'll just leave you with this. There's a reason this task fell to you, Leigh D'Alessandro. You know the hearts and minds of the people we serve."

"Is this the part where you hand me the staff that'll help end this? 'Cause I could use it right now. If not to work a miracle, then to kick some asses with it."

I'm scared, I didn't say.

"Anything you need," Carla said. "Just let us know and we're on it. You're not alone."

Not alone, I told myself as I drove home, doing my best to ignore the burning unease in my stomach. Pulling into the drive, I felt a tinge of relief. I'd feel better after talking to Walker.

I turned off the car, squinting at the unfamiliar Maserati SUV in the adjacent driveway lane. Who was visiting Walker? It wasn't anyone in his family.

I was startled to hear raised voices as I walked in the house. Walker and Miles, in my bedroom. I raced down the hallway, panicked.

"I don't want any part of this," Miles said, frustration leaking from every syllable. "You're not known for doing dumb shit, but boy is this dumb."

"You don't agree," Walker said, sounding tired. "I'm clear on that. I'm not asking you to. I'm just asking for your help."

"I don't want to help with this. Maybe she'd understand if you did it the right way. But sneaking out like this, without even giving her a heads-up?"

"I'm not sneaking, Miles. I'm only thinking of her. She'll come to understand. If I told her in advance, you know what she'd say."

I turned the corner to my room. Walker stood at the foot of my bed, next to a nearly full duffel bag. Miles stood a few feet away from the door, his back to me.

"Let's end the mystery," I said, and they both jumped. "Why don't you tell me what's going on, and then nobody has to guess what I'm going to say."

Walker let out a defeated sigh. Miles groaned.

Neither said anything.

"What, is this a game? Do I have to put together the clues and guess?"

Silence.

"Alright," I said, coming farther into the room to peer into the open duffel bag. Walker looked pained as he watched me, his temples working.

"Let's see, we've got Walker's boxers, his socks, his sweats, and T-shirts. Even his house shoes."

"Leigh," Walker began, and I held up a hand to stop him.

"No, please. This is fun, guessing. Let me see ... hmmm. I'd say it looks like you're leaving me. And since you can't lift anything heavier than a gallon of milk and you can't drive yourself, you recruited Miles as the getaway driver. Nice car, by the way, Miles."

"Thanks," he said, sounding subdued as he scrubbed a hand down his face.

"I didn't want it to happen like this. Why are you back so soon?" Walker said.

With no intention of answering that question, I stared at him, expecting any minute that he would tell me there was another explanation for what I was seeing. When interminable seconds ticked by and he did no such thing, I felt my chest splinter into a million pieces as I took in the misery, the strain on his face.

"I guess you figured me coming home to an empty house would have felt better than this does, huh?"

"I'm doing this for you," Walker said.

Miles made a scornful noise. "I'll be out front," he said, shooting Walker one last pointed look before he turned and left.

Calm. I would stay calm. Now that we were alone, I could get him to talk to me. "What's going on, Walker?"

He sighed, then turned and sat stiffly on the bed against the headboard, grimacing.

I walked over and wedged a pillow behind his back.

"I need some time to think," he said, reaching up and catching my arm to hold me in place beside him. My heart turned over at the turmoil I saw in his eyes.

"Okay," I said, doing my best to be brave for the second time that day. "I want you to think. Thinking's good. Any way I can help?"

He hesitated. "I want you to be able to think, too."

"What does that mean?"

"Everything's happened so fast. With everything that's going on with Visage, you haven't had time to really think about what you want for your life."

"I'm not sure what you mean. I want you."

"But things have changed, and given that, you should have the chance to re-evaluate the situation."

Icy, frozen heartbreak settled over me. "*I* need to re-evaluate? I'm not the one who's leaving, Walker. Don't project your issues, whatever they are, onto me. At least take ownership of whatever it is you feel, and your actions."

I stepped away, out of his reach.

"Leigh. Please. I just—" He ran a hand over the back of his neck. "I'm just trying to figure this all out. I didn't see the heart thing coming. I didn't know the future would change this drastically for us."

"What's the drastic change? Walker, you will recover from this surgery. You will feel better."

"Yes. I already feel better in some ways. But I still might not be able to give you all I thought I could."

I closed my eyes, welcoming the merciful, familiar numbness. "You fooled me alright, with the happily ever after bullshit. I bought it, hook, line, and sinker."

"This is not about loving you. I do love you," he said, his voice urgent as he reached for me. I took another step away, grateful for his slower response time. "That hasn't changed, and it never will. It's why I'm giving us both a little space right now. I just need some time to think. And you need to know ..." His voice broke and he seemed to gather himself. "You need to consider that you can have another chance at starting over with someone who can give you everything you're going to want from life."

"What can't you give me that you haven't already?"

His eyes closed. "If we had kids one day, there's a chance they could have my condition. I don't wish that kind of worry for you. And my condition could get worse. I can't take a chance that I'd ever be a burden to you."

"All I want is you, Walker. You."

"You say that now, but it wouldn't be enough."

"Are you serious right now?" I realized I was yelling when Walker's eyes closed briefly. I took a slow breath and attempted to moderate my tone. "Let me get this straight: I tell you it doesn't matter to me, and you insist that might change, as if I don't know my own mind? This isn't about me, Walker. If you have to leave, leave. I won't keep you here. I want you to have all the space you need." Thank God anger was trumping heartbreak at that moment, because the last thing I wanted to do was cry.

Walker slowly pushed to his feet. "I just want the world for you. I want to *give* you everything. And if I can't, I'd rather be honest with both of us about that. Now."

"Honesty isn't really what we're talking about here. You want me to accept your hypocrisy. You see this relationship as lopsided. Everything is fine as long you're Superman, the hero, the guy who's always rescuing me. But the minute you're the one who's vulnerable, the second you might have to lean on me, you're out the door. 'You can trust me with the hard stuff,' you said after the baptism. I guess that only goes one way, huh?"

I headed over to my closet and pulled out his robe. "Make sure you pack this too."

"Don't be angry."

"Walker, if I'm angry at anyone, I'm angry at myself. I deluded myself into thinking this was real."

His face twisted. "What's between us *is* real. It's the realest thing I've ever experienced."

"You pull strings to make things easier for me, to support me like you did today. But God forbid I try to support you."

"I want you to be able to focus on what's important to you, what's happening with the hospital. I *don't* want you to be preoccupied with taking care of me." That last he said with an edge that conveyed just how much he detested the idea of accepting my help.

Now, *that* was bitter irony for you. Here I was, thinking he would make this day better. That he'd provide the respite I needed after a day of nerve-wracking uncertainty. And he was leaving me. What the fuck?

"I'm going to go. Give you and Miles space to get whatever you need," I said, moving back to the doorway.

Walker followed after me. "Don't leave like this."

I couldn't help my bitter laugh. "Why the hell not? Isn't that exactly what you were going to do before I got here?"

He stopped in his tracks.

"Are we even together anymore, Walker? Or is that what you're trying to figure out?"

His silence and the way he averted his gaze from mine told me all I needed to know.

I bit my tongue, hard, and the answering rush of pain briefly overrode the searing pain in my heart.

"I didn't think anything could hurt more than what I'd already been through," I said, shaking my head at myself. "But this? This is worse. 'Cause I never loved or trusted anyone like I love and trust you."

"Leigh."

"I'll be gone for the rest of the day. You and Miles can take your time clearing out."

CHAPTER TWENTY-THREE

Walker

One Week Later

"Are you eating the food I'm bringing?" My mother wore a severe frown as she stood, arms folded, glaring down at me.

"Somewhat."

"Are you sure? Because you look like you've been losing weight."

I shook my head, shifting on the couch as she scrutinized me even more closely. "I haven't been losing weight. I've been walking a lot, but I've been eating too."

She set her purse down on the end table with a thump. "I don't like this."

I let out a mirthless laugh. "I know, Mama. You tell me that every day. Really, I'm fine."

"You are *not* fine. You are miserable in this crappy little apartment that's way too far from home. I *hate* this place." She sent a dark look around my furnished executive apartment, her brows further lowering as if she suspected the furniture of foul motives.

"Knoxville isn't all that far away, and you know it."

Honestly, I hated it too, even if it was a perfectly acceptable, generic, soulless box of an apartment. But I didn't spend all my time in it. Now that I was slowly recovering and gradually feeling stronger, I spent more and more time exploring the long trails that surrounded the complex. I walked and walked, until either my body or thoughts exhausted me enough that I had to retire back inside.

When I wasn't walking, I was writing. Transposing my thoughts and ideas into endless reams of paper I printed from my laptop.

"You lonely?" My mother sat at the end of the couch, smoothing her dress over her lap.

"I don't know how I could be, between Miles practically living here, Zora, Nick, and Pops coming by all time—"

"You know what I'm asking. Leigh answering your calls or texts yet?"

My shoulders fell inward.

"No. Any news?"

"Visage hasn't backed down. Folks are still marching outside the hospital, but the crowds are getting much smaller."

I couldn't help but worry and wonder how Leigh was taking that. For the millionth time, my mind rifled through possible ways of helping her.

"They're not giving her a hard time at work, are they? Does she need anything? Is there anything I can do for her?"

And then, taking in my mother's smug expression and raised brows, I remembered Leigh's request that my family not pass any information between the two of us.

"Leigh has asked—"

"I know what Leigh asked. I guess I was just hoping you could tell me something."

"Ask her yourself."

"She won't speak to me, you know that."

"It's understandable."

I pushed myself to standing. "Okay, Mom. Get it out of your system. Please. It's been a week. Let's stop circling around it. I'm lower than pond scum for leaving Leigh, right?"

"I respect others' personal boundaries—"

"Since when?"

"So I won't talk about Leigh," she said in a prim tone, lifting her chin. "But I would be more than happy to discuss matters involving you."

"Might as well," I said, moving toward the kitchen on sore, wooden legs. I might have overdone it with the walking.

My mother followed, arms crossed as she watched me retrieve a sparkling water from the fridge.

"What's the last thing you ate, Walker?"

I held back a sigh. "I can't remember."

"So you're taking your pain meds on an empty stomach?"

"I don't take them anymore." I unscrewed the cap to the bottle and leaned against the fridge, returning her narrow look. "I can manage the pain just fine now."

"At least you haven't been idle all this time. You've mastered self-deception."

"Mama. Isn't it you who's always going on about catching flies with honey?"

"You don't need me to be kind and indulgent. You need me to kick your butt in gear, and that's what I'm doing. I've done my best to be patient and mindful of what you're going through. I talked to people in the support group who said it's normal to feel this way after heart surgery."

"What support group?" I frowned.

"They have a support group for people with your condition. I've been talking to some of the people there."

I stared at her for a helpless moment, fighting back a sudden tide of emotion.

"I know, baby," she said quietly, walking over to me with her arms open. "I know. It's been a lot all at once. A lot to process."

"I didn't know you joined a support group."

"Well, you haven't been talking much, and I wanted to know how to help you."

I slung an arm around her, loosely hugging her back. "I know I haven't been easy to deal with lately. I'm sorry. I'm really sorry."

"It's okay," she said. "I know you'll need time to understand and accept your new normal. But, son, this struggle you're having right now, this fight to accept yourself? You put all that on Leigh, and that wasn't very fair."

"I'm only thinking of her. She deserves someone who can take care of her."

"Having heart surgery makes you ineligible for that role? Suddenly you're a different person because you found out about an anomaly in your heart that you've had your entire life? That makes you a different man now? C'mon, son. You know better than that."

"It's not that simple."

"You're right. There's also the issue of your pride. It hasn't exactly helped things."

She left my side then and went to open the refrigerator. "You haven't eaten *anything*. The same food is in here."

"I don't think there's an issue of pride."

"Oh, of course there is," she said, taking out a Tupperware container and stretching to reach for the paper plates atop the fridge. "Tell me, Walker. When I was diagnosed with breast cancer, did it make me any less your mother?"

I stepped behind her and pulled the plates down to the counter. "Of course not."

"Should your father have left me? Better yet, would he have been better off never meeting or marrying me?"

My throat tightened. Her remission was the answer to my most fervent prayers. I hated remembering the terror of that time.

"Of course not, Mama."

She paused in the act of popping the Tupperware lid to look back at me. "Why not? There's a pretty lengthy history of breast cancer in my family. I've always been aware of it. And just because I'm in remission doesn't mean it won't come back. I could still die from it."

"Don't say that," I snapped.

"You're the one making decisions based on worst case scenarios. According to your way of thinking, I should have walked away from Ezra when we met in high school. Spared him potential heartbreak, just like you're trying to do with Leigh."

I stood still, transfixed, as I considered her words.

"Your father, he's not always easy. You know that. But I've never doubted that he would fight like hell for me, whatever the reason, regardless of how scary the threat might be. And he has, with you kids right alongside him. That's what happens when you choose to share your life with someone, Walker. It's a commitment to the other. An agreement to shoulder whatever burdens may come."

"I know."

"You're strong for each *other*, Walker. It's not just one person who does the heavy lifting. You remember when Zora and Tavia came early? How Zora was barely more than three pounds?"

I nodded.

"I thought I wouldn't survive it, seeing my tiny baby struggling to live in that incubator all those months. And when your father's mother died, I thought he would never smile again. Not him or Pops. We've endured a lot together, your father and I. Sometimes we took turns being strong, but we've always leaned on each other to get through all of life's unexpected surprises."

I studied the floor, biting back my objections, unable to meet her gaze.

"Your refusal to allow Leigh to support you as wholeheartedly as you want to support her, it's an appalling lack of trust. And it shows a reluctance on your part to be as vulnerable as you expect her to be with you."

I cleared my throat. "She said something like that."

The microwave chimed and she pulled the plate out, then filled a glass with ice water. "Come on, let's sit down."

I followed her back into the living room. She set the plate and glass on the end table next to the couch and motioned for me to sit.

I blinked at the plate's contents.

"You made cinnamon rolls?"

She settled in the nearby armchair, squinting at me in obvious disapproval. "See, you obviously have no idea what's in that kitchen. 'Cause you're not eating. Take a bite, please."

There was no point in mentioning my lack of appetite, not when she looked ready to spring up at a second's notice and cram it in my mouth for me. I took a bite of the roll and affixed a pleasant expression to my face as I chewed.

It tasted like ash and regret.

I settled back against the cushion and closed my eyes. "I miss her so much. I love her so much. I don't know how I went from having everything to nothing in the space of a few weeks."

My mother let out a long breath. "I know, baby. I know how hard this is."

I nodded, not trusting myself to speak.

"Do you know why I gave you your name?" she asked, and I smiled before I opened my eyes to find her watching me.

"Yes. You and Bethany Winston thought it would be cute if your kids were named after your favorite authors—"

"First of all, your name isn't Ezra. Not like your father, or your grandfather."

"I know."

"That was intentional," she said, raising her eyebrows. "And required more than a little wrangling with your father to accomplish."

"I can imagine," I said, having heard my father grouse about it on more than one occasion.

"I wanted you to have the opportunity to set our own course in the world. To find a path outside the one your feet were already planted on when you were born, without the weight of that name and all its expectations," she said. "You should give me credit for knowing you'd eventually need to escape and break away."

I looked at her with sharp interest. "You know I don't want to work at the bank anymore?"

"Long before you did."

"So—"

"I named you for Alice, Walker. Alice Walker, whose characters overcome incredible obstacles to survive in this merciless world. Characters who live in the ugly underbelly of life and still fight for hope and redemption. You're in a hard spot right now, but you're a fighter. Decide what you want, what *you* want, not what's expected. Then fight for it. Start with your first obstacle: You. Then fight your way up from there, son."

CHAPTER TWENTY-FOUR

Leigh

"Well. I didn't expect to find you back here. I've been knocking on your door for fifteen minutes. Hello again, Loretta."

I squinted against the blinding light of the sun, fighting to make Adesola out from my prone position in the lawn chair on my back patio.

From beside me in her matching chair, Loretta gave a disbelieving snicker. "Well, why'd you walk your ass back here, if you didn't think you'd find us?"

I cracked up. The liter of sangria I'd slowly downed over the course of the afternoon only enhanced the hilarity of the moment. "Good one." I fashioned my free hand into a fist and Loretta obliged me by bumping it with her own. "What's up, Adesola? You looking for me?"

Adesola moved out of the sunlight's glare and stepped closer, her tiny fists propped on either side of her hips. Her mouth twisted with displeasure. "So, this is where you've been? What you've been doing?"

"Did you go to work today?" Loretta's head bobbed slightly as she tried to focus on Adesola.

"Yes," Adesola said, with great patience.

"Well, so did we, and we're not at work right now," Loretta said.

"We're adults and free to do what we want, so this is right where we're supposed to be."

Adesola ignored her to focus on me. "Is that a cigarette?"

I looked at the lit cigarette in my right hand. "Why, yes, I believe it is." I giggled, then took a long draw.

"Why?" Adesola sounded bewildered.

"'Cause she's been smoking it," Loretta all but yelled, and we both fell over in helpless laughter. The burning sting of falling ashes on my neck didn't even give me pause.

"She's right," I said, gesturing to Loretta with the cigarette. "I have been smoking it. And I'll tell you a secret: before this one, there were others."

"Several," Loretta slurred, and we cracked up again.

"Leigh. It took you forever to quit. Don't do this."

Loretta struggled up to one elbow and aimed a comical squint at Adesola. "It's Friday. TGIF. *Why* are you trying to kill our buzz? It took me all day and four of these to get her loose," she said, pointing at the half-full pitcher of sangria on the card table between us. "What, you want her sober and crying? Leave. Her. Alone."

Adesola stood watching me, saying nothing.

I took another long draw, held the smoke in my lungs as long as I could, then let it out in a series of perfectly shaped O's. God, this felt good. Why had I ever quit?

"Aww, shit. Here we go," Loretta said as Adesola walked over to the patio set and dragged a chair in our direction. "Time for your lecture."

"I'm not trying to hear it," I said, closing my eyes at Adesola's approach.

From beside me, Adesola said, "May I have some sangria, please?"

I kept my eyes closed. "You'll just drink and keep your mouth shut?"

"I won't push," she said. I just want to know what's going on with you."

"Just this," I said, slurring a little. "What you see." I was vaguely aware of Loretta pouring Adesola a glass of sangria and passing it over me.

"I see you have on your pink shirt," Adesola took a noisy sip. "I thought I saw you out there marching today. God, what's in this?"

"Everything," Loretta said, sounding satisfied. "Usta be a bartender. Guess that's what I am now. Again."

"It's amazing," Adesola said, sounding genuinely impressed. I knew she took her sangria seriously. "Is that cinnamon?"

"Mmmhmm," Loretta said. "Brandy gives it the kick."

"I'll say," she agreed.

The three of us sat in blessed silence for a while. I kept my eyes screwed shut against the threat of reality Adesola represented and focused instead on the faint breeze against the back of my neck.

"It's really admirable, you and Leigh still going out there to march every day," Adesola said. "I'm proud of you both."

"Yeah, the twenty or so of us that are left," Loretta sniffed. "While everyone else falls for Visage's fake-ass apology tour. You see that sickening commercial?"

"I did," Adesola said. "But I'm sure no one believes it."

"Everyone's falling for it hook, line, and sinker," Loretta said, getting louder, "with the damn 'community advisory board' they're talking about starting. Who do they think they're fooling?"

"I heard about that," Adesola said, sounding despairing.

"Bullshit," Loretta said. "That's just, 'Let's pretend to be friends, I'll look you in the eye while I screw you from behind.'"

"That's what it amounts to," Adesola said.

"Visage is not going anywhere," Loretta said, and I heard her pouring another glass of sangria. "We did all of this for nothing."

"Don't say that." Adesola's hand rested on my shoulder. "It's not over yet, and we're not past the window where they can withdraw from the sale. It's not over. We just gotta have faith."

"Awww, listen to you. You sound like one of those inspirational posters at work. It's over," Loretta said, slurping. "I'm going to make more sangria." I heard the sound of the lawn chair scraping against the ground, followed by Loretta's footsteps and the screen door to the house banging closed.

The weight of Adesola's hand left my shoulder.

"What?" I asked, from behind the darkness of my lids. "What is it you just have to say?"

She was quiet for a long time. "I just wanted to ask if you'd spoken to Walker," she finally said.

I pulled my legs into my chest and hugged them. "No."

"You think you guys will talk soon?"

"No."

"Okay." Adesola let out a long breath. "But he's been trying to reach you?"

All too easily, the memory of Walker standing in my bedroom watching me walk away bloomed to life, and my breath snagged in my chest. "He left *me*, Adesola. He needed time to think. And now, so do I. I'm not waiting around for Walker Leffersbee."

"This has been a really bad week for you. I don't blame you for being in this state."

"Is that why you came? To remind me?"

"No, I ..." She trailed off. "I wanted to remind you that you're the same bad bitch you've always been. You're still The General, even if it feels like life has you retreating at the moment."

"Thanks for the reminder."

"Walker loves you, Leigh. That hasn't changed because he's not here."

I opened my eyes and found Adesola watching me with sad eyes.

"Thanks for coming by." I give her the best smile I could summon in my brandy-addled state. "Now, it's time for you to go."

LOUD BANGING BROUGHT me out from under my comforter the next morning.

"Who is it?" I yelled from under my pillow, unwilling to face the unrelenting sunlight. It was Saturday, I didn't have work and there was no escaping the sharp edge of my hangover. Whoever was waiting for me on the other side of the door could kiss my ass.

The answer was more hammering.

"Whoever that is, I'm gonna kill them." I cracked open one eye, straining to peer at the digital clock at my bedside.

1:38 p.m.

Huh. Later than I thought.

Well, still. This was highly annoying.

Pushing back the covers required herculean effort. Finding my robe and stumbling down the stairs called for even more heroic measures, enough that I was plotting a profanity-laced attack on my surprise visitor.

Unless it was Walker. Walker would only get cold silence and the door slammed in his face.

I hope it's Walker.

I wrenched open the door and stared at the older man standing on my porch. His hands were shoved into the pockets of weathered jeans, his face shadowed by an ancient Mets hat. The after-effects of one too many glasses of sangria slowed my mental processing time, but when the recognition hit, I about fell over.

"*Dad*?"

Shrewd blue eyes rose and met mine. "You look like shit. 'Bout what I expected."

I stared. "What are ... how ... Dad?"

He shifted his weight back on his heels, saying nothing as he ran a narrow glance over me.

"How did you get here?"

"Flew into Knoxville not too long ago." He pinched the end of his nose in the way that always signaled his irritation or discomfort. "We just gonna stand here and look at each other?"

I blinked. "Uh. No. I—" I gestured weakly, shoving the tangled snarls of hair back from my face. I still hadn't recovered from the shock of seeing him standing on my porch. I'd lived here six years, and he'd never once come with my mother to visit. I'd have sooner expected the horsemen of the apocalypse to come blazing past the horizon. But here he was, looking expectantly at me, as if we'd ever had more than ten words to say to each other.

"Can't even bring yourself to invite me in." His tongue poked around the inside of his cheek. He'd attempted a jocular tone, but I caught the edge underneath.

"No, it's not like that." But my words rang false and hollow as we regarded each other with all the warmth of strangers. I wasn't sure what the hell he was doing here, but I wasn't going to reassure him or pretend he wasn't the architect of my most deep-rooted pain. All of his betrayals, big and small, had marked my heart with dense, impenetrable scar tissue.

I didn't hate him. I guess that was something.

"They got decent coffee in this godforsaken town?"

"Yeah," I said, grateful for the change of topic and something concrete I could respond to. "There's a place I think you'd like. I'll grab my shoes and we can go."

He gave a single nod, then headed back to the rental car in the driveway.

The ride to Daisy's Nut House was painfully awkward. We chatted about the specs of his rental for a total of a minute ("Best thing to come out of Detroit in a while") before he finally turned on the radio and freed us from the burden of small talk.

Silence persisted even as we sat across from each other in a booth by a window. I started in on one of the two donuts I'd selected, washing it down with a gulp of coffee. He ignored his coffee and donuts, casting anxious glances out the window as the fingertips of his right hand alternated between drumming the table and circling his thumb.

"Sweetheart." He gestured to the waitress approaching with a carafe of coffee we didn't need. "Can I trouble you for a minute?"

He flashed what I'd always thought of as his "wolf" smile, the wide toothy one he always put to work while closing in on his desired prey. Those sharp blue eyes glinted up at her under shaggy salt and pepper brows, and his mouth twitched as if laughing at a shared secret.

The waitress dimpled.

"I know there's rules against smoking inside most places nowadays," he began. He colored his voice with enough "aww, shucks" that the waitress actually looked sympathetic as he made his pitch. "I already get an earful about quitting as it is. But I'm sitting right next to a window. I've been on a flight all day and I only need one ..."

A familiar routine ensued.

She dutifully recited the law. He charmed her past her protestations. Three minutes later, he was drawing on his lit cigarette, exhaling out the open window as promised.

"Haven't lost your touch, I see." My stomach twisted in derision.

"Jesus. Ten minutes in, already I fucked up."

"Just saying." I pushed the dish of donuts away.

"Give me a break, kid. I flew all this way to see about you."

I raised a disbelieving brow. "Does Ma know you're here?"

That got a rusty laugh out of him. "What, you need her here to referee?"

"I've never needed that."

"Nah, you wouldn't." Another gravelly laugh as he tapped ash into the saucer of his coffee cup. "You always come out swinging. It's one of the things I always liked about you."

"I'm not one of your women. You can't charm me."

He blew a long stream of smoke out the window. "I get it. My old man was a piece of shit too. I hated him."

I gaped at him, too preoccupied with this stunning admission to make any token protests. "You hated Grandpa?"

He let out a mirthless laugh. "He was a rotten sonofabitch. Mean drunk, so he never held onto a job. Always chasing some skirt and dragging me along, then I got the black eye if I let it slip to your grandmother. I swore I'd never be like him."

I sat back and stared at him, stunned. I'd never heard him say anything like that about my grandfather. Then again, he rarely talked about his childhood. And he and I rarely talked at all since our communication always gave way to mutual rancor.

"Your mother hated him, too," he said, taking another drag. "It's why you and your sister only saw them on holidays."

"So, Grandpa was like you," I said, piecing it together. "And then you—"

"Hold on now, I'm not as bad as he was." He looked highly offended. "I mean, I've done my shit, but I've always been a good provider. All of you always had a roof over your head. And I never drank."

"But you got the womanizing down."

"It'd be nice if just once, *just once*, you surprised me and didn't throw that shit in my face. I know you've taken it upon yourself to punish me on your mother's behalf."

"Someone had to. She would never hold you accountable."

He waved that away, his scowl deepening. "When do I get out of your jail?"

"You slept with my high school geography teacher."

He gave a rough exhale, expelling twin plumes of smoke. "Christ on a stick. I can't take it back! Do you get that? I can't take it back."

The angry defiance, his inability to acknowledge, just once what he'd done, set my teeth on edge. He was Gio, standing in my sister's backyard and complaining about what he couldn't undo, heedless of all that was already broken because of him.

"How can you expect forgiveness when you won't even admit to what you've done or acknowledge the damage you've caused? I'm supposed to pretend nothing ever happened? Are you even sorry?" Anger coalesced to ignite a hot, searing fire in my chest. I tensed for the familiar combat, forgetting we were in an emptied restaurant and not in the familiar battleground of my parents' kitchen.

He stabbed out the cigarette and folded his arms. "Hate me all you want, but at some point you gotta look in the mirror and tell the ugly truth. If you can't see how much like me you are, you're lying to yourself."

I recoiled at that. "I've never—"

"You got the same lousy temper. Can't let go of a grudge." He ticked items off with his fingers. "Same compulsions. You'd give an eyetooth for a pull of this right now," he said, holding up the stub of his cigarette and nodding at my twitchy fingers. "You swore you'd never hook up with a lowlife like me or make your mother's mistakes." His brows raised as he gave a satisfied smirk. "And what'd you go and do?"

Damn it.

I deflated, feeling hammered by each indictment. Bad enough that all those things were true, but my father's self-satisfied grin stoked a growing flare of resentment.

"I might be all those things, that's true. But I didn't lie to Ma and betray her all those years. I didn't crush her self-esteem. That was you. All you."

He scowled, drumming his fingers on the table. "I made my peace with your mother. We have an understanding now. You don't know what goes on in a marriage."

"What does that even mean? 'An understanding?' You sure as hell don't have an understanding with me and Lucia. Our childhood was fucked up, you know that? You know what it was like having everyone in school and the neighborhood know what you'd been up to? Having to watch Ma cry all the time? Living with one of our aunts every time Ma decided to try to teach you a lesson? A lesson you never learned, by the way."

I didn't realize I was yelling, a napkin clenched in my fist, until the waitress standing at my elbow cleared her throat.

"Refill?" Her face was frozen in a grimace.

"No, thank you," I said, taking a deep breath.

Wordlessly, my father nudged his cup to the end of the table and nodded.

We sat in silence as the waitress beat a hasty retreat. I took another deep breath, trying to calm down. Why did I let him do this to me?

"See?" Dad's grin was sly as he raised his coffee mug to toast me. "Same temper."

"Bye, Dad." I slid to the end of the booth. "I don't know what you came here for, but I'm not sitting here for you to gaslight me into making your point. You wasted your airfare and my time."

"How you gonna get back?"

"I'll walk," I snapped, slinging my purse over my shoulder as I stood up. His hand grabbed my arm and stopped me.

"I'm sorry, okay? I'm sorry for all that stuff."

I'm tired, I thought. Tired of trying to convict him of all the pain he'd so selfishly meted out to our family and never acknowledged.

On the heels of that thought, another new voice piped up: *But aren't you tired of doing the same thing with him, over and over again?*

I looked down at my father. "Why are you here, Dad? What do you want from me?"

Behind the counter, the waitress watched us with ill-concealed fascination, her eyes huge as she pretended to wipe down the counter.

My father held up his hands as if in surrender. He suddenly looked as weary as I felt. "I just wanna talk. That's all. Sit down. Please."

I tossed my purse down and balanced at the very edge of the booth, ready to leave again if need be. "So talk."

"I hate me, too, you know."

"I don't hate you, Dad." *But I'd never be stupid enough to trust you again.*

He waved that away. "I fucked up, okay? I always hated that part of me that didn't know how to walk the straight and narrow for you and your sister. And your mother. I know it made for hard times. I wish it never happened."

"That's the first time you've ever attempted anything resembling an apology," I acknowledged. "But ..." I shook my head at the inadequacy of his words, remembering the crippling uncertainty of those early years.

His gaze went to his hands on the table as he laced and unlaced his lanky fingers. "Like I said. I can't take it back," he said, his voice heavy with finality. "I can't change it. But this, the ways things are with me and you? That I'd like to change. Plus, I want to help you."

"Help me? How?" I asked, not bothering to hide my disbelief. "All of a sudden you want to reconcile the past and help me. So much so you fly to Green Valley for the first time ever? How'd I get so lucky?"

We stared at each other for long, charged moment.

Then he surprised me by laughing.

"Goddamn if your grandmother wasn't right. She always said I'd catch it from my own kids for being such a badass when I was growing up. And here I am, sitting across from *myself*. You're not gonna give me an inch, are you, Lee-Lee?"

"Don't call me that," I said irritably. "And you don't deserve an inch."

He acknowledged that with a half shrug. "True. But we both know you could use the help. You've got yourself in a bad situation with that hospital—"

"How do you know about that?"

"Your sister, she talks to your mother. It works its way to me. Now, listen. You may not remember, but I dealt with the same kind of thing when I was working that mechanic gig at the plant—"

"I remember. You led the protests, it went on for weeks."

His face cleared in obvious surprise. "You remember that? You weren't all that old, probably still in grade school."

"No, I remember. It made things better for everyone they hired afterwards. It didn't make things alright for you, though. You lost your job in the end," I said, remembering how worried and anxious my parents had been. Things had been tight, and my mother had explained to Cia and me that we'd need to make sacrifices to make ends meet. But she'd always spoken of our father's stand with glowing pride and quiet conviction.

I'd been proud of him, too. For a time.

"It was brave." I glanced up in time to see him shift uncomfortably.

He wouldn't meet my eyes. His throat worked. "Yeah, well. That bravery cost me a lot in the short-term. I'd do it again, though."

"It's probably what put a fire under my ass to even try to pull this off. And I'm about to go out the same way."

"Yes, you are," he agreed, so quickly that I felt a twinge of alarm. "They try to bargain with you, get you alone and cut a side deal yet?"

"Yeah."

"Well, then, it's coming," he said. He gaze slid in the waitress's direction as he pulled the pack of cigarettes from his breast pocket and tapped it until one came out. "They're about to fire your ass. Gotta cut the head off the snake."

"You told the waitress you only needed one cigarette."

He scoffed. "She knew that was a lie."

I shook my head.

"Companies like that, usually they're betting you'll fold under the financial pressure. You know, give in when the mortgage gets more than a month behind. But you don't have that problem," he said, lighting the cigarette and taking a long pull.

"Why's that? I do have rent, you know—"

"Because I'm gonna back you," he said, exhaling out the window. "And I'm gonna help you with whatever you need while you see this through to the end. I've got money saved up. I'll make sure you don't miss a step. This fight you picked, it's important. It's the principle of the thing, you know?"

"I have money," I said absently, staring at him in open bewilderment. What kind of crackpot morals or backward-ass creed let him cheat on my mother without a second thought but go balls to the wall over corporate wrongdoing?

"You ain't got to understand it," he said, and I wondered if he'd somehow read my thoughts while he blew smoke contentedly out the window. "Or me. Bottom line is, I'm your dad. And I've got your back."

CHAPTER TWENTY-FIVE

Leigh

"Hell of a day." My father groaned as he loaded his overnight bag into the trunk of his rental. "My feet are killing me. Glad I'll be sitting down on that flight."

I scowled at him in the growing darkness, swatting at the gathering cloud of insects. "You're hoarse. I told you to quit the protest hours ago." I deposited a jug of cider and bag of donuts from Daisy's for my mother next to his duffel bag, then stood back to study him.

It was awkward, *we* were awkward, even after spending almost two days together. After we'd left the diner the previous day, I'd surprised myself by offering up my guest room to spare him a drive back to his hotel in Knoxville. He'd taken me up on it, and we'd spent the night on either ends of my couch in stark silence, both of us having exhausted our quota of words, watching vintage episodes of *The Twilight Zone*. He'd surprised me that morning by announcing he planned to join me marching at the hospital.

"You plan on changing that shirt before you board the plane? They might not let you on with that, uh, language. I did offer you a pink shirt."

He looked down at his T-shirt, pulling the hem away as if examining the printed words for the first time: *These fuckers are going down.*

"I like my shirt. It's multi-purpose. Works in a lot of different situations. In a march. When your mother's sisters come over."

"Jesus, Dad."

He gave a tired shrug, rocking on his heels as he folded his arms. "We are what we are. And spare me, you're the last one to be delivering sermons. I've heard your mouth. And to think you've been hanging out with clergy at work."

"Alright, alright." I folded my arms, then realized I'd unconsciously mirrored his stance. We'd never been good at small talk, and neither of us knew how to broach this goodbye. For once, I missed my mother's anxious chatter.

"Remember what we talked about." Dad pursed his lips. "Admit to nothing. They hint at suing your ass, shut up in a hurry. Call the number on that card I gave you. Lou at Local 743. His kid's a lawyer and he owes me big. He knows you might be calling."

I bit at the inside of my lip. All of this was ... strange. I didn't know how to reconcile this new side of my father, or the conflicting emotions his visit aroused.

"Dad—"

"Flag's up on your mailbox. It's Sunday. You haven't checked your mail since Saturday?" He ambled up to the porch, slower than usual on his tired feet, and pulled the mailbox open. I joined him, using the well of light from the porch to peer at the face of the single envelope he held.

"No postage. Wasn't mailed," my father observed, his brows going up. "You know who might have hand-delivered this?"

"Yeah," I said, my throat going dry. I recognized the aggressive slant of the letters in my name.

He sent me a questioning glance. I hesitated, unsure if I wanted to open this can of worms. After all, we'd managed to survive over twenty-four hours together. He'd made a big effort to demonstrate his support of my protest and even copped to his wrongdoing in the past. Inviting his opinion about the current mess with Walker could strain our fragile cease-fire.

"It's that young man, isn't it? Walker?"

I looked up, surprised, and found his gaze steady on mine. "Uh—"

"Don't bother lying. You don't want to be any more like me, not if you can help it," he said with a dry laugh. "I figured something was up. Why haven't I seen or heard from him since I've been here? He struck me as a respectful young man who had serious intentions." He held the letter out.

I took the letter, lowering it to my side. "Things are different now. I don't think we're together anymore."

"How is it you don't know?"

I hesitated. "You really want to get into this?"

"I do. Tell me."

For some reason, I did. My father and I sat on the steps, bathed in the wan illumination from the porch light as I recounted all that had happened since we'd returned from Fairlane.

He astonished me by laughing when I was done.

"What's funny about this?" I demanded as he chortled, his forehead bouncing against the steeple of his thumb and forefinger.

"Many things. Starting with the fact this man wants to protect you from what, his genes, and what they might do to children you don't even have?"

"I knew I shouldn't have told you—"

"No, listen," he said, still choking on his laughter. "Does he have any idea of all the crazy that's in *you*? In *your* genes? Even after he met all of us back home and we dragged him into our madhouse? He's worried about what *he* might contribute?"

For the first time since Walker left, I cracked a smile.

"Leigh," my father said conspiratorially, and I think we both were shocked when he laid a calloused hand on my arm. "Your nephew, your sister's oldest ... I caught him chewing on the toilet brush. Makes me wonder if he's eating out of the toilet."

I reared back, torn between shock and laughter. "Dad, don't say that, that's not funny. Cia would kill you."

"If it's not funny, why are laughing? Don't tell me you don't think, with all that boy's fascination with the toilet—"

The memory of nephew gnawing on the toilet brush surfaced and we whooped together as darkness fell.

My father pushed to his feet, his stiff movements betraying his fatigue and arthritis. *He's gotten older,* I realized with a mild bolt of shock. Somehow, with all the fighting and avoidance, I hadn't noticed.

"You working tomorrow?" I followed as he cut a path back to the rental car.

"You think cars in Jersey don't need fixing anymore, just 'cause I was here with you all weekend?"

"I guess not," I said, suppressing a grin. It was the standard line he'd given Cia and me when we were kids.

"Of course I'm working tomorrow." He retrieved a key ring from his pocket, engaged the power locks on the car. "That guy, Walker, he isn't me. Not this time. Be patient with him," he said, nodding at the letter in my hand. "It's misguided, what he's done, but it's because he's a better man than I ever was." He shrugged his shoulders, his gaze downcast. "I have a lot of respect for what he did, teaching Gio to shut the fuck up for once. Maybe I'd have turned out better if someone had done that for me when I was young and thought I knew everything."

He'd opened the car door and eased one leg in the footwell when the question escaped me, floating over us in the chilly spring air.

"Why'd you take his side, then, Gio's? When I left him for cheating on me. If you agree with what Walker did."

He went still, one half of his body still in the car, the other foot anchored on the pavement. The silence was so complete and profound, the chorus of crickets and katydids seemed deafening.

I held still, waiting for the answer. Waiting for an explanation, a rationalization for the inexplicable. But he didn't respond, only tucked himself fully in the car. The door closed with a soft *thunk*.

You were hoping for too much, I chided myself as the engine of the car turned over. Two days of civil conversation did not a rehabilitated relationship make.

He put the car in gear and reversed a few inches down the driveway before abruptly braking. The car window rolled down.

I edged closer, curious.

"I looked at him and saw me." His gaze never left the rearview mirror. "I saw me and my mistakes. Doesn't make it right, and it's not like I condoned what he did. But ... that's what happened."

With no further comment, the car continued to back down the driveway.

And then he was gone.

~

MY FATHER'S WORDS, and the significance of his visit, stayed with me as I attempted to unwind. As I soaked my aching muscles in the tub, I reflected that it felt like a lifetime had passed over the last day.

And now, there was finally word from Walker. Not that I was in a hurry to read it or anything.

But the letter taunted me all night from its perch on the kitchen table. *Open me*, it whispered when I slipped into the kitchen for a snack after my bath. *Read me*, it called as I sat watching television trying not to remember better times with Walker on that very couch. I resisted its lure until I was in bed, under the covers with the light off.

Then curiosity finally won out.

"Okay, fine," I said out loud, throwing back the covers and stalking into the kitchen to snatch the letter up before climbing back in bed. My hands shook slightly as I ran a finger along the adhesive seal, and my heart assumed a galloping rate when the folded pages fell in my lap.

Whatever it is, you can handle it. It may hurt, but you will handle it.

Leigh,

It's so hard being apart from you, sometimes I ask myself why I ever left. So I figure it can't hurt to let you in on my thinking, though I know I'm probably the last person you want to hear from right now.

I always knew I wanted children. I looked forward to the day when I, like my father and grandfather before me, would teach my child how to bait a hook. I've anticipated sharing Pops's oft-recited treatise on why Motown is the best era of music, and Stevie Wonder is the best musician of all time. But I've always been frightened for my children, even now, before they even exist. I can't wait to teach my children what a privilege it is to be Black, but I know I'll also need to teach them to survive in a world where many may treat them unfairly, or worse, for simply having black skin. Like my father and grandfather before me, I know I'd do my very best to protect them from all that. But this heart condition is a whole other thing. What if I can't protect them from that? What if they can't be protected from losing their dad prematurely? Please understand. I didn't leave because I don't want to be with you. I love you, madly. I left because I want the best for you. I want you to have the children you've dreamed of. I won't stand in the way of that, even if you think it won't matter later. I love you enough to want you to have all your dreams. Even if they can't include me.

Walker

CHAPTER TWENTY-SIX

Walker

"You know, I think she can read an email just as easily as she'd read a handwritten letter."

Tavia offered her unsolicited two cents as she lounged on my couch, her head on the armrest, her feet stretched across the cushions. She was completely dressed down in shorts and a Notorious RBG T-shirt. The long curly wig she favored was gone, revealing her short, tightly curled afro.

The present scene wasn't what I would have imagined for either of us a mere month ago. But here she was, for the second time. She'd managed to honor all the terms of our truce so far.

That was something, for her.

"I don't recall ever asking your opinion." I folded the pages of my letter and slid them into an already addressed envelope. "You're here to drop this off just like the last time. Nothing more, nothing less. It better still be sealed when it gets to her."

"I've got better things to do than read your stupid love letters anyway," she sniffed, her head lolling on the armrest as she turned down the volume on the TV. "You seem like you're getting better. Feeling stronger."

I considered that as I sealed the back of the envelope and followed it with a strip of industrial tape. "I am. Different, in a good way."

"You know you still can't drive," she said, and it sounded accusatory somehow.

I looked back. She'd muted the TV and was watching me, biting her lip in earnest. Moments like this, when I remembered how she and Zora shared the same affectations, I especially wished things were easier with Tavia.

"Who said anything about driving? I'm quite aware that I'm not ready for that yet."

"Tried it, didn't you," she said, a smile breaking across her face, and I laughed.

"Yeah. I snuck Miles's car keys while he was using the bathroom. Just wanted to see if I could make it around the parking lot." I shook my head. "It's been three weeks since the surgery, and my chest muscles still remember being sawed through. Man."

She sat up, running a hand over her hair. "If you're feeling that trapped and isolated, why don't you come home? I swear Mama must be cutting side deals with Jesus by now to get you back in her clutches. Daddy tries to act like he knows you've got it under control, but he interrogates anyone who's been to see you in between his visits."

"And to think that I'm missing out on all that."

"I like that you can't drive," she said quietly. "It's nice to feel needed. Also, you're the only one talking to me right now."

I rose from the desk and walked over to the couch to hand her the envelope. "Sounds like something to work on, then."

"Why aren't you mad at me?" She snatched the envelope from my hand. "After all, you're the one I supposedly owe an apology to."

"Is that what you've been told?"

"Over and over again. I just asked the doctor a question, Walker. The vote was coming up—"

"You're three seconds from being thrown out."

"Right, right. No business talk. Sorry."

I lowered myself at the end of the couch, and she scrambled to move her feet. "Tavia, you and I have a long way to go as brother and sister. I can't speak for everyone else, but I'm willing to bet you've got inroads to make with the rest of the family too."

"Even Nick won't speak to me."

"Nick's usually pretty neutral."

"Ever since that day in the ER, he gives me that dry-ass smile with no teeth," she said. She turned, wearing such a perfect imitation of Nick's frigid "polite" smile that I cracked up.

"Like I said, you've got work to do."

"You can't put in a good word for me?"

I shook my head. "I'm over here in purgatory. Leigh may never speak to me again. This heart surgery and the recovery will seem like a walk in the park if I lose her. I've gotta focus all of my effort into fixing that somehow, and it's probably too late. It's time for you to figure out your own shit. Deal with the consequences of your behavior."

Silence.

"Did you just say 'shit?'" Her eyes were huge in her head.

I gave a humorless chuckle. "Yeah, I did."

"Mr. Perfect cusses now?"

"Don't call me that."

"What? Isn't that why you're over here and not with her? Because you can't accept that you might be not perfect?"

That stung. "That's an oversimplification. I'm here because—"

"Yes?"

"Because I didn't want to saddle her with a future that included me getting sick or dying on her or passing on this heart condition to our kids."

"Screw her, then," Tavia said, her face tightening. "If she makes you feel inferior for something you can't control, she doesn't deserve you."

"Don't talk that way about her, and that's not—"

"No, fuck her," Tavia said heatedly. "Anyone who would blink twice because of your heart stuff and not see what a wonderful person you are—"

"She said she didn't care about my diagnosis. She said that." I closed my eyes, remembering Leigh's stricken expression, how her eyes had grown dark with pain right before she left me alone in her bedroom. "She said all she wanted was me."

"Exactly," Tavia said, sounding smug. I opened my eyes to find her smirking at me. "That's what I heard through the grapevine."

"'The grapevine' must mean Mama since no one else is speaking to you."

"Yeah. And Miles. Leigh told you she didn't care, and you still walked away from her. After all she'd been through with her ex, she trusted you. And you left her."

That was a pretty damning summary. "I wasn't in the right head space."

"I know. So, what's stopping you now?"

"She stopped taking my calls. I won't have the results of the genetic testing back for several weeks and I'm feeling my way through the dark here. That's why I'm writing the letters. I just want her to know where I am mentally, that I'm getting myself together so I can beg for another chance."

She sucked her teeth. "Then you still don't get the lesson, Walker. You're still not ready to let her love you the way you love her, not if you still think you need to 'get yourself together.' It has nothing to do with the results of that genetic test, whatever they are. We're not friends, me and Leigh. But I respect her, and I know she wouldn't appreciate being treated like some damsel that needs to be rescued or protected from life."

"That's true."

"Well, okay," Tavia said, sounding exasperated. "Then just go to her. Enough with the letters."

"Just drop it off, okay?"

"Fine." She stood with a huff. "I'll leave you alone. What's that mountain of papers by the printer, your manifesto? Do you need me to deliver that anywhere before you drive yourself off a cliff?"

"Goodbye, Tavia."

"Only you have the power to end this, Walker," she said, turning back to me with the doorknob in her hand. "For god's sake, put us all out of our misery."

~

"LOOKING BETTER," Pops said with a satisfied grunt. He deftly shuffled a deck of cards and dealt to us both. "You're not sleeping through those judge shows all day anymore."

I laughed. "I never did that. I think you're confusing your midafternoon routine with mine."

"Watch yourself." He laughed. "I'll have you know, I'm far too young and spry to be sleeping through *Judge Judy*. I'm over here trying to get you up to *my* speed."

"Alright, alright, playboy. Listen." I waited until Pops was done sliding cards across the table and his eyes were back on mine before I continued. "You're right, you're still young and spry. Now, I haven't asked what's been going on with the bank and Consolidated."

"No, you haven't. It's not anything you need to be bothered about while you're recuperating anyway. I'm not letting anyone make any moves until you're up and better."

Taking a deep breath, I exhaled the words I'd alternatively longed for and feared for so many years. "Pops. I'm done with bank."

He sat back and studied me, saying nothing. He interlaced his hands on the table, his cards apparently forgotten for the moment.

"It's not the right fit for me. I don't know that it ever has been. I've always considered it my responsibility to preserve what you built. But it's not meant to be my life's work. I'll throw my support behind you with this Consolidated thing, and you know you can always count on me. But the bank can't be my responsibility anymore."

"Fine," Pops said. A tiny smile played around his lips.

I stared. "That's all you're going to say?"

"Fine," he repeated. "I hear you, and I understand. It's not a complete surprise. I'm proud of you for speaking up, saying what was on your mind."

Relief and guilt weighted my conscience in equal measure. "So ... that's it?"

"That's all it takes, Walker," he said. "You know your mind. If there's anything these last few weeks have taught us, it's that life is short. I thank God every day that you're still with us, and I don't begrudge you wanting to chase your passion. Hell, I encourage it. It's what I did when I was a young man. I can't wait to see what *you* build. Do it, grandson. Start building your future."

I let out the breath I hadn't even realized I was holding. "Thanks, Pops."

"You need anything, any startup money?"

"No, I've got plenty of money," I said. When I gave him an estimate of the capital I had on hand, he blinked.

"Flipping houses pays a lot better than I thought," he said, looking taken aback.

"That and careful investment all these years, but yeah. I'm ready to roll this out on a larger stage. It's time. I've got a plan. My attorney is drawing up the paperwork and Miles and I are putting out feelers."

"Want me to take a look anything?"

"No, sir. Not right now. I'm still laying the groundwork for a few things."

He nodded quietly, his dark eyes prying into mine from under his heavy gray brows. "You look relieved. Probably a load off, getting that out."

"Yes."

"When are you gonna get Leigh back so you can be happy? So you can go home?"

"Trying to figure that out. I made such a colossal mess of everything. I think it's going to take time."

"Last thing you need is more time in this situation, youngblood. You need to *act*."

"You hear anything from her?" I asked, unable to suppress the eager note from my voice. Leigh's silence was killing me. I was desperate for any news, any update, anything.

Pops studied me from under hooded eyes. His smile was wry. "I'm not telling you anything, but I'll gladly give you a ride over there if you want. We can leave right now."

Yes. Let's go. Right now.

"Not just yet, Pops," I said, feeling the pulse in my neck break into a syncopated rhythm.

What if she turned me away?

"Fine," he muttered, picking up his cards and scowling down at them. "But the longer you wait, the harder it'll be."

CHAPTER TWENTY-SEVEN

Leigh

"Heads up, Leigh," Mark, the security guard, spoke out of the corner of his mouth as I approached. His gaze darted over his shoulder before returning to mine.

I slowed, pausing in the act of stuffing my pink protest T-shirt in my oversized purse as I noted the knot of officious suits in the lobby. Their eyes were trained on me and my approach. A lone security guard stood with them, his hand resting on his belt. "Oh. Oh no," I breathed.

Mark nodded. "Yep."

Courage, dear heart.

"Ms. D'Alessandro." The eagle-eyed crisis manager strode forward to meet me as I emerged from the vestibule. I resisted the urge to wipe my clammy hands on my scrub bottoms and met her hard gaze. *She's enjoying this*, I thought, taking in the satisfied purse of her mouth and the triumphant glitter in her eyes.

I would not give her the satisfaction of backing down or breaking down.

"Would you come with us, please?" She gestured to the suits behind her. "We'd like to have a word with you."

"Wow, an entourage. I feel special." I kept the fear off my face. "Lead the way."

We all crowded into an elevator and rode it to the professional building, where I once again found myself seated across a huge glass table from ever more suits.

"Ms. D'Alessandro." One of the staff lawyers sifted through a pile of papers before meeting my eyes again.

"Leigh."

"Fine, Leigh," she said, giving me a smile that held little warmth. "It's admirable, really, what you've accomplished up until now. You did engineer this little uprising, did you not?" She waited expectantly, her expression pleasant.

My gaze flicked over to the security guard who'd accompanied us upstairs. He'd posted himself right outside the glass door, looking bored but ready for whatever task befell him.

Like marching my ass outside after they fired me.

My father's instructions came back to me. *Admit nothing. Shut up in a hurry.*

I met the lawyer's expression with my own sugar-sweet grin, folding my hands in front of me as the silence thickened.

Her smile slipped a bit. "I hope you realize we are fully within our rights to bring charges against you. Stealing documents, disclosing sensitive information—"

"Get to the punchline." I gave myself major credit for holding her gaze and straightening my spine even as anxiety roiled in my guts. "You intend to terminate my job today. Isn't that why he's here?" I nodded in the security guard's direction. "And why she's here." I flicked a glance toward the kind, soft-spoken HR rep assigned to our unit. "This is just some last-minute information-gathering attempt, right? Well, I have nothing to say. So, you might as well give me my box now."

"We're not giving you anything," the lawyer said crisply, all pretense of friendliness gone now. "Not a box, and certainly not a chance to go back to your workstation and pilfer more privileged materials. We'll mail your belongings to you."

"Works for me." I pushed back from the table and stood. "Let's get the perp walk over with, then."

I kept my shoulders back and my head high during the entire guard-accompanied march to my car. But the longer I sat in the ominous quiet of the car, gripping the steering wheel for dear life, the closer I came to crying. When my phone rang, I immediately answered it, grateful for the distraction.

"They walk you to your car like a criminal too? With a guard, like you might bust out some kung fu moves?" Loretta's indignant voice flooded my car speakers.

I let out a pained sigh, casting a brief glance at the folder on my passenger seat. Its contents detailed the terms of my termination. "Yeah. Loretta, I'm so sorry about all this. I never meant for you to lose your job."

"It's alright," she said, but I heard the melancholy in her voice. "I've been at that place over twenty years. It hurt, a lot, to see it in the rearview mirror this morning and know I'd never be going back. But I'd rather leave it now than see it become an ugly version of what it used to be."

"Yeah," I said, but I was thinking of all of my kids. Wondering who would take my place to help them. Probably no one, and that was heartbreaking. "I knew this was a likely outcome. I just didn't expect it to hurt so badly."

"Same," Loretta said on a noisy exhale, and I wanted a cigarette more than I wanted my next breath as I listened to her puff away. "Shit stings, doesn't it?"

"It does. I don't think I fully understood how much that place meant to me until I got put out like garbage at the curb. Listen, I'm going to help you find another job, I will."

"I got me, alright? I knew the risk I was taking when I gave you those documents. I just didn't know they were tracking everything that was scanned, copied, or faxed," she said on a strangled laugh. "But I'd do it again. They're some shady assholes, you know?"

Shady assholes who won, I thought.

"Listen, we'll get together and have drinks again," Loretta said. "Several times if need be. Hell, it's not like we got to go to work, right?"

"Right. Talk to you soon," I said weakly before we disconnected. It was beyond disconcerting to realize I didn't know what would come next. I didn't know where I'd find another job or even what to do with myself when I woke up the next morning.

My phone dinged with a text. My eyes got big when I saw the sender.

You alright, kid?

I stared at the phone, shaking my head at the cataclysmic turn of events. Maybe the earth really was flat. It seemed everything I knew had been turned on its head.

I texted back with numb fingers. *I'm alright, Dad. Just got fired. Kept my mouth shut.*

His response was immediate. *Good girl. Good for you. The basement's finished. I can move my shit to the garage if you need to move back home.*

I let out disbelieving laugh. *Let's hope it doesn't come to that,* I sent back. But honestly, it was impossible to rule anything out.

"Oh hell no. Not 1980s Whitney Houston." Adesola groaned as she pushed through the back door to my kitchen, her hands full of paper bags. "Turn that shit off, Leigh. We're trying to get it turned up and lift your spirits. Put on something with a decent bass line, for god's sake."

"Shut up," I said from my perch on the kitchen counter where I was coring avocados. "It's not going to kill you to listen to a little Whitney."

"I remember this song," Zora said, trailing behind Adesola with more bags in hand. "My parents loved Whitney when I was a kid. *Didn't we almost have it all?*" Zora sang along with Whitney, sounding like a tortured cat.

Adesola set her bags down on my kitchen table and pointedly raised an eyebrow at Zora, who at that point was making discordant vocal runs while twisting her hand through the air à la Mariah Carey. "If you weren't in the dumps before, I'm sure you are now."

"Fine, fine," I said, changing the song on my iPhone until P!nk's voice blasted through the nearby Bluetooth speaker.

"Much better," Adesola said, moving to the fridge to put groceries away. "That's the vibe we're looking for here. So, you've had some employment and relationship setbacks. You're still a rock star. God, your fridge should not be this empty. Since when do you not have food?"

"Since my brother is an idiot," Zora answered. "You know, as happy as

I was that you two got together, I always worried about this moment," she said, stretching to reach one of my overhead cabinets.

"What moment?"

"The moment when you and Walker might be at odds and I'd feel like I was in the middle."

I studied her as I sliced another avocado open. "Do you feel like you're in the middle?"

"Careful," Adesola singsonged under her breath to Zora, and I threw her a glare.

"I heard that," I said.

Adesola shrugged. "Your temper is guillotine sharp lately. I'm just trying to keep her safe. She's carrying innocent lives, you know?"

I laughed despite myself. "Is that going to be her get out of jail card for the next however many months?"

"Yes," Zora yelled as she pulled down my quesadilla maker. "Yes, it is. I'm terrified and completely inept, yet I'm bringing two lives into the world, God willing. You should have mercy on me."

"Do you really feel like you're in the middle of all this, between me and Walker?" I asked, hacking the knife lengthwise into the avocado core.

"It's a weird position to be in," Zora said, her eyes riveted on the knife in my hand as she washed the removable hot plates to the quesadilla maker. "It's not like that time we thought we caught Nick cheating on me in undergrad, remember?"

"Ohhhh, I remember that." I smiled, thinking back to our Northwestern days. "Yeah, I agree. It would be weird to have you serve as my wing woman while I went on a revenge tour with hot guys. And I don't even want to do that."

"Right," Zora said. "And we can't do any of the mean tricks we played on Gio when you first came to live here."

"What mean tricks?" Adesola paused in the act of settling a half-gallon of almond milk in the fridge. "Tell me. I need to know."

Zora and I exchanged glances.

"We can't," I said. "You need plausible deniability, in case the authorities ever get wind of what we did."

"But that's my point," Zora said. "It's a strange set of circumstances.

It's actually really sad. Both you and Walker want nothing more than to be together."

"Your brother left *me*," I said automatically, then sighed in defeat. "But I'm not angry with him. I better understand where his head has been." I closed my eyes, thinking of the letter that had nearly brought me to tears. My immediate reaction after reading it was an overwhelming urge to find him, to shake some sense into him and ask him to come home so I could show him how much I loved him.

But he'd left me.

I looked down and realized I was squeezing the avocado in my hand into a fine green paste that was currently escaping, excrement-like, between my fingers. I didn't know how to articulate my dilemma to these two women I loved dearly. Admitting out loud that Walker had broken my heart by finally overcoming my defenses and then abruptly leaving me wasn't something I could easily confess to.

And yet, there was no denying that my heart was broken. I wasn't in any rush to deliver the remaining pieces to Walker so he could pulverize whatever was left.

"Are you okay?" Adesola looked at me strangely as she pried the avocado carcass out of my hand and wiped at the mess with a paper towel.

"Yeah, I'm okay. Maybe we shouldn't talk about Walker," I said.

Zora held up the leather-bound tablet on my kitchen table. "You have another iPad?"

"It's Miles's," I said, feeling my spirits sink just a little lower. "He wants me to use one of his software programs to play around with potential designs for this side of the duplex. Although now, I don't know if I'll even be living here."

"It'll be fine, chica," Adesola said, throwing a pointed look over her shoulder. "Just you watch."

"It will. And we have good news," Zora said. She rooted around in one of the reusable bags and retrieved a huge Tupperware container. "This is from Mama. Oxtail stew. She said it's only for you and that we'd better not ask for any of it because you shouldn't have to share right now." Zora rolled her eyes.

I rushed forward to take the container from her. "I love your mother. She's a woman after my own heart."

"And the Winstons hooked you up with a huge care package. Jennifer sent another compassion cake, Cletus made chili and homemade sausage, and Drew contributed a pie," Adesola said, unloading said items in the fridge. "And I don't care how down you are, your ass is sharing some of this lemon pie."

I smiled.

"The best part," Zora added, "is that they're all heading to the protest today and tomorrow, and they've been shaking the trees to get other people to join you. They wanted Adesola and me to tell you just how proud of you they are." Zora pulled me into a hug. "And so am I, for the record. I'm proud of you. Proud that you're my friend."

I hugged her back. What an embarrassment of riches, to have these wonderful friends, this supportive community. What an honor to have them marching beside me every day.

But all I wanted was Walker.

A knock sounded at the back door.

Adesola and Zora looked at me.

"I'm not expecting anyone," I said.

"I'll get it." Adesola headed to the door. For a wild moment I hoped I'd see Walker on the other side of the door.

It wasn't Walker, but the visitor's identity was surprising.

Tavia.

"Hi," Tavia said, looking as nervous as I'd ever seen her as she waved at me from the doorway. When her eyes settled on Zora, she lost her tentative smile.

The two sisters stared at each other for an endless moment.

"Let me know when she's gone," Zora said with a derisive sniff as she turned to leave the kitchen.

"Zora, wait," Tavia said, coming into the kitchen.

Zora paused in her path out of the kitchen but kept her back to sister.

"I just wanted to drop this off," Tavia said, walking over to me and depositing an envelope in my lap. I recognized the handwriting immediately.

"Another letter from Walker," I said, and Adesola's eyes widened as she closed the kitchen door.

"*Another* letter?" Zora retraced her steps back toward me, though she kept her eyes carefully averted from her sister.

"Walker sent me a letter the other day," I said. "It was in my mailbox but it didn't have postage. So, you're the messenger," I said, watching Tavia.

"He would kill me if he knew I was delivering it in person," Tavia said, frowning. I noticed for the first time that she wasn't as perfectly put together as usual. She wore a T-shirt and jeans with no jewelry or makeup, and she was suddenly sporting a super-short tapered haircut that showcased her natural hair texture.

"So why are you here?" Zora asked, her tone so cold Tavia looked shocked. "Is this about the bank? God knows you don't do anything unless there's some benefit to you."

"Zora, I'm sorry," Tavia said, but by then she was talking to empty air because Zora had already turned and left.

Adesola and I barely managed to hide our winces as we watched Tavia look after sister. Tavia seemed bereft, without her usual brash confidence, and I had no idea what to say to help heal the sisterly conflict.

"Thank you for bringing this," I told Tavia, nodding. "I appreciate it."

She nodded back, lifting her chin as she deliberately cleared her throat. I realized she was doing her best not to cry. My mind flashed back to the memory of her weeping in Eddie's arms, and I felt an unexpected rush of sympathy for her.

"I know you probably weren't happy about what I said in the ER," she said. I internally applauded her bravery in giving me unflinching eye contact, but I didn't bother to temper my words.

"No, I wasn't. I love your brother, and I thought the topic and timing of your question was really callous and uncaring. If your sister hadn't addressed it first, you wouldn't have any teeth left," I said.

She blinked. "I get it. I've come to understand it was poor timing on my part. For that I apologize. But I hope you understand, my wanting additional details had nothing to do with how much I love my brother. Sometimes I'm not good with ..." She trailed off, then lifted her shoulders in a shrug. "I won't make any excuses. But I do apologize."

"I accept your apology, although it's Walker you should—"

"Yeah, yeah, I know," she said. "I'm working on that. Anyway, I'm putting this in your hand instead of in the mailbox as instructed because I want to say something."

"Let's hear it," Adesola said, and Tavia narrowed her eyes at her.

"Leigh, my brother loves you. His whole life, he's always been the responsible, dependable guy for everyone around him. I realize now that I took advantage of that and I haven't been a very good sister. To any of my siblings."

"No, you haven't," I said.

Her lips firmed. "I'm aware, and I regret it. I never meant to let business get between us that way. I was just trying to create a space for myself, and I've been going through my own shit trying to get over some—whatever, that's not the point," she said.

Adesola and I exchanged surprised glances.

"The point is that I'm here on my brother's behalf, even though he'll probably let me have it for stepping in all of this. But if you know my brother, and I know you do, you know he doesn't know how to not do the honorable thing. When he found out about his condition, it shook him. I'm not saying it was right, him leaving and making the decision for you, but he thought at the time it was the right thing to do. He knows better now, and he misses you so much. Just, just keep an open mind, okay?"

"Okay, Tavia," I said, nodding. "I will. I'll keep an open mind."

"Good." She looked genuinely relieved at my response. "Alright. I'll go."

"Thanks for stopping by," I said, tapping the envelope on my leg. "And for bringing this."

She nodded at Adesola and me and headed to the back door. She'd just slipped out when the front doorbell chimed.

What now?

"Leigh," Zora yelled. "Are you expecting someone else? Like a camera crew and a reporter?"

Adesola and I stared at each other for a charged moment.

"What's going on?" I asked.

Adesola shook her head. "I have no idea."

We scurried to the front of the house to find Zora holding the front door open. A woman with big hair and TV makeup stood on the front porch. Above the waist, she wore a professional ensemble of a camisole and jacket, with jeans and athletic shoes on the bottom. Two men stood behind her, one with a large camera resting at his side.

"Ah, there you are," the woman said, thrusting her outstretched hand in my direction as I neared the door. "I'm Brooke Knowles. I'm a reporter down at the local station. I wondered if we could have a moment of your time."

"What's this about?" I peered past them, sighting several cars parked in the driveway and in front of the house, including a van bearing the station's logo and a broadcasting dish.

"Maybe I should explain," a new voice said. Everyone made room for Mrs. Bowers, Maddie's mother, to move forward until she was at the front of the crush of bodies. "Hey, Leigh," Mrs. Bowers said, and I blinked in disbelief.

"Mrs. Bowers?"

"Yeah," she said, looking flushed and excited. "Can we come in?"

Once everyone was seated, with Adesola and Zora looking on from the nearby corner, Mrs. Bowers started her explanation.

"So, someone nominated our family for a Local Heroes spotlight." Mrs. Bowers nodded to the TV crew seated around her. "They wanted to create public awareness about Maddie's treatment and hopefully drum up some contributions to cover her medical bills. So they came to interview us today, but the more I thought about it, the more I felt like they were interviewing the wrong person."

I shook my head. "I can't think of anyone more deserving than Maddie. She's been through so much, and there's so many more challenges ahead of her. Not to mention all the bills."

"Well, we're still going to do the showcase on Maddie," Brooke slid in smoothly, "but the more Mrs. Bowers talked about you, the more we realized we needed to cover the good deeds of yet another hero."

"I'm not a hero," I began, until I was interrupted by Adesola's insistent voice.

"Of course she is, and we quite agree."

"They'll still do a feature on Maddie," Mrs. Bowers said, "but we think your story needs to be told sooner, because of the situation at the hospital. And since Walker paid all her hospital bills, I *still* can't believe he did that—"

"*What did you just say?*" I blinked, wondering if I'd heard her right.

She blinked at me. "Walker. He paid all her outstanding medical bills. He didn't tell you?"

I stood stock still, my mouth hanging open as I struggled to formulate a reply. "No," I finally managed. "He didn't."

Oh, Walker.

"Yes," Mrs. Bowers said, beaming. "It wasn't all that long ago. We figured you told him about my husband losing his job at the mill too. Walker managed to pull some strings and got my husband a job managing an axe throwing restaurant in Knoxville," she said, sounding euphoric. "And the benefits started on day one!"

Miles, I thought, struggling to keep my grateful tears at bay. Dear God, Walker and Miles had worked together and invested so much in saving this family they hadn't even known until several months ago.

"We loved the story about Mr. Leffersbee dressing up as Karney the Kangaroo," Brooke said. She was biting her lip, her eyes narrowed, and I knew the big pitch was coming. "So, we've decided to reconceptualize these two segments and instead come at it from the angle of what the hospital's Peds program means to our community."

"Smart," Zora said approvingly. "And I'm guessing you plan to be perfectly candid in discussing how that's threatened at KCH, now that there's no longer a Child Life program?"

"Oh, we do," Brooke said, her smile wide and hungry. "If we do this right, which we will, this segment should cast a long shadow of doubt about what this community should expect from this hospital if Visage remains in control."

"We already did an exposé on Visage, and it didn't work," I said. I didn't feel nearly as encouraged as everyone was looking.

Brooke shook her head. "This is different. That piece was all about facts, which many people can, to a shocking degree, resist. This will be a personal story that people will see and hear for themselves. It'll get at the heartstrings."

"We're in," Adesola said, and when I looked askance at her, she laughed out loud. "If Leigh says yes, we're in. And she should say yes if she knows what's best for her."

"We'll start with Leigh. I've gotten several statements from other hospital employees in just the last few hours attesting to Leigh's role in sounding the alarm about Visage's past and planned misconduct. We have file footage of her marching outside. And now we want her story. I think it's remarkable that this movement started with a Child Life Specialist who loved her kids so much she made lasting connections with families and sacrificed her own job and welfare. Oh, and we'd love to interview Walker. Does he live here? Where can we find him?"

The brief bubble of happiness I'd momentarily felt burst at the mention of Walker. Zora stepped in and responded for me, for which I was exceedingly grateful.

"I'm his sister. He's not available at the moment. If this is time sensitive and, well, it should be, you might want to proceed without him. I'm sure he'll be flattered by your intentions when I tell him."

"Alright," Brooke said, looking momentarily deflated. But her eyes brightened when they landed on me, and I got the distinct impression that she was holding her breath. "So, Leigh ... are we a go for this?"

"Yes," Zora and Adesola said together, and I nodded and laughed.

"Yes," I said.

"Alright," Brooke said. "Where's a good place for us to set up? The lighting is good in here. We could just move the furniture a bit—"

"Uh-uh," Adesola said, waggling a perfectly manicured red-tipped finger at the crew. "First, we get her makeup, hair, and wardrobe together. Then you get her heroic story."

CHAPTER TWENTY-EIGHT

Walker

"Thanks for coming, everyone." Pops presided from the overstuffed armchair in my executive apartment as if it were a throne, running his hands over his knees with a restless glee. He seemed many years younger as he glanced at each of us in turn. "Let's go ahead and get started."

I shook my head, wondering what he was up to. The modest-sized living room was filled with my immediate family members and Mrs. Watkins. Zora and Tavia were on opposite sides of the room, Zora having given Tavia very little pre-game conversation. Mrs. Watkins sat on the couch alongside my parents. In the corner of the room, a laptop was open and strategically angled toward the sitting area.

Just then a noisy burst of music spilled from the laptop. My mother turned back and glared at it. "Audre," she said, frowning, "you should be listening. At the very least, mute yourself."

"No problem, Mama," Audre said, her face briefly filling the screen before the computer went silent. I suppressed a snicker when she disappeared completely, leaving us with a view of her messy side of the dorm.

Zora's eyes met mine, and we both gave an amused shake of our heads.

"I asked you all to come here today so we could discuss where things stand with Consolidated," Pops said. "I won't take too long, Walker has to leave soon. He's got someplace to be," he said, flicking an amused glance over the perfectly pressed suit I wore and the bouquet of roses resting near the front door. I'd already told my family I planned to bite the bullet and finally visit Leigh to throw myself at her mercy, but he'd strangely insisted on having everyone over at that specific time. I gave Pops a shrug. When Miles showed up to drive me, I was leaving. No matter how far they'd gotten into the agenda.

The family business, well, it wasn't my business anymore. But fixing things with Leigh for damn sure was.

"As you all know, we took a break from our formal talks when Walker had his surgery so we could focus on him getting better. And he has been," Pops said, relief audible in his voice as he turned to run an assessing eye over me. I nodded back at him from where I was leaning against the wall. "He looks good," Pops said.

"I feel good," I said, giving everyone an assuring nod. "And no, I don't want to sit down. It's been almost four weeks since the surgery. I could do with more time on my feet and I'm leaving soon."

"Fine by me," Zora teased. "I'll just keep your seat warm over here."

"Alright. Your father and I have had informal talks with Consolidated, more or less off the record," Pops continued. "We think we've come to terms that are agreeable for the bank overall. We've also identified unexpected opportunities for several of you, and we wanted to outline those as well. We're not voting today, but I did want to give everyone a rundown of what we'll consider and vote on over the next three weeks or so."

"You did good, Dad," my father said, nodding at Pops. "It's a hell of a better deal than we started out with, and it keeps us in the driver's seat."

"Which should have always been the point," Pops said, narrowing his eyes at my father and Tavia until they both looked more than a bit chagrined. "That's why you keep the Big Dog here informed of the moves you're making. I've been around the block more times than you can count. I know what's up. Now, here's what's going to happen," he said, and proceeded to outline a plan so masterful I was stunned.

So were my family members, from the looks of them.

"Pops," Zora said, looking delighted. "How in the world did you get Consolidated to agree to a merger where we retained the controlling share? Why would they ever agree to that?"

"Because," Pops said, grinning, "Consolidated's sins are many and well-publicized. They're dismantling their entire exec board and leadership team in an effort to clean house. But the stain of cheating everyday, hardworking folk out of their money isn't going away anytime soon. The way I structured this deal, Consolidated gets one non-voting seat on our board. They get no say. We, however, get access to a wider selection of resources and products that give our customers more choices and help build the community."

"It's a win for us," Audre's voice said from the laptop, "but how is it a win for them?"

"Because," I said. "when critics monitor Consolidated's rebranding and reorganization efforts, they can always point to our bank and tout all the good they're doing for the community. For them, this isn't about making money. It's marketing, making amends."

"Precisely," Pops said, giving me a quiet smile. "Which is why I will be transitioning out of full retirement to semi-retirement." He playfully wagged his neck at Mrs. Watkins. "I want to keep an eye on all these new developments, and I've heard that place is boring without me."

Mrs. Watkins's grin told me just how thrilled she was by this news. "The customers will be so happy to see you back," she said.

"We're going to promote Jamal," my father said, nodding at me. "I got to spend a good deal of time with him in Florida. I like him, and Mrs. Watkins speaks highly of him. He's going to take over your daily responsibilities. Pops and I will be a guiding hand for him while he learns the way of things."

"And what about you, Walker?" Pops asked, looking way too pleased with himself. "Do you accept my proposal?"

I smiled, probably for the first time in weeks. "I've conferred with my business partner and the answer is yes. Miles and I agree that Leffersbee & Green Construction will work with the bank."

"Proud to be your partner, in a different capacity." Pops nodded, as a world of understanding passed between us. This new business was mine, to shape and mold however I wanted. It could conform to the rhythm of my life and any unknowns that occurred. I could follow my passion on my own terms while still contributing to my family's legacy.

"Thanks, Pops," I said, clearing my throat.

He nodded back. "Don't thank me. I'm not asking because you're blood. You're good at what you do and you've got an impressive head for business. The bank is fortunate to be working with you and Miles, period."

"Which makes me even more curious about the position you've offered me," Tavia said, her gaze hard as she looked between me and Pops. "A Managing Director spot with *Consolidated*?"

My father squared his shoulders. "They were impressed by you, Octavia. They have been since you pitched the deal to them in the first place. They love your strategic thinking, and they'd like to have a mind like yours on their side."

"On their side," Tavia said with quiet bitterness. "Not with my family."

My father looked to Pops.

"Tavia," Pops said. He paused, studying his hands as he seemed to consider his approach, and I held my breath to hear whatever was coming next. "I know you think we kept you from the bank all this time, that we never considered you when we tapped Walker to lead it. But that's not the case. Really, it just came down to fit. You and your brother have always had very different ways of seeing the world, and that influences how you see the bank and its potential. Neither of your perspectives are wrong. But Walker has a love for the people in this community that balances his thinking about profit. I've always been more comfortable with him driving decisions for that reason."

"This new deal wouldn't have even been an option if it hadn't been for me," she shot back, then subsided when Pops lifted a brow. No matter how angry she was, she knew better than to tussle too hard with Pops.

"The deal as you envisioned it wasn't going to make you happy," Pops said. "Not in the long term. You would have been hungering for more,

more clout, more recognition, more money before the taste of victory even faded from your mouth. It's not the bank that you want. You want the kind of success you won't find from your family's business. And I don't want to find out what kind of shape we'd be in by the time you realized that."

"Well, you've got me right where you want me," Tavia said. "Out of Green Valley, exiled to Chicago. I'd rather go anywhere but Chicago."

"Moving to Chicago's not a hardship," Pops said. "Wonderful city, and you'll likely enjoy the change of pace. You've got goals. Chicago's as fine a place as any to reach them."

"I've had a few lessons of my own," my father said, swallowing hard. "Tavia, don't think of it as a punishment. Try to see this as an opportunity." My mother squeezed his hand briefly.

"Just not a good fit here," Pops said, tone gentle and his eyes kind as he took in Tavia's stiff posture and tight jaw. "You belong in that corporate world for right now, and I know you'll shine there. You've always shone to me, baby girl. I've always been proud of you."

She gave a brief nod, stood, and collected her purse as she walked out the door. We all watched her in silence, none of us able to find anything appropriate to say.

"That was hardcore," Audre said from the laptop, and my father looked pained.

I barely listened as they discussed my father's new liaison role with Consolidated. I was struck by how quickly the satisfaction of hearing about my new role had diminished.

The one person I wanted to tell wasn't in the room.

I needed to get to Leigh. I was beyond ready to throw myself at her feet and beg for mercy. Imperfect as I was, as uncertain as my future was, all I wanted was her. If she'd just take me back

I opened my mouth to excuse myself and realized the topic had changed to something lighter. Audre had signed off, and my mother got up to assemble the food she'd brought over.

"Glad we got that done before the program started," Pops said.

I shook my head. "Pops, you all are welcome to stay here, but whatever it is, I'm gonna watch it later. I really need to—"

"Oh no you don't," Zora said, her mouth twisting as she stood. "We're all about to watch something that I think you'll find pretty interesting."

"That's right," my mother said, re-entering the living room with a platter of chips and dips. "Miles'll be here when it's over. You're going to want to see this."

By the time my loud-talking, disruptive family located the remote and squabbled over the correct channel, we were six minutes past the hour.

And suddenly Leigh's beautiful face was there, filling the television screen. Her voice, the voice I'd missed so much, flooded the room and left me breathless.

"—things are hard for you right now," the interviewer was saying, her eyes overwide and earnest as she waited for Leigh's reply.

"Yes. You could say that," Leigh said, looking down at her lap for a long moment.

Something inside me rose up, incensed that anything or anyone had given her cause to bow her head.

And then I listened in disbelief as Leigh answered questions about her termination and the bleak outlook for the hospital's future.

"When did she get fired?" I yelled, pushing to my feet.

"After you left," my mother said, looking as she if was enjoying herself immensely as she slid a chip in her mouth.

"Why didn't you tell me?" I looked around at all of them, unable to believe they'd kept something that important from me.

"Following orders," Pops smirked. "You wanted space to clear your head, remember? And she didn't want us telling you anything. She wanted you to be able to think."

God, I was dumb. And the lowest of the low. *I* was why she looked so sad.

I did that, in the name of trying to protect her.

"Sit down," my father said, looking amused. "You don't want to miss the rest. I think your name comes up in a few places."

By the time the video ended, I was beside myself.

"There's Miles," my mother said, peering out the front window. "Alright, son. Get your woman back. Do what you have to do. Make it count."

"Gross. That sounds hella questionable," Zora said, grimacing.

My mother ignored her. "The roses are fine, Walker, but Leigh likes food. Take the pound cake I brought for her," she said, gesturing to the foil package on the table, and the rest of my family groaned.

"I wanted some of that pound cake," Zora said, sounding resigned. "But take it. I have a feeling you're gonna need all the help you can get."

CHAPTER TWENTY-NINE

Leigh

"She'll be down in just one moment." The receptionist in the KCH Human Resources office offered me a saccharine smile as she hung up the phone.

I didn't bother smiling back. My guts were a bubbling cauldron of unease. "Sure."

When I'd gotten the call to come and retrieve my belongings, I'd known something was up. I expected Visage to mail my belongings as promised, perhaps even spit on them first. I'd tried to guilt Aaron and Layla into standing in as my proxy, but they'd both refused, suggesting I might find it "nice" to be inside the hospital again.

Nice?

So I'd consulted the lawyer my father referred me to, who'd reinforced the importance of "getting my shit and keeping my damn mouth shut." I could do that, easily.

The receptionist had gone back to studying her cellphone, content to ignore me while my mind raced with admittedly paranoid thoughts.

Maybe the crisis manager had laced the water cooler with an untraceable poison, and they were just waiting for me to keel over, empty Dixie cup in hand, so they could dispose of my body.

Maybe they were secretly recording me right now, with plans to analyze my body language and use the results as evidence to sue me for everything I owned or would ever own.

I barely managed not to jump up and bolt from the office. And then I remembered something.

Leaving my house earlier, some instinct had urged me to grab the still unopened letter from Walker that Tavia had dropped off a few days ago. It was a ridiculous notion, the idea that having Walker's letter with me would somehow substitute for his presence. But now, sitting in the hideous quiet and waiting to find out what Visage had planned for me, I wanted to hear his voice.

Even if it was just in my head.

I ripped the tape off the back of the envelope with trembling fingers and pulled out the single page. It was short.

Leigh,

That day, when you covered my eyes and dared me to dream about the future?

I did.

And I saw you. I was certain of how much I loved you, and how beautiful our life would be.

So, when I was faced with the uncertainty of the genetic test results, I wanted to protect you. But now, weeks later, I realize I'm the one who lost track of what mattered. I'm certain that I love you, and that there is no life for me without you. You're what I know for sure.

Walker

Oh, Walker, I thought, closing my eyes. Why couldn't he understand that his love and him in my life were all the things I'd ever wanted or needed in the first place?

"We're ready for you," a chipper voice said, and my eyes flew open in panic.

A shiny, perfectly groomed woman I'd never seen before stood in front of me, a clipboard in her hand.

"Who's 'we,'" I demanded. I put the letter back in my purse and pushed to my feet, smoothing the fabric of my perspiration-soaked skirt down the back of my legs as I peered around her.

"Just me so far," she said, her eyes growing wide at my outburst as she turned to lead me out of the office.

"I guess I thought my things would be here in HR. Where are we going?" I fished in my purse for my phone, readying my thumb to execute a call to my lawyer.

We stepped onto the elevator and she pressed the button for the floor of administrative suites. The elevator was in motion before she responded.

"We have your belongings elsewhere." Her tone was vague enough that I couldn't help but wonder if I would soon be sleeping with the fishes.

Stepping out of the elevator, it was almost eerie seeing the familiar landmarks again, posters and offices I'd passively observed a million times whenever I'd visited this part of the hospital. It seemed like a lifetime ago.

Where were we going?

My anxiety mounted.

"We're here," the woman said, stopping in front of one of the offices. And then, suddenly, she gave me an exuberant smile.

I froze, unsure whether my flight or fight reflex should kick in.

And then I saw it. The nameplate on the door.

Leigh D'Alessandro, Director of Child Life Services.

I squinted at the nameplate, expecting the words to change.

The HR rep watched my struggle, smiling. "That's your name, alright," she said.

My mouth opened, closed, opened again. "But I'm not the director. And I'm ... I'm fired."

She keyed open the door and pushed it in. I stepped past the threshold into the office, still fighting stupefaction as I gaped at the view from the floor-to-ceiling windows, the fancy office furniture, the separate meeting area. Items from my old cubicle were seamlessly integrated into the décor, from my Wonder Woman mug on the desk, to my worn copy of *Between the World and Me* nestled in the bookshelf alongside my work binders, to the framed pictures of Zora and me at Mardi Gras on a side table.

"So, what do you think?" a new voice asked, and I whirled around.

Nick stood behind me grinning, merriment dancing in his wicked green eyes.

"Nick." I gestured around the office. "What is this? What the hell is going on?"

He eased further into the office, past the HR rep. "This is me, holding your belongings hostage to stage a job offer. Is it working?"

I stared at him. "Why are ... How did you ... What is *going on?*"

He laughed, and reached out to gently squeeze my shoulder. "What's going on is you won. Yesterday, Visage got wind of the fact that your interview would air today. It was the final straw that got them to withdraw from the deal. They completely underestimated your staying power," he said.

I burst out into incredulous laughter. "Are you kidding me right now?"

"Not kidding at all," he assured me. "Woe unto anyone who crosses you."

"Damn right," I said, finally letting out a relieved breath. "So, why are you here?"

"I'm buying the hospital." He grinned. "I couldn't do it until you ran them off. You deserve all the credit for that, so thank you very much. Zora's already picked out the wing she wants to name after my mother," he said, his eyes going slightly unfocused as his gaze went to his feet.

I couldn't help giving him a hug, HR rep be damned. I knew how hard it was for him to talk about his mother, who had worked in the hospital as a nurse for years before she died from drug addiction.

"Nick, this is amazing. But do you know what you're doing?"

"Oh, hell no," he laughed. "Hospitals aren't my thing, but healthcare innovation is. We're going to put the two together here. I'd been hoping they would succumb to your pressure, so I've already assembled a team of experts way smarter than me to help with the transition and running of the hospital. We're turning it back into a non-profit that provides supportive services to its community members, and we plan to add to the offerings. We've heard from some of Ellie's friends in high places who plan on hosting fundraiser shindigs year-round to help families with their medical expenses."

I stared at him, overwhelmed. "You're serious."

He rocked back on his heels, tucking his thumbs inside his belt loops. "I am. So, do you accept my offer? I need you to re-build and expand Child Life here."

"Well," I said, feeling my heart lighten for the first time in days, "I might. I've gotta see the terms you're offering."

"Smart woman," he said, holding up his hand for a high five. I obliged him. "We're still in transition, but I'll have someone courier over the paperwork soon. For now," he smiled gently at me, "why don't you take a week or two and relax? Now that your mission is accomplished, I bet you could use a break. You've been through a lot."

"Yeah," I said. All of this was so wonderful, far more than I'd ever dreamed of being possible. But it felt incomplete without Walker there to share in it.

"Some people want to talk to you," Nick said. As if on cue, the doorway to an adjoining waiting room flew open. Aaron, Layla, Ebony, Adesola, and Loretta all spilled in, their raucous yells and laughter filling the room.

"You did it!" Layla crowed as they crowded around me, all of us screaming and jumping and hugging and crying in a joyful huddle.

"You did it," Ebony screeched, and Aaron grinned.

"You kicked ass, chica," Adesola said, loudly smacking my forehead with a kiss. "I told you no one could break The General down!"

"*We* did it," I reminded them, overcome. In this moment, all the angst and anxiety and fear was more than worth it. "We saved the hospital. For everyone."

"Yes, you did," Nick said, smiling and nodding at me. "The community is safer now, because of you. And now it's time to reap the rewards."

~

THE EMPTY, gnawing feeling was back in the pit of my stomach as I piloted my car back home. The high I'd been riding from our champagne-soaked monumental victory an hour before paled in comparison to the knowledge that I was going home to celebrate alone.

Without Walker.

This has to end, I thought. Walker wanted me. I wanted him. It wasn't complicated. Neither of us needed any more space or time to think. I was ready to overcome my fear of rejection and bring him home.

By the time I pulled into my drive, my mind was made up. I was so lost in my thoughts, I made it out of the car and all the way to the porch before I realized I wasn't alone.

I froze midstride, inhaling sharply at the sight of Walker Leffersbee sitting on my front porch, his long legs trailing down the steps. A bouquet of flowers was balanced across his knees.

An entire lifetime seemed to pass as we stared at each other wordlessly. Slowly, and somewhat awkwardly, he rose to his feet, never taking his eyes off me.

"Golden Boy," I said, finally finding my voice.

He nodded. "Maleficent."

Courage, dear heart.

I watched, hardly breathing as he made his way toward me, trying to temper my wild excitement at the sight of him.

"What brings you to my neck of the woods?" I ran a glance over all his suited finery, taking in the precisely cut lines of his beard and hairline. "You look nice. Got a date?"

He came to a stop before me, and I blinked at the tenderness and determination in his gaze.

"I hope so," he said, nodding. "I made a real mess of things, but I really hope so."

"I missed you, Golden Boy." I reached to grasp his hand, and his eyes closed briefly at my touch.

"I was hoping we could talk," he said, inclining his head to the door. "I know I should have called first—"

"Why would you call first? You're home," I said, unlocking the door and pushing it open. "Come on in."

Something like relief flooded his expression and he nodded, following behind me as I led him into the kitchen and gestured to the table.

"I don't want to sit," he said, shaking his head. "I want to get this said. There are no adequate words to apologize for how I hurt you."

"Not gonna lie." I set my purse on the kitchen counter and faced him. "You broke my heart when you left."

"I know," he said, nodding, his eyes on mine. "I know I did. I didn't realize it at the time. I thought I was protecting you."

"I've never needed you to protect me from hypotheticals, Walker. I was tough long before I met you. I might get knocked down, but I'll always end up kicking ass. Being in love with you," I raised my brows meaningfully and watched his shoulders fall in relief, "that doesn't make me weaker. It makes me even stronger."

"All true," he said, a wry smile curving his lips. "I never should have forgotten that. You don't need me to fight your battles or save you."

"That's right." I got up and went over to him finally, because I couldn't help myself. Because he was mine. He pulled me into him, and I reached up to run my fingers over the high blade of his cheekbone and along the crisp line of his beard. *Thank you, God*, I thought, closing my eyes as I inhaled the familiar smell of him. How had we gone this long apart? "If you'd stopped packing that day and stayed long enough to listen, I could have told you what a dumb decision you were making," I said, fighting to steady my voice.

We stared at each other for a minute, Walker's mouth twitching, then we both burst into relieved laughter.

"Dumb decision, huh?" Walker said, cracking the barest hint of a smile. "Still the diplomat, I see. Some things don't change, thank God."

"You were so worried about something you can't control and that I don't give a shit about anyway. I could have listed all the other ways you're not perfect, if that would have made you feel better." I reached out and lightly fingered the button on his suit coat before I slipped it out of the hole and pushed the halves of his suit coat open.

"Deeply flawed, am I?"

"You have no idea. You have Adam Sandler's movies memorized."

"You love Adam Sandler now. What else is on this list of flaws?" he asked, running a callused finger over my bottom lip. I leaned in even closer without thinking.

"Well," I said, pretending to think. "You're anal about cleaning, you clearly never learned that a treadmill is meant to serve as a secondary closet for clothes."

"Guilty," he said, with a straight face.

"You're only capable of swearing when we have sex, which points to repressed tendencies that will take me years to undo."

"I'll take that under advisement," he said, ducking his head to hide a smile. "But, sugar. Our kids can't be sent home from kindergarten for using your favorite words."

I sighed. "Agreed. No 'F is for fuck' until college, at least." I hesitated, struck by the significance of his words. "Wait. You're okay with ... the kid thing now?"

"I don't have the test results back yet—"

"I don't care about those results, and I never will. That's not what I asked you."

"I was still struggling with it, yes. Then I got an unexpected note that made me rethink things." He retrieved something from the inner pocket of his suit jacket. "One of the tellers gave me this. Seems someone dropped it off one weekend. Threw it in the dropbox."

I raised a brow at the rental car brochure in his hand. "What is that?"

He pushed it toward me. "See for yourself."

Frowning, I opened the heavily creased brochure, unfolding it until I found familiar writing straddling the free white space at the periphery.

Walker, take it from me. Any kids you have, you're going to fuck them up no matter what you do. So, just have them. However you want to have them. Who cares if you scramble eggs in a petri dish, take a swing and hope for the best, or get them from elsewhere? It's nobody's business but yours and Leigh's. You're already a better man than I am. You'll be a better father too.

"DAD," I murmured, shaking my head at my father's bold signature. I looked up to find Walker watching me closely.

"He called me too," he said, pushing a curl back from my temple.

"I can't imagine how that conversation went."

"Great, actually. He wanted me to understand some things. Decisions he made when you were growing up. Things he wished he could change. It helped me understand you better."

"What did it tell you about me, exactly?" I bit my lip.

"That I'd hurt you in the worst possible way, leaving after gaining your trust. And that you'd never wanted perfection from me. Just honesty."

I bit my lip again to stop an onrush of tears. "My dad told you that? He got that?"

Walker nodded. "He did, sugar. He did. He also told me to get my head out of my ass and come back home. He said you were capable of granting mercy if I was accountable for my behavior."

I stared at Walker, speechless. I never would have thought my father capable of understanding my issues with him, and *me*, so very well. The fact that he'd reached out to Walker and tried to help ... It didn't make up for the past. But it made me hopeful for a new start.

New starts all the way around.

"I want to know if you can find it in your heart to forgive me." Walker's gaze was steady on mine. "I'll do whatever it takes to earn your trust again."

I waved away his words. "I already forgave you. But I need something from you. Several things, actually."

"Done," he said promptly. His entire body seemed to sag in relief. "What's first?"

"Remember what you told me that night after the baptism?"

"I do," he said quietly. Our gazes locked in an electric moment as we remembered that earth-shattering coupling. "And I meant every word of it. I still do. I guess I just didn't expect that I would test those words so soon."

"Thought I'd be the one to bolt, didn't you?" I said, and we both laughed. "Which leads to the second thing. Hold on one sec."

"Okay," Walker said, frowning as I turned and ran out of the kitchen. Soon enough, I found what I needed in my room. When I returned, I found him seated at the kitchen table.

"Isn't this Miles's iPad?"

"Yep," I said, smiling to myself. This was working out perfectly. "Turn it on. Open the design app."

I opened the fridge, searching.

Walker's voice came from around the refrigerator door. "What is this? You, what? Created a design for a whole *house?* This is really detailed. When did you have time to do this? *How* did you do it? You hate this stuff."

"I was motivated."

Bingo. Found what I needed.

Walker was so immersed in studying the iPad he didn't notice my approach until I was already seated across from him. "What is this you have here? The "*Star Wars* Study." Is this—?" He glanced up at me, his gaze widening as it moved from my face to what sat in front of me.

"It's for you," I told him, sitting back. "I tried to include all the things I thought you'd like. There's plenty of room in the yard, a vaulted ceiling in the foyer." I grabbed his hand. "I tried to make a safe space just for us. A place that looks like us. Where we'll grow together with our family, whatever that family looks like."

He swallowed, his throat bobbing. "Leigh. You'd already done this. Before I even—"

"I believe in us. Which is why I'm proposing a new arrangement." I slid the old jeweler's box across the table.

Walker blinked at its contents. "Is that ... is that raw bacon?" he asked, and I almost cracked up at the awe in his voice.

"I'm trying to get your attention. You and I, we're going to make mistakes. Hopefully not the same ones, if we can help it. But no matter who makes the mistake or whatever winds may blow, I want us together. Forever."

Walker's eyes closed.

And then, slowly, creakily, he lowered himself until he was on one knee.

"Walker," I said, aghast. "What the hell are you doing?"

"Counter-proposing. " He reached into the pocket of his suit coat and pulled out a velvet box. "I'd worried it might seem like a leap to you, especially because we've been apart for the last three weeks. But I've never been more sure of anything," he said, opening the box.

I got down on the floor with him, throwing my arms around his neck and nearly upsetting his precarious balance. We laughed, the both of us, as we slid to the floor in a slow topple, with me in his lap.

"I think this is how it all started," Walker said, his smile bemused. His eyes were soft as he freed wayward strands of hair from my mouth.

"Nah. We started long before Zora's wedding. Many years before." My mouth fell open when I finally paid attention to the ring. It was beautiful. And huge. "When did you buy that?!"

He smiled. "When I flew out to New York for the baptism. I was sure then. I'm sure now. This is an iron-clad no-escape clause," he said, and I lost my breath. "I know this is probably scary for you. I know marriage for you was, well, a terrible experience. But you've got to know—"

"Oh, please." I blinked against the sting of tears. "I'm the one trying to lock you in, now that you have a history of bolting," I said, and he shook his head at me and laughed. "Yes. I'll marry you. And you don't have to explain how marriage will be different with us. You're a different man, and I'm a different woman. I believe in us like I've never believed in anything."

Walker let out a long breath. "Okay," he said, smiling. "Okay."

I gave up on holding the happy tears at bay as he slid the ring over my finger. "Then we're agreed," I said, nodding at him to indicate that we'd sealed the deal. "But I still have unfinished business with you, and I think we might as well settle it now."

Walker stood. "You just agreed to marry me. You can have whatever you want."

"I'm going to quote you on that later," I said, and he laughed, offering me his hand as I got to my feet. "How's your pain? You take anything lately?"

"I've got some Motrin on board, I'm good. Why?"

"Then follow me," I said, leading him back to the bedroom. "We've got some reuniting to do. I'll do the heavy lifting this time. You just hang on and enjoy the ride."

"Yes, ma'am." He laughed. The scruff of his beard from behind pleasantly scraped at my neck as he grabbed me, pulling me into his side. "But

I may have some tricks up my sleeve. And there is the matter of the pound cake my mother sent along."

"There's pound cake?" I threw a glance over my shoulder, grinning. "This is why I'm marrying you. You get my kink. Bring the cake. We'll need it."

EPILOGUE

Leigh

Four Months Later

"Your family is wild," Walker whispered in my ear, laughter rumbling in his voice. He stood behind me, one hand anchored at my waist as he reached over me to grab a glass from the open cabinet above.

I instinctively leaned back against him, delighting in the hard surface of his chest and the woodsy notes of his aftershave. His arm snaked around my waist and I jumped as his beard scraped the side of my neck in the just-right-way that never failed to ignite my libido.

Damn, I love him. The thought, and the ooey-gooey feeling that accompanied it, felt as natural as breathing.

"You smell good," I said, sniffing his chest over my shoulder. "It's getting me in the mood—"

"Nuh-uh," he said under his breath, planting a kiss on my forehead while laughing. "Don't try to distract me. This has been the craziest July Fourth picnic I've ever experienced. Do you know how many times I've had to re-route your nephew from the bathroom?"

I cracked up, going limp over the kitchen counter.

In the nearby window, lightning arced across the gray gloom. The subsequent rumble of thunder was loud enough to rattle the windowpanes. None of it, I noticed, seemed to faze our houseful of guests who'd been forced indoors when the heavens opened. The adults kept talking, raising their voices even louder to be heard over the shrill yells and cheers of Lucia's children.

"Also," he continued, "your sister is currently traumatizing my sister with her labor stories, and I don't think Nick will ever be able to peel Zora off the ceiling."

I snuck a look through the crook of Walker's arm at the long dining room table in the center of our massive kitchen. Peering past the nearly twenty-five seated diners, I quickly zeroed in on Lucia, who was seated next to Zora. Lucia was using the forefinger and thumb of each hand to create widening, overlapping circles. Zora appeared stricken as she gripped Nick's sleeve.

"What is Lucia doing?" Walker murmured.

I choked on another laugh. "Oh my God. I think she's showing Zora what happens during crowning. I should get over there and derail that conversation before Zora goes into early labor."

"Nick's got it," Walker said, just as Lucia rammed her balled-up fist through the half-circle of her other hand and Nick made a "time out" gesture while trying to keep Zora from bolting.

"Yup, it's under control," I said, lying, while my nephew flung a handful of macaroni salad against a nearby wall from his highchair. Ellie didn't even pause in her conversation with my mother as she pulled his highchair closer, angling him away from the wall. She caught my eye, pointed to my niece, who was currently vomiting down my mother's shoulder, and mouthed, *I want one.*

Don't be greedy, I mouthed back to Ellie, pointing to a visibly pregnant Zora. Ellie grinned back at me.

"We are wild," I acknowledged. "But you love it."

"I do, sugar. And I love you."

"I know." I let myself go boneless against him, savoring the support of his strong arms around me. "Who knew we'd be this good together?"

"Or that our families would produce such a combustible amount of fun together. Take a good look." Walker rested his chin in my hair as we took in the wild scene. "This is what our July Fourths will look like for the rest of time."

"Damn straight."

Walker and I both jumped at the sound of the new voice right behind us. Paul looked smug as he wrestled a six pack of beer from the over-crowded counter of food. "Glad you know how this works, Walker. You're one of us now, forever. No take-backs, brother." Paul lifted the back of his hand to tap his wedding band against the gold band Walker wore on his left hand.

"Nah," Walker said easily. "I'm not taking anything back. I don't have a future without her. We're an inevitability."

"Damn straight," I said, already calculating how long it would be before I could get him alone in our newly rehabbed master suite.

"Good job getting a ring on him, Lee-Lee, and locking him down so fast," Paul said.

"Didn't you propose to him first?" I grinned at Paul. "Maybe you get some of the credit."

"Team effort." Paul and I slapped palms as Walker rolled his eyes.

"If nothing else, this scene is entertaining." Paul popped the top of a beer. "The Osbournes meet the Huxtables. Thank God we already broke Walker's family in at the wedding reception. Now that it's official, we can officially unleash all our mayhem."

Walker snorted. "There's more? And both of you are can stop congratulating yourselves. There was no way our story ended any other way." He lifted my chin to face to look in my eyes, and I fought the urge to climb him like a tree in front of my family.

"I loved your reception," Lucia said, sidling up to Paul. "It was so dreamy and romantic."

"It was a sublime." Walker's cheeks bunched up in a quiet smile, and I knew we were both remembering the spectacle of both of our families and practically the entire town boogeying down on the electric slide and the chicken dance. My aunts and cousins had fallen so hard for the town and the Winston brothers, they couldn't wait to come back for the Fourth of July.

"Here, here," I said, returning the kiss he dropped on my lips.

"I came to check on the drink you were getting Mom, *favorite new son*," Lucia said with a playful roll of her eyes.

"You know, I resent that," Paul said, pointing to Walker with his beer. "If I'd known knocking out that bastard's front teeth would forever cement me as the favorite son, I'd have done it years ago."

"He knocked his own teeth out when he put his hands on Leigh," Walker said, his grip on me tightening. "And he'll be gumming his words if he ever tries it again. That pavement in your backyard can handle a repeat performance."

"I don't think Gio wants to take the risk of tangling with you," Paul said, laughing. "And now that you've hammered out that agreement with your father-in-law, I doubt you'll bump into Gio again."

"What'd you tell Dad, Walker? Every other Thanksgiving?" Lucia asked.

"I didn't *tell* him anything," Walker said, shaking his head, and I joined Paul and Lucia in making scornful noises. "I merely suggested that it would be good if Leigh could come home for a major holiday without having to see Gio there."

"And it was as good as done," Lucia said. "Years of dysfunction, ended by Walker talking to Dad."

"Give him more credit than that," Walker said, getting serious. "He just needed to understand how badly that boundary needed to be drawn for Leigh's sake. He wanted to do the right thing, and he did."

"You and Dad still talking every week? Every time I see Dad, he's always telling me what you said. 'Walker said the market's due for an upturn. Walker says I can replace that vinyl kitchen tile with a stonework that's almost as cheap.'" Lucia folded her arms, smirking. "Admit it. You're besties."

"Yup, they talk every week," I said, closing my eyes. "Walker invariably hands me the phone at some point. As if Dad and I are gonna do anything more than grunt at each other."

"I've gotten to know him, and I have a lot of respect for him," Walker said. "It's true, he's made a lot of mistakes. He knows it, but he's trying."

"It does seem different this time," Lucia said, studying her sneaker-clad feet. "Ever since he had that conversation with you, Leigh, he's been more open to talking about the past. He still gets irritable, but he's let me get it all out. Finally. And that's made helped me lower my guard a lot more. Baby steps, but maybe we'll get there."

"Must be this country air," Paul said, watching as my father, Ezra, and Pops animatedly conferred over the specs for a particular sports car. "Or Walker's charm. Whatever it is, I'm grateful. It's made a difference with him."

"That's why we're adding a mother-in-law suite." Walker's gaze went to the backsplash where we'd tacked up copies of the ever-evolving floor plans for the house. "So they can come and be with us whenever they want."

"When do you plan to start work on the nurseries?" My sister's smile was sly.

Walker gave her an equally sly smile. "What, are you trying to give away one of your children?"

"*Hell* yes," Paul said, just as a clatter sounded from the other side of the kitchen. My nephew looked down from his highchair perch at the overturned plate on the floor before him, his mouth rounding before he yelled, "Shit!"

"Shit," Lucia hissed, covering her eyes, and I had to turn away from the shock on Ellie's face before I completely lost it.

"We've got to get most of the construction done before we introduce any sleep-dependent newborns," Walker said, laughter in his voice.

"It doesn't even look like the same place," Paul said, looking around, and I nodded, taking in the open concept layout of the first floor. When Walker had the idea to buy the duplex from Zora and renovate it to our specifications, I'd been surprised. I'd wondered if the duplex could ever measure up to the grand plan we'd drawn up together. But I trusted him completely. And now, I was constantly surprised at the almost daily transformation of the house. Knocking out the wall between the two sides had unlocked endless possibilities, and I was excited about exploring them all with Walker.

"I wanted to start right away," I admitted. "With kids. But Walker wants to travel for a while first. More and more, I see his point."

"Tavia didn't want to come?" Lucia maneuvered a chunk of ice from the nearby bag and filled a glass of water from the tap. "She decided to skip out on this family circus?"

Walker's lips thinned. "I haven't heard from her since she left. She's in Chicago, still a little pissed over having to move there. I figure when she's ready to talk, she'll call."

"A break from her might not be the worst idea," Paul mused, and I reacted without thinking.

"Give her a break, okay? She just moved to a new city and she's trying to get over some shit."

Walker pulled back to look at me. "How do you know that?"

I hesitated, then sighed. "We talk."

His brows shot up to his hairline. "We who? You and *Tavia?*"

"Yes. What, you thought you were the only one doing outreach?"

"Let me get this water to Ma," Lucia said, snickering as she retreated back to the table.

"I guess I can't hide from the kids anymore," Paul said, following in her wake.

Walker and I watched them ago, bemused.

"She's okay, you know," I told Walker, taking in the speculation in his gaze. "I think she's even starting to have fun. And with Eddie there—"

Walker balked. "What is *he* doing there?"

"That's not my business to be telling," I said, realizing my mistake. "But what *is* my business is what I'm doing to you in bed tonight."

"You can't distract me," Walker said, watching me from under slitted eyes. "But we'll see who does what to who first."

"That's what I love about you, Mr. Leffersbee. You're full of surprises," I said, drawing him in for a deep kiss. All around us, our family erupted into cheers.

"Buckle up, Mrs. Leffersbee," Walker said. "We've only just begun."

ACKNOWLEDGMENTS

Many, many thanks to Penny Reid and Fiona Fischer at Smartypants Romance. It is an honor to write for such an amazing, empowering platform. Special thanks to my editor, Angela Houle, who faithfully accompanied me through the journey of BAAY. All my gratitude to Brooke Mann Nowiski, who bestowed invaluable insight and dared me to write fearlessly.

ABOUT THE AUTHOR

Hope Ellis is a health outcomes researcher by day and writes romances featuring sexy nerds by night. She hopes to one day conquer her habit of compulsively binge-watching T*he Office*.

Facebook: https://www.facebook.com/hopeelliswrites/
Goodreads: https://www.goodreads.com/author/show/19916500.Hope_Ellis
Twitter: https://twitter.com/HopeEllisWrites
Instagram: https://www.instagram.com/hopeelliswrites/

Find Smartypants Romance online:
Website: www.smartypantsromance.com
Facebook: www.facebook.com/smartypantsromance/
Goodreads: www.goodreads.com/smartypantsromance
Twitter: @smartypantsrom
Instagram: @smartypantsromance

ALSO BY SMARTYPANTS ROMANCE

Green Valley Chronicles

The Love at First Sight Series

Baking Me Crazy by Karla Sorensen (#1)

Batter of Wits by Karla Sorensen (#2)

Steal My Magnolia by Karla Sorensen(#3)

Fighting For Love Series

Stud Muffin by Jiffy Kate (#1)

Beef Cake by Jiffy Kate (#2)

Eye Candy by Jiffy Kate (#3)

The Donner Bakery Series

No Whisk, No Reward by Ellie Kay (#1)

The Green Valley Library Series

Love in Due Time by L.B. Dunbar (#1)

Crime and Periodicals by Nora Everly (#2)

Prose Before Bros by Cathy Yardley (#3)

Shelf Awareness by Katie Ashley (#4)

Carpentry and Cocktails by Nora Everly (#5)

Love in Deed by L.B. Dunbar (#6)

Dewey Belong Together by Ann Whynot (#7)

Hotshot and Hospitality by Nora Everly (#8)

Love in a Pickle by L.B. Dunbar (#9)

Scorned Women's Society Series

My Bare Lady by Piper Sheldon (#1)

The Treble with Men by Piper Sheldon (#2)

The One That I Want by Piper Sheldon (#3)

Hopelessly Devoted to You by Piper Sheldon (#3.5)

Park Ranger Series

Happy Trail by Daisy Prescott (#1)

Stranger Ranger by Daisy Prescott (#2)

The Leffersbee Series

Been There Done That by Hope Ellis (#1)

Before and After You by Hope Ellis (#2)

The Higher Learning Series

Upsy Daisy by Chelsie Edwards (#1)

Green Valley Heroes Series

Forrest for the Trees by Kilby Blades

Seduction in the City

Cipher Security Series

Code of Conduct by April White (#1)

Code of Honor by April White (#2)

Code of Ethics by April White (#3)

Cipher Office Series

Weight Expectations by M.E. Carter (#1)

Sticking to the Script by Stella Weaver (#2)

Cutie and the Beast by M.E. Carter (#3)

Weights of Wrath by M.E. Carter (#4)

Common Threads Series

Mad About Ewe by Susannah Nix (#1)

Give Love a Chai by Nanxi Wen (#2)

Key Change by Heidi Hutchinson (#3)

Educated Romance

Work For It Series

Street Smart by Aly Stiles (#1)

Heart Smart by Emma Lee Jayne (#2)

Lessons Learned Series

Under Pressure by Allie Winters (#1)

CPSIA information can be obtained
at www.ICGtesting.com
Printed in the USA
FSHW012012081221
86804FS

9 781949 202649